Finland

Leningrad

Estonia

Novgorod

Baltic Sea

Demyansk

Latvia

Riga

Kalinin

Lithuania

Moscow

Vitebsk

USSR

Königsberg

Orsha

Smolensk

Tula

Minsk

Bryansk

Kaluga

Bialystok

Orel

Bobruysk

Warsaw

Pripet Marshes

2

Poland

Kursk

Belgorod

Kiev

Kharkov

Don River

Dnieper

Lvov

5

6

River

lovakia

Stalingrad

Dniester River

Rostov

Volga River

Hungary

Bessarabia

Odessa

3

Rumania

Sea of Azov

Crimea

Krasnodar

Caspian
Sea

Yugoslavia

Sevastopol

Kerch

Novorossisk

Bulgaria

4

Black Sea

Caucasus Mountains

Albania

Aegean Sea

Greece

Turkey

Europe in June 1941

Germany, its allies and occupied countries

Key to inset maps

1 Operation Barbarossa, June 1941
2 The Battle for Moscow,
. December 1941 to November 1942
3 The Battle of Stalingrad, November 1942
4 The Kuban Bridgehead, 1943
5 The Battle of Kursk, July 1943
6 The Belorussian Offensive, June 1944
7 The Berlin Offensive, April 1945

Crete

Mediterranean Sea

Cyprus

MECHANICS' INSTITUTE
MECHANICS'
MERCANTILE LIBRARY

RED PHOENIX

The Rise of Soviet Air Power, 1941–1945

VON HARDESTY

SMITHSONIAN INSTITUTION PRESS
Washington, D.C.

Library of Congress Cataloging in Publication Data

Hardesty, Von, 1939–
   Red phoenix.
   Bibliography: p.
   Includes index.
   Supt. of Docs. no.: SI 1.2:R24/941–45
   1. World War, 1939–1945—Aerial operations, Russian.   2. World War, 1939–1945—Aerial operations, German.
3. Soviet Union. Voenno-Vozdushnye Sily—History—World War, 1939–1945.
4. Germany. Luftwaffe—History—World War, 1939–1945.   I. Title.
D792.S65H37   940.54′4947   82–600153
ISBN 0–87474–510–1   AACR2

Printed in the United States of America
First edition

Photographs not otherwise credited belong to the National Air and Space Museum, Smithsonian Institution.

The paper in this book meets the guidelines for permanence and durability of the Committee on Production Guidelines for Book Longevity of the Council on Library Resources.

Contents

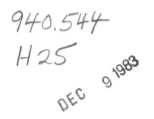

940.544
H25
DEC 9 1983

Preface

The Russo-German war, 1941–1945, or the "Great Patriotic War," as it is known to the Soviets, occupies a central place in the Soviet experience. As history, it marked a triumph of epic scale against a formidable enemy, Nazi Germany. For the Soviet military this brutal four-year conflict with all its challenges and sacrifices provided an accelerated passage to modernization and power. Even in the nuclear age, the Great Patriotic War lingers as a vivid memory in the national psyche, shaping public attitudes and serving as a conditioning and limiting factor in the evolution of Soviet military doctrine.

The air war in the east, as well as the larger military conflict, began with near disaster for the Soviet Union. Caught unprepared, the Soviet Air Force (*Voyenno-vozdushnyye sily*, or VVS) became the first victim of the German blitzkrieg. No air force has ever endured the brutal attrition the VVS experienced in the summer of 1941. Following crushing defeats, the story of the Soviet Air Force became one of heroic sacrifice and recovery. At Moscow during the winter of 1941–42 and then at Stalingrad, the Kuban (North Caucasus), and Kursk in 1943, the Soviets fought back, achieving the strategic initiative in the air. During the final phases of the war, the reborn Soviet Air Force overwhelmed the waning Luftwaffe. The Soviet Union concluded the war with the largest tactical air force in the world.

This historical study provides a survey, if not an exhaustive history, of the Soviet Air Force in World War II. Systematic reference has been made to Russian-language memoirs and histories to identify pivotal themes and events in the growth of Soviet air power between 1941 and 1945. The supplementary Appendixes and Bibliography are designed to supply the reader with the necessary references for study and further research. The magnitude of the air war in the east, by itself, should beckon Western military historians to study the Soviet Air Force in greater depth in order to shed light on this neglected aspect of World War II. Given the floodtide since 1960 of Soviet historical literature on the subject of the air war, much of it excellent in quality, Westerners can no longer justify their silence with lamentations over the paucity of historical materials.

At the heart of contemporary Soviet military doctrine is the concept of combined-arms operations. Forged in the difficult years of World War II, combined-arms warfare involves the cooperative interaction of air, ground, and, if required, naval forces. The Soviet Air Force, then and now, cannot be understood apart from this doctrine. For this reason Soviet air operations between 1941 and 1945 have a special meaning: they are both air history and a vast reservoir of battle experience for modern practitioners of combined-arms warfare. Much of the peculiar "style" of the Soviet Air Force in World War II—organization, operations, and aircraft design—reflects this doctrine of combined-arms warfare. Such a doctrine, articulated in the prewar period and necessitated by the exigencies of the Eastern front, meant that the Soviet

Air Force evolved along lines markedly different from the Anglo-American experience.

Another Soviet military priority during the war was the perfection of an air force administrative structure, one which would provide simultaneously centralized direction and decentralization at the lower levels to promote initiative and flexibility. The organization, or more properly the reorganization, of the air force structure was an imperative throughout the war years, beginning with the creation of air armies in 1942 as part of a series of reforms instituted by Air Commander A.A. Novikov. Other war-induced changes dealt with air-combat tactics, the expanded use of radio for more efficient air-ground coordination, a logistics system capable of sustaining large-scale "air offensives," and the mobilization and training of a vast cadre of pilots and air personnel. Behind the Soviet air juggernaut, of course, was the aviation industry, relocated beyond the Ural Mountains in 1941–42, which provided in its ever-expanding productivity an awesome Soviet capacity for the concentration (and reinforcement) of combat aircraft. These crucial themes gave shape to the history of the Soviet Air Force, not only for the years 1941–45, but for the modern era as well.

The term "Soviet Air Force" has been used in this study for the time frame of the Great Patriotic War, although the name technically belongs to the post–1945 period. The choice reflects current Soviet usage, but does not exclude the occasional employment, if appropriate, of "Red Air Fleet" or "Red Air Force" to describe the air forces of the Soviet Union. The transliteration of Russian-language names and words follows the system of the United States Board on Geographic Names. Physical quantities are given in metric in the Appendix to provide a complete profile of Soviet aircraft and their performance.

Since the air war in the east remains an obscure episode of World War II, photographs—to the extent they are available—provide an important avenue for historical study. Without visual reference, it is difficult to comprehend fully the impact of the Russian landscape and diverse climate on air operations. Careful attention has been given here to the identification of appropriate illustrations from Soviet, German, and American sources. As a collection, they evoke images of an unknown air war.

A number of individuals have made significant contributions to this project, which began in the fall of 1978 when I received a Guggenheim Fellowship at the National Air and Space Museum (NASM). Having joined the staff of the Aeronautics Department of NASM in October 1979, I received the valued supervision and counsel of Donald S. Lopez, who as department chairman has done much to make NASM an important center for research in aviation history. Also, Walter Boyne, assistant director of NASM and an aviation historian, provided welcome encouragement. Among my colleagues, Glen Sweeting and Jay Spenser stand out as frequent and important contributors in the field of German military history and as assistants in the gathering of Soviet Air Force illustrations. Carl-Fredrik Geust, an authority on the Soviet Air Force, enriched the photo-illustrations with contributions from his own remarkable collection. John T. Greenwood, chief of the Historical Division, United States Army Corps of Engineers, played an important role in the preparation of this book. His pioneering research on the Soviet Air Force, in particular his analysis of recent Soviet historical sources, helped to direct the focus of this study in manifold ways. I wish to thank him, along with Jeff Ethell and Dale Dickey, for their willingness to read and comment on the original manuscript.

Others who helped in diverse ways include Stephen Hardesty, Judy Hardesty, Dom Pisano, Karl Schneide, Patricia Najjum, Phil Edwards, Hermann Neff, Norman Polmar, Tom Crouch, Mary Pavlovich, Mimi Scharf, Tim Wooldridge, Dorothy Cochrane, Natalie Rowland, Susan Owen, Judy Engelberg, Dana Bell, Dale Hrabak, Jim Vineyard, Lonnie Rabjohns, John Bessette, Williamsom Murray, Bob van der Linden, June Chocheles, Melinda H. Scarano, Frank Winter, and the late Benjamin S. Kelsey.

Special thanks go to a number of librarians and Soviet specialists who assisted with the Bibliography: Linda Lester; Lt. Col. William A. Burhans, USAF; Lt. Col. Robert S. Makinen, USAF; Robert P. Moore; Carl-Fredrik Geust; and Michael Parrish. Don Gillmore provided expert references on Soviet aircraft types and contributed a number of illustrations from his own collection of materials.

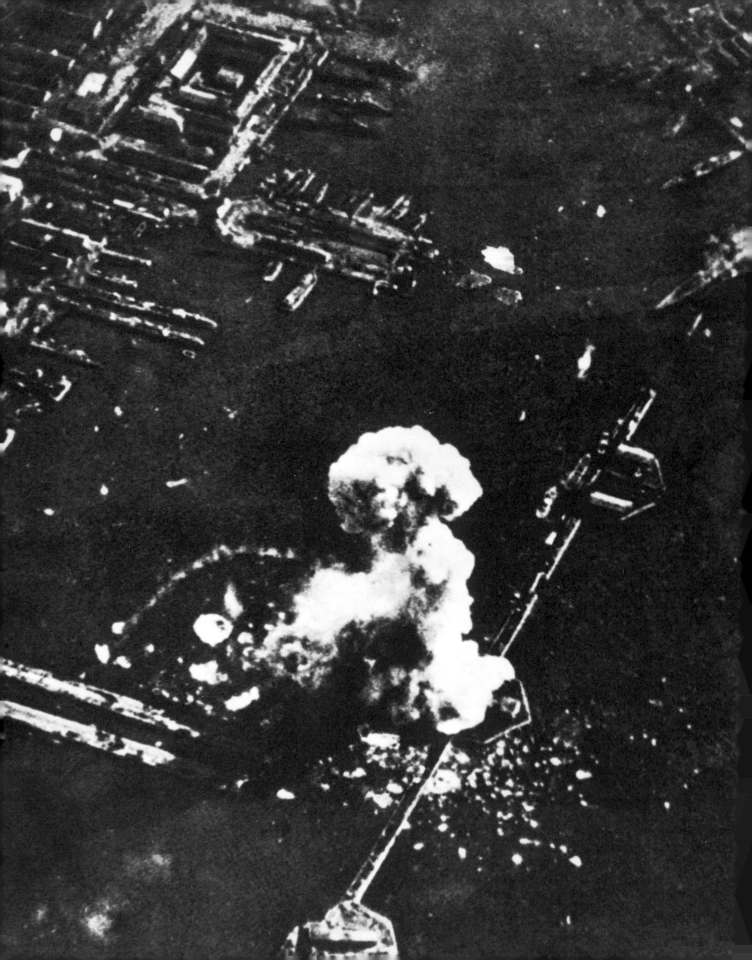

Chapter 1

The Arduous Beginning

The Soviet Union passed abruptly from peace to war at 03:30 hours on Sunday, June 22, 1941. Thirty hand-picked Luftwaffe bomber crews, flying He 111s, Ju 88s, and Do 17Zs in groups of three, struck ten Soviet airfields in the predawn darkness. As the first wave of a carefully orchestrated blitzkrieg (Operation Barbarossa), the German bombers approached the western periphery of the Soviet Union at maximum altitude to avoid detection. Once over the Soviet territory, the bombers swept down on their targets at the very moment that German artillery signaled the advance of a ground force consisting of 3,800,000 men.

This initial air strike was aimed to create havoc at the forward Soviet air bases. At sunrise, the major Luftwaffe force of 500 bombers, 270 dive bombers, and 480 fighters hit 66 airfields containing nearly three-quarters of the Soviet combat aircraft.[1]

Wave after wave of German aircraft struck Soviet airfields on June 22 with only token resistance from interceptors or anti-aircraft fire. There was no evidence of an air alert or any effort to disperse the numerous aircraft deployed at the forward airfields. Few Soviet fighters escaped the fury of the first preemptive air sorties to challenge the Luftwaffe in the air.

Soviet air divisions faced near annihilation within the space of one day—the 9th Mixed Air Division of the Western Special Military District lost 347 planes out of 409 deployed, the 10th lost 180 out of 231, the 11th, 127 out of 199, and so on.[2]

The Soviet Air Force (*Voyenno-vozdushnyye sily*, or VVS) had been caught by surprise. Its movements were incoherent and sluggish, much like those of a large animal stricken by sudden and repeated blows. At one airfield, Luftwaffe fighters discovered more than 100 VVS aircraft—bombers, fighters, reconnaissance planes—parked in long rows, as if on display. In the course of twenty minutes, German fighters made repeated sweeps of the airfield, destroying the aircraft in place.[3]

The sudden Soviet air paralysis meant the Luftwaffe could strike at will against defensive fortifications, rail junctions, troop groupings, and communications. For the Soviet pilots who managed to get airborne on the morning of June 22, there was the formidable task of air combat with the battle-seasoned Luftwaffe units. Those who entered into combat with the Luftwaffe faced such skilled pilots as Werner von Molders, who had eighty-two victories to his credit, fourteen in Spain and sixty-eight on the Western front. Before his death in an accidental air crash in November 1941, Molders notched another thirty-three victories against the VVS. Not all German pilots possessed Molders's skills, but many took full advantage of superior training and equipment to become aces. Many roaming squadrons of Messerschmitt Bf 109s found VVS fighter units unaggressive, some fleeing on the approach of the German fighters.[4]

In the midst of burning airfields and staggering confusion, some Russian air units struck back boldly at the invaders. But the VVS reaction to the Luftwaffe assault, as I. V. Timokhovich has stated, was generally "spontaneous, uncoordinated and purposeless."[5] Soviet bombers spared destruction in the opening hours of the war flew into action in a desperate attempt to stem the relentless German advance. Soviet air commanders, following confused directives from Moscow, recklessly sacrificed scores of bomber squadrons in the vain hope of destroying Luftwaffe staging areas. At 11:00 hours, Soviet SB-2s and DB-3s, all slow-flying medium bombers, attempted to attack several Luftwaffe air bases north of Warsaw. At one airfield the Soviet bombers appeared five times during the day—each time without fighter escort. German fighters and flak crews had a field day against the lumbering Soviet aircraft. During one strike by twenty-five Soviet bombers, German fighters downed twenty of the attackers.

The attrition of Soviet bomber strength remained high through June 23, when SB-2s and DB-3s appeared in regimental strength—and again without fighter escort. Their goal was to interdict the advancing German army at crucial road and river crossings.[6] The Soviet bombers attempted to hit the German targets from altitudes of 10,000 feet, an approach altitude prescribed in their prewar training. The results proved ineffectual, prompting a decision to lower the altitude to 3,000 feet. Already vulnerable to Luftwaffe fighters, the Soviet bombers now found their slow approach speeds at that low altitude against German anti-aircraft units to be near suicidal. German fighter pilots and flak crews watched in amazement as the unescorted Soviet aircraft made repeated sweeps with extraordinary losses. Once ordered to attack a German target, the bombers maintained their course despite withering fire.

The destruction of Soviet bombers continued from the first day of the invasion into July. When his airfield was attacked by twenty-seven Soviet bombers on July 9, Maj. Guenther Luetzow of the Luftwaffe's 3d Fighter Wing took to the air with his unit and shot down the entire regiment in fifteen minutes without a loss.[7] One Luftwaffe fighter unit, J-52, or the Green Heart, scored sixty-five aircraft in one day.[8]

There was no frame of reference for the Luftwaffe's air triumph of June 22 and the subsequent phases of the German offensive. For the Soviets it was an air debacle of unprecedented scope and devastation. Few Soviet air com-

Soviet fortifications in Moldavia under attack by an He 111 bomber, flown by a Rumanian crew. Courtesy of Glen Sweeting.

June 22, 1941: German Ju 87 Stukas attack the Soviet-held fortress at Brest on the Bug River. Courtesy of Glen Sweeting.

German Stukas hit Soviet positions south of Leningrad during Operation Barbarossa, 1941. Courtesy of Glen Sweeting.

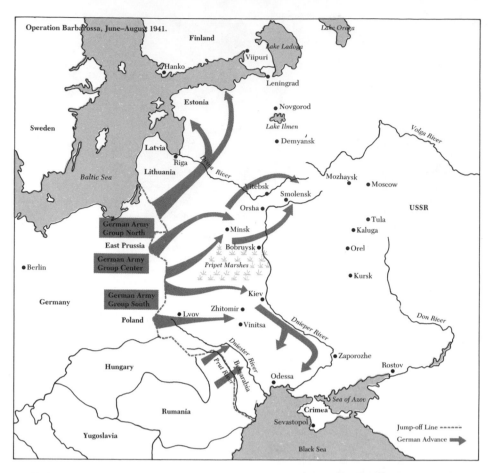

Operation Barbarossa, June–August 1941.

A Messerschmitt Bf 109 fighter makes a low-level "victory" sweep over a burning Soviet bomber during Operation Barbarossa, 1941. Courtesy of Glen Sweeting.

manders in the midst of chaos and retreat had the opportunity, or the inclination, to measure the quantitative dimensions of the German air victory.

Once the Germans began the process of tallying the results, the triumph surpassed their boldest expectations. At 13:30 hours, Gen. Franz Halder had recorded in his diary 800 Soviet aircraft destroyed, compared to German losses of only ten! By the end of the day, the tally had reached 1,811 aircraft—1,489 on the ground, 322 in the air. During the next twenty-four hours, another 1,000 Soviet planes were destroyed, reaching 4,017 by the end of the first week of the war. German losses at that point stood at 150 aircraft.

Hermann Goering, a man accustomed to hyperbole, found the reported Soviet losses for June 22–24 to be exaggerated. He ordered a recount and verification. The subsequent report, to his amazement, added 300 more Soviet aircraft to the original figure.[9] By the end of one week, the Luftwaffe had achieved firm control of the air, and in the first week of July the Germans turned their attention to ground support of their army, which now was advancing along a front approaching 1,800 miles in width.

Operation Barbarossa Unfolds

Nazi Germany's projected *coup de main* on the Soviet Union, Operation Barbarossa, had dictated a preemptive air strike as a prerequisite to victory. With the Luftwaffe in firm control of the air, the German Army planned to move into Russia along three diverging avenues of conquest—toward Leningrad in the north, Moscow in the center, and Kiev in the south. Hitler's bold Drang nach Osten, if successful, would eliminate a potential enemy and hasten the end of World War II on German terms. Implicit in this blueprint were other considerations linked with Hitler's own personal vision: the destruction of Bolshevism and the establishment of the Nazi New Order in Europe.

The plan was not without risk. Germany could ill afford a prolonged, two-front war. If the risks of such a war of attrition were real, Hitler and the German High Command feared a still greater threat: a rearmed Soviet Union attacking at a moment of its own choosing, perhaps before the defeat of Great Britain in the west. A more practical motivation, however, was the German expectation that the campaign in Russia would be short and decisive. Soviet Russia, in Hitler's estimate, was vulnerable: "We have only to kick in the door and the whole rotten structure will come crashing down."[10]

The Wehrmacht, with its mobility, massive striking power, and battle experience, advanced into the Soviet Union in 1941 on the day after the date chosen by Napoleon for the invasion of tsarist Russia in 1812.[11] The ambitious campaign to bring down the Soviet regime involved a series of envelopment battles west of the Dvina and Dnieper rivers; the capture of the Baltic republics and Leningrad; the liquidation of surviving Soviet forces around Moscow; and concluding forays in the Volga and Caucasus regions.[12] Germany's dramatic victories over France, Poland, and Yugoslavia in 1940–41 fueled an attitude of supreme confidence in the Wehrmacht's ability to defeat Russia.

The genesis of Operation Barbarossa can be traced back to Directive 21, issued by Hitler on December 18, 1940. Named after Frederick I Barbarossa (Red Beard), who marched to the Holy Land in 1190, the plan called for "armored spearheads" to penetrate deeply into the hinterland of the Soviet Union, destroy the Red Army, and erect "a barrier against Asiatic Russia."[13]

The word "Barbarossa" itself evoked a historical meaning which John Erickson has described as "arrogant in its recall of medieval splendors and menacing in its hints of medieval cruelties."[14]

The concrete planning for the invasion began after nearly sixteen months of diplomatic cooperation between Germany and the Soviet Union, an alliance growing out of the Nazi-Soviet Nonaggression Pact of August 1939. Both sides had entered the diplomatic rapprochement with cynicism, anticipating immediate political and military advantages. Each moved into these dangerous diplomatic maneuvers fully conscious of the important factor of time.

Playing for time had prompted Germany and the Soviet Union in the first instance to reach an understanding, despite the seemingly insurmountable ideological differences between the fascist and communist regimes. Hitler's changing perception of the time factor eventually required the abandonment of cooperation for a fateful military confrontation. Speaking to his close associate Martin Borman, Hitler confessed his fear of a two-front war, but he argued that time was working on the side of Soviet Russia. Only when Germany possessed the territory of the Soviet Union, Hitler asserted, would time once again work on the side of Germany.[15]

Stalin, no less concerned with the strategic implications of the calendar, had pushed the Soviet military in 1940 toward a rapid reorganization and modernization. This hurried effort to prepare for a potential conflict with Germany required a prolongation of the Nazi-Soviet Nonaggression Pact. Stalin's timetable anticipated war in 1942, at the very moment his air force and army would be reequipped and in a state of readiness. As events demonstrated, Stalin had permitted his fervent hope for additional time to be transformed into a firm conviction that Hitler would not strike until 1942. This illusion became fixed Soviet policy. Much of the Soviet inaction and confusion in response to Operation Barbarossa stemmed from Stalin's dogged refusal to face the reality of Hitler's intentions.

Approaching the conquest of Russia, Hitler took pains to make the conduct of the war brutal and repressive. Civilians who resisted the Wehrmacht were to be regarded as outlaws and shot without trial. Special Action Groups (*Einsatzgruppen*) were organized under Heinrich Himmler and given the task of eliminating political and racial types considered incompatible with the Nazi New Order.[16] Following the German Army into Russia, four SS *Einsatzgruppen* of 3,000 men each rounded up Communist party members, particularly political commissars, for liquidation. This policy quickly transformed the Eastern front into a cruel campaign where little quarter was given, prompting both sides to fight to the extreme on the ground and in the air.

The harbingers of war in the winter and spring of 1941 should have been apparent to any astute observer, let alone Joseph Stalin, with his access to foreign and Soviet intelligence data. Only Stalin's stubborn refusal to act upon the ominous warnings prevented the Soviet military from taking appropriate steps to prepare for war. The German troop build-up had gone forward in measured steps, beginning as far back as the fall of 1940.[17] The final stages of German troop transfers to the east had begun on May 25, 1941, with one hundred military formations ordered into place every twenty-four hours.

Such massive shifts in military power by Germany did not escape notice in the West. On two occasions Great Britain and the United States warned the Soviet Union about the German plans; the last warning was delivered on June 21 by Sir Stafford Cripps, the British Ambassador to Moscow. Always suspicious of Western motives, however, Stalin received these warnings with ill-concealed contempt, seeing in the Anglo-American messages a cynical effort to provoke a war between Nazi Germany and the Soviet Union. If these warnings were suspect to him by virtue of their origin, Stalin also had credible intelligence reports from his own sources. Richard Sorge, the Soviet master spy in the German Embassy in Tokyo, cautioned in a dispatch sent on June 14, 1941: "War begins June 22."[18]

Luftwaffe overflights into Soviet territory in 1941—as arrogant as they were frequent—provided telltale signs of German intentions. Beginning in February, high-altitude German reconnaissance aircraft gathered target intelligence through repeated flights over the western periphery of the Soviet Union. Airfields were photographed in detail and studied, along with Soviet defenses. A German reconnaissance aircraft, equipped with camera and exposed film of Soviet territory, crashed near Rovno on April 15. Despite these aerial incursions, reaching a high frequency by June, Stalin forbade Soviet fighters or anti-aircraft units to intervene.[19] Soviet air commanders viewed these bold overflights with alarm, but they bowed to the Kremlin's presumed strategic wisdom. Later, many of the Soviet officers who survived the fighting wrote bitterly about the lack of preparedness in the months preceding the war.[20]

German intelligence reports on the Soviet Air Force underscored the overall impression of military vulnerability. A German General Staff report, dated January 1, 1941, estimated that the VVS had 12,000 to 14,000 combat aircraft, but only 4,000 (two-thirds of them fighters) were operational as first-class machines.[21] Furthermore, German intelligence analysts in 1941 discerned other, more fundamental, weaknesses behind the facade of Soviet air power. Soviet fighters (largely I-15, I-153, I-16 models of Spanish Civil War vintage) were now obsolescent and had proved in 1939–40 to be ineffectual against the minuscule Finnish Air Force. Moreover, the command structure of the Soviet Air Force had been brutally repressed, along with other branches of the armed forces, by the Stalinist purges of the late 1930s. Successive commanders—Ya. I. Alksnis, V.V. Khripin, and Ya. V. Smushkevich—had been arrested or executed. Pilot training, ground services, equipment, and organization were all deficient by Luftwaffe standards.

For the execution of the preemptive air strikes, the Luftwaffe had deployed four air fleets, or *Luftflotten*, numbering approximately 2,000 aircraft—880 bombers, 280 dive bombers, 60 ground-attack planes, 60 twin-engine fighters, 600 single-engine fighters, 120 reconnaissance aircraft, and 230 transport and liaison aircraft.[22] Soviet sources suggest a higher figure, around 5,000 combat aircraft.[23] Air Marshal K.A. Vershinin has stated that on the eve of the war the Luftwaffe had deployed 4,950 machines in the east, out of a total of 10,980. Most Western sources accept the lower figure.[24]

Soviet air strength on the eve of Barbarossa is less certain. No official Soviet figures have been published to date. A probable estimate would fall between 8,000 and 10,000 aircraft. The fury of Operation Barbarossa fell on the Soviet Air Force at the very moment a program had begun to reequip forward air units with a new generation of combat aircraft. This transition was

This Soviet I-15 fighter was destroyed in place by the Luftwaffe in the opening hours of Operation Barbarossa. Courtesy of Glen Sweeting.

Pictured here is one of the countless I-16 fighters, called the "Rata" by the Germans, which were destroyed during the opening weeks of Operation Barbarossa. (SI–74-2941)

German soldiers look at an I1-4 bomber shot down near Kaluga. Courtesy of Herman Neff.

Luftwaffe personnel inspect a rare YAK-4 twin-engine bomber and reconnaissance aircraft used briefly by the Soviet Air Force at the beginning of the war. (SI 74-2903)

A German soldier relaxes in the nose well of an abandoned TB-3 bomber, the mainstay of the Soviet Union's bomber force in the 1930s. (SI 80–18481)

An SB-2bis bomber—one of many downed in the futile Soviet efforts to stem the German advance in the summer of 1941. (SI 80-1848)

not advancing smoothly or quickly. Such a program inevitably brought disruption in its wake as air and ground crews trained in the newer aircraft—MIG-3s, Yak-1s, LaGG-3s and Pe-2s.

To add to the confusion, the VVS in 1940–41 had moved into a network of new airfields in the territories recently annexed following the Nazi-Soviet pact. Having occupied the Baltic republics, portions of former Poland, and Moldavia, the Soviets worked hurriedly to fortify the new western border. The Soviet blueprint for establishing its new defensive perimeter called for construction of new airfields and the expansion of existing ones.[25] On the eve of Barbarossa, VVS airfields in the western border regions were packed with combat aircraft; old and new types were mixed chaotically as Moscow attempted simultaneously to provide for an air defense network and to reequip its forward air units.[26]

The confusion at the forward airfields stemmed from the rapid pace of the transition program, not from the failure of the Soviet aviation industry to bring on line new aircraft types. Under A. I. Shakurin, the plants had retooled and reorganized their production lines in 1940, achieving considerable momentum by the spring of 1941 toward reequipping the VVS with modern combat aircraft. Whereas the Soviets produced fewer than 100 new aircraft in 1940, the production of modern types for the first half of 1941 (up to June 22) surpassed 2,600 machines. Another few months, as VVS commanders lamented, would have made a real difference.

Stalin as Leader

Stalin's role in the events of June 22, 1941, remains confused and contradictory. Reports of the Luftwaffe air strikes reached the Defense Commissariat in Moscow shortly after 03:30 hours. Gen. G.K. Zhukov, later to emerge as a prominent Soviet Army commander, who was then assigned to the General Staff, passed the information on to Stalin shortly afterward. The latter's initial reaction was to view the attacks as "a provocation on the part of the German generals."[27] Three hours earlier Stalin had approved a confusing directive to the frontier military districts, after a day of discussion about the growing menace on the western border. Issued through Marshal S.K. Timoshenko, defense commissar, to the Leningrad, Baltic Special, Western Special, Kiev Special, and Odessa military districts, it warned of a possible German attack on June 22–23. The directive called for concrete steps to be taken by local commanders to assure combat readiness: troops were secretly to man the fire points of fortified districts; aircraft were to be dispersed and camouflaged before dawn on June 22; all units were to be placed at combat readiness; other measures, such as the blacking-out of towns and installations, were to be implemented.[28]

These same commanders, however, were told in explicit terms to take no other steps without special authorization. The belated Timoshenko directive embodied some half-measures toward preparedness, largely in response to the overwhelming weight of intelligence data suggesting a German invasion, but it failed to make the grim prospects of war clear to Soviet commanders.

Coming just after midnight, the Timoshenko directive did little to reduce the vulnerability of the Soviet Air Force. In the Baltic area, for example, the air commander ordered his units not to intercept or fire upon German aircraft in Soviet airspace unless the enemy aircraft undertook overt military opera-

Table 1
Number of New Types of Aircraft Produced
on Eve of Great Patriotic War

Type	1940	1941 (June 22)	Total
YAK-1	64	335	399
MiG-3	20	1,289	1,309
LaGG-3	—	322	322
Pe-2	2	458	460
IL-2	—	249	249
Total	86	2,653	2,739

Source: TsGASA (Central State Archives of the Soviet Army), quoted in M. N. Kozhevnikov, *Komandovaniye i shtab VVS Sovetskoy Armii V Velikoy Otechestvennoy voyne, 1941–1945 g.g.* (Moscow: Nauka, 1977), p. 16.

tions. In the Western and Kiev military districts, dawn arrived with Soviet aircraft still in place on their crowded runways. Only the Odessa Military District reacted promptly, dispersing much of its aircraft before the arrival of the Luftwaffe.[29]

By 07:15 hours on the morning of June 22, Timoshenko, after further consultation with Stalin, had issued a second directive.[30] At this point the full brunt of the Wehrmacht had fallen on the exposed and disorganized Soviet defenses. War now raged from the Baltic Sea to the Ukraine as German mechanized spearheads penetrated deeply into the Soviet Union. Overhead, the Luftwaffe swept toward its various targets with massive and lethal concentrations of firepower. Soviet air defenses appeared almost nonexistent as the communications network collapsed and Moscow lost effective contact with the frontier.

In this murky and ever-deepening crisis, Timoshenko directed "active offensive operations" to begin against the invading German troops where they had violated the border. Soviet aircraft, at that very moment facing the full fury of the Luftwaffe, were ordered on the offensive, to "destroy with powerful blows" the enemy aircraft and ground forces. For the first time, Moscow permitted the VVS to conduct air strikes to a depth of 100 miles into German territory.[31]

Another Moscow move, no less confused or unrealistic, followed at 21:15 hours. Timoshenko's third directive called upon the Soviet military, now roughly redefined into the Northwestern, Western, and Southwestern fronts and coextensive with the avenues of invasion, to go on the offensive and carry the war into enemy territory. Such a projected counteroffensive to push the German forces back from the frontier coincided ironically with the collapse of Soviet forward defenses. At Minsk and other sectors, the Soviet Army faced encirclement and disintegration. The Soviet Air Force, already in ashes, was simply incapable of providing sustained air support for offensive operations.

Wherever this directive managed to evoke feeble Soviet efforts to expel the enemy, the Germans quickly adjusted and crushed the attackers. Stalin's directives of June 22, based on a gross misunderstanding of the forces at play, committed the shattered Soviet armed forces to a series of foolhardy counterattacks. Grim farce had followed tragedy.

On the Frontlines

In the midst of this vast military catastrophe, there were moments when Soviet fliers, air commanders, and air units responded with extraordinary courage. One pilot, I. I. Drozdov of the 127th Fighter Air Regiment (IAP), flew four sorties against German bombers near Brest on June 22. According to Soviet sources, he downed five "fascist airplanes" during the course of the day.[32] The 123d Fighter Air Regiment, also stationed near Brest, fought an uneven ten-hour duel with the Luftwaffe on the opening day. Under constant enemy fire and frequent air raids, the ground crews managed to keep the airfield operational. The regimental commander, Maj. B. N. Surin, engaged in the four dogfights, only to lose his life. He was credited with three victories.[33]

The Luftwaffe first appeared over the Leningrad sector in the early hours of June 22, when twelve aircraft, flying in three groups, dropped mines in the Gulf of Finland. The following night, the air raid sirens warned the citizens of Leningrad of an impending German air attack, but no massive raid materialized. Being remote from the enemy breakthrough zones, the Leningrad Military District and the Red Banner Baltic Fleet enjoyed a brief reprieve. By the second week of the war, however, this area found itself drawn into the vortex of battle.

Gen. A. A. Novikov, then VVS air commander in the north, demonstrated decisive leadership in the air defense of Leningrad. As the German Army Group North approached, Novikov mobilized existing air units for a spirited defense of Novgorod and Leningrad. In a context of confusion and increased enemy air presence, Novikov pieced together an air armada drawn from the shattered Baltic Military District, the Navy fleet air arm, air defense units stationed at Leningrad, and his own Leningrad Military District.

Responding to the urgent requirement to blunt advancing enemy armored units, Novikov also committed large numbers of slow-flying SB-2 bombers. The effort here as elsewhere to use air power to halt the German forward movement proved to be ineffectual. Losses were high, fighter aircraft were in short supply, and reinforcements were modest, but Novikov had displayed impressive skill and energy in asserting Soviet air power in the north. Moscow took note of his effective command, promoting him to the post of VVS deputy commander.[34]

Soviet frontal air commanders found only small numbers of the newer type aircraft available for the winter months. Highly prized were the modern Pe-2 bombers and Il-2 Shturmoviks, which gave the VVS a powerful tactical air capability even with all their teething problems. The new fighter types, the MiG-3s, Yak-1s, and LaGG-3s, shared sleek, modern silhouettes, and replaced the older I-15, I-153, and I-16 models. Among these new fighters only the Yak-1 survived the initial challenge of combat in 1941–42 and earned approval for continued series production, subject, of course, to further and radical refinements during the war. The MiG-3, originally designed for high-altitude interception, had proved ineffectual at lower altitude where most of the air combat took place in 1941. It was dropped from production.

Perhaps the LaGG-3 symbolized best the mixed characteristics of Soviet combat aircraft in 1941. With its wooden construction, the LaGG-3 bespoke another era in aviation. While sturdy, the Soviet fighter demonstrated a unique and devastating blend of sluggishness and poor maneuverability. Even with a boosted M-105PF liquid-cooled, 12-cylinder engine with

slightly over 1,200 hp, the overweight LaGG-3 displayed little advance over the prewar I-16 in acceleration; it was also short in range and fearfully unpredictable in handling. The LaGG-3's low performance quickly produced a reputation for odds-on-death in the minds of many Soviet fighter pilots. Its highly polished skinning (wood impregnated with plastic) suggested to these wary pilots, using the acronym "LaGG," that the new fighter was a *lakirovanny garantirovanny grob*, or a "varnished guaranteed coffin."

In combat, the LaGG-3 endured a high loss rate, a fact aggravated by the inadequate conversion training provided in the chaotic war conditions of 1941. Soviet pilots found the plexiglass canopy, once closed, so opaque that it drastically reduced vision, and in emergencies it proved to be extremely difficult to open. For safety's sake, they flew with the canopy open, which penalized performance. Some skilled pilots, however, mastered the LaGG-3's built-in adversity and went on to score impressive victory tallies. V.I. Popkov, later to emerge as the VVS's fifteenth-ranking ace, scored his initial victories in a LaGG-3. Capt. G. A. Grigoryev, also in a LaGG-3, reportedly downed fifteen enemy aircraft in the first six months of the war. These pilots, however, were exceptional and in no way suggest in their combat records the typical script for the LaGG-3.

If lacking in agility and power as a fighter, the LaGG-3 was resilient. The fact that it could absorb punishment led to the decision to use it increasingly in a ground-attack role. Consequently, some LaGG-3s saw action in 1941–42 as fighter bombers armed with RS-82 rockets and/or bombs.

During its short combat life, the LaGG-3 underwent several modifications in powerplant and armament—but the Messerschmitt Bf 109G outclassed it in almost all respects. Rather than totally abandon the LaGG-3 under the severe wartime conditions for a newly designed fighter, the decision was made to retain the airframe and wed it to the ASh-82 air-cooled engine.

The transformation, which took place in late summer 1942, was a practical and expedient move that resulted in the Lavochkin La-5. The "varnished coffin" had a happy ending in the production of the La-5, and the later La-7, which ultimately challenged the Focke Wulf Fw 190, its German counterpart, in the skies over Kursk in the summer of 1943.

Aleksandr I. Pokryshkin, later to be the second-ranking VVS ace, with fifty-nine victories, began the war as a senior lieutenant in the 55th Fighter Air Regiment in Soviet-occupied Moldavia near the Rumanian border. His experiences, related in his autobiography *Nebo voyny* [The war sky], convey dramatically the crisis of the VVS during the opening phases of Operation Barbarossa.

When the war began, Pokryshkin found himself and his MiG-3 fighter temporarily assigned to Mayaki airstrip, living in a primitive tent encampment with his regiment, while a concrete runway was being constructed at Bel'tsy, his home air base. The stillness of Sunday morning, June 22, was broken with shouts of "alert! scramble! There's a war on!" Pokryshkin bolted from his tent to watch the dark silhouettes of three bombers and four fighters pass to the side of the Mayaki airstrip and then, in clear view, turn toward the parked Soviet aircraft. After a series of explosions, the enemy aircraft departed to the west unscathed. Pokryshkin soon learned that Bel'tsy had been attacked and a close friend had been killed in a dogfight with German fighters.

Pokryshkin's memoirs convey not only a fighter pilot's frustrations on the first day of the war, but a profound indictment of the lack of Soviet air preparedness. Prior to June 22, Pokryshkin had observed with growing impatience the German aerial reconnaissance overflights. In May 1941 a Junkers Ju 88 had passed over Bel'tsy airfield in broad daylight. Ordered not to intercept the enemy aircraft, Pokryshkin and his air regiment looked on in anger: "We crowded around the commander, as if he had given the order not to intercept and could rescind it. 'An order from above . . . diplomacy,' he replied. Realizing the injustice of it, we sought answers, but could not find them. It seemed that the bold overflights gave evidence of terrible events to come."[35]

For Pokryshkin, the spectacle of German aircraft flying freely over Soviet airspace, photographing defense installations and then carrying away the film unmolested, made a mockery of the Soviet Air Force. It suggested that the Soviet Union lacked power or courage. Expressing his bitterness, Pokryshkin remembered in his memoirs the sentiments of his squadron commander, Anatoliy Sokolov, a burn-scarred veteran of Khalkhin-Gol air skirmishes (1938) with the Japanese in the Far East, who exclaimed: "We must burn the vultures! Burn them! You won't scare them off with diplomatic notes! Use MiGs!"[36]

During the first hours of combat Pokryshkin faced many other grim truths about Soviet "military preparedness." Flying in his new MiG-3 fighter to intercept on-coming German bombers, Pokryshkin caught sight of a group of aircraft approaching Mayaki airfield out of the sun in a wedge formation. These bombers, perhaps light-bomber types, appeared strange to him. They did not fit the description of any known enemy aircraft: single-engine, a single cockpit for the pilot and navigator-bombardier, a camouflaged paint scheme.

"I quickly closed in on the nearest bomber," Pokryshkin recalls, "and gave him a short burst. I felt I had aimed accurately and hit him. The backwash from his engine flipped me over at close quarters, throwing my MiG to the right and above. Looking down from my inverted position, I saw to my horror, red stars on the bomber's wings! They were friendly aircraft! I had fired upon Soviet aircraft!"[37]

Stunned and wondering what to do next, Pokryshkin hovered above the mysterious aircraft for several seconds, watching his intended victim begin to fall behind. Quickly his attention turned to the other MiG fighters approaching to attack. Since the MiG-3 fighters did not have radio sets, Pokryshkin dipped his wings and tried to maneuver between the attacking fighters and the bombers. The crippled aircraft made a belly landing, but Pokryshkin's squadron mates continued to attack the surviving bombers. By darting in front of the fighters and firing warning shots, Pokryshkin managed to halt the attack, but only after one near collision with a fighter.

The strange aircraft were Su-2 dive bombers, stationed at a nearby airfield at Kotovsk. None of the fighter pilots had been introduced to these new-model aircraft, or, as yet, to the new Pe-2, which would become an important frontline dive bomber. Pokryshkin and his fellow pilots, angered over the loss of the Su-2 air crew, complained bitterly to their squadron commander about the absurd military secrecy, the fact that "every day all the women in the marketplace at Kotovsk saw them," but that the fighter pilots had observed the Su-2s—part of their own air division—for the first time in the air on a combat sortie against the Luftwaffe![38]

Soviet air commanders quickly realized how ill prepared their units were to match the flying technique of the Germans. VVS fighters, largely defense-minded toward their aggressive enemy counterparts, normally flew in tight formations of three aircraft, or flights (*zveno*). Against the looser, more flexible two- and four-aircraft combinations of the Luftwaffe, this prewar Soviet pattern of fighter deployment proved ineffectual, if not suicidal. Once attacked, VVS fighters often adopted a defensive circle (*krug samoletov*) to provide cover, or the snake (*smeika*) formation to draw enemy fighters into the range of Soviet anti-aircraft fire. There were frequent instances when VVS fighters proved to be unreliable, abandoning their escort duties on the arrival of Luftwaffe fighters.

Su-2 short-range ground-attack aircraft. Known for its sluggish performance in combat, the Su-2 gave way to the Il-2 Shturmovik as the standard Soviet ground-attack plane. (SI 81-2818)

K. A. Vershinin, wartime commander of the VVS 4th Air Army, suggests that the defensive circle tactic was a deliberate effort in 1941 to exploit fully the high maneuverability of I-16 and I-153 fighters.[39] He implies that VVS fighter tactics became more aggressive when the newer Yak and Lavochkin fighter aircraft arrived in large numbers at the front.

Another commentator on VVS operational art, I. V. Timokhovich, has described the defensive tactics as "deficiencies," reflecting a whole pattern of passivity toward the enemy.[40] Consequently, VVS operational tactics were too cautious and inflexible, limited largely to horizontal maneuver, and lacking in coordination with the land army. This latter defect became crucial from the standpoint of Soviet air doctrine because the VVS, as an integral part of the Red Army, existed primarily to work in close harmony with the ground forces.

In theory, the VVS sought to establish air superiority over the battlefield, and then to provide effective ground support for the army in both its defensive and offensive operations. In the face of the German invasion, the VVS was unable to provide more than feeble resistance, let alone fill the ambitious role Soviet air doctrine had defined for it. Soviet air commanders and pilots quickly realized how ill-prepared they were to match the flying technique of the Luftwaffe. New types of aircraft, even in vast numbers, were not alone a sufficient answer to the challenge of the Luftwaffe.

At the same time, Soviet bomber tactics displayed an absence of caution. From the opening moments, bombers had been thrown into battle in large numbers to slow the German advance, particularly at river crossings. Except for a few modern Pe-2s, these air units flew Il-4s (DB-3F) and SB-2s, even some vintage TB-3s. All these bomber types were slow, limited in range and payload, and extremely vulnerable to German interceptors and anti-aircraft units.

Soviet bombers typically flew in "wedge" and "line" configurations. The preferred mode became the wedge formation, consisting of three to twelve aircraft echeloned in altitude. A bomber squadron at this juncture in the war numbered nine aircraft. To reduce losses and maximize their defensive firepower, the bombers flew in tight formations. Despite these tactical adjustments, VVS bombers suffered high attrition during the summer of 1941.

In the midst of all this bloodletting at the hands of the Luftwaffe, Soviet bombers made a symbolic counterstrike against Berlin itself on the night of August 7–8, 1941. A group of thirteen DB-3 bombers, drawn from the 1st Mine-Torpedo Air Regiment of the Baltic Fleet Air Force, made the night strike, taking off from Soaremaa Island off the coast of Estonia. They caught the Berlin air defenses off guard, and returned to their base without a loss. Damage to Berlin was slight.

By August 11, two bomber air regiments from Long-Range Bomber Aviation (*Dal'naya aviatsiya*, or DA), flying Il-4s and Pe-8s, had joined the naval aviators. On one raid, launched from Pushkino near Leningrad on August 11, the Soviet bombers ran into determined German air defenses. Of the eleven Pe-8s sent from the 332d Bomber Air Regiment, only five returned safely. One Pe-8, in fact, was downed near Kronstadt by Soviet anti-aircraft and interceptors. Soviet naval air units attacked Berlin ten times in August-September.

A year earlier, the Royal Air Force (RAF) had bombed Berlin in a reprisal raid for the Luftwaffe's bombing of London, but the German capital in 1941, still largely unscathed after two years of war, found the Soviet night bombing a modest and ineffectual undertaking. Soviet crews displayed little bombing proficiency and, to make matters worse, their aircraft lacked range and payload capacity. For the Soviets in 1941, as with the British in 1940, the effort expressed the will to resist even in the darkest hour.[41]

One harbinger of the future was the Il-2 Shturmovik (ground-attack) aircraft. Unlike Soviet bombers, the Il-2 displayed considerable promise as a ground-attack weapon in the summer of 1941. Il-2s, soon to be dubbed the "flying tank," made effective, low-level attacks on German infantry, mechanized columns, and airfields. Its heavily armored shell was immune to small-arms fire, and Shturmovik pilots already were demonstrating an aggressiveness the Germans grudgingly respected. The problem for Soviet ground-attack units in 1941 was numbers: fewer than 400 Il-2s were available to the VVS during the first months of the German invasion.

In the desperate struggle with the Luftwaffe, the VVS employed the *taran*, or ramming technique, first used by the Russians in World War I. The deliberate ramming of a German aircraft occurred less than one hour after the invasion began, at 04:25 hours on June 22, 1941.[42] Lt. I. I. Ivanov of the 46th Fighter Air Regiment rammed a German bomber after his ammunition had been exhausted. This incident took place in the skies over the Zholkva region, near the spot where P. N. Nesterov, on August 26, 1914, had rammed the plane of Austrian Baron von Rosenthal. Following Nesterov's historic example, Ivanov drove his I-16 fighter into the tail of an He 111 bomber. Ivanov did not survive this bold maneuver, but he received posthumously the gold star, Hero of the Soviet Union.

Eight other Soviet pilots resorted to this tactic on the first day of the war.[43] Lt. D. V. Kokorev of the 124th Fighter Air Regiment, stationed in the Western Military District, rammed a Messerschmitt Bf 110 after exhausting his ammunition. More fortunate or skillfull than Ivanov, Kokorev survived the unorthodox maneuver by guiding his crippled fighter to a forced landing. In the southwest, A. I. Moklyak downed two German aircraft and then rammed a third. In the first two years, many VVS pilots scored multiple vic-

Luftwaffe airmen look in amazement at an He 111 bomber damaged in an aerial ramming by an I-16 Soviet fighter. Despite the severe damage to the fuselage and control surfaces, the German bomber made it back to its home base. Courtesy of Glen Sweeting.

tories by ramming. Lt. Boris Kobzan of the 184th Fighter Air Regiment became the top-scoring flyer in this demanding maneuver during the war, with four successful ramming assaults. Alexander Khlobystov followed Kobzan with three aerial victories by *taran*. Seventeen other VVS pilots are credited with two ramming victories. A total of more than 200 ramming attacks were made on the Luftwaffe during the war.[44]

Ramming differed from kamikaze attacks employed by the Japanese toward the end of World War II, although both reflected a blend of patriotism and desperation. For the Soviets, the tactic stemmed strictly from practical considerations. It was used at decisive moments, when there was no hope of knocking down an enemy plane by other means.[45]

A. I. Pokryshkin described the *taran* as an extreme measure, to be employed only after all ammunition had been exhausted. Frequently, it was the last-ditch means to down a crippled German bomber. Soviet air commanders did not issue specific orders for pilots to ram. Instead, the pilots exercised their own discretion, employing the technique when they felt it was necessary. If the pilot was skillful, he might survive, as many did, by parachuting to safety after ramming an enemy aircraft. Others, at considerable risk, flew their disabled fighters to the ground. For a successful *taran*, there was the significant achievement of downing a valuable German bomber and its five-man crew.

At the start of the war, the trade-off was in the Soviet favor—an obsolete I-16 fighter for a modern He 111 or Ju 88. Ramming became in time an established, if unconventional, air-combat technique. It never was merely a brutish suicidal plunge at an enemy plane. For the Soviets, it was a blend of flying skill and daring—always dangerous, but worthy of effort if one's ammunition was expended in the heat of battle. Unlike other air-combat tactics, the *taran* could not be practiced, only attempted with the confident expectation that one's flying skill equalled the challenge.

Three ramming methods were developed by Soviet aviators. The first, the one requiring the greatest skill and providing the best chance for survival, was to ram the control surfaces of the enemy aircraft. This was accomplished by approaching from the rear, adjusting to the speed of the enemy at close quarters, and then pushing the tip of the propeller into the opponent's rudder and/or elevator. As soon as firm contact was made, the Soviet pilot would drop away quickly, fearing he might become entangled with the stricken aircraft as it spun out of control. The resulting impact of the *taran* on the enemy aircraft and on the Soviet fighter was never predictable. Frequently, both fell into a spin. If propeller damage was minimal, the Soviet pilot might retain control and land safely.

A second method required more courage than artistry—ramming the fighter into the enemy aircraft at a moment of opportunity. This direct blow (*tarannyy udar*) proved to be the most dangerous. Being more spontaneous, it was frequently employed on those occasions when the Soviet fighter itself was damaged and a direct blow was the only way to score an aerial triumph in a context of diminishing options.

The third variant involved the skillful use of the wing of the Soviet plane as a weapon. Here, the pilot rammed one of his wings into the rudder of the enemy aircraft. A variation was to dip the wing of the fighter into the wing of German aircraft, forcing it out of control at a low altitude. Whatever method was used, the chances for survival were not high. The virtuoso pilot was one who could down the enemy and preserve his damaged aircraft in the uncertain aftermath.

Less publicized was another practice, mentioned by Pokryshkin, of flying head-on, at full throttle, at a German aircraft. Such feigned rammings demanded equal daring and were designed to make the enemy adopt evasive maneuvers. The tactic also had a supposed psychological impact, evoking fear and confusion in German air crews.

One of the most spectacular ramming feats occurred several weeks after Ivanov's effort in the first hour of the war. On August 6, 1941, a young, inexperienced pilot named Victor Talalikhin performed the first night ramming in history, a feat requiring extraordinary courage. Talalikhin, of the 177th Fighter Air Regiment PVO, was flying against Luftwaffe bombers on a night patrol over Moscow when he spotted an He 111 at about 15,000 feet and attacked from the rear. The German bomber swerved and dived to a lower altitude, but Talalikhin managed to retain visual contact and continue his pursuit, firing at the enemy with little effect.

At around 7,500 feet, Talalikhin had exhausted his ammunition. For several seconds he followed the He 111 in a mood of futility, pondering his next move. After some hesitation, he then maneuvered his I-16 interceptor to within thirty feet of the enemy bomber in order to ram it. As the threat to ram became apparent, the German gunner opened fire. At close range, the fire was intense and accurate, piercing the right side of Talalikhin's cockpit and searing his right arm. Simultaneously, Talalikhin opened his throttle and rammed into the rear of the He 111, which then spun out of control and crashed.

At 2,500 feet, the wounded Talalikhin, now flying upside down and out of control, managed to free himself and parachute into the night sky. He landed in a small lake, and later was feted in Moscow as the first major air hero of the war. His wartime career, however, was cut short on October 27 when he was killed in aerial combat over Moscow. For the Soviets in 1941, the feats of Talalikhin and others provided a measure of pride in a dark period of military defeat.

The phenomenon of ramming, in its active phase, lasted into 1943 and then disappeared, except for isolated incidents. Always an extreme tactic, it reflected the mood of national crisis and heroic sacrifice of 1941–42. After 1943, the VVS had acquired the strategic initiative in the air war, and the *taran* became less attractive as a combat tactic. The sacrifice of a modern Yak-9 or La-7 fighter for a German bomber was then considered a more expensive exchange.

One Soviet wartime pamphlet, *Ram Them!* (1943), expressed well the nationalistic fervor behind the *taran*. Written in English for an Anglo-American audience, the pamphlet described a simplistic air struggle between Stalin's "Falcons" and Nazi "Vultures." The pamphlet also portrayed with wild hyperbole the He 111 bomber crew which Talalikhin downed over Moscow:

> The fascist bomber plowed heavily through the air like a sinister bird of ill omen. It was commanded by a Lieutenant-Colonel, a regular fascist werewolf, gloating over the prospect of dropping his diabolical load upon the metropolis of the Soviet Union. With fiendish glee he pictured to himself the stars on the spires of

Victor Talalikhin, one of the first Soviet air heroes of the war, is shown with a bandaged hand after his historic night ramming of a German bomber over Moscow in August 1941. This photograph was taken by Margaret Bourke-White. Courtesy of Time–Life, Inc.

the Kremlin towers crashing to the ground, the cries of agony of women and children, which sounded to him like celestial music.[46]

The language in *Ram Them!* mirrored the emerging fierce brutality of the Russo-German war. Little chivalry animated the behavior of Soviet pilots in their struggle against this "fascist" enemy. Behind the unorthodox tactic of ramming, at first glance inexplicable to most Westerners, there was a profound patriotism, the willingness to risk one's life for the "Motherland." Emblazoned on many Soviet planes was the motto *za Rodinu*—"For the Motherland." The *taran* represented a higher calling for VVS pilots, a way of making a meaningful sacrifice for the nation. Since it was not an act of suicide, bravery alone was not sufficient: only pilots with flying skill could execute the maneuver properly. From the Soviet perspective, the ramming was a legitimate air-combat tactic, differing from other techniques of air warfare only in the sense that the entry-level requirements for courage and flying skill were so extraordinary.

Fateful Decisions

The German invasion of Russia appeared to follow the script of the fall of France in 1940. Operation Barbarossa in its opening phases had been punctuated with rapid breakthroughs, skillful displays of air-ground coordination, dramatic victories, and a series of encirclements of Soviet troops. The collapse of the Soviet Army appeared at hand. Few gave the Soviet regime any chance for survival, particularly after July 19 when Smolensk fell, opening the way to Moscow. By August, Army Group Center was at the gates of Moscow. Luftwaffe bombers had inaugurated a series of air raids which appeared to signal the imminent German assault on the Bolshevik capital.

Under Gen. Ritter von Leeb, Army Group North had occupied the Baltic republics in July, in a campaign coordinated with the Finns, who had advanced into their former territory in Karelia. On August 16 the Germans overran Novgorod and within a week had reached Krasnogvardeisk on the outskirts of Leningrad. By early September, the Germans had placed Leningrad under siege, which turned out to be one of the most protracted (900 days) and costly phases of the war for the Soviet defenders.

In the south, the Germans scored additional successes, but with much more difficulty. Army Group South, commanded by Field Marshal Karl von Rundstedt, had advanced into the vast Ukraine, with Kiev as the initial objective. Here Col. Gen. M. P. Kirponos held out bravely, but ultimately fell victim to German encirclement on September 16, a disaster aided in part by Moscow's unwillingness to let Kirponos withdraw to the east in time. Three days later Kiev, the ancient capital of the Ukraine, finally surrendered to the advancing Wehrmacht. Subsequently, Army Group South pushed on toward Rostov and into the Crimea.

The Soviet position at the end of August 1941 was precarious, but not hopeless. Already, there were signs of renewal and resiliency. The Nazi blitzkrieg had achieved dazzling tactical victories, but in a strategic sense it had failed to bring a total victory. The Soviet military, severely weakened and disorganized, persisted as a viable force. The Soviet political structure remained intact, even ready to evacuate Moscow, if necessary, to continue the struggle. On the eve of the battle for Moscow, the VVS could still muster 2,516 combat aircraft (638 in operational condition). Another factor, concealed in the confusion of Soviet reversals, was the survival of a significant number of VVS pilots, other air personnel, and technicians. For the prolonged struggle ahead, the Soviet Air Force did not face, as one might have expected, an acute shortage of flight crews.

The fate of the VVS rested ultimately on the crucial decision of the State Defense Committee, in early July 1941, to evacuate the Soviet war industries to the east. The herculean effort to transplant more than 1,500 industrial enterprises beyond the Ural Mountains at the height of the German invasion marks one of the most impressive Soviet wartime achievements.

The migration of workers and industrial machinery beyond the reach of the German Army required enormous effort and organizational work. Great hardships accompanied the workers, around 10 million during the great trek eastward, particularly during the winter of 1941–42, when they resumed industrial production under the most primitive conditions. By November 1941, Soviet aircraft production had dropped to 500–600 aircraft per month.[47] The war-making capacity of the aircraft industry, however, had been preserved. During 1942 the relocated plants produced nearly 25,000 aircraft. Most of these were newer models—Il-2s, Pe-2s, and Yak-1s. The rebirth of the Soviet Air Force after 1942 stemmed from this remarkable achievement.

The vestiges of the once-powerful Soviet Air Force enjoyed a brief respite in early September 1941, as the Germans moved into position to launch an offensive against Moscow. The decisive Battle for Moscow raged through the winter of 1941–42. The continuation of the war at Moscow signaled clearly that the Soviet Union had survived.

The military situation, however, remained grim and foreboding. Operation Barbarossa had shattered Soviet air power. The Communist party in the prewar years, especially under Joseph Stalin's leadership, had stressed preparedness. Yet, Operation Barbarossa had made a mockery of Soviet military capacity and had come close to toppling the Communist regime. Stalin and the Soviet military leadership behaved with hesitation and ignorance in the moment of crisis. Gross deficiencies in equipment, training, and organization emerged as the Soviets clumsily, if heroically, fought back.

In the air, the Soviet Air Force demonstrated little combat prowess, and reflected the overall Soviet technological backwardness. The magnitude of the air defeat prompted disbelief among the Soviet people and a profound sense of inferiority within the ranks of the surviving VVS crews. Military victories evoke celebrations; decisive defeats, even when redeemed at a later date, give rise to reflection and historical debate. For the Soviet Air Force leadership in the fall of 1941, there were many questions to ask about the pathway to June 22, 1941.

The Dnieper River Bend

This sequence of aerial photographs, taken boldly at tree-top level by the Luftwaffe, shows clearly the collapse of Soviet air defenses at Zaporozhe in 1941. The objective of the reconnaissance mission was the dam (the Dnepogas) at Zaporozhe on the Dnieper River bend. Already evident here is the Soviet effort to destroy the dam in advance of the German arrival. Opposite, top: the German reconnaissance aircraft approaches the dam at low level from the south over Khortitsa Island; opposite, bottom: the damage to the dam is clear from this close-up view. Shown on this page (top to bottom) are a view from the west bank of the river, a destroyed barge located on the east bank, and a final view of the destroyed bridge below the dam.

Chapter 2

Where Was Our Air Force?

A poster of a Soviet airman, one of Stalin's "Falcons," is removed from a building in German-occupied Ukraine. This photograph was taken by a German cameraman. Courtesy of Glen Sweeting.

"Where was our air force?" When Aleksandr Yakovlev, the Soviet aircraft designer, asked this question in the summer of 1941, he echoed the sentiments of a stunned Soviet public. Operation Barbarossa had exposed the myth of Soviet air power. The ashes of the once vast Soviet Air Force, the world's largest in 1940, now littered the flight lines of countless airfields in German-occupied Russia. The Luftwaffe had demonstrated in the summer skies of Russia its supremacy over the VVS in machines, flying technique, and combat experience. Soviet air preparedness had proved to be an illusion.

For twenty years the Soviet people had been conditioned to think of their air force as the most powerful in the world. Pilots of the Red Air Fleet had helped secure the Bolshevik Revolution in the 1918–21 Civil War. In the interwar years, Soviet pilots had flown over the North Pole, set numerous speed and endurance records, and established air links between Moscow and the remote hinterlands of the Soviet Union.

Propaganda organs portrayed the heroism of "Stalin's Falcons" in the Spanish Civil War, where Soviet "volunteers" struggled against the "forces of fascism." At the end of the 1930s, Soviet pilots again engaged in aerial skirmishes, apparently with success, against the Japanese in the Far East. Following the example of Igor Sikorskiy's "Il'ya Muromets," the Soviet Union under Stalin had built huge bomber and transport aircraft, best symbolized in the forty-two-ton "Maxim Gorkiy." These behemoths suggested in their size and payloads the great advances of the Soviet Union in aviation; the air triumphs, real and imagined, prompted in the public a sense of pride and confidence.

The Bolshevik regime, the survivor of a brutal civil war and foreign intervention, had stressed throughout the interwar years the importance of mili-

35

tary preparedness. The advent of Hitler and the Anti-Comintern Pact in the 1930s reinforced the propaganda claim that the Soviet Union faced aggressive external enemies. The Stalinist program for rapid modernization under a succession of five-year plans firmly established the impression that the Soviet Union had acquired the industrial base to wage modern warfare. The aviation industry, for example, boasted at the end of 1940 approximately 100 active plants with an annual production exceeding 10,000 planes. Besides the military schools, there were 125 aeronautical training centers, helping to build a vast cadre of pilots and aircraft technicians. On the surface the foundations of Soviet air power appeared secure, even at the moment the world drifted toward war.

The air debacle of 1941 prompted serious doubts, at least momentarily, about prewar Soviet aviation and its vaunted achievements. The perception of a powerful Soviet Air Force, so carefully nurtured by Stalin in the propaganda organs and public ritual, now appeared ludicrous. As the war progressed, however, the calamities of 1941 gave way to a period of extraordinary growth in Soviet air power. The taproots for this growth were to be found in the interwar decades.

Birth of the Red Air Fleet

The Bolsheviks inherited in 1917 a vast empire and a small air force. They came to power on November 7–8 through a carefully planned and executed coup d'état. For the next three years, the revolutionary party headed by Vladimir I. Lenin fought off a series of challenges to emerge as the successors to the Romanovs.

From the beginning, the Bolsheviks (after 1918, the Communist party) displayed an ardent interest in aviation. Lenin himself supervised the creation of a Bureau of Commissars for Aviation and Aeronautics as early as December 1917. The leadership of the new Soviet regime quickly embodied an air mindedness which fully appreciated the airplane as a weapon of modern warfare. To build an air arm for the Red Army, which had been organized by February 1918 to defend the revolution, an All-Russian College for the Administration of the Aerial Fleet, headed by K. V. Akashev, took shape that spring. Akashev, "a professional revolutionary, aviation engineer, and pilot," led a campaign to salvage aircraft from the old Imperial Air Force and to recruit flying personnel.

On May 24, 1918, "Order No. 385" of the People's Commissariat on Military and Naval Affairs created the Main Directorate of the Workers' and Peasants' Red Air Fleet (*Raboche-Krest'yanskiy Krasnyy Vozdushnyy flot*). M. A. Solovev headed the new directorate and assumed all the functions formerly exercised by Akashev and the All-Russian Aviation Board. With this move the Red Air Fleet became an integral part of the Red Army.[1]

These formative steps established important precedents, which influenced the subsequent evolution of Soviet air power. Akashev's appointment expressed the Bolshevik tendency to blend military expertise and political orthodoxy at leadership levels. The new Red Air Fleet, as part of the Red Army, served the revolution (i.e., the Communist party). In a context of revolutionary disorder, civil war, and foreign intervention, the Bolsheviks displayed a tough-minded pragmatism. For the new Soviet regime to survive, aircraft factories had to be reopened, pilots recruited, and air units reorganized—all under the tutelage of political commissars. The Bolsheviks promoted technical expertise, always in short supply, but the primacy of politics became firmly established.

Moreover, the new leadership learned in these early days the importance of tactical aviation. The Red Army fought on a variety of fronts against an ever-shifting set of foes. The Russian landscape was immense, and the army placed a priority on an air arm which could be deployed rapidly at decisive points. To meet these diverse requirements, the Red Air Fleet required rugged, easy to maintain aircraft. To keep the Red Air Fleet operational, the Bolsheviks resorted to a ruthless mobilization of human and material resources and improvisation in the battle zones.

The year 1918 presented enormous challenges for the All-Russian Aviation Board. Most aircraft factories had been destroyed or abandoned. Many pilots and technicians had defected to the counterrevolutionaries, or Whites. Others had been caught up in the vortex of the revolution, to be jailed or executed as counterrevolutionaries. For those air units which fell under Bolshevik authority, there were acute shortages in spare parts, fuel, and operational aircraft. Order No. 84, issued to the Peoples' Commissariat on Military and Naval Affairs in January 1918, called for the preservation of all aviation units and schools. The Aviation Board worked zealously against enormous obstacles to supply aviation stores, fuel, and aircraft to Soviet-held centers such as Moscow, Tula, and Petrograd.

Tsarist aviation, despite a tendency among many Soviet historians to downplay its achievements, provided the means, even the ideas, for building the Red Air Fleet. During World War I, the small Imperial Russian Air Force had flown more than 31,000 sorties. Russian air units had obtained considerable combat experience, flying diverse missions in all kinds of weather. Much had been learned about the uses of air power. Former tsarist fliers and technicians supplied a trained cadre for the new Bolshevik-led air force.

At the start of the First World War, the Russians had seven aircraft factories, producing over 400 aircraft in 1914. Although production did not expand dramatically during the years 1914–17, it sustained the effort of the Imperial Russian Air Force. As was to be the case with their revolutionary successors, tsarist air planners struggled with the restraints of a modest industrial base, chronic shortages in raw materials, bureaucratic incompetence, and dependence on the West for aero engines.

Between the time of the abdication of Nicholas II and the Bolshevik takeover, elements from the old Imperial Russian Air Force convened an All-Russian Congress of Military Pilots and Aviation Mechanics in Petrograd. The representatives, drawn from air units at Petrograd and from the front, met in April 1917 with the goal of preserving a viable air force in a context of war and revolution. By May 1917 the organizing effort had expanded to include representatives from the Petrograd All-Russian Aero Club, as well as engineers, teachers, journalists and aviation figures from Moscow. They launched a publication, *Vestnik letchikov i aviatsionnykh motoristov obnovlennoy Rossii* [Messenger of pilots and aviation mechanics of a reformed Russia]. In his inaugural statement, "A Bright Dawn After a Dark Night," the editor praised Russian military pilots for their bravery at the front and appealed to the entire aviation community on a nonpartisan basis to advance the cause of aviation. N. A. Rynin', "engineer, aviator, professor," ex-

Russian interest in aviation was high under Nicholas II, the last Tsar. Pictured here in 1911 is the military Bleriot XXI. (SI 81-13185)

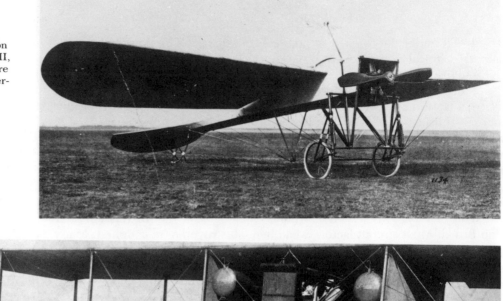

The Imperial Russian Navy purchased twenty Curtiss Flying Boats. This Curtiss airplane was assigned to the Black Sea Fleet at Sevastopol.

The Imperial Russian Air Force made a significant contribution to the war effort against Germany. Here a Russian pilot receives final instructions before a mission in front of his Morane Parasol fighter. (SI 81-9023)

A Voisin bomber, Imperial Russian Air Force. A Captain Stariparlov is pictured with his assistants and mechanics on the northwestern sector of the front. (SI 81-13187)

World War I prompted Russian avant-garde artist Natalie Goncharova to portray the airplane in visionary images. This was part of a series called "Voyna" (War), Moscow, 1914.

A group of Nieport 11 biplanes equipped by the Russians with skids for winter operations on the Eastern front. (SI 81-13186)

Igor Sikorsky's four-engine bomber, the Il'ya Muromets. At the outbreak of World War I the Imperial Russian Air Force possessed around fifty of these giant aircraft. (SI 81 2813)

A Russian-flown Albatros B-2 is shown at the front during World War I. (SI 81-9022)

pressed the vision of many in the Russian aviation community when he called for an "Aeronautical Institute." This projected institute, with its many departments and facilities (airfields, laboratories, and factories), would make Russia self-sufficient in both civil and military aviation. Much of the vision and goals of Rynin' and his associates entered into the Bolshevik air-mindedness of the post–1917 period.[2]

A Neuport 23 with red star insignia, Red Air Fleet, about 1918. (SI 81-2811)

The aircraft inherited by the Bolsheviks from the Imperial Air Force were largely of British or French origins. This mixed air flotilla consisted in the main of Nieuport, Caudron, Morane, Farman, Sopwith, Napier, and Spad machines, which had been imported or manufactured under license during World War I. The few Russian-built aircraft available to the Soviets were the Grigorovich M-9 and M-15 seaplanes and the Il'ya Muromets bombers. Ten of the latter machines survived and were used by the Soviets for transport duty. During the Civil War, the Soviets captured many aircraft—the German Albatros, Fokker, Halberstadt, and Brandenburg types, Spads, D.H. 4, D.H. 9, D.H. 11, and Sopwith two-seaters.[3] The Red Air Fleet was further diversified after 1921 by the importation of Italian, Dutch, German, and English aircraft of various types. Such a diverse aircraft inventory created enormous problems for the poorly trained Soviet maintenance and aviation support services.

The acute shortage of operational aircraft had limited the combat role of the Red Air Fleet in the Civil War. The total inventory consisted of approximately 980 aircraft in the spring of 1918;[4] of these perhaps 100 to 150 were operational at any given time.[5] By September of that year, 266 aircraft were operational, but the fleet faced enormous problems in providing logistical support, particularly fuel and spare parts.

Under the harsh conditions of Lenin's "War Communism" policy, the Soviets attempted to augment the numbers of operational aircraft through the ruthless use of force. A decree issued on January 12, 1918, by the Council of Peoples' Commissars of the Republic put all aircraft factories under state control. Always fearful of sabotage and counterrevolution, the Soviets ordered all technical and professional personnel to remain at their posts with the explicit threat that "willful negligence of assigned duties" would mean an appearance before a revolutionary court. Further mobilization of the aviation industry continued through the Council of Labor and Defense. These emergency measures achieved some modest successes: Soviet-controlled aviation industries repaired for combat use 1,574 aircraft and 1,740 engines, and manufactured 669 aircraft and 270 engines,[6] during the course of the Civil War.

The effort to destroy the old imperial military establishment in the immediate aftermath of the Bolshevik takeover had created an acute shortage of trained personnel. Most pilots came from the social classes least sympathetic to the revolution in general, and the Bolsheviks in particular. Having been officers in the Imperial Air force, they were largely aristocratic in background and were perceived by the Bolsheviks as political risks. Some fliers, including Russian air ace Kazakov, joined the Whites against the Bolsheviks. Others, like Alexander Severskiy, had gone into exile.[7] But a significant number of flight personnel volunteered for the Red Air Fleet.

To maintain party control, a military commissar system exercised authority over the military specialists recruited from the ranks of former tsarist officers. Communist party members assumed key positions, and party cells

The Airplane and Propaganda Warfare

From its inception the Red Air Fleet served political purposes. Sometimes political and military activities merged, as evidenced by these leaflets, which were dropped on German troops in two wars.

This historic leaflet, signed by Trotsky and Lenin, was dropped on German lines by the Red Air Fleet in January 1918. (SI (SI 80-4204)

Der Rat des Volkskommissare in Petersburg verschickt durch Funkspruch folgendes Telegramm, dessen Veröffent-lichung der deutschen Presse verboten wurde und das wohl wie gewöhnlich von der deutschen Presse dementiert werden wird. Denn das deutsche Heer und das deutsche Volk dürfen die Wahrheit nicht erfahren:

Tsarskoie-Selo, 6. Januar 1918.

Deutsche Deserteure berichten, dass alle unter 35 Jahren alte Soldaten der Ostfront nach Kowno und Wilna geführt werden, wo sie ein für die Westfront bestimmtes Heer bilden sollen. Diese Massnahme bildet einen formellen Bruch der Bedingungen, die für den Waffenstillstand vereinbart wurden.

Gez: TROTZKY, LENIN.

A pass through Soviet lines was offered to German officers and soldiers of the 57th and 168th infantry divisions in 1942. A quote from no less a person than Joseph Stalin promises safe passage to all German deserters. Courtesy of Herman Neff. (SI 79-5025)

"Wenn deutsche Soldaten und Offiziere sich ergeben, nimmt sie die Rote Armee, gefangen und schont ihr Leben,,,

Aus dem Befehl STALINS Nr. 55

Passierschein für die Offiziere und Soldaten der 57.I.D. und 168.I.D.
Пропуск для офицеров и солдат 57 пд. и 168 пд.

Jeder deutsche Soldat ist berechtigt, mit diesem Passier-schein die Front zu überschreiten und sich den Russen gefang-enzugeben. Jeder Angehörige der Roten Armee und jeder Sowjetbürger ist verpflichtet, ihn in den nächstgelegenen Stab der Roten Armee zu führen.
Das Kommando der Roten Armee garantiert dem Kriegsgefangenen das Leben, gute Behandlung und die Heim-kehr nach dem Kriege. ▭ ▭ ▭
Bei der Gefangengabe — Hände hoch, und niemand Schiesst auf Euch!

---

were organized at various levels to reinforce political conformity. One Orwellian measure, the so-called "group of three system," organized all military personnel in a given air unit into groups of three; the desertion or treason of one member brought the entire triad under "revolutionary justice for treason."

These harsh measures and the use of tsarist officers and technical personnel were expedient ways of making the Red Air Fleet operational in a war emergency. At the same time, the Bolsheviks sought to recruit and train Communists or Communist sympathizers. Some of these men, who met the minimal physical requirements to be pilots, were ordered arbitrarily into flight training regardless of their aptitudes or personal inclinations. By the end of the Civil War, in late 1920, more than half of the pilots in the Red Air Fleet were Communist party members. Some Soviet sources claim that a total of 730 pilots or observers had been trained during this period. The figure may be exaggerated, but the entire training program, with all its coerciveness, demonstrated the Communist regime's determination to build a viable air arm. By threat and appeals to revolutionary duty, the Red Air Fleet made significant strides in the recruitment and training of flight personnel during the difficult years of the Civil War when the fate of the revolution itself hung in the balance.[8]

Already in the chaotic period of the Civil War, the Red Air Fleet articulated a basic air doctrine which emphasized the tactical use of air power in support of the Red Army. The Red Air Fleet's limited striking power dictated that its units not be diffused, but concentrated at selected points for maximum effect. Sometimes as many as fifty Soviet aircraft were mobilized for a single air operation, as in the defense of Petrograd in late 1919. A draft manual on the combat use of aircraft, published in June 1919 by the Field Directorate for Aviation and Aeronautics, embodied these operational principles. One of the authors of this manual, A. N. Lapchinskiy, went on to become a major Soviet air theorist in the interwar years.

The magnitude of Red Air Fleet operations during the Civil War remains uncertain. Soviet sources do not always agree, but one of them listed a total of nearly 20,000 sorties, including 144 air battles. Most combat sorties appear to have been low-level strafing and bombing missions. Others included aerial reconnaissance and liaison between the widely deployed Red Army units.[9]

Improvisation became an established tradition in the Red Air Fleet. To meet the demands of the Red Army, aircraft were shipped by rail from front to front. Such measures enhanced the mobility and striking power of the Red air arm, but chronic shortages in men and machines severely limited the scope of operations. Captured enemy aircraft were repaired or cannibalized to support Soviet air operations. Whenever possible, experiments were conducted in night fighting, dive bombing, and cold-weather operations.[10]

To meet a serious shortage of aviation fuel in 1919, one air unit in the battle against the Whites, under General Denikin, concocted the "Kazan mixture," a make-do fuel consisting of alcohol, ether, toluene, and other additives. The Kazan mixture failed to supply full power, while corroding metal and hoses, but it proved to be a workable expedient. In the same spirit, when Red air units faced a shortage of rubber tires, they wrapped several layers of towing ropes around the aircraft's wheels.[11] This seeking of common-sense, primitive solutions to problems in the field foreshadowed the shrewd pragmatism of the VVS in World War II.

By 1921 the new Soviet regime had defeated its rivals and consolidated its political power. The triumph, however, was accompanied by diplomatic isolation and military weakness. In a speech to the All-Russian Congress of Soviets in December 1921, Lenin defined the mood and purpose of the new Soviet Union: "the first precept of our policy . . . is to be on the alert and to remember that we are surrounded by people, classes, and governments which are openly expressing the most bitter hatred toward us." In this same speech Lenin articulated the notion of a state and society under siege, "always on the edge of invasion." This condition of perpetual threat called for "constant military preparedness" and the need "to strengthen the combat capability" of the Red Army.[12] Lenin's goals, as outlined in this speech, became state policy in the 1920s and 1930s. Given the Bolshevik air mindedness, this stress on military preparedness meant a rapid expansion of the Red Air Fleet.

The building of a strong air arm required a large modern aviation industry, and the Soviet leadership decided to move in this direction despite limited resources and competing economic priorities. The Soviets were fortunate in having a talented group of aeronautical engineers and designers to provide leadership for their embryonic aviation industry. In 1918 N. E. Zhukovskiy, supported by Lenin, had established the Central Institute for Aerodynamics and Hydrodynamics (*Tsentral'nyy aero-gidrodinamicheskiy institut*, or TsAGI). Other research institutes for aeroengines and aviation materials also appeared; the Bolshevik stress on technical education as a key component in their cultural revolution provided an incentive to expand the aviation schools. At Moscow, the Institute of Red Air Fleet Engineers School (later the Zhukovskiy Military Air Academy) opened its doors in 1919.[13] In a few short years, the institutional base for the expansion of Soviet aviation had been established.

M. V. Frunze, a Soviet military theorist, argued in the 1920s that military preparedness could not be achieved without a modern industrial base.[14] The Soviet Press echoed this viewpoint. "During the war," *Izvestiya* lamented in 1923, "our pilots gave proof of their skill, but we have no airplanes or air industries."[15] The Soviet aviation industry in the year prior to this *Izvestiya* article produced a meager forty-three aircraft and eight aero engines.[16] At the Tenth Party Congress in 1921, Lenin had inaugurated the New Economic Policy (NEP), which allowed an awkward mixture of socialism and foreign capitalist investment to revitalize the nation's economy.

Economic recovery, even the goal of achieving 1913, pre–World War I levels, advanced slowly in the 1920s. Despite the economic crisis, the Soviet regime in 1921 allocated three million rubles, a considerable sum for the time, to provide the seed money to rebuild selected aircraft factories. The following year, 35 million rubles were designated for the development of the aviation industry. In 1924 a new three-year plan for the expansion of the Red Air Fleet was approved. Dependence on foreign aero engines persisted, however, as a crucial problem area, and this technological gap defied any quick solution. Self-sufficiency had not been achieved in the Soviet aviation industry by 1928, despite a decade of growth.

The Communist party put its considerable weight behind the effort to support the Red Air Fleet. To make the Soviet Union more air-minded, the party in 1923 established the Society of Friends of the Air Fleet (*Obshchestvo druzei vozdushnogo flota* or ODVF).[17] With more than five thousand branches and around one million members, ODVF became a nationwide repository of Soviet air consciousness. Participants donated a portion of their salary, usually a day's wage, for the building of aircraft. ODVF called upon the workers and peasants for hard work and personal sacrifice. It became a conduit to express Bolshevik enthusiasm for the benefits of modern technology. Slogans, hyperbolic language, and organized events to dramatize Soviet devotion to air power punctuated the life of ODVF.

In 1925 ODVF merged with the Society of the Friends of Chemical Defense to form the Association for the Promotion of Defense, Aviation and Chemical Warfare (*Osoaviakhim*). This paramilitary organization for Soviet youth became an important and ubiquitous buttress for Soviet aviation in the interwar years. Its wide-ranging activities included civil-defense drills, flight training, navigation, aircraft maintenance, and the aggressive propagation of air power.

Through a clandestine program of collaboration with Weimar Germany in 1922, the Soviet Union found a way to obtain valued technical assistance in building its aviation industry. The Soviets offered the Germans training facilities, outlawed at the time by the Treaty of Versailles, in exchange for the modern aircraft factories.[18] Gen. Hans von Seeckt argued forcefully for the covert arrangement as a vehicle to build German air power. At the same time, he attempted to convince German aviation industrialists that the Soviet Union under the NEP was a place for profitable investment. Soon after the agreement was reached, a group of German pilots began training near Smolensk. In 1924 a training base was established at Lipetsk in central Russia, where more than 450 German air force personnel received instruction over the next ten years. Various types of experimental aircraft were tested under strict secrecy. Soviet airmen obtained valuable training in the latest German flying techniques, and also participated in joint air maneuvers with the Germans. (After Hitler came to power in 1933, he ordered the Lipetsk school closed.)[19]

The Soviet government anxiously sought German-built aircraft factories as part of the Russo-German exchange program, but General von Seeckt encountered difficulty in attracting German private industry to work in Soviet Russia on any sustained basis. Through subsidies, however, he did manage to recruit token German investment. Junkers established an aircraft factory at Fili, near Moscow, in October 1922. Once completed, the company agreed to produce 300 planes per year, sixty to be purchased by the Soviet government. Representatives from Junkers were responsible for equipping the plant and supplying the skilled labor;[20] the Soviets provided raw materials and the nonskilled work force. In less than two years, however, the Junkers plant found itself in difficulty as a result of the financial crisis in Germany and poor management,[21] and in time the Soviet government discovered that it was less expensive to purchase equipment outright from abroad. Nevertheless, the plant was a major undertaking, with more than 400 German engineers and skilled workers. It represented a type of technology transfer which the Soviets eagerly desired in the 1920s. In addition to German aid, the Soviet Union obtained technical assistance from the United States, Italy, France, Britain, and other western countries during the same period.

The Soviets, meanwhile, did not neglect to expand their indigenous aviation industry during the austere NEP period. *Glavkoavia* (the Chief Administration for the Aviation Industry), organized under the Supreme Economic Council, worked diligently to build aircraft and aero-engine plants. The program advanced slowly because of acute shortages in machine tools and materials. There were also chronic organizational problems, the competing priorities of civil and military aviation, the dependence on foreign aircraft and engine types, and the small available pool of skilled workers. By the end of the decade, the Soviets had only about eighteen aircraft and engine factories.[22] Significant growth was not achieved until the 1930s, during the Stalinist drive for rapid industrialization.

While the industrial base for aviation was expanding in the 1920s, the air force command structure prospered under the tutelage of Air Commander P. I. Baranov. A Bolshevik since 1912 and the son of a St. Petersburg worker, Baranov assumed the post of head of the Main Directorate of the Air Forces of the Workers' and Peasants' Red Army in 1924.[23] Ably assisted by Deputy Air Force Commander Ya. I. Alksnis, Baranov brought continuity and professionalism to the Red Air Force. He expanded air force programs in training, meteorology, and navigation. During his tenure, a group of theorists emerged to debate the problems of air power. Men such as A. S. Algazin, V. V. Khripin, A. N. Lapchinskiy, and B. D. Teplinskiy endeavored to define a Soviet air doctrine.[24]

At the conclusion of the first decade of Communist rule, the Soviet Air Force had made significant progress; it constituted about 10 percent of the Soviet armed forces in 1928 and the leadership had acquired experience and professionalism. Behind Soviet air power was an expanding industrial base, a network of new research and design institutions such as TsAGI, new aviation schools, a growing cadre of pilots and mechanics, broad public support of aviation, and also the vital imprimatur of the Communist leadership. Despite these real accomplishments, the technological gap with the West persisted. The year 1928 also saw the emergence of Joseph Stalin as the political successor to Lenin, who had died in 1924. The advent of Stalin's rule signaled a new era. For the Soviet Air Force the next decade would bring both triumph and tragedy.

Stalinist Aviation

Joseph Stalin presided over a series of profound changes in Soviet life in the second decade of Bolshevik rule. Having consolidated his political authority after a four-year struggle for power, he ruthlessly pushed a program of industrialization, the forced collectivization of agriculture, and the building of a totalitarian state under the aegis of the Communist party. Since Stalin fully embraced the goal of modernization, the Soviet aeronautical world at first became a beneficiary of the regime's largess and propaganda. Soviet fliers, called "Stalin's Falcons," received lavish public praise for their exploits, and occupied a role in Soviet life comparable to that of the Soviet cosmonauts a generation later. Self-sufficiency became the watchword in the aviation industry. Stalin gave concrete support, as reflected in budget allocations, to the expansion of aviation design bureaus and factories. Within a short period of time, the Soviet Air Force acquired a new generation of combat aircraft. The fast I-15 interceptor and the large TB-3 bomber, dramatic examples of Stalinist achievements in aviation, gave the VVS status as a first-rank air force in the turbulent decade of the 1930s.

An early Soviet aerial spectacular. Between August 23 and October 30, 1929, S. Shestakov with a crew consisting of a copilot, navigator, and mechanic flew the all-metal *Land of the Soviets*, a twin-engine TB-1 (ANT-4), on a flight from Moscow to New York City. The Soviet crew is pictured on October 19, 1929, upon their arrival at Sandpoint Naval Airport, Seattle, Washington. (SI 81-6998)

Stalin launched a series of "Five-Year Plans," the first in 1928, to transform the Soviet Union into a modern industrial society. The construction of new aircraft plants became a high priority for his economic planners. One Soviet source listed six aircraft and four aero engine plants built in 1930.[25] Non-Soviet sources suggest a different figure, perhaps eighteen plants in 1929 and thirty in 1931.[26] Whatever the base figure, the Soviet aviation industry expanded dramatically during the decade, reaching new levels of productivity.[27] In the first year of the initial Five-Year Plan the aircraft plants, depending on the source, produced 500 to 1,000 aircraft,[28] The average yearly totals for the period of this plan may have been 1,250 to 1,500 aircraft.[29] By 1936, at the time of the second Five-Year Plan, the figures were 7,000 to 8,000 aircraft. During the final year of peacetime production, 1940, Soviet factories produced 10,000 to 12,000.[30]

Growth was steady during this period of the Five-Year Plans, but quality frequently fell below Western standards. Dependence on foreign technology, particularly in aircraft-engine development, continued to compromise the goal of self-sufficiency. Even as the Five-Year Plans expanded the indigenous aircraft production facilities, Soviet representatives negotiated agreements to build American-made Wright engines and Douglas DC series aircraft under license. The importance attached to aircraft production became evident in a symbolic way at the end of the 1930s when Stalin created a separate People's Commissariat of the Aviation Industry.[31]

The Soviets designed and produced a whole new generation of military aircraft during this period of rapid expansion. In the 1920s, N. N. Polikarpov designed the highly derivative I-2, I-2 bis, and I-3 fighters. These undistinguished biplane fighters gave way to the I-5, designed by the team of N. N. Polikarpov and D. P. Grigorovich. The I-5 entered VVS units as the standard fighter aircraft in the early 1930s. Despite these advances, however, Soviet fighters lagged behind comparable Western models in speed, maneuverability, and armament. One Soviet source has claimed that the VVS inventory consisted largely of Soviet-built aircraft before the start of the first Five-Year

Plan, but this claim could be made only at the end of the 1930s, not in 1928.[32]

The Soviets displayed an enthusiasm for large, powerful aircraft during the interwar years. A. N. Tupolev, associated with TsAGI from its earliest days, became the preeminent designer of large bombers and civilian transports. The Soviet affinity for such behemoths grew more out of the Bolshevik mind-set than any belief in Giulio Douhet's notion of strategic bombing. "Giantism" became a measure of technological progress. In 1925, Tupolev designed the ANT-4 (TB-1), a prototype for his giant aircraft of the 1930s. The Topolev-designed TB-3, an all-metal, four-engine bomber, entered mass production in the mid-1930s as the standard Soviet heavy bomber. The SB (fast) bomber, designed by A. A. Arkhangelskiy, and the DB-3 long-range bomber, designed by S. V. Il'yushin, diversified the growing Soviet aircraft inventory by adding medium-range bombers. By 1935 the Soviet Union had the largest bomber force in the world.

For a brief period in the thirties, the Soviets produced some of the best fighter aircraft in the world—the I-15 and I-16, both designed by Polikarpov. The I-15 was a snub-nosed biplane powered by a Soviet-built 715-hp Wright cyclone engine, called the M-25. It was first flown in October 1933 and entered into serial production the following year. It achieved considerable fame in 1936 when it became the standard fighter used by the Loyalist forces in the Spanish Civil War.

The I-15 was armed with two 7.62mm machine guns. It could achieve a maximum speed of 225 mph, a performance sharply reduced when it was equipped with bombs or rockets. By 1936 the Soviets had produced the I-15 *bis*, powered by the M-25B engine with 775 hp. This variant displayed little improvement over the I-15, the more powerful engine providing only a marginal increase in range.

The gull-winged I-153 "Chaika," coming in line in 1938, represented an important step forward in performance. Armed with four 7.62mm machine

Joseph Stalin's stress on giant aircraft is best illustrated by the ANT-20 *Maksim Gorkiy*, an eight-engine behemoth with a crew of twenty and a variable passenger capacity of forty-three to seventy-six. The *Maksim Gorkiy*, equipped with a cinema in the rear fuselage, a printing press, and a photolab, was destroyed on May 18, 1935, in a collision with an I-4 fighter. (SI 79–9505)

guns, the I-153 boasted a speed of 275 mph. While heavier than the I-15 types, the I-153 was powered by a M-62, 1,000-hp engine. The I-16, a monoplane introduced in the same year as the I-15, followed the same pattern of refinement. The original version of the I-16 was powered with the same M-25 engine used on I-15, but the I-15 powerplant was improved to achieve the speed—282 mph. The improved I-16, flown in the late 1930s, was powered by the M-62 engine and achieved a speed of 326 mph. Compact, snub-nosed, and highly maneuverable, the late-model I-16, called the "Rata" by the Germans, was armed with two 7.62mm machine guns and two 20mm cannon. Compared to the I-15 and I-153 biplanes, the I-16 had greater performance and firepower, but slightly reduced range. These VVS fighters, particularly the I-16, represented performance characteristics equal or superior to their counterparts in the West in the mid-1930s.

Keeping pace with the rapid changes in aeronautical technology required considerable effort, but the Soviets claimed important advances. In armament, the ShKAS machine gun, designed by B. G. Shpital'nyy and I. A. Komaritskiy, entered operational service with a claimed (and unlikely) rate-of-fire of 1,800 rounds per minute.[33] Optical sights, the electrical bomb release, the oxygen support system, improved parachutes, and aviation medicine became additional measures of the Soviet technical advancement.[34]

Aviation provided benchmarks in "socialist construction" in the same way as the building of the Moscow subway, canals, or factories. Stalin's Falcons established new record-breaking flights in the 1930s, and quickly assumed a prominent place in Soviet public life. The propaganda organs systematically exploited air feats such as Valeriy Chkalov's historic flight over the North Pole, anticipating Sputnik and the flight of Yuri Gagarin a generation later. For those living under the brutal regimen of the Stalinist years, the aerial spectaculars gave substance to the claim of the Communist party that it was leading Soviet society from the backward tsarist stage toward modernization. Such achievements in the technological sphere reinforced the political legitimacy of the Stalin regime.[35] The Communist party exercised authority and leadership over culture and industrial progress. The precise flybys of hundreds of Soviet aircraft over Red Square on May Day dramatically embodied all these rehearsed images of air progress.

Between 1934 and 1938 Stalin's Falcons attracted worldwide attention through a series of air feats. In February 1934 a Soviet icebreaker, the *Chelyuskin*, sank in the icy Choukchi Sea. A group of six Soviet fliers rescued the trapped crew. All received a specially commissioned medal, Hero of the Soviet Union.[36] V. P. Chkalov, the most famous of Soviet fliers in this period, flew to Udd (now Chkalov) Island in the Arctic Circle in 1936, a nonstop flight in an ANT-25 with crew members G. F. Baydukov and A. V. Belyakov. The following year Chkalov with the same crew flew across the North Pole to Portland, Oregon. A second flight in 1937, led by M. M. Gromov, extended Chkalov's route by flying an ANT-25 from Moscow to San Jacinto, near San Diego, California, a total of 6,262 miles in 62 hours, 17 minutes. A third crew was lost attempting the same feat, but Soviet prowess in long-distance flights had been firmly established by 1937.

That same year saw the Soviets achieve other records. A total of ten altitude records were set by V. K. Kokkinaki, A. B. Yamashev, and M. A. Ninkhtikov. This era of spectaculars drew to a close in 1938 when three women—V. S. Grizodubova, P. O. Osipenko, and M. M. Raskova—flew an ANT-37, the *Rodina* (Motherland), across the vast terrain of the Soviet Union (eleven time zones!) to achieve a women's record of 3,672 miles in 26 hours, 29 minutes.

At home, the Soviets used aircraft in orchestrated displays to dramatize technological achievement. The annual Aviation Day was held on August 18, a public holiday to celebrate the aerial prowess of Soviet fliers and their aircraft. At Tushino Air Field near Moscow in 1937, squadrons of Soviet aircraft flew in precise formations spelling out the names of Lenin, Stalin, and USSR. Soviet aircraft also appeared on carefully arranged time schedules to provide drama at May Day and other public celebrations in the Soviet calendar. "Aviation," Politburo member L. M. Kaganovich stated in 1938, "is the highest expression of our achievements. Our aviation is a child of Stalinist industrialization; flyers are our proved falcons, raised lovingly and with care by Stalin."[37]

In retrospect, the excessive interest in aerial spectaculars and the funds expended on the development of large aircraft functioned to the disadvantage of Soviet aviation. It was a grandiose misuse of limited resources. The construction of bombers and the flirtation with Douhet's doctrine of strategic bombing diverted attention from the design of tactical aircraft which could provide air support to the army in a future war. The aerial achievements of Soviet pilots helped to create a myth of Soviet air power. Defense requirements were not served by these expensive activities. The only justification was political: Soviet mastery of the air, a carefully orchestrated myth, helped to consolidate Stalin's power by diverting public attention from the somber realities of forced industrialization and the purges.

Air Battles and Purges

Military conflict in Spain in 1936, the Far East in 1938, and Finland at the end of the decade had a profound effect on Soviet aviation. These military encounters provided opportunities for the Soviets to test their combat aircraft and air crews against the latest technology of Germany, Italy, and Japan. The results were mixed, but the frustrations encountered helped to redirect VVS development. In the immediate context, these air skirmishes exposed to Soviet leadership critical weaknesses in organization, aircraft design, air tactics, and strategic planning. For the long-term development of the VVS, the reversals were important, for they stimulated a process of modernization. The combat with German, Japanese, and Finnish air power set into motion new ideas about tactics, aircraft development, and technological innovation. It was unfortunate for the Soviet Air Force that these developments had not reached fruition by June 1941 at the time of Operation Barbarossa.

The Soviet military intervention in the Spanish Civil War in 1936 remains even today a confusing and controversial episode. Soviet military aid in fact did not prove decisive in the effort to preserve the Spanish Republic from defeat at the hands of Italian- and German-backed Nationalists under Gen. Francisco Franco. The Civil War in Spain lasted for three years, 1936–39, and provided the first sustained opportunity since the Bolshevik Revolution to measure the technological advances in Soviet air power.

The Soviets made their appearance in the Spanish war in the summer and fall of 1936 in order to "repel fascism." Moscow sent in a "volunteer"

Ya. V. Smushkevich (second from left), a hero of the Spanish Civil War and one-time Soviet Air Force commander, is pictured in prewar Moscow attending sessions of the Supreme Soviet. He died in the Stalinist purges.

group of 141 pilots, accompanied by a support group consisting of nearly 2,000 technicians and mechanics. They sailed from Odessa to the Spanish ports of Alicante and Cartagena.[38] The Soviet air units flew I-15 and I-16 fighters, along with a smaller number of SB-2 bombers. Command of the air contingent remained strictly in Soviet hands under the leadership of the able Gen. Yakov Smushkevich. Before his assignment in Spain, Smushkevich had served as a deputy to General Alksnis, air commander of the VVS. Coincidental with the arrival of Smushkevich's unit, the Germans sent in their own "volunteer" group, consisting of eighty-five men. This initial air component was augmented in November 1936 by the arrival of the Condor Legion. By the end of the year, the German air commitment to Franco's Nationalist cause numbered 370 pilots, with 50 fighters and 150 Junkers Ju 52 transports.[39]

The Soviet air operations in Spain began with high expectations and some measure of success, only to decline in effectiveness as the war progressed. Soviet-built SB-2 bombers sank the German cruiser *Deutschland* off Saragossa in May 1937. At the beginning of the conflict, the Soviet I-15 and I-16 fighters proved to be superior against the German Heinkel 51 and the Arado fighters, although the superiority of German training frequently tipped the scales against the Soviets. Smushkevich and his fellow fliers found themselves hampered by shortages in spare parts and the absence of efficient maintenance services. Despite reinforcements in aircraft and personnel, the Soviet air contingents did not achieve air superiority over the enemy.

During the crucial summer campaign of 1937, at the very moment that Soviet commitment had reached full stride, the Germans introduced a new generation of aircraft—the Messerschmitt Bf 109 fighter, the Ju 87 Stuka, the He 111, and Do 17 bombers. This dramatic leap forward in technology dramatically altered the course of the air war over Spain. The Bf 109 quickly demonstrated its superiority. The Ju 87 Stuka provided the Franco side with an effective ground-attack weapon. The He 111 and Do 17 bombers, with their increased speed, range, and payloads, gave the Nationalists a formidable striking power, which the SB-2 could not match. Having been suddenly and embarrassingly outclassed, the Soviet air units could do little to regain the initiative in the air. Once the Spanish Republic appeared to be on the road to defeat, a reality by the summer of 1938, Stalin began the gradual withdrawal of his Falcons from Spain. The Soviets, by one estimate, had sent more than 1,400 combat aircraft to Spain, about two-thirds of them being I-15 and I-16 fighters.[40]

Even with such an enormous commitment of aircraft and personnel, the Soviets had been unable to turn the tide. For Soviet air commanders in Spain, there was also the sobering realization that the Germans had displayed superior air-combat tactics. Wolfram von Richthofen's experiments with radio-controlled ground-attack sorties and Werner von Molders's fighter tactics based on the "Rotte" (two aircraft) and "Schwarm" (four aircraft) configurations had also contributed to German air dominance.

The German ascendancy in equipment and tactics made a deep impression on returning Soviet airmen in 1938–39. The need for the Soviet Union to design a new generation of aircraft, especially fighters and ground-attack types, became apparent. Other lessons came in the wake of the Spanish experience: the importance of tactical aviation, the need to develop greater coordination between air and ground forces, the use of fighters in air defense, the ineffectiveness of heavy bombers, and the shortcomings of Soviet engines and armament.[41]

Soviet intervention extended as well to the Far East. Between 1938 and 1940, the Soviet Union gave extensive military and technical assistance to China in the struggle against Japan. On two occasions, Soviet air power came into sharp conflict with the Japanese, first at Lake Khasan in July 1938 and then at Khalkhin-Gol in May 1939. Both encounters ended with Soviet claims of victory.

The Lake Khasan incident began with the Soviet fortification of a hill (Cheng fu-keng) in the summer of 1938 near the ill-defined Soviet-Korean border. In retaliation, the Japanese attacked, an effort which soon escalated the border dispute into a small-scale war. At the height of the conflict, the Soviets committed twenty-seven infantry battalions, supported by artillery and tanks.[42] Before the end of the twelve-day skirmish the Soviet Air Force had appeared in strength to assist the ground forces: a total of 70 fighters, 180 bombers, including 50 lumbering TB-3 heavy bombers.

Flying largely ground support for units of the First Independent Red-Banner Far Eastern Army, the VVS launched large-scale air strikes against Japanese positions. These operations foreshadowed the massed application of Soviet air power during the Great Patriotic War. The Japanese withdrew from the disputed territory near Lake Khasan with significant losses, the Soviets claiming more than 3,000 Japanese dead and wounded.[43]

At Khalkhin-Gol, a river near the border of Outer Mongolia and Manchuria, the Soviets accepted another military challenge from the Japanese, in May 1939. As with the Lake Khasan incident, a Japanese border intrusion set into motion a sequence of military escalations which nearly erupted into full-scale conflict. On May 28, 1939, General Smushkevich arrived with a group of experienced fliers from the Spanish war to help regain air supremacy. By June, intense air battles had erupted over the disputed border area as each side flew air strikes against opposing airfields. According to one Soviet account, an air battle on June 22, 1939, pitted 120 Japanese aircraft against 95 Soviet fighters. In the ensuing aerial struggle, which continued for two and a half hours, the Soviets downed thirty-one Japanese aircraft, losing only eleven of their own.

In another encounter, on June 29, the Soviets claimed to have downed twenty-five enemy fighters while losing only two aircraft. One of the downed Soviet fliers, Maj. V. H. Zabaluyev, parachuted nineteen miles behind Japanese lines. Maj. S. I. Gritsevets boldly landed and rescued Zabaluyev, even as enemy troops advanced and Japanese aircraft threatened them from the skies. For Gritsevets's bravery, he was awarded the gold star, Hero of the Soviet Union.[44]

The Khalkhin-Gol fighting extended from May to September 1939, and soon acquired the dimensions of a small war. The Soviet 1st Army Group under General Zhukov, launched a counteroffensive against the Japanese on August 20, 1939. By September 15, the Japanese had been expelled, and the Soviets claimed a significant victory. Before the offensive, the Soviets recorded 355 Japanese planes destroyed, 320 of them downed in aerial combat. In the period of the counteroffensive, the VVS claimed another 290 Japanese planes downed. For this dramatic victory, the Soviets admitted only modest losses—thirty-four aircraft lost, for example, in the last two months of the conflict. The magnitude of the air war over Khalkhin-Gol was impressive, involving as many as 250 aircraft, according to some Soviet sources. In the end the Japanese withdrew, surrendering the field to the Soviets.[45]

Against Finland in the Winter War of 1939–40, the VVS enjoyed fewer successes. The Nazi-Soviet pact, signed in August 1939, allowed the Soviet Union the freedom to "rectify" its borders with several nations. The efforts to pressure the Finns into territorial and military concessions failed in the fall of 1939. As a result, the Soviet Union launched a military invasion of Finland on November 30. The Soviet effort began with confidence of a quick victory, but soon the Soviet military found itself stalemated as the Finns displayed fierce resistance. The Finnish Army, numbering a mere 200,000, held on under heavy Soviet pressure. The Soviet Army deployed forty-five rifle divisions, 1,500 tanks, and 3,000 aircraft to subdue the Finns.[46]

At the outset of the Winter War, the Finnish Air Force consisted of only 145 aircraft organized into twelve squadrons;[47] the inventory included mostly obsolete types of mixed origin—sixty-five Fokker C-10s, C-5s, and D-2s, ten Bristol Bulldogs, fifteen Blackburn Ripons, and other assorted aircraft. As the war progressed, the Finns received 200 additional aircraft and volunteer pilots from sympathetic countries.[48] Despite these reinforcements, the Finnish Air Force could rarely commit more than 100 operational aircraft to meet the expanding VVS contingent.

Such a minuscule air power nevertheless displayed extraordinary skill. Soviet losses numbered 700 to 900 aircraft, depending on the source.[49] The Finns lost only sixty-two in aerial combat, another fifty-nine damaged beyond repair.[50] Nearly half of the Soviet aircraft losses were bombers, which were committed in larger numbers—TB-3s, SB-2s, and the new DB-3Fs (I1-4). As in Spain, Soviet bomber operations displayed poor navigational technique, inadequate coordination with fighter escort units, equipment failures, minimal bombing accuracy, and high attrition to Finnish fighter interceptors and anti-aircraft fire.

One Finnish source indicated that the most successful single air strike by the VVS occurred on February 29, 1940, when forty I-153 and I-16 fighters attacked the airfield at Ruokalahti. The Soviet fighters struck at noon, catching the Finnish air units on the ground. Three Gloster Gladiators were shot down by the Soviets as they attempted to get airborne. In the subsequent air melee, the Soviets destroyed two more Gladiators and one Fokker. The Finns managed to down only one I-16 fighter.[51] Otherwise, Soviet fortunes in the air war were disappointing, even with a numerical advantage reaching ten to one at times. One measure of the skill of the Finnish pilots was the extraordinary feat of Jorma Kalevi Sarvanto, who in four minutes shot down six DB-3 bombers in a formation of seven on January 6, 1940. The small Finnish air contingent flew sorties almost daily in January–February 1940. Eventually, the quantitative superiority of the Soviets prevailed. In March 1939 the Soviets compelled the Finns to sign an armistice and to cede the disputed territories.

The course of the air war in Finland revealed in stark outlines the crisis in Soviet military aviation. The melancholy pattern of substandard performance touched most categories of equipment, technique, and organization. If the VVS had entered the decade of the thirties as one of the premier air forces of the world, it found itself in a position of obsolescence by 1940. The

whole matter of air preparedness assumed critical importance. If Soviet air officers felt acute fears about the readiness of the VVS for war, they could do little more than hope that the "*lyubimyy vozhd*"—the beloved leader Stalin—perceived the dangers.

Stalin viewed the military officer corps with suspicion. Through the "Great Purges" of the late 1930s he seriously weakened the Soviet military at the very moment external dangers arose. The purge phenomenon, initiated by Stalin in 1934, had swept first the party ranks and, after 1937, the top leadership of the armed forces. Although the darling of party propaganda, the VVS was not spared; its leadership was badly demoralized and depleted. The origin of the "purge" was deeply rooted in Communist party theory and practice; periodic distillations of the ranks were viewed as necessary, even positive, in their consequences. The Stalinist purges, however, acquired an intensity and arbitrariness which extended beyond the rational bounds of party discipline into a sphere of paranoia and self-destructiveness.

The purge of the military began in May 1937, when Stalin arrested Marshal Mikhail Tukhachevskiy. On June 11, 1937, Tukhachevskiy was executed after a secret trial. The shadowy circumstances of his arrest for "treason" signaled a purge of exacting cruelty against the entire military hierarchy from the highest ranks down to regimental commanders. Alksnis, now holding the positions of deputy commissar of defense and commander-in-chief of the VVS, followed Tukhachevskiy in 1938. He had been associated with Tukhachevskiy too closely to escape the purge dragnet.[52] He was arrested on the night of November 23, 1937, on his way to a diplomatic reception, and was executed on July 29, 1938.

Other senior officers shared Alksnis's fate: V. V. Khripin, chief of Air Staff and head of the Special Purpose Air Arm (*Aviatsionnyye armii osobogo naznacheniya*, or AON); B. V. Troyanker, of the Air Force Political Directorate; A. I. Todorskiy, head of Zhukovskiy Air Force Academy; and most VVS military district air commanders.[53]

Another prominent victim of the purge was General Smushkevich, who had assumed command of the VVS in September 1939. He had served in both Spain and Khalkhin-Gol, winning the gold star, Hero of the Soviet Union, twice. He had been given the VVS command during the grim three-and-a-half month struggle against Finland. Stalin ordered Smushkevich removed in April 1940, and replaced him with Gen. Pavel Rychagov, another hero of Khalkhin-Gol. Smushkevich's sudden demise came in the wake of the embarrassing failures in the aerial campaign against Finland; Rychagov was destined to be sacrificed for the VVS losses endured during the first days of Barbarossa. Soviet sources differ on the nature of Smushkevich's death, but it is probable that he was executed on October 28, 1941.[54]

The purge also extended to designers, engineers, and aviation industry leaders, and the dragnet enveloped the research institutes as well, victimizing personnel from the top administrative levels down to clerks. TsAGI, for example, felt the full impact of this program of arbitrary police repression. A. N. Tupolev, the renowned Soviet aircraft designer, was not spared. He was arrested, briefly imprisoned, and then released to continue his work in a shadowy context of internment.[55] His internee design bureau performed important work during the war. There may have been as many as 450 aircraft engineers and designers arrested with about 300 surviving to work in police-supervised design bureaus.[56]

Others, such as K. A. Kalinin, who designed experimental K4 aircraft, were less fortunate. After a K4 crashed during a test flight near Kharkov, killing four party members, Kalinin was arrested and shot for sabotage. His previous record of competent work, such as his design of the first delta-wing aircraft in the early 1930s, counted for little in a political atmosphere where even old Bolsheviks, Lenin's comrades-in-arms, were being accused of "wrecking," "Trotskyite opposition," or being an "enemy of the People."[57]

The purges had a devastating impact on the VVS, leaving the command structure crippled on the eve of the German invasion. Viewed in broader perspective, the purges eliminated three of the five marshals of the Soviet Army. Between 1937 and 1940 the army's loss of top leaders exceeded the subsequent wartime losses to Nazi Germany.[58] At the height of the purges, Stalin repressed all corps and military district commanders, almost all the brigade and divisional commanders, one-half of the regimental commanders, and a vast number of political commissars extending down to the regimental level. In addition to the sacrifice of Alksnis, Smushkevich, and Khripin (all VVS air commanders), the aviation community lost through execution important air theorists such as A. N. Lapchinskiy, A. C. Algazin, and A. K. Mednis.

The purges severely compromised the Soviet Union's national security, since the chief victims were the senior professional military officers. Their replacements came to the newly vacated posts with minimal training and experience. No military establishment, losing half of its senior officers, could maintain any high level of preparedness. Such a bloodletting satisfied certain opaque political requirements, but it left the Soviet military in a vulnerable position at the end of the 1930s.[59] One of the most remarkable aspects of the history of the Soviet Air Force was its impressive capacity for renewal. It endured the twin body blows of the purges and the ravages of the Barbarossa attack, to emerge in 1945 in complete mastery of the air.

The Eleventh Hour, 1940
The year 1940 became the pivotal one in the shaping of Soviet air preparedness. The purges had diminished in intensity, but the VVS leadership had been left in an anemic state because of the removal of most of the experienced commanders. The difficulties of asserting air supremacy over the tiny

Finnish Air Force in the Winter War had revealed a serious pattern of operational inefficiency and technological obsolescence. Together, these events evoked a mood of cynicism about the capacity of the VVS to meet the challenge of the Germans and Japanese in a future war.

Adding to the growing sense of crisis, the Luftwaffe had begun the photographic mapping of the Soviet military districts in the western border regions in October 1940. This aerial reconnaissance project under the leadership of Lieutenant Colonel Rowehl took on an ominous character, signaling that war with Germany was near at hand. Soviet sources suggest that the Luftwaffe conducted more than five hundred overflights, one hundred fifty in the last six months before the German invasion. The Nazi-Soviet Nonaggression Pact of August 1939 had permitted the Soviets to expand their territorial holdings and to enjoy a short reprieve. It was during this period—1939–1941—that the Soviet leadership attempted hurriedly to resolve some of its most pressing defense problems.

Although Stalin demonstrated a certain naïveté in 1940–41 about the precise nature of German intentions vis-à-vis the Soviet Union, he did not abandon entirely the high priority of military preparedness during this Indian summer after the Nonaggression Pact. In fact, he accelerated the process of modernization in anticipation of a future struggle. On September 1, 1939, the Soviet Union instituted universal military service, which extended the length of military training from two to five years. The effect was dramatic, mobilizing a force of 4,207,000 men by January 1, 1941 (80.65 percent ground troops; 8.65 percent air force; 7.35 percent navy; 3.35 percent air defense).[60] The Soviet Union was divided into sixteen military districts and the naval forces were organized into four fleets and five flotillas. The ineffectual K. E. Voroshilov, a long-time crony of Stalin, was replaced as People's Commissar of Defense by Marshal Timoshenko. General Zhukov, recent hero of Khalkhin-Gol, assumed the post of chief of the General Staff and Deputy People's Commissar of Defense. The VVS acquired a new leadership as well, with General Rychagov at this juncture replacing General Smushkevich as chief of the Main Administration of the Air Forces of the Red Army.[61] Other top level personnel shifts followed as Stalin attempted to revitalize his decimated military high command.[62]

Consequently, the entire Soviet military establishment found itself in 1940 subject to a thoroughgoing reorganization. The question remained, however, as to the effectiveness of such eleventh-hour changes. Could an active program of reorganization in 1940 be completed before war erupted with Germany? For Stalin and his military planners it became a race against time.

The fundamental reorganization of the Soviet Air Force required a corresponding shakeup in the aviation industry. In January 1940 A. I. Shakurin, known for his tough-minded efficiency as an administrator, replaced the party functionary M. M. Kagnanovich as head of the Aviation Industry Commissariat. Shakurin's tenure of power signaled the rapid transition to a new generation of Soviet-designed aircraft. Already in 1936, there had been a dramatic increase in expenditures related to the military, climbing upward by 80 percent in one year.[63] Stalin had removed the aviation industry from the control of the civilian-led Commissariat of Heavy Industry in November 1936, and placed it under the aegis of the Commissariat of Defense Industry.

In 1938 the third Five-Year Plan was launched, again stressing the high priority of defense expenditures. Despite the enormous strides made in establishing an industrial base for the manufacture of military aircraft, certain weaknesses persisted which could not be eliminated by changes in leadership. The dependence of the Soviets on Western designs for aero engines and airframes remained a critical problem. Technical assistance arrangements had been negotiated with American aircraft companies, for example Douglas and Consolidated, but these contracts only shortened the technological gap. Soviet emphasis on the construction of bombers in the early 1930s now appeared foolhardy; Germany had demonstrated the importance of fighters and ground-attack aircraft in their campaigns against Republican Spain, Poland, France, and the Lowlands. The Soviet Union found its aircraft production high, but falling behind capitalist and fascist countries in crucial qualitative measurements.

One important change was the expansion of design bureaus for both aero engines and airframes. Tupolev and Polikarpov, who had dominated the Soviet aircraft design world for two decades, were compelled in the late 1930s to share the limelight with a new generation of designers—Yakovlev, Sukhoi, Lavochkin, Ilyushin, Mikoyan, and Gurevich. These men forged a new series of fighters and ground-attack planes, which would establish by 1943 near parity with German and Allied types. To reinforce this process of modernization, the Soviet aviation industry was encouraged to develop fewer designs, particularly fighters and ground-attack models, and to provide for greater standardization and interchangeability of parts. By 1941 Soviet productivity reached the reported level of 12,000 to 15,000 air planes produced each year.[64]

During these hectic months of 1940, Stalin endeavored to reorganize the VVS command structure along more rational lines. The VVS remained as an organic part of the Soviet Army, but Stalin agreed to permit a more unified and professional air force command. During the purge years the old political commissar system had been restored, creating a pattern of dual authority. With the stress once again on military expertise, the air commanders assumed their traditional authority. This "unity of command" did not eliminate political officers; it only placed them in a subordinate position in those areas where strictly military decisions were required. VVS commanders remained subordinate to army commanders in all tactical operations. For administrative functions, the VVS had a chain-of-command structure extending from the Commissariat of Defense to the squadron level.

The 1940 Soviet Air Force consisted of several components: the Long-Range Bomber Aviation (*Dal'ne bombardirovochnaya aviatsiya Glavnogo Komandovaniiya*); the Front Air Forces (*Frontovaya aviatsiya*); and the Army Air Forces (VVS *Armii*). The Long-Range Bomber Command operated under the direct supervision of the High Command;[65] the Front Air Forces were attached to the individual military districts; and the Army Air Forces were subordinate to the various commanders of the ground forces. Additional air units served as liaison units. Such an organization diffused the VVS across the vast matrix of the Soviet army command structure. It was a rational system, designed to serve the diverse requirements of a military structure extending from Europe to Asia, but its chief defect was its decentralization.

Apart from the VVS there was the naval and air defense aviation, which in 1940 amounted to about 20 percent of Soviet aviation. Each of the Soviet Navy's four fleets had its own air force in 1938. In addition, the Air Defense Forces had within their structures a number of fighter air units.

A crew member of an SB-2 bomber emerges from the nose hatch after a training flight in the late 1930s. (SI 80-13021)

Logistics, airfield construction, and technical services required extensive reform in 1940–41. To provide for greater efficiency, air base regions (*Raion aviatsionnogo bazirovaniya*, or RAB) were created. Each RAB served a front or, in special circumstances, certain designated air divisions. By the eve of the war, thirty-six RABs had been organized.[66] Soviet efforts to build new airfields and modernize existing ones took on new momentum as war approached. This involved the transfer of 25,000 workers to airfield construction in March 1941 alone. The VVS set the ambitious goal of providing three airfields for each regiment (a main airfield, a standby, and a field facility). In the spring of 1941, more than 250 airfields were built, but this fell far short of the projected goals.[67]

Complaints about the low serviceability of VVS combat aircraft prompted a full-scale reordering of maintenance units into special battalions (*batal'on aerodromnogo obsluzheniya*, or BAO). Each BAO served two fighter regiments or one regiment of twin-engine aircraft. The momentum of these changes in logistics and rear services carried over into the war years, giving the VVS an effective mechanism to handle the dramatic expansion of air operations after 1943.

Further deficiencies existed in the VVS training program. Bold steps were taken in 1940–41 to improve the quality of training for VVS pilots and support personnel. In December 1940 the Soviets abandoned the volunteer recruitment program. Henceforth, recruitment for aviation schools and training programs became a function of the draft.[68]

Three types of schools were established for flight training: basic training, normally for four months in peacetime; combat pilots' schools, a nine-month course in peacetime, six months in war; and advanced aviation schools for command pilots, to be shortened from two to one year of training in wartime. Curricula and training procedures became more standardized and demanding. To provide a more permanent institutional structure for flight and navigation training, the VVS established the Red Banner Military Air Academy. The Zhukovskiy Air Force Academy became the center for advanced training in command and leadership.[69]

A third institution, the Military Engineer Academy (today named after A. F. Mozhayskiy), was opened near Leningrad. These institutions did not significantly improve Soviet air preparedness in 1940–41, but they did represent important steps toward the creation of an adequately trained cadre of air force leaders.

By 1940–41, the Soviet aviation industry began to deliver a new generation of combat aircraft. More than 1,900 MiG-3, LaGG-3, and Yak-1 fighters arrived in the first six months of 1941. During the same period, 458 Pe-2 bombers and 249 Il-2 Shturmoviks reached operational air units.[70] Conversion training to these new models required time and effort. They were too few in numbers to alter the course of the air war in 1941—about 20 percent of the VVS inventory. In the strategic sense, the retooling by the Soviet aviation industry provided a base for achieving eventual parity with German aircraft.

The VVS command demonstrated a belated sense of concern for the combat readiness of its forward air units just on the eve of the war.[71] The program for the transition to the newer aircraft had revealed a pattern of inefficiency. In April 1941 Gen. A. V. Nikitin, chief of the VVS Organization and Manning Directorate, conducted an inspection of the 12th Bomber Air Division of the Western Special Military District. Nikitin, an old veteran of the

Luftwaffe Overflights on the Eve of War

A dramatic air encounter between the Soviet Air Force and the Luftwaffe occurred on April 17, 1941, two months before the Germans launched their invasion of Russia. During an aerial reconnaissance flight over Grodno, the Germans took a sequence of photographs of the western approaches to the city. Alerted to the presence of the intruder, the Soviets sent an interceptor up to observe. The Soviet aircraft, probably an I-153, appears in several of the frames (see opposite page). The German reconnaissance plane (a Junkers Ju 86P) flew this mission at 39,000 feet, well above the ceiling of the Soviet interceptor. In this cat-and-mouse game, the Soviet pilot was under strict orders to shadow—not to fire on—the German aircraft.

Civil War and an experienced military pilot, found the retraining program proceeding at a glacial pace. He discovered that 104 of the air division crews were still undergoing retraining. The purges were still a vivid memory and had prompted a caution toward the transition program to new aircraft. Fear of flying accidents, an understandable reflex, given the purge specter of "wrecking" or "sabotage," had made the retraining program grossly inadequate. Retraining flights were few in number. Nikitin's critique of the "impermissibility of such a faulty retraining method" led to an accelerated program to achieve combat effectiveness.

Beyond the confusion associated with the retraining program there was an absence of consensus over the military uses of air power. In the 1920s the Bolsheviks had applied Marxism-Leninism to all aspects of life, including military science. Leon Trotskiy, M. V. Frunze, M. N. Tukhachevskiy, and others had written on this important topic in the rapidly changing context of the interwar years.[72] By 1941 the Soviet military theory was in disarray, with many of its leading theorists already victims of the purge. Tukhachevskiy, one of these victims, had proved in the 1930s to be an outstanding leader, whose ideas would be largely vindicated during the course of the Great Patriotic War. He saw the importance of air power, particularly in close coordination with tanks, artillery, and airborne troops. Tukhachevskiy stressed mobility, combined-arms offensive, and the concentration of forces at decisive points. Only after enormous losses and drastic reorganization did the Soviet military forge these concepts into a powerful mode of operation in 1942–43.

In the context of crisis in 1940, General Rychagov, then chief of the Air Force Main Directorate, submitted a report on air power to a conference of higher command officers. In this report, called "The Air Force in the Offensive Operation and in the Fight for Air Superiority," Rychagov argued for an offensive posture, aimed at the destruction of the enemy's aviation both in the air and at forward airfields. Rychagov mirrored the lack of realism toward VVS capabilities among the top air force leadership. Looking back on this conference and its posture toward the war, M. N. Kozhevnikov, a modern Soviet historian, has recorded candidly the confused state of Soviet thinking. Too many commanders, Kozhevnikov argued, exaggerated their successes in Spain and Khalkhin-Gol and foolishly dismissed Luftwaffe capabilities recently displayed against Polish and French aviation. The fact that these commanders did not arrive at a settled notion on the operational application of airpower compromised Soviet military preparedness.

Khalkhin-Gol and the Finnish War—at best minor skirmishes—cast a long shadow over these deliberations, obscuring the need for a more centralized control of air power. The lessons of Barbarossa would bring clarity of purpose, but only after painful sacrifices. Few commanders understood or anticipated the lethal impact of suprise attacks, the critical importance of coordination of air and ground units in "strategic defense" operations, and the need for high-level combat readiness.

The question of Soviet military unpreparedness in 1941 cannot be explained, as some Soviet writers have done, by the element of surprise and the tactical superiority of the Luftwaffe. Hitler's blitzkrieg merely exposed the confused state of Soviet air power in 1941. The Soviet Union, along with other major powers, had faced in the prewar years the problems of defining its air strategy, of providing the requisite industrial and technological re-

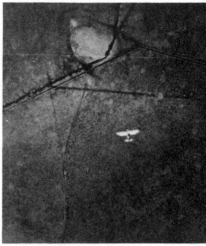

Frame 1 (right camera): The Soviet airplane makes its first appearance in the sequence of photographs. It is visible in the lower left corner.

Frame 2 (right camera): Close-up of Soviet interceptor made from the original print, showing lower wing and open cockpit.

Frame 3 (left camera): The Soviet aircraft makes its last appearance, again a close-up, over a small village.

Courtesy of National Archives via Jay Spenser.

sources for a modern air force, and of organizing air units to effectively serve the strategic and tactical military requirements of the nation. Various factors—historical, ideological, economic, political—shaped the evolution of Soviet air power prior to 1941. The story is one of trial and error, dramatic achievements, and a complex sequence of adjustments.

Lenin, founder of the Soviet state, had challenged the Communist party to guard "the military preparedness of our country and the Red Army like the apple of our eye."[73] Soviet historians and writers have asserted that this demanding task had been achieved in its fundamentals through the rapid industrialization of the 1930s. The events of 1941 revealed serious inadequacies, but the essential industrial, technological, and organizational factors were in place to guarantee an ultimate Soviet victory. I. V. Timokhovich in his recent book, *Operativnoye iskusstvo Sovetskikh VVS v Velikoy Otechestvennoy voyne* [Operational art of the Soviet Air Force in the Great Patriotic War], has provided a characteristic Soviet analysis of Soviet military preparedness. He argues that the German attack, while effective in its initial states, was restricted in its impact to the forward positions. Soviet losses were the result of a skillfully executed preemptive strike, the limited airfield network near the border only recently under construction, the absence of shelters and antiaircraft defenses, the preponderance of outdated aircraft, and the incomplete process of conversion training to new aircraft. Despite these vulnerabilities and enormous losses, the VVS displayed "massive heroism" against the German invaders.

From this Soviet perspective, the reversals in the summer of 1941 were not decisive because they were temporary. The reversals were tactical, not strategic. The Luftwaffe had destroyed large numbers of aircraft, but these losses consisted largely of obsolete types, already scheduled for retirement. Moreover, most VVS pilots and ground-support personnel had escaped the German onslaught to fly into combat at a later date. Consequently, Soviet historians view the German air offensive against the VVS as a failure in the strategic sense. Soviet "deficiencies" had assisted the Luftwaffe, but they were not of a nature to bring about the destruction of Soviet air power. The dramatic character of the German aerial sweep exaggerated the Luftwaffe's strength even as it concealed the fundamental strategic abilities of Soviet air power. These capabilities became evident only in the crucial air battles of 1943.

The Soviet interpretation of "preparedness" in 1941 pivots the overarching strategic considerations. Soviet historians look to May 9, 1945—not June 22, 1941—as the crucial point of reference. In their view, the Soviet victory in the air, as on the ground, came as a result of the Soviet Union's superior industrial capacity and organizational skill.

Battle for Moscow

Operation Barbarossa had been breathtaking in its scope and devastating in its impact on Soviet aviation. Dramatic air victories by the Luftwaffe had accompanied the rapid advance of the German infantry and panzer units in July–August, 1941. German air supremacy, forged swiftly on the first day of the war, continued in almost absolute terms throughout the summer months.

The enormity of Soviet aircraft losses surpassed even the initial exuberant German estimates, reaching an unprecedented 7,500 machines destroyed by September. At Leningrad, Moscow, and in the Soviet rear areas, vestiges of the once mighty Red Air Force—perhaps 25 percent of the prewar inventory—survived the German blitz. With the concurrent relocation of Soviet industry beyond the Ural Mountains during these desperate months, there were few replacement aircraft or spare parts, although a substantial number of VVS air personnel had managed to escape the enveloping pincers of Hitler's armies.

Reduced in power and humiliated in combat, the VVS, along with the Soviet regime itself, approached the inevitable clash with the Germans at Moscow in a mood of desperation. The extraordinary aircraft losses could not be attributed merely to the element of surprise or, grudgingly, to Luftwaffe flying prowess. They stemmed as well from glaring deficiencies in Soviet equipment, organization, and air crew training. These factors prompted among Soviet air crews an acute sense of inferiority toward the Luftwaffe. Having mobilized its modest air strength, the VVS was prepared at Moscow to offer determined air opposition. Such fierce resistance—even the ultimate tactic of ramming—would not close the technological gap or make up for an overall lack of skill, but it would compel the Germans to make sacrifices, to endure high attrition for each step forward. The scenario of Paris in 1940, it was fervently hoped, would not be repeated at Moscow in 1941.

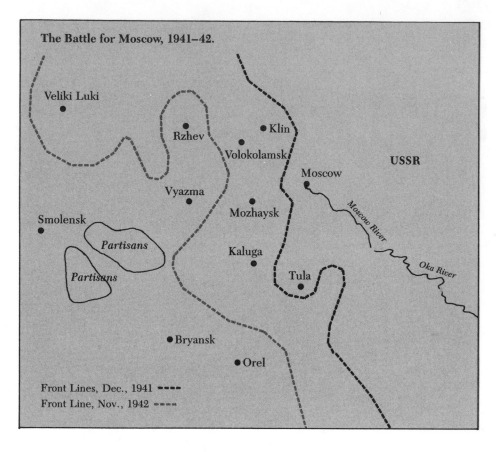

The Battle for Moscow, 1941–42.

Veliki Luki

Rzhev   Klin
        Volokolamsk
                          USSR
Vyazma   Moscow
                    Moscow River
Smolensk   Mozhaysk
    Partisans
              Kaluga   Oka River
    Partisans
                      Tula

              Bryansk
                    Orel

Front Lines, Dec., 1941 ▪▪▪▪
Front Line, Nov., 1942 ▪▪▪▪

German fighter pilots consult maps before a mission against the Russians in the combat zone west of Moscow during the summer of 1941. Courtesy of Glen Sweeting.

At the Gates of Moscow

The German invasion of the Soviet Union advanced through Smolensk to the western edge of Moscow, laid siege to Leningrad, and captured Kiev and much of the Ukraine. The fall of Smolensk to the Germans on July 16 placed Moscow in imminent danger. Rather than continue the drive on Moscow, however, Hitler ordered Army Group Center to stand in place. Hitler remained confident that the fall of the Soviet regime was close at hand, but he decided to postpone the final blow in order to consolidate German positions at Leningrad in the north and in the Ukraine in the south. Consequently, Moscow received a reprieve during the crucial weeks of late July and August 1941. Hitler's Directive 33, issued on July 19, had ordered a series of air raids on Moscow, but the tactic only appeared to stiffen the Soviet will to resist. With its gift of time, the *Stavka* (Headquarters Supreme High Command) worked to organize the defenses of the city.

The belated German assault on Moscow, code-named Operation Typhoon, began at 05:30 hours on September 30, 1941. Gen. Fedor von Bock's Army Group Center planned a double envelopment of Soviet troops guarding the approaches to Moscow. German pincers, advancing to the north and the south of the Smolensk-Moscow highway, were to close the trap at Vyazma, while another panzer spearhead moved below Bryansk toward Orel. Once these initial encirclements were completed, the Germans would be in a position to make the final assault on the Soviet capital some eighty miles away. The German High Command remained optimistic about the potential of Operation Typhoon for success. It represented a concerted effort to bring the war in the east to a dramatic conclusion.

Operation Typhoon possessed all the attributes of a well-planned military campaign save one—good timing. The German offensive came late, at the end of September, just when the Russian weather turned foul. During autumn the heavy rainy season, or *rasputitsa*, fell on central Russia, turning the landscape into a vast, muddy wasteland. German military planners failed to appreciate fully the impact of the *rasputitsa* on the primitive roads (in reality dirt passageways without roadbeds). Only widetrack vehicles could move, with difficulty, and air operations from grass fields became nearly impossible.

For Operation Typhoon to achieve success, a quick victory over the Russians west of Moscow became urgent. Otherwise the *rasputitsa* would deny the German Army mobility, the very life force of the blitzkrieg. The *rasputitsa* ended abruptly each fall with the arrival of the winter frosts. With the descent on the land of the long Russian winter, the ill-prepared German Army would face a greater challenge: trying to keep men and machines in fighting condition in an icy environment of heavy snow and numbing cold.

During the Napoleonic war, Count Simon Vorontsev had seen clearly the impact of Russia's vast distances and short summers on invading armies. In a letter to Tsar Alexander I in 1812, Vorontsev stated that the invasion by Napoleon's Grand Army prompted little fear: "Even if at the start we should suffer military reversals, we might win nevertheless by persisting in a defensive war and by fighting while we retreat. If the enemy pursues us, he is lost because the further he is from his stores of foodstuffs and arms, and the deeper he advances into a country which had no roads and no supplies . . . the sooner he will be reduced to a pitiful state." Knowing well that Russian geography and weather favor the defender, Vorontsev concluded: "he will end by being annihilated by our winter, which has always been our most trusted ally."[1] The battle for Moscow in 1941–42 (and by implication the larger Russo-German War) rested in large measure on the enduring validity of Vorontsev's analysis. Could modern warfare with all of its mobility, range, and striking power give the invader a technological edge to overcome Russia's natural advantages in a prolonged defensive war?

For three months, the Soviets had traded geography for time. For them, too, time was now short, dictating a shift from strategic retreat to the manning of fixed, echeloned defenses at Moscow. The defense of the Soviet capital occupied the full attention of Joseph Stalin on the eve of Operation Typhoon. On his orders, the *Stavka* organized Soviet forces facing Army Group Center into the Western, Bryansk, and Reserve fronts. Together these three fronts could muster 391 combat aircraft with more than 50 percent of the air inventory being older models.[2] By contrast, the Luftwaffe's 2d Air Fleet had 950 aircraft, according to Soviet reckoning, with slightly more than half being bombers.[3] Both air forces experienced a dramatic drop in the number of operational aircraft in September. The long summer campaign produced a low serviceability rate among German air units assigned to frontline duty, a condition aggravated by logistical problems, primitive airfields, and the debilitating regimen of maintaining air operations over the vast, ever-advancing Russian front.

The VVS faced critical shortages in day bombers and ground-attack aircraft, having on the eve of Operation Typhoon a mere five Shturmovik (ground-attack) regiments for the entire zone of the Western, Bryansk, and Reserve fronts.[4] Nevertheless, Col. Gen. P. F. Zhigarev, then VVS air commander, could muster a significant number of fighters for frontal aviation. He could count on the 6th Fighter Air Corps of the Moscow Military Air Defense (PVO) zone. In addition, the Air Corps of the *Stavka* Reserve (AK-RVGK), consisting of six air groups of four to six regiments each, provided the VVS at Moscow with some modest reinforcements. For the long run the VVS, along with the 6th PVO Fighter Corps, enjoyed the benefits of flying from established airfields around Moscow—Vnukogo, Fili, Tushino, Khimki, and the Central Aerodrome.[5] With the advent of the *rasputitsa* and the Russian winter, the possession of good basing facilities by the VVS became a distinct advantage.

The Soviet frontal aviation units, deployed on the critical Western front, mirrored in their composition the plight of the VVS at Moscow. Col.-Gen. I. S. Konev, army commander of the Western front, outlined in a report to the Peoples' Commissariat of Defense on September 25, the thinned ranks of the VVS one week prior to the onslaught of Operation Typhoon—106 operational fighters and 63 bombers. Konev's bomber force consisted of twenty-five TB-3s, lumbering behemoths from the thirties with a cruising speed of 150 miles per hour, along with twenty-eight obsolete and outclassed SB types. He complained that he had only five Pe-2 bombers and four Su-2 ground-attack planes, eleven reconnaissance planes, and eight Shturmoviks. He urgently requested a regiment of Pe-2 bombers and another of Il-2 Shturmoviks. Against the Luftwaffe and advancing panzer units, Konev's VVS air flotilla could offer at best only token air resistance.[6]

Despite its reduced numbers, the VVS played an active role in the period just prior to the German offensive. Frontal aviation assigned to the Western front flew 4,101 sorties and delivered 831 tons of bombs on enemy positions during September. The Soviets also claimed to have destroyed 120 enemy aircraft on the ground and another 89 in air combat. Aviation of the Reserve and Bryansk fronts recorded similar levels of air activity. Bombers from DA, or Long-Range Bomber Aviation, followed the same pattern. According to the Soviets, the 81st Bomber Air Division, down to a mere forty operational aircraft by September 30 (twenty-one Yer-2s, seven Pe-8s, and twelve Pe-3s), hit the staging airfields for the Luftwaffe's air raids on Moscow. More than 80 percent of these strikes took place at night.

While air crew courage and sacrifice abounded in the VVS bomber units during this period, the number of sorties claimed by the VVS seems inflated. From German sources, VVS air operations appear to have been more occasional than sustained in character. German observers acknowledged the fierce determination of some Soviet airmen, particularly the Shturmovik pilots, but in general viewed the overall impact of Soviet air power as negligible. Only during Operation Typhoon did the VVS begin to reassert itself, bolding attacking advancing German troops and armor by day as well as at night.[7]

Night bombing, mostly by Po-2 (U-2) biplanes in the tactical zones, became commonplace in 1941. Attacks occurred throughout the year and sometimes in extreme weather, but the ideal conditions selected for night bombing sorties were the long moonlit or starry nights. Soviet women pilots, the so-called "night witches," acquired considerable fame in this dangerous pursuit. The Po-2s approached their targets singly at predetermined intervals, usually five to fifteen minutes apart, and at varying altitudes, ranging from 700 to 5,000 feet.[8] While bomb loads were light (up to 135 pounds), the Po-2s made a significant impact on German troops by maintaining a sustained air presence over the battle zone.[9]

Such harassment raids worked well because the Po-2 was highly maneuverable, and its slow speeds made night interception by the fast German fighters a difficult undertaking. Often VVS pilots would stop their engines and glide stealthily to the target, dropping their bombs by hand. Any campfire or German target sighted became fair game. These ubiquitous night attackers—nicknamed by German troops "sewing machines" or "duty sergeants"—forced the enemy on all fronts to take precautions, lose sleep, and on occasion suffer the loss of a storage area or fuel depot. Sometimes the only warning for exposed German units in advance of a Soviet fragmentation bomb was the wind whistling through the wing struts of a low-flying Po-2.[10]

The opening drive of Operation Typhoon had struck southwest of Bryansk toward Orel, spearheaded by Gen. Heinz Guderian's 2d Panzer Group. Here the Germans quickly established a breakthrough corridor, pierced the Soviet tactical defense zone, and advanced rapidly toward Orel. On October 2, a second German drive began to the north against the Soviet Western front. VVS frontal aviation commanders, Gen. F. G. Michugin (Western), Gen. Ye. M. Nikolayenko (Reserve), and Gen. F. P. Polynin (Bryansk), found themselves overwhelmed by the rapid German advance on the ground and the spirited Luftwaffe air action.[11] VVS frontal air strength proved to be incapable of air resistance except for occasional sorties against isolated targets of opportunity. The German blows shattered the entire forward structure of Soviet defenses in the Vyazma and Bryansk sectors.

The German advance quickly gained momentum. Orel fell on October 3 after bitter fighting. By the end of the first week Bryansk had been taken and forward units of the 2d Panzer Group had reached the outskirts of Tula. On October 7 the Germans successfully closed the trap at Vyazma, encircling a large contingent of Soviet troops. The *Stavka's* refusal to allow retreat, fearing panic and disintegration, had kept Soviet forces in place in the Vyazma sector. This tactic assisted the Germans in their aim of trapping the Soviets, and afforded the Luftwaffe in the first days of Operation Typhoon a multitude of static targets with little or no air cover.

For the Soviet regime this was the moment of truth, and no effort was spared to blunt the German offensive. Committed in force, the VVS steadily increased its air activity, flying 700 sorties against the advancing Germans in the opening week. Soviet aircraft of various types airlifted men and material from rear areas to reinforce the precarious defenses.[12]

During these frantic opening days the VVS transported 5,500 troops and thirteen tons of supplies to the forward defense zones.[13] At several crucial moments and against the hovering menace of the Luftwaffe, Zhukov ordered massive strikes by VVS combat aircraft against German tanks and motorized units. Soviet bomber units, already depleted by the carnage of the summer campaign, also flew numerous sorties against the enemy. Following prewar training, bomber crews operated normally at 8,000 feet, an attack altitude which proved to be risky and ineffectual, since the slow-flying bombers became easy prey to roaming German fighter squadrons and displayed little bombing accuracy when they reached the target zone. Such raids became at best a ritual sacrifice of aircraft and brave bomber crews. Finally, VVS air commanders ordered the attack altitudes lowered to 3,000–5,000 feet. While this tactic enhanced accuracy, it made the bombers more vulnerable to German anti-aircraft fire, which by the fall of 1941 had taken a fearful total of Soviet aircraft.

At Moscow, the VVS managed to provide the German ground forces with an unpleasant surprise—the Il-2 Shturmovik. Small numbers of these effective ground-attack planes had reached frontal air units prior to Operation Barbarossa, but they had not made any significant impact. For the first time at Bryansk, the Il-2 "Ilyushas," as they were referred to by Soviet pilots, made an appearance in force, boldly attacking German infantry and tanks.

Guderian's 2d Panzer Group at Orel, according to one German account, faced an aggressive display of Soviet air power: "Enemy air activity was very lively, with Soviet bombers and ground attack aircraft flying in small formations of three to six planes."[14] Guderian found himself under air attack on October 4, shortly after his plane landed at Sevsk airfield, an experience repeated shortly afterward when he moved forward with the 3d Panzer Division.[15]

The Luftwaffe, however, remained supreme in the air. According to the Soviets, the Germans flew more than 4,000 combat sorties in the first nine days of October against the Western front alone. At the same time the Luftwaffe renewed its attacks on Moscow, flying forty-one missions over the Soviet capital between November 15 and December 5, 1941. In the course of these raids, Soviet air defenses claimed an average of thirty to forty enemy planes destroyed per day.[16]

While Soviet accounts speak of extraordinary acts of bravery and sacrifice

German He 111 bomber on a night mission to Moscow during the summer of 1941. Courtesy of Glen Sweeting.

Another downed Soviet bomber, an SB-2bis, is shown just east of Vyazma, September 1941. (SI 80-9449)

Moscow under bombard-
ment, August 1941. This
dramatic photograph was
taken by Margaret Bourke-
White. Courtesy of
Time—Life, Inc.

by VVS air crews against the superior enemy, the same historical sources also candidly record "serious shortcomings" of the Soviet Air Force, particularly in the crucial sphere of coordinating air and ground actions. Under the chaotic conditions of retreat, communications broke down and VVS air division commanders frequently directed air operations with minimal contact or interaction with ground commanders.[17]

By October 10 Soviet troops of the Western, Bryansk, and Reserve fronts had retreated to the Mozhaisk Line, a secondary tier of defense situated a mere fifty miles west of Moscow. The Germans offered no reprieve, applying constant pressure on the regrouping Soviet forces. At this crucial juncture, the Western and Reserve fronts were combined into a single Western front under a new commander, General Zhukov. Stalin's choice of the talented and tough-minded Zhukov reflected a realistic appraisal of the extreme peril facing the Soviet Union. Stalin could no longer blissfully allow political orthodoxy or cronyism to remain as criteria for the selection of military commanders. The caprice of the purges had ceased by 1941, but their destructiveness had not been exorcised. Earlier, Zhukov had displayed considerable organizational skill and military leadership at Leningrad, prompting Stalin to select him as commander of the Soviet defenses at Moscow. With Zhukov's appointment, a war-generated pragmatism prevailed in the higher Soviet military councils.[18]

Having enveloped the Soviet defensive group at Vyazma, Army Group Center moved relentlessly against the Mozhaisk Line. Rather than assault this position directly, the Germans applied pressure on its flanks, at Kalinin (Tver) in the north and at Kaluga in the south. Under these grim circumstances, Zhukov's debut as overall commander did not bring immediate success. On October 12 German forces occupied Kalinin, and two days later Kaluga fell, forcing the Soviets to abandon Mozhaisk for fear of another envelopment. Fierce battles raged on the ground and in the air along the path of the advancing German spearheads. Borodino, the site of the dramatic battle with Napoleon in 1812, fell after bitter fighting; Tula, the pivot for Soviet defenses southwest of Moscow, found itself momentarily surrounded.

The fall of Moscow now appeared imminent. On October 19 Stalin ordered a state of siege, which threatened execution for "spies, wreckers, diversionists, and agents provocateur."[19] On the same day General von Bock reported to the German High Command that Army Group Center had captured 573,000 prisoners at Vyazma. At this moment of ultimate peril, Stalin ordered a number of government offices to evacuate to Kuibyshev, a move accompanied by contingency plans to relocate important armaments factories out of the Moscow area. The Moscow Communist Party organization, the State Defense Committee, and the *Stavka* remained to organize the capital's defenses.

Beginning on October 12 a *levée en masse* of more than 450,000 Muscovites, three-quarters of them women, began the construction of massive defensive fortifications, tank traps, and trenches on the outer ring of the city. "Communist Battalions," consisting of 12,000 untrained civilian volunteers, also moved into "gaps" along the frontlines in a desperate effort to stem the German advance. During the time of these emergency measures, a panic of sorts gripped the populace, prompting many to flee the city in advance of the German troops. The Communist regime, to firm up the shattered confidence of the Red Army and the civilian population, blended patriotic appeals and explicit threats to those who digressed from duty in word or deed.

On October 17 it was announced that Stalin still remained in Moscow. This reality, combined with the iron discipline of the party organization and the secret police (NKVD), helped to instill a tenuous sense of confidence. Stalin's famed speech, delivered in Mayakovskiy station of Moscow's subway system on the night of November 6, provided another significant gesture of defiance. The Soviet leader spoke confidently of ultimate victory—and made a direct appeal to Russian nationalism, reminding the people of past heroes, such as Alexander Nevsky, Dimitri Donskoi, and Generals Suvorov and Kutuzov, who had led Russia against past invaders.[20]

Even as Moscow prepared for the German assault, the Russian weather, until now a hovering specter, intervened to halt Operation Typhoon. First came steady rains mixed with snow, which turned roads and airstrips into impassable bogs as the mud sometimes reached a depth of three feet.[21] Suddenly, the Luftwaffe's 2d Air Fleet found itself nearly immobilized as the offensive entered the second half of October. From October 18 to the beginning of November, the German Army made little progress, although at this juncture it was less than fifty miles from Moscow. Soviet resistance, not just the extremes of the weather, halted the Germans during this period. Threatened with encirclement, the Red Army held on to Tula with fierce determination. At Kaluga, Volokolamsk, and other points west of Moscow, Soviet troops harassed the enemy. During the same defensive phase, the VVS

The *rasputitsa*, or rainy season, transformed Russia's primitive roads into muddy quagmires in the autumn of 1941. This photograph was taken by Margaret Bourke-White west of Moscow, near Vyazma. Courtesy of Time–Life, Inc.

flew 26,000 sorties in support of the ground forces.

Winter frosts and snow arrived in mid-November, abruptly ending the muddy season. The Germans renewed their offensive. The sudden arrival of cold weather froze the ground and allowed mobility once again. But the changing weather brought new rigors as one of the worst winters in memory descended on both sides. Soon, movement ceased again. The subzero temperatures brought untold hardships on the German Army, which was not properly equipped or clothed for the extremes of the Russian winter.

While the VVS enjoyed a number of relatively well-equipped airfields, the Luftwaffe operated under the most primitive field conditions, a situation constantly worsened by the unexpected severity of the snow, fog, and freezing temperatures. Airstrips had to be continually cleared of snow. Starting aircraft engines, particularly the liquid-cooled engines, became nearly impos-

MiG-3 fighters in the winter air campaign of 1941–42.

sible in the extreme cold. Ground crews found routine maintenance almost impossible when exposed skin froze to metal. Rubber tires at these extreme temperatures became brittle and deteriorated rapidly with use. Ground crews frequently had to work in the open or in unheated work areas; tools had to be heated before use; engines and armament defied the elaborate efforts of skilled technicians to make them operative; and work efficiency dropped sharply. There were no manuals or established procedures to accommodate the impact of "General Winter" on Luftwaffe operations.[22]

By contrast, the VVS increased the tempo of its air operations to take full advantage of the enemy's immobility. Dropping out of low clouds, Soviet aircraft repeatedly hit the hard-pressed German troops. Soviet air units, long accustomed to cold-weather operations, controlled the skies above the frozen ground. For the twenty-day period, November 15–December 5, 1941, the VVS, according to Soviet sources, flew 15,840 sorties as opposed to 3,500 for the Luftwaffe.[23] These same Soviet accounts claim that the Luftwaffe lost 1,400 aircraft in the Moscow sector during this time.

The Wehrmacht, which had won battle after battle since 1939, now found itself nearly frozen, exhausted, and incapable of sustaining the drive on Moscow. The campaign in the east had placed enormous strain on the entire German war machine, a fact which only became apparent with the sudden collapse of Operation Typhoon. If Soviet casualties and losses in 1941 appeared catastrophic, German losses had mounted steadily as well. By September 25, 1941, German casualties had reached 534,000 with more than one in five being killed.[24] Russia had proved to be more formidable in its defensive capabilities than either Great Britain or France on the western front in 1940. While Soviet resistance was uneven, it displayed a ferocity and toughness unparalleled in the west. The enormity of the landscape appeared to absorb the German infantry, mechanized units, and aircraft with ease. The military triumphs of the Germans, now projected over four months, had ended in exhaustion rather than inevitable victory.

During the summer campaigns in the center sector around Smolensk and across the steppe to the south, the German fighting efficiency began to falter at the very moment the Soviet military appeared near collapse. There had been long marches, heat, dust, and bloody encounters with the determined Soviet defenders. The monotony and immensity of the landscape added to a growing demoralization born of fatigue. By fall, the situation worsened as the weather complicated an already difficult situation. Logistical support had become irregular and inadequate.

The desperate plight of the invaders in October–November has been expressed well by Albert Seaton:

> Infantry companies, twenty men strong, led by second lieutenants or sergeants, were bearded and filthy, not having bathed or changed their clothes for months. Tormented by lice, they lay all day cramped and stiff in the narrow weapons pits filled with water, their feet so cold that they had lost all feeling. Sickness and cold caused more casualties than enemy action. Rain fell incessantly and the Luftwaffe seemed unable to cope with the Red Air Force fighters and bombers which dropped out of the low clouds, bombing and machine gunning.[25]

These privations were soon intensified by a logistics crisis. The resupply problems continued into December 1941 as the desperate, ill-clad German troops attempted to maintain themselves against a revitalized Soviet air and ground offensive.

The power of the Luftwaffe also proved to be illusory in facing these challenges of the Eastern front. The air supremacy achieved in June–July 1941 quickly dissipated, as the strains of a 2,000-mile front took their toll. With increasing commitments in the west, the Luftwaffe had few reserves to sustain a prolonged air-support role in the east. At the end of 1941, Hitler withdrew Field Marshal Albert Kesselring's 2d Air Fleet from the support of Army Group Center at Moscow to meet new requirements in the Mediterranean theater. Up to that time the Luftwaffe, even with a beginning strength of 3,000 aircraft, found itself incapable of covering the vast distances. In 1941 the Luftwaffe deployed on the Eastern front about two aircraft per mile, as compared to ten to fifteen per mile in earlier campaigns in Poland, France, and the Balkans.[26]

The Messerschmitt Bf 109F demonstrated early its superiority over Soviet fighter aircraft, including the modest numbers of newer models such as the MiG-3, LaGG-3, and Yak-1. Luftwaffe bomber units, however, were still using many obsolescent Dornier 17s. Also, the Ju 87 Stuka dive bomber appeared in Russia in large numbers. These models, along with the He 111 and Junkers 88, reflected a continuity in equipment already displaying the telltale marks of obsolescence. The Soviets, on the other hand, had established in 1940–41 the momentum for the reequipment of their fighter and ground-attack units, a process that would be strengthened by the acquisition of Anglo-American models—Hurricanes, Spitfires, Tomahawks, and Airacobras. Time would demonstrate that the technical inferiority of VVS combat aircraft, so evident in the summer of 1941, would disappear as the war progressed.

In the first month of the war, the Luftwaffe had flown an average of 2,500, sometimes 3,000, sorties per day,[27] and all during the summer, German air crews had displayed considerable skill and efficiency—destroying VVS machines on the ground and in the air, providing effective ground support, and covering ever-extending lines of communication. But the serviceability of the Luftwaffe aircraft inventory began to decline perceptibly by the end of the summer, a condition which became even more critical during the Operation Typhoon period (October–November 1941) when bad weather intervened to halt nearly all aerial operations. Combat losses mounted steadily, prompting concern within the operational units. Though crippled, the VVS continued to operate and, in some sectors, make Luftwaffe operations difficult. The use of *taran*, or ramming, only added to German frustrations over Soviet doggedness and resilience. The use of Messerschmitt Bf 110s, He 111s, and Ju 88s for ground strafing resulted in unexpected and unacceptable losses.[28]

Again, the Polish and Western front experiences provided a poor frame of reference for the unfolding realities of the harsh Eastern front. The Luftwaffe approached the Russian winter of 1941–42 exhausted, overextended, and depleted in numbers. At best, the German air arm—despite unparalleled air victories—had only a tenuous hold on tactical air superiority.

The Soviets demonstrated an impressive capacity to strike back even under extraordinary pressure. While faced with the menace of a catastrophic German breakthrough at Moscow during the second week of October, the

VVS made a bold air strike at Luftwaffe airfields. Soviet intelligence had learned that on October 12, the Luftwaffe planned to make a massed attack on the Western front, aimed at industrial centers, airfield complexes, rail terminals, and logistical support facilities. The Soviets estimated that more than 1,500 planes would participate. To blunt this enemy raid, the *Stavka* ordered the hard-pressed VVS to mobilize a preemptive strike for the night of October 11–12, to be followed by an air raid on the morning of October 12. The *Stavka* directive, part of a larger blueprint for VVS air operations for the period October 11–18, called for VVS air units to hit Luftwaffe staging airfields along the northwestern, western, and southwestern axes leading to Moscow. This plan drew heavily upon the existing frontal and long-range bomber units deployed around Moscow.

According to the Soviets, the preemptive air strikes achieved dramatic success, descending with force on Luftwaffe airfields at Vitebsk, Smolensk, Orel, Orsha, Siversk and other points. The reported tally of destroyed enemy aircraft for that period reached 500 aircraft, a figure not confirmed by German accounts.[29] Whatever the exact figures, this whole operation reflected boldness and resourcefulness on the part of the Soviet Air Force in the most difficult climatic conditions.

The Soviet Counteroffensive

Operation Typhoon had pushed forward with determination during the difficult days of November 1941 against an increasing tempo of Soviet resistance. The ferocity of the Soviet defenders soon matched the extremes of weather to slow the German advance. By the beginning of December, the German offensive against Moscow was in deep trouble. This fact became evident on December 1, when German army units attacked the small towns of Akulovo and Golitsyno on the western approaches of the city in an environment of heavy snow and fierce Russian opposition. The German attack ceased after 10,000 casualties and the loss of fifty tanks.

In its episodic fury, the fighting at Akulovo and Golitsyno typified the overall crisis of Operation Typhoon. Four days later Guderian entered into his journal a fitting epitaph for the German assault: "The offensive on Moscow has ended. All the sacrifices and efforts of our brilliant troops have failed. We have suffered a serious defeat."[30]

Guderian's somber assessment of German military fortunes at Moscow coincided with the Soviet decision to launch a winter counteroffensive. Bloodied by more than five months of war, the Soviet Army remained viable despite its reduced numbers and equipment shortages. Sensing the opportune moment, Stalin called upon his troops to roll back the invaders. Timely reinforcements from Siberia and the *Stavka*'s reserves gave the Soviets enhanced striking power for a counterattack against a weakened and vulnerable enemy. Nine new armies began to arrive at the end of November from formation sectors as distant as Lake Omega in the north and Astrakhan in the south.

At the beginning of December, Zhukov's Western Army Group consisted of 787,000 men (of whom 578,000 were in frontline units), 1,794 field guns, 2,973 mortars, and 618 tanks (205 the latest T-34 and KV models). Zhukov approached the counteroffensive with the reinforced Kalinin and Southwestern fronts on his northern and southern flanks. For the air war, the VVS had in the western sector alone 1,376 aircraft (859 listed as operational) against the Soviet-estimated 580 Luftwaffe aircraft.[31] Many of the VVS machines were obsolete, but they operated out of established airfields with concrete runways, and profited from a more accessible logistics base. Given the severe winter weather, these advantages in facilities and support services became important to the VVS in a prolonged conflict.

At dawn on December 5, troops of the Kalinin front went over to the offensive, crossing the frozen Volga River against stubborn German resistance. The following day Soviet troops from the Western and Southwestern fronts joined the battle. Now the Russian counteroffensive moved foward along the entire Moscow front, a distance of 560 miles, stretching from Kalinin in the north to Yelets in the south. Fierce fighting erupted along the entire length of the Soviet advance, and the Soviets quickly established dramatic progress through mobile pursuit and flanking tactics. Despite poor weather—low clouds, fog, and snow storms—the VVS covered the Soviet advance in force.

The German Army fell back in disorder. Fighting became brutal and exacting. Soviet troops pierced the tactical zone of the enemy defenses during the first three days despite aggressive opposition and the numbing cold. For the first time the Russians had advanced in force and threatened the Germans with encirclement in several sectors. By December 9 Soviet air reconnaissance confirmed a massive withdrawal of German troops west of Klin. Fearing entrapment, many German units along the entire front withdrew in panic, abandoning their guns, tanks, and equipment along the snow-drifted roads. At Kaluga, a city earmarked by Hitler to be defended at all costs, the Germans offered stubborn opposition, which forced the Soviet attackers to take the city street by street and house by house in some of the heaviest fighting of the war.

Already at Kaluga, there was ample evidence of the brutality of the Russo-German War now in its sixth month: Soviet troops found seven men and one woman, accused of partisan warfare, hanging from a gallows in the main square. In other places the retreating German troops set torch to buildings, large and small, in an effort to make Russia a landscape of charred ruins.

Along the entire sweep of the Moscow front both armies struggled against the bitter cold and the heavy snow.[32] For the Germans the impact of the winter became more severe and debilitating in the absence of cold-weather clothing, proper equipment, and lubricants for operations in subzero weather. Frostbite took a fearful toll of German soldiers. By contrast, Soviet replacements from Siberia arrived west of Moscow fully equipped with winter issue clothing—fighting in their white camouflage combat clothing designed for maximum protection against the rigors of the Russian climate.[33]

Moscow confidently announced on December 11 that the German drive on the capital had been pushed back. A week later, the momentum of the counteroffensive began to slow perceptibly, but the Soviets had recaptured the cities of Klin, Kalinin, Yelets, Kaluga, and Volokolamsk, forced Guderian's panzers back from besieged Tula, and now threatened the encirclement of the forward elements of Army Group Center. Fearing a total collapse of the German forces at Moscow, Hitler ordered his troops on December 16 to stand fast "without retreating a step." This move, taken against the urging of many of his generals, stiffened German resistance, particularly in the center in the Rzhev-Gzhatsk-Vyazma triangle located between Smolensk and Mos-

cow. Here the residual strength of the German Army once again asserted itself against the determined but faltering Soviet counteroffensive. There
would be no repetition of the retreat of Napoleon's Grande Armée of 1812.

The resuscitated Soviet air arm made a dramatic, if limited, show of force
on the western approaches of Moscow in December 1941. On the first day of
the counteroffensive, the VVS attacked German troop concentrations and artillery positions in support of the advancing 31st Army on the Kalinin front.
After the fall of Kalinin, Soviet air units flew support missions to assist five
armies in the northwest sector in a drive on Rzhev, between December 17
and 26.[34] Frontal air units made 1,289 combat sorties in close air-support missions, reconnaissance flights, and sporadic attacks on retreating troops in rear
areas. During these actions, Soviet fighters claimed sixteen air victories over
the Luftwaffe. Gen. S. I. Rudenko, who replaced Gen. N. K. Trifonov as
VVS commander for the Kalinin front in January 1942, demonstrated energy
and skill as a commander during the winter counteroffensive. His subsequent
career would include command of the 16th Air Army at Stalingrad, Kursk,
and Berlin.[35]

At the other end of the Moscow front, in the airspace around Tula, the
VVS frontal aviation under the command of another talented leader, Gen.
F. Ya. Falaleyev, made a forceful appearance. Here the VVS targeted as its
major goal the destruction of Guderian's 2d Panzer Army, now in retreat. In
the Tula sector, the *Stavka* deployed a concentration of ground forces, drawn
from the Western and Southwestern fronts, which included the 50th and 10th
armies plus some cavalry units. During the first ten days of the offensive, the
Soviet forces pushed the enemy back fifty to sixty miles. Soviet air units
made a valiant effort to destroy Guderian's tanks. For the Southwestern front,
the VVS had only 236 operational aircraft, while the Western front could
muster five air divisions with 183 combat aircraft of mixed composition. Despite difficult weather and such a modest number of operational aircraft, the
VVS claimed an important role for itself during December in this sector. The
frontal aviation of the Western front mounted 5,066 combat sorties alone,
which scored a significant tally of enemy tanks and vehicles, according to Soviet records. The steady air pressure from VVS units also restricted the general movement of German troops, now in desperate retreat, and compelled
them to feverishly set up anti-aircraft defenses.

During the December counteroffensive, the Soviets attempted to slow
the German retreat through the use of airborne troops. On the night of December 15, 415 men were dropped behind the German lines in the district of
Teryayeva Sloboda in the northwest. The VVS aimed to block the escape
route west of Teryayeva Sloboda in coordination with the advancing 30th
Army. While some Soviet sources describe this operation as successful, there
is evidence that it failed in its purpose. It was a bold maneuver, but it lacked
organization and adequate cover from VVS fighter squadrons. The Soviet par-
atroopers suffered heavy casualties and only with great difficulty escaped annihilation. In January 1942, another paratroop drop, numbering 2,000 men,
took place at Medyn, near Tula. Such operations, launched under severe
weather conditions, displayed boldness and heroism, if not efficiency.[36]

For the air operations over the crucial Western front of General Zhukov,
the VVS concentrated nearly 80 percent of its strength. Aviation from the
Moscow Air Defense Zone (PVO) joined with frontal air units to assist the

5th, 33d, and 43d armies in breaking through the enemy's defenses. Fighting in this sector had been bitter and progress slow for the Soviet armies until late December 1941. By January 4, 1942, the Soviet 43d Army had retaken Borovsk and Maloyaroslavets, two key cities located on a line directly south of Mozhaisk.

During these difficult days, Gen. N. F. Naumenko commanded the Soviet air operations (to be replaced by Gen. S. A. Khudyakov on February 7, 1942). Naumenko, a veteran of the Winter War with Finland, went on to command the 4th Air Army briefly in the Kuban and then the 15th Air Army at the battle of Kursk.[37]

The 6th Fighter Air Corps (PVO), commanded by Col. I. D. Klimov (and after November 1941 by Col. A. I. Mitenkov), played a prominent role in the defense of Moscow and the subsequent Soviet winter offensive. While maintaining its role as a protector of Moscow proper, the 6th Fighter Air Corps assisted VVS frontal aviation in the vital air-support role, attacking enemy troops, airfields, and railroad centers.[38] During November this unit alone, according to Soviet records, destroyed 170 enemy aircraft and in December, another eighty planes.[39] The 6th Fighter Air Corps had switched to ground-attack missions in December as the Luftwaffe's threat to Moscow diminished. Between December 9 and 14, in a period of heavy snow and extreme cold, fighter pilots from this air defense unit harassed retreating columns of enemy troops at various points west of Moscow, including the areas around Klin and Solnechnogorsk.[40]

The flexible use of PVO air units in the Soviet counteroffensive complemented their earlier heroics in the defense of Moscow in the summer and fall of 1941. Victor Talalikhin, who had made the first night-ramming of a German bomber in August, was killed in action on October 27, 1941. Another Soviet pilot, Lt. A. N. Katrich of the 120th Fighter Air Regiment, PVO, made two aerial rammings, including the first high-altitude *taran* of a German aircraft. A total of twenty-three fliers from the 6th Fighter Air Corps received the gold star, Hero of the Soviet Union, during the battle for Moscow.[41]

Along with the 6th Fighter Air Corps, other special air units participated in the assault on retreating German infantry and tanks. Reserve air groups (under Generals A. A. Demidov and I. F. Petrov) joined selected bomber units from Long-Range Bomber Aviation to bolster Soviet air power during the defensive struggle at Moscow and subsequent Soviet general offensive. The mobilization of all available units for these crucial operations provided Soviet air commanders with valuable experience in the coordination of diverse forces over a vast geographical area. Not only had Soviet aviation survived in 1941, it had conducted offensive operations in extreme winter conditions to the surprise of an enemy who now appeared to be something less than invincible.[42]

At the time, the Moscow Military District had sufficient air strength to form a special air group under the command of N. A. Sbytov. Once reinforced by the 46th Bomber Air Regiment, equipped with the new, fast Pe-2 airplanes and the 65th and 243d ground-attack regiments flying Il-2s, Sbytov's air group entered combat along the Mozhaisk line in support of the Soviet 5th Army. During the defensive stage of the battle of Moscow, further reinforcements came from the military school instructors and recent graduates from *Osoaviakhim* pilot training courses who were thrown into night-flying air regiments equipped with Po-2, R-5, and R-2 aircraft. More than seventy-one air regiments were organized between October and December 1941.[43]

The first phase of the Soviet counteroffensive at Moscow lasted for thirty-three days. The VVS flew a total of 16,000 combat sorties, about half in direct support of the ground forces. Under severe conditions, the Soviet air units demonstrated their impressive capacity for maintaining flight operations. Only the most extreme weather—heavy snow storms or fog—grounded Soviet operational aircraft. Low clouds and marginal visibility provided challenges, but no insurmountable obstacles to the low-flying VVS pilots intent on attacking the retreating enemy columns.

At Moscow, the *Stavka* deployed its small rump air force against the enemy along the main avenues of attack in an effort to maximize its impact. Frontal aviation massed 70 percent of its sorties against the northern grouping alone, a concentration of air power which made a significant contribution to the advance of Soviet ground forces in this dangerous sector. Along the entire front, VVS air units, often using two crews for each aircraft in round-the-clock operations, accelerated the pace of the counteroffensive. In the enemy rear, attacking Soviet aircraft created confusion by applying pressure on retreating units, command posts, and lines of communication.

Stalin still hoped to annihilate the German Army before the end of winter, to repeat the great triumph against Napoleon. Before a conclave of top leaders at the Kremlin on January 5, Stalin had announced his decision to launch a general offensive. The bold plan called for the envelopment of Army Group Center, then situated between Smolensk and Moscow, the lifting of the siege of Leningrad, and the liberation of the Donets Basin and the Crimea. From January to April, 1942, the Soviets attempted in a sequence of attacks to make this ambitious scheme for ultimate victory a reality. In the end they faltered and suffered enormous losses.

West of Moscow, Army Group Center held on in January–February 1942 and successfully resisted the Soviet effort to close the trap at Smolensk. To the north at Leningrad and in the south at Kerch, the Soviet general offensive also proved inconclusive. The Wehrmacht, if exhausted and vulnerable, had proven resilient. For the Soviet armed forces the general offensive exposed their own strategic weaknesses. The strain of the prolonged conflict (even with a powerful assist from "General Winter"), the enormous losses in men and materiel, and the lack of adequate reserves made the general offensive a difficult, and ultimately impossible, undertaking.[44] By the spring of 1942, it was apparent to both sides that the war was going to be a prolonged one.

During January–March 1942, the VVS flew by its own account a total of 49,000 sorties against Army Group Center. This high level of air action, even adjusted to correct probable Soviet exaggeration, revealed the remarkable vitality of the VVS in the difficult months of the general offensive in 1942.[45] Frontal aviation, according to Soviet sources, played a significant role in this offensive against Army Group Center. Between January 4 and 7, 1942, for example, VVS frontal aviation units attacked forward Luftwaffe airfields at Rzhev and Velikiye Luki during a period of transition as increasing numbers of transport aircraft were making an appearance to resupply hard-pressed German ground units. Participating in the raid were the 5th Guards (GvIAP)

Lt. P.A. Brinko, of the 13th Fighter Air Regiment of the KBF (Red Banner Baltic Fleet), demonstrates air-combat technique to fellow fliers during the summer of 1941. Brinko was killed in combat on September 14, 1941. At the time of his death he had fifteen air victories to his credit and had earned the gold star, Hero of the Soviet Union. Courtesy of Carl-Fredrik Geust.

and 193d fighter air regiments and squadrons drawn from General Petrov's air group.[46] The Soviets claimed they destroyed nine Ju 52s on the ground and one Do 217 in aerial combat. The element of surprise and the impressive capability of the VVS to operate in poor weather were key elements to the Soviet success.

Although the rigors of combat and weather had reduced drastically the total number of available VVS aircraft, the proportion of newer types increased. The VVS Kalinin front inventory, for example, numbered ninety-six machines at the end of January 1942: five Pe-2s; seventeen Il-2s; seven MiG-3s; twenty-three LaGG-3s; fourteen Yak-1s; eight I-15bis; and twenty-two I-16s.[47] This meant that only one-third of the inventory consisted of obsolete I-15 and I-16 models. The Soviets accelerated this process of transition to the newer models in the summer and fall of 1942, once the aircraft production in the newly relocated aviation factories reached full capacity.

Soviet chroniclers of the winter offensive have described a quickening of air combat activity during February and March 1942. In February, they record sixty-seven air battles in the Moscow region involving 344 aircraft. During March 258 air battles took place in wide-ranging combat encounters, which saw 656 Soviet aircraft committed against 971 German machines. The Soviets explain this increased tempo of air combat by pointing to the aggressive posture they assumed during this period.[48] Viewed from this historical perspective, the Soviet air arm, still numerically inferior to the Luftwaffe, took the initiative against Army Group Center. Soviet pilots flew combat missions along the entire German salient, from Smolensk to the approaches of Moscow, attacking enemy troops, tanks, communication centers, and airfields.[49]

German accounts, however, have suggested a much lower level of combat activity by the VVS in the early months of 1942. Walter Schwabedissen, one German commentator on this campaign, acknowledged that by the turn of 1941–42 the Soviet Air Force had survived its worst crisis and was display-

Soviet I-16 (Type 18) fighter of the 7th Fighter air regiment, Leningrad front, autumn 1941. Courtesy of Carl-Fredrik Geust.

MiG-3 fighter at Leningrad in 1942. Courtesy of Carl-Fredrik Geust.

ing a renewed vitality. Soviet units, however, varied in combat aggressive-ness, depending on time and circumstance. The shift to a more offensive ori-entation became apparent in the summer, rather than the spring of 1942. Soviet fighter units showed a new confidence as their aircraft approximated in performance the German models. The Soviet ground-attack arm, in particu-lar, became more aggressive and strong as 1942 progressed.[50]

At the start of the war, VVS combat aircraft were austerely equipped as compared to Luftwaffe airplanes. The Soviets introduced radio during 1941–42, a technological leap forward of great significance for the VVS planners who strove to improve the control and discipline of air operations. With radio-control techniques, the VVS command structure gained a powerful tool to coordinate air-ground operations. Some Soviet accounts explain the in-creased effectiveness of VVS frontal aviation in the winter offensive to this ra-dio air direction teamwork.[51] German accounts, however, have recorded that the system was primitive and poorly run.[52] Since the transmissions were made by voice, the Luftwaffe monitored them regularly and exploited the in-formation to their advantage.

For the first time the Soviets organized their rear services for an arduous winter offensive. A total of seven new air-basing regions (RAB) were orga-nized, consisting of thirty airfield service battalions (BAO), nine airfield engi-neer battalions, and other support units. Soviet rear services also established large storage depots along the front at intervals of 150 to 250 miles to serve the forward airfields. The organizational difficulties were enormous, given the disruption following in the wake of the invasion, but the ruthless applica-tion of centralized control began to bear fruit.

A network of airfields was established, technical and logistical personnel were distributed, and stores of ammunition, fuel, and foodstuffs were fun-neled in a rational fashion toward the frontline airfields. Moreover, the entire logistical command was organized to serve an advancing, offense-oriented air arm. Mobile railway aviation workshops provided the flexibility required for offensive operations. The entire system, by definition, was designed to sus-tain a massive counteroffensive rather than a number of static or territorially based air units. These pragmatic efforts at mobilization and centralization an-ticipated the great Soviet "air offensive" operations of 1943–45.

The Soviet winter offensive brought in its wake an important and precedent-laden conflict at Demyansk. Here in the seam between Army Group North and Army Group Center, the advancing Soviet troops in Febru-ary 1942 encircled the German 2d Army Corps, a force numbering around 100,000 men. The Soviet advance also swept around another smaller pocket of German troops at Kholm, just southwest of Demyansk. The Demyansk-Kholm region, located south of Lake Ilmen, offered a challenge to both ar-mies with its numerous forests and swamps. During the January–February Soviet assault on the exposed right flank of Army Group North, heavy snows had fallen in the region, blunting both Soviet mobility and German efforts to stabilize their defensive positions. As part of their general offensive, the So-viet effort in the Demyansk sector placed Army Group Center in distinct jeopardy of encirclement by the northern wing of the Soviet pincer move-ment. Fierce fighting accompanied the Soviet penetration into the area.

Faced with a crisis of considerable magnitude in mid-February, Hitler boldly decided to order his encircled forces to remain in place rather than ac-

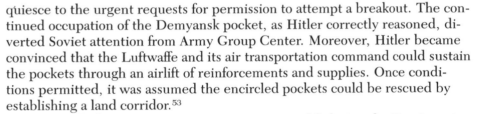

quiesce to the urgent requests for permission to attempt a breakout. The continued occupation of the Demyansk pocket, as Hitler correctly reasoned, diverted Soviet attention from Army Group Center. Moreover, Hitler became convinced that the Luftwaffe and its air transportation command could sustain the pockets through an airlift of reinforcements and supplies. Once conditions permitted, it was assumed the encircled pockets could be rescued by establishing a land corridor.[53]

Now called upon to execute an emergency airlift during the Russian winter, the Luftwaffe responded with impressive vigor and capacity for improvisation. The smaller Kholm pocket, consisting of 3,500 soldiers, posed real problems with its constricted area and lack of adequate airfields. Initial efforts to land Ju 52 transports ended in disaster, since the small Kholm airfield fell within the range of enemy guns. The Luftwaffe then resorted to air drops and the use of gliders.[54]

For the larger Demyansk pocket, there were enormous obstacles to a large-scale airlift in the midst of an enemy offensive and the severe weather. The Luftwaffe's 1st Air Fleet, assigned to Army Group North, had only one air transport group at the outset of the crisis. Demyansk, it was quickly determined, required a minimum of 300 tons of food and materiel daily.[55] By February 19 a total of seven air transport groups were available to the airlift, an air flotilla that was steadily reinforced during late February and March. Given the low serviceability in winter air operations, the Luftwaffe needed 500 Ju 52s deployed for the airlift to ensure 150 operational aircraft, each loaded with two tons of cargo, to meet the 300 tons-per-day requirement.[56]

Of the two fields within the Demyansk pocket, the one suitable for airlift operations was located at Demyansk and had been a VVS airbase; the other, at Peski, was little more than an emergency strip. To save Demyansk, both airfields had to be prepared for maximum use even in the absence of adequate ground facilities. The Luftwaffe began its airlift effort in an atmosphere of urgency. Various ad hoc measures followed to initiate the vital flow of materiel. The Soviets quickly moved forward, as a coiled spring, suddenly applying intense pressure on both pockets—setting up anti-aircraft batteries on the approaches to Demyansk and deploying fighter units for air interdiction.

The Demyansk airlift worked, but barely. It established the fateful precedent that air power could be used to supply surrounded troops even in the rigors of the Russian winter. From January 1942 to the final removal of the Soviet threat to Demyansk early in 1943, the Luftwaffe flew a total 64,844 tons of ammunition, supplies, weapons, spare parts, and fuel. Moreover, German reinforcements amounting to over 30,000 troops reached Demyansk by way of the airlift, while return flights brought out over 35,000 wounded. During the most critical phase in late winter (February 18–May 19, 1942), the Luftwaffe managed to deliver an average of 302 tons per day. This achievement narrowly exceeded the required daily needs of Demyansk. The price tag for the entire airlift was high: 265 aircraft lost. In addition, Luftwaffe transports assigned to the airlift consumed 42,155 tons of aviation fuel and 3,242 tons of lubricants.[57]

Throughout the Demyansk airlift operations, German fighters made sweeps over the approach and return routes, providing necessary fighter cover for the slow-flying Ju 52s. Soviet anti-aircraft batteries, however, displayed considerable skill against the German transports, often with mobile, self-propelled guns. Consequently, the dangers from anti-aircraft fire compelled the Ju 52s, formerly flying in pairs at low level, to cross the enemy zone in groups of twenty to forty aircraft at altitudes ranging from 6,000 to 8,000 feet.

Air drop by an He 111 over Kholm during the Demyansk airlift operation, 1942. Courtesy of Glen Sweeting.

German fighters and transports found VVS fighters unaggressive at Demyansk, always avoiding direct contact with fighter escorts or large groups of Ju 52s. They preferred to attack stragglers or single, unprotected transports. This assessment of Soviet fighter units fits the overall negative estimate of the VVS fighter air operations by the Luftwaffe during 1941–42. Yet, these same sources are quick to acknowledge the prowess of VVS pilots in low-level bombing and strafing attacks, which, according to one German spokesman, "invariably resulted in German personnel and aircraft losses."[59] Within a year the VVS brought these same skills for surprise attack, along with a much more aggressive fighter interceptor role, to Stalingrad, where an "air blockade" worked with Soviet ground forces to annihilate a German pocket three times as large as the Demyansk pocket.

Soviet sources have remained largely silent about the role of VVS fighter units over Demyansk in 1942. One source, a memoir by Gen.-Maj. F. A. Kostenko, describes in graphic detail the aggressive role assumed by Soviet fighter units over Demyansk the following winter. At that time (February–March 1943), a renewed Soviet offensive to destroy the German army grouping at Demyansk began in earnest.

Kostenko's account suggests that VVS fighters, largely late-model Yaks (Yak-7b) with some La-5's, flew cover for Il-2 Shturmoviks, which were often used to draw German fighters into air combat. Against Bf 109s and Fw 190s, the VVS deployed in this sector some of their best fighter units. The results, as Kostenko records, were often quite successful, particularly the efforts of VVS fighters to resist sweeps by enemy fighters, normally from six to twelve aircraft, to clear the air prior to the arrival of German bombers. Soviet fighter pilots, many now proudly flying with the guards designation, boldly challenged the German fighters for control of the air.[60] As Kostenko points out, the enemy again anticipated easy victories, but the skies over Demyansk were now hotly contested, thanks to Kostenko's 1st Fighter Air Corps (as well as the 6th Air Army), which were not available in 1942 during the crucial first days of the Demyansk encirclement. Part of the German success of the Demyansk airlift rested on the anemic state of Soviet fighter aviation in the winter of 1941–42.

Both sides had learned their respective lessons at Demyansk. The Luft-waffe victory—once disembodied from its accompanying high costs—became an illusory model for subsequent German airlift operations. With the advent of Stalingrad, Hitler and the German High Command turned to this precedent to bolster their contention that a large encircled army grouping could be resupplied effectively by air. The Soviets, always keen to perfect their skills at combined-arms operations, saw in the Demyansk experience the demanding requirements for an air blockade. By the time of Stalingrad, the VVS would possess the requisite aircraft and battle experience to attempt another air blockade on a larger scale.[61]

The Novikov Reforms

The Soviet Air Force emerged from the winter offensive tattered, sobered by cruel attrition and gross inefficiency, a survivor of ten months of debilitating air operations against a technically superior enemy. The abundant heroism and dedication of Soviet air and ground crews could not conceal the serious deficiencies in air force organization. The major problems, first evident on June 22, 1941, was the lack of effective interaction between aviation and the ground forces. There had been a number of ad hoc measures, such as the October 1941 Directives at Moscow, but these fell short of solving the fundamental problems.

The imperative for a major reorganization of the VVS weighed heavily on the *Stavka* and air force planners in the spring of 1942. Already the Germans were planning a second summer offensive. A renewed German drive, perhaps against Moscow, would place an enormous burden once again on the hard-pressed Soviet Air Force. The aviation industry, now safely relocated beyond the Urals after extraordinary human effort and sacrifice, had acquired a momentum in the winter months to reach (and soon to pass) the prewar production levels. This meant a steady flow of modern combat aircraft during the coming months.[62] To make these new aircraft a powerful component in the overall striking power of the Soviet Army, the *Stavka* decided to refashion the structure, operational character, and tactics of the air force. As with the 1940 reorganization, these changes grew out of the frustrations of war. The context of 1942, however, prompted a sense of urgency comparable only to the Russian Civil War, when the survival of the Soviet regime had rested squarely on its ability to mobilize a potent military organization.

The first move came on April 11, 1942, when Gen. A. A. Novikov replaced Gen. P. F. Zhigarev as VVS commander. The choice of Novikov proved to be a wise one. Known for his talent and energy, Novikov quickly presided over a series of far-reaching reforms of the Soviet air arm in the spring of 1942. His rise to the top leadership had been rapid. In February he had assumed the post of first deputy commander of the VVS, a short-term assignment which sent him to the various fronts to coordinate air operations as

Winter air operations in Russia, 1941–42, required primitive expedients by the Luftwaffe. A Junkers Ju 52 flies overhead as a horse-drawn panje (sled) carries supplies across the snow-covered landscape. Courtesy of Glen Sweeting.

part of the Soviet general offensive then in progress.

Returning to Moscow in the second half of February, Novikov helped to plan air operations on the western axis. In March he moved to the north to plan and lead VVS air operations in the area of the Volkhov and Leningrad fronts. With subordinate air commanders drawn from frontal aviation, long-range aviation, and the Air Corps of Stavka Reserve, Novikov planned and executed the first massed air strikes in support of troops on two fronts. For this strategic achievement, he received the appointment of commander of the Soviet Army Air Force, and, concurrently, Deputy Peoples' Commissar of Defense.

The *Stavka's* appointment of Novikov reflected a war-induced preference for military talent over political caprice. The subsequent appointment of his predecessor, General Zhigarev, to the command of the VVS in the Far East suggested a refreshing example of how a reassignment did not necessarily mean the end of a professional military career.

Novikov provides an interesting profile of a top-ranking VVS commander during the Great Patriotic War period. As a youth, he had participated in the Civil War, joining the Communist party in 1920. His decision to pursue a military career led him ultimately to the Frunze Military Academy, from which he graduated in 1930. Following the older pattern in the Red Army of moving talented officers frequently from one post to the next, Novikov soon found himself assigned to aviation after serving in the headquarters of the 11th Rifle Corps of the Belorussian Military District. There was a shortage of experienced military officers in the expanding Soviet aviation in the early 1930s, and Novikov's appointment, among many others, was a practical means of solving the personnel crisis.

Serving as chief of staff of an air brigade, Novikov showed a genuine interest in aviation, passing the observer-pilot examination in 1933. His prewar career, however, advanced as a result of his skills as a commander, not as a pilot: he became in 1938 Air Force chief of staff of the Leningrad Military District, and in 1940, VVS commander for the Leningrad Military District. Gen. S. I. Rudenko found Novikov to be "an open minded person." His attention to detail and brisk efficiency impressed Rudenko, who first encountered him during the Leningrad-Volkhov air operations of 1942. Novikov, Rudenko noted, considered the introduction of new and proven techniques into VVS operations to be his "sacred duty".[63]

If Novikov displayed an aggressive desire to modernize the VVS, he did not emulate the Luftwaffe in a slavish fashion. Expediency dictated selective borrowing. The rites of copying, always with refinements, were as familiar as the elasticity of Bolshevik ideological program in the interwar years. Being behind the Luftwaffe at the outset of the war in technical and operational terms was not unique to the Soviet Air Force. During the Battle of Britain, for example, the Royal Air Force had made a series of changes in air tactics to conform to the *Rotte* and *Schwarm* formations. The VVS, by necessity, struggled with the same problem, among others, making similar tactical adjustments in 1942–43. Through the Air Force Military Council, Novikov organized the War Experience Analysis and Generalization Section to study systematically the "lessons" of the air war in the east. In part, this meant a close scrutiny of Luftwaffe organization, tactics, and equipment. The larger task, however, required an adaptation to the peculiarities of the Eastern front, that is, changes in lock step with Soviet air doctrine, which had dictated the building of a strong tactical air force.

To achieve these ends, Novikov blended proven Luftwaffe techniques with an indigenous operational style. Thus, the VVS under Novikov forged many innovations, and with time, this narrowed and closed the gap in equipment and technique with the Luftwaffe, a fact recently acknowledged by Gen. Adolf Galland.[64] There were also areas in which the VVS surpassed the Luftwaffe in technique and experience—such as cold-weather air operations. Moreover, the Soviets had a powerful and effective ground-attack capability with the Il-2 and Pe-2 aircraft.

Novikov began his tenure as air commander (a post he held for the duration of the war) with a group of able associates. His first deputy was Maj. Gen. Grigori A. Vorozheykin. General Falaleyev, who served as chief of staff until June 1943 (replaced by Gen. S. A. Khudyakov), played a key role as operational deputy.[65] Other important and long-term assignments included General Zharov (Rear Services), General Repin (Engineering-Technical Service), General Turkel' (Inspector-General), General Shimanov (Political Directorate), General Nikitin (Air Formations Directorate), and General Zhuravlev (Air Operations Directorate). These men provided continuity in leadership for the VVS in a period of rapid expansion after 1942.

Soviet military planners had viewed VVS organization in 1941–42 with a critical eye, seeing a persistent pattern of inferior performance and coordination. Some of this disarray, of course, stemmed from the disruption of the command and logistics structure as a result of Operation Barbarossa. At Moscow, however, the situation had stabilized enough to test the existing air force organization. Enormous problems continued throughout the winter, particularly air operations associated with the general offensive. The increased scope of the war required better command and control, more effective means of mobilizing air resources, and improved training for air crews.

Spearheading the entire program of reform was the Air Force Military Council, a group of high-ranking officers who attended to both the military and political affairs of the VVS. This group reviewed a series of staff proposals in 1942 for the improvement of the air force central administration. As a consequence, the various sections and directorates were redefined, including the creation of the aforementioned War Experience Analysis and Generalization Section with A. A. Vasil'yev as section chief. The sweep of reform altered rear services as well, which included the important spheres of airfield construction, technical and supply functions. All these changes extended the work of the 1940 reorganization program.

At the same time, Novikov supervised the reorganization of the Soviet bomber command. Although this command was called Long-Range Bomber Aviation (DA), the VVS in reality possessed only a depleted fleet of medium-sized bombers at the end of the first winter of the war. During the previous summer, DA had struck Berlin in a bold effort to bring the war home to the enemy, a symbolic gesture much like the Doolittle raid on Tokyo in 1942.[66] But the prevailing climate in air force planning circles suggested tactical, not strategic, bombing. Such an inclination pivoted on wartime expediency, and on Soviet air doctrine, which had shifted away from a brief flirtation with Douhet's concept of strategic bombing at the end of the 1930s. Lend-Lease reinforced this important shift by making available in 1942 shipments of A-20

By 1942 Lend-Lease aircraft had begun to arrive in the Soviet Union in significant numbers. With a P-40 as a backdrop, two Soviet pilots on the Karelian front play chess between sorties. Courtesy of USAF.

and B-25 medium bombers. The Soviet aviation industry also committed itself to the production of the highly regarded Il-4 (DB-3F) bomber in 1942 in
hopes of expanding its inventory of bomber aircraft.

A new structure for long-range aviation appeared in March 1942 with the
creation of ADD, or *Aviatsiya dal'nego deystviya*. As the successor to DA,
the newly formed "strategic aviation" component operated in direct subordi-
nation to the *Stavka* command. Maj. Gen. A. Ye. Golovanov assumed the
post of ADD commander, with Lt. Gen. M. I. Shevelev as chief of staff.
Golovanov, like Novikov, would hold his post throughout the war. The ADD
bomber command had at the start seven bomber air divisions, one transport
air division, and one reserve air brigade. In May 1943 ADD underwent further reorganization and expansion, adding to the command eight bomber air
corps of two divisions each (a division consisting in this case of two
regiments). Later, in December 1944, ADD became the 18th Air Army, again
with Golovanov as commander.

Bomber operations remained a problem for the VVS throughout the war.
The numerous reorganizations in many ways only hampered combat efficiency. Among all the components of the VVS during the war, the bomber air
units suffered some of the highest losses, particularly in the first two years.
Toward the end, however, a significant degree of combat efficiency became
apparent in VVS bomber operations. The commitment to the tactical deployment of bombers left the VVS with little real capacity for strategic bombing in
1945. The Pe-8, a large, four-engine Soviet bomber, existed, but in modest
numbers. Despite Moscow's interest, Lend-Lease did not provide B-17s or
B-29s to the VVS, although four of the latter were interned by the Soviets at
the close of the war after they made a forced landing in the Soviet Far East
after a raid on Japan.[67]

Novikov and the air force command had been frustrated in the first
months of the war with the cumbersome VVS organization. Toward the end of
the winter offensive, Novikov spearheaded in the Leningrad sector the organization of ten air strike groups (*Udarnyye aviatsionnyye gruppy*, or UAG).
Each unit consisted of six to eight regiments of mixed composition.[68] This effort at centralized control anticipated the *Stavka's* reorganization priorities.
Once Novikov assumed the post of VVS commander, he presided over the
creation of the air army organization, which brought centralized control into
the entire scope of VVS air operations. The Air Force Military Council for-
mally adopted the new air army structure in April 1942. The resulting air armies (*Vozdushnaya armiya*) fused together the fragmented army and frontal
aviation. With such an organization, Novikov and his planners were confident
that Soviet air power, now on the threshold of rapid expansion, could be concentrated quickly in strategic theaters of conflict for maximum effect.

Mobile air armies under centralized control provided the VVS with enormous flexibility in future campaigns. The 1st Air Army, with Gen. T. F.
Kutsevalov as commander, appeared in May 1942. It combined the air units
of the Western front for the purpose of "heightening the striking power of
aviation and allowing the successful application of massed air strikes."[69] In its
initial formulation, the 1st Air Army had modest strength: two fighter air divisions of four regiments each; two mixed air divisions, made up of two fighter
and two ground-attack regiments, along with one bomber air regiment; a
training air regiment; a long-range air reconnaissance squadron; a liaison

squadron; and a night bomber air regiment equipped with Po-2s. While army aviation, per se, was scheduled to be phased out, this did not take place quickly. Other air armies took form during the spring and summer of 1942: the 2d, 3d, 4th, and 8th air armies in May; the 5th and 6th in June; the 14th and 15th in July; and the 16th in August. By November three more air armies had been organized (the 7th, 13th, and 17th), completing the dramatic transformation of Soviet frontal aviation. Except for regimental air units performing reconnaissance and liaison work, all operational aviation entered the mobile air armies.

The air army gave the Soviets the capability for a rapid build-up of air power to meet the shifting requirements of battle. This capability became crucial in the last stages of the war, 1943–45, when large-scale summer and winter offensives along a 2,000–2,500-mile front required swift orchestration of forces to keep the enemy off balance. The demise of army aviation (*armeiskaya aviatsiya*) and the older frontal air command (VVS *fronta*) meant that control of the VVS passed to the air army commander who was subordinate in operational terms to the front's army group commander. By working as an air deputy to the frontal army commander, the VVS air army commander was able to coordinate his air operations more effectively with the requirements of the front for either defensive or offensive action.

No less important for the ultimate success of the air armies was the creation in 1942 of the Air Corps of *Stavka* Reserve. Again the Air Force Military Council assumed a leading role in the establishment of this powerful air reserve.[70] Each reserve air corps consisted normally of two or more air divisions with a total strength of 120 to 270 aircraft. Armed with the latest-model aircraft, the Air Corps of *Stavka* Reserve numbered thirteen air corps at the end of 1942, and comprised 43 percent of all Soviet combat aircraft inventory by January 1945, according to one Soviet source. Whatever their actual numbers, these strategic air reserves served as a conduit from the aviation industry to the air armies. They reinforced VVS aviation at crucial junctures in the war, augmenting air armies according to the requirements defined by the *Stavka*. Such a system gave the air armies an impressive capacity for maneuver and concentration.

With an ample supply of reserves, the average air army grew dramatically in size within a short period of time. During the 1942–43 period, at the time of the VVS challenge to the Luftwaffe for the strategic initiative in the air, an air army normally consisted of 900–1,000 aircraft. By 1944–45, the average reached 1,500, and for the final campaigns on the approaches to Berlin, the size of participating air armies mushroomed to 2,500–3,000. The formidable air production allowed the Air Corps of the *Stavka* Reserve to make massive augmentations in frontline air strength, sending more than 3,000 aircraft (eleven air corps) forward to buttress the 1st, 3d, 4th, and 16th air armies during the important Belorussian campaign in June–August 1944.[71] (See Appendix 7 on VVS air armies.)

Along with the creation of the air armies, the VVS began a gradual shift to homogeneous air units on the division and regimental levels. Air commanders argued for such units, particularly in fighter regiments, to provide for greater efficiency, more effective maintenance and supply, and better training of air and ground crews. This type of organization facilitated centralized control of Soviet air power. The shift also foreshadowed the sudden expansion of combat aircraft inventory in 1943, when VVS regiments increased in size by the average of twenty-two to thirty-two aircraft. By 1943 VVS fighter air regiments began to appear with single-type aircraft, for example Yak-7bs. For tactical reasons Shturmovik air divisions retained their composite character, with one fighter regiment attached for escort and reconnaissance duty. Novikov endeavored to reshape VVS squadron, regiment, and division configurations to meet the exigencies of air combat.

The Soviet Triumph at Moscow

The winter counteroffensive achieved its fundamental objective of removing, at least temporarily, the German threat to Moscow. But the larger goal of destroying Army Group Center had not been achieved despite extraordinary effort and sacrifice. The VVS claimed the destruction of more than 1,600 enemy aircraft. If true, this was a singular accomplishment for an air force which had suffered in the summer and fall of 1941 the worst air defeat in military history.

During the long winter months, the Soviets had pushed the Germans back as far as 240 miles in some sectors, inflicting, by Moscow's reckoning, 300,000 casualties.[72] German tallies of the war losses confirmed the high attrition. General Halder, chief of the general staff, listed 1,005,000 Germans killed, wounded, or missing by the end of February 1942, with 262,000 casualties alone over the course of the Soviet winter offensive.[73]

The role of the VVS at Moscow, however, had been peripheral in deciding the outcome. At times aggressive, the Soviet air units managed to survive the German blitz in the first months and go on the offensive in the winter of 1941–42. For the VVS to have survived amazed both German and Allied observers. Next, Soviet air force planners, assured of the support of the relocated aviation industry and Lend-Lease aid, sought to refashion the VVS organizational structure in 1942 to meet the realities of the Russo-German conflict.[74] Novikov, the new VVS air commander, pushed for dramatic changes in organization and tactics in advance of the renewal of the German offensive. These efforts presaged a prolonged conflict with the strategic initiative passing to the Soviet side in the short term.

Under Novikov's leadership, the air armies became a reality. They reflected in 1942 a crucial transition to a more efficient coordination of frontal aviation with the ground forces. Long-range bombers, once the centerpiece of Soviet aviation, began to assume a major role in tactical operations. The offensive air operations of 1942, as General Vershinin has noted, gave birth to the "air offensive," later to be elaborated in more precise terms. It emerged in rudimentary form as the VVS developed techniques for air support and the coordination of air and ground attacks.[75]

At Moscow, VVS air-combat operations fell short of any conventional notion of operational efficiency. Tactical coordination of air and ground forces had been haphazard, attrition remained high, and the sporadic displays of bravery by individual pilots and air crews failed to conceal a melancholy pattern of disorganization. Germans marveled at the occasional aggressiveness of Russian aviators, but rarely praised VVS air combat technique or equipment.[76]

The failure of the VVS to systematically apply air power on the retreating Wehrmacht at Moscow stood out as a major tactical error in the minds of Ger-

In one of the most impressive wartime achievements, the Soviets evacuated their war industries east of the Ural Mountains in 1941–42. Pictured here is a relocated YAK fighter assembly line. (SI 79-9509)

man observers.[77] Much of this apparent inertia can be explained by the peculiarities of Soviet operational practice. VVS air units remained close to the ground units providing cover. They rarely flew wide-ranging attacks in the enemy rear. Soviet air units at Moscow had only meager resources to press the attack. Both operational practice and circumstance kept the VVS close to the battle zones.

Gen. A. I. Yeremenko, in his memoir, *The Arduous Beginning*, has described the anemic striking power of the VVS in the January 1942 offensive operations: "the 4th Shock Army of the Northwestern front possessed a mere sixty planes, of which fifty-three were battleworthy, including sixteen LaGG-3s, 17 I-15s, two SB (bombers) and eighteen Po-2 airplanes."[78] With this small flotilla of obsolete aircraft, Yeremenko planned to cover advancing troops, ambitiously attack German strong points, and interdict enemy reserves and retreating troops in the rear. In 1941–42, the VVS could be aggressive, but material shortages and organizational flaws precluded anything approaching combat effectiveness.

Already at Moscow both sides in alternating offensives grappled with the enormity of the Russian landscape and climate. For the Germans, space more than the extremes of weather made invasion a problematical undertaking. The Wehrmacht had been absorbed, rather than frozen in place in 1941–42. As Soviet historians correctly note, the subzero temperatures and snow storms did not spare Russian troops or their equipment, but the Soviet military entered the winter campaign better prepared for cold-weather operations. The Luftwaffe, for example, had been reduced to half its invasion strength at the end of 1941, approximately 1,700 aircraft for a 2,000-mile front from Murmansk to the Black Sea.[79] The ratio of aircraft for distances covered was low (fewer than two aircraft per mile of front), which allowed the VVS—even in its reduced strength—to operate with relative freedom.

In 1812 R. V. Rostopchin saw clearly that invading armies, even those well-armed and numerous, became vulnerable with each step eastward. The irony was that Russia's defenses gained strength through Russian retreat: "the emperor will always be formidable in Moscow, terrible in Kazan, and invincible in Tobolsk".[80]

Chapter 4

Stalingrad

Stalingrad became the epic backdrop for the Soviet Air Force to wrest air supremacy from the Luftwaffe. The air war at Stalingrad, like the war on the ground, was a watershed in the Russo-German conflict. For the first time, the Soviets began to assert the strategic initiative in the air, marking a shift of balance that became complete after the Kuban and Kursk campaigns of the spring and summer of 1943. These air battles—Stalingrad, the Kuban, and Kursk—occupy a pivotal position in the history of Soviet air power in World War II. As a triad of air victories, they gave evidence of the new aggressiveness among Soviet pilots, the more effective VVS air-combat tactics, and the growing numerical superiority of the VVS over the Luftwaffe. Through the bitter Stalingrad conflict the VVS established the momentum for eventual victory. The great air offensives of 1944–45 were first tried on this strategic bend in the Volga River in the winter of 1942–43.

Stalingrad also became the occasion for the VVS to introduce new combat aircraft and to execute successfully a large-scale "air blockade" of the Luftwaffe. Over Stalingrad as well, a new mood of confidence animated Soviet pilots and air crews. No longer did the VVS view the Luftwaffe as invincible. This shift in attitude alone signaled a turning point in the war.

Soviet historians divide the air war at Stalingrad into two distinct phases: a defensive stage, beginning in July 1942 and extending into the fall, in which the VVS endeavored to blunt German air and ground operations on the Don and at Stalingrad; and the Soviet counteroffensive, November 19, 1942–February 2, 1943, which encircled and destroyed Gen. Friedrich Paulus's 6th Army.

The two periods were uneven in terms of the quantity and character of VVS activity. During the defensive stage, Soviet air operations, at best, were occasional and in no way a serious challenge to Luftwaffe supremacy. This reduced level of air action by the VVS contrasted sharply with the fierce ground resistance offered by the Soviets on the approaches to Stalingrad. Only in the second phase, beginning with the November 19 Soviet counteroffensive, did the full brunt of Soviet air power fall with a vengeance on the overextended German positions.

The Soviets had curtailed their air operations during the summer and fall of 1942 to build up the newly formed air armies to full strength in preparation for a winter counteroffensive. By the fall of 1942, the Soviet aviation industry had regained its productive capacity, supplying a steady stream of newer model La-5s, Yak-7bs and Yak-9s, and Il-2s to the forward air units.[1] Stalin prudently channeled the growing number of VVS aircraft into the Air Corps of *Stavka* Reserve. Stalingrad became an important testing ground for the reorganized VVS command structure to make effective use of these resources.

To the Volga River

After the abortive Soviet offensive at Demyansk and Kharkov in May–June 1942, the German High Command ordered Army Group B under Field Marshal Fedor von Bock to begin the long awaited German summer offensive. Stepping off in the Bryansk sector on June 28, Army Group B moved toward Voronezh. Concurrently, Army Group A, under the command of Field Marshal Wilhelm von List, attacked through the Donets Basin toward the Volga River. Across the flat, almost limitless steppe of the eastern Ukraine, German panzer units pushed forward in clouds of dust and in sweltering heat. Overhead the Luftwaffe, resuming its customary ground-support role, attacked the retreating Russians in force. Having overrun the Soviet defenses on the Don, the Germans, with Paulus's 6th Army as a spearhead, managed to reach the Stalingrad Oblast (region) by July 12. To the south, German forces moved into the Caucasus.

Moscow reacted desperately in an effort to halt the German advance, sending reinforcements to Voronezh and organizing the defenses of Stalingrad. The Luftwaffe, deployed along the attack zones of the German armies, had more than 1,200 aircraft. By contrast, the VVS found itself awkwardly situated to meet the challenge, being outnumbered by nearly four to one in the attack zones. The *Stavka* sent an operational group under P. S. Stepanov to organize the air defense of Stalingrad.

Stalin feared a possible collapse of Soviet defenses. In the face of the unfolding crisis, he issued Order No. 227 (July 28), which stated: "*ni shagu nazad*," or "not a step backward." The decree was harsh and determined. For potential "deserters" or "panic mongers," it threatened swift retribution. It was also patriotic in its appeal, committing the Soviet Army to the strategic defense of Stalingrad—a city hitherto outside the sphere of combat. At the moment of this decision, Paulus's 6th Army was approaching the great bend in the Volga River.

Stalingrad, called Tsaritsyn in prerevolutionary days, occupied a narrow strip of land nearly twenty-five miles long on the west bank of the Volga. In earlier times the city had been an important tsarist military and trading center; now, in 1942, it was a burgeoning industrial center with a population of 500,000. The approach to Stalingrad from the west resembled a table top, giving way at the city's perimeter to a series of hills and ridges. Winding

1. Industrieanlage
2. Tanklager
3. Zerstörte Kessel
4. Holzlagerplatz
5. Flakstellung
6. Ausgef. Brücke, teilw. zerst.
7. Panzer, teilweise verladen
8. Holzflöße
9. Bombeneinschläge
10. Flakstellung

German aerial reconnaissance photograph of Stalingrad and the Volga River. Translated key: (1) industrial plants; (2) tank storage; (3) destroyed area; (4) wood storage area; (5) flak installations; (6) partially destroyed bridge; (7) partially loaded armor; (8) barges; (9) bomb craters; (10) flak installations; (11) oil slick. Courtesy of Glen Sweeting.

through this asymmetrical geography was the deep Tsaritsa Gorge. In the middle of Stalingrad, overlooking the Volga River, was the Mamaev Hill. The long, tightly arranged urban strip which was Stalingrad proper faced a bend in Volga and the vast, flat terrain stretching to the east. Tsaritsyn had been renamed Stalingrad (the city of Stalin) because Joseph Stalin had led the Bolshevik forces there during the Civil War. Once the German summer offensive began, the city acquired strategic importance, since its loss would sever the north-south waterway between Moscow and the Caucasus.

The *Stavka* had moved slowly to prepare the defenses of the threatened city. Not until July 14 did Moscow place Stalingrad on a war footing. The previous summer, during the hectic days of Operation Barbarossa, the Soviet authorities had ordered the construction of three defensive lines on the western perimeter of the city, but these projects remained unfinished. Work had begun again in late June just on the eve of Army Group B's thrust eastward.

Other defensive measures followed in the wake of the German advance—the creation of a peoples' militia, the organization of partisan groups, the evacuation of children. All these measures fell under the aegis of the Stalingrad front, which had been created by the *Stavka* on July 12. Since German air raids, as expected, preceded the main assault on the city, desperate efforts were made to provide adequate air cover. The 8th Air Army of the former Southwestern front assumed an important role in the air defense of Stalingrad.

Stepanov, the *Stavka* representative, inspected the situation at Stalingrad and reported to Moscow that the entire network of air defenses was inadequate. He toured the various airfields and established communications with the command of the PVO *strany* for Stalingrad. The 102d Fighter Air Division (PVO) possessed a mere eighty aircraft, mostly obsolete I-15 and

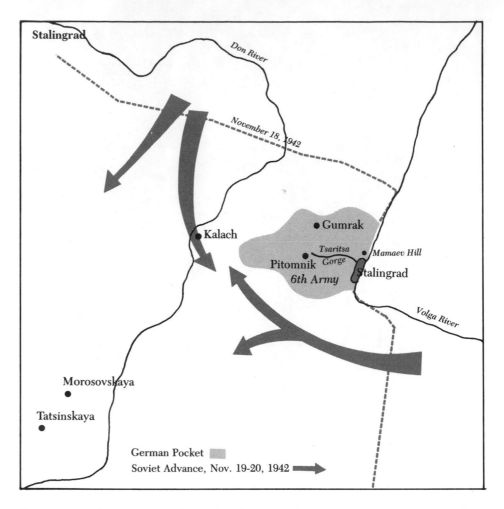

Stalingrad

Don River

November 18, 1942

Gumrak

Tsaritsa Gorge

Mamaev Hill

Pitomnik

6th Army

Stalingrad

Kalach

Volga River

Morosovskaya

Tatsinskaya

German Pocket
Soviet Advance, Nov. 19-20, 1942

I-16 types. The newer model Yak and Lavochkin types were in short supply, and Stepanov appealed to Novikov and the *Stavka* for the immediate deployment of a fighter regiment equipped with Yak-1s.

This appeal did not go unheeded: Air Commander Novikov ordered forthwith a crack fighter air regiment from Moscow to Stalingrad, and the *Stavka* deployed ten air regiments to reinforce the 8th Air Army. For frontline air commanders these timely reinforcements were most welcome and necessary. The fact that nearly 75 percent of the aircraft in these regiments were the newer types—Yak-1, Yak-7b, Il-2, and Pe-2—prompted greater confidence in the ability of the VVS to frustrate the Luftwaffe at Stalingrad.

Already the Novikov reforms were shaping the character of the VVS response. General Falaleyev, appointed air force chief of staff in July, spearheaded a number of crucial operational changes. During the first week of his tenure as chief of staff, Falaleyev issued a directive instructing all frontal air commanders to concentrate their aviation along the main avenues of Soviet Army operations. Falaleyev sought to make the VVS an effective weapon. No longer would it be dispersed to perform myriad tasks without reference to the larger combat priorities. The diffusion of Soviet air power had led to extraordinary attrition and minimal efficiency in the first year of the war.

Falaleyev's directive embodied as well the on-going effort to centralize Soviet air operations. VVS strikes against secondary targets were still possible, but only after the larger requirements had been met. Reflecting

Novikov's stress on competence and efficiency, Falaleyev pushed for better operational planning. This meant greater use of air reconnaissance. For the headquarters staff in Moscow, there was the difficult task of walking a tight rope between increased need for centralization and the desire to encourage initiative among frontline air commanders. VVS personnel, from squadron to divisional levels, were now displaying considerable élan in their struggle with the Luftwaffe. At the same time, the Soviet air commanders, still intimidated by the purge era and fearing retribution for any mistakes which might result from excessive battlefield "initiative," exercised caution in all things. Men such as Falaleyev encouraged a higher level of flexibility, but these problems defied any permanent solution.

Stalin himself monitored VVS air operations through daily briefings. These reports, based on the major air operations of the previous day, provided a profile of missions flown, targets hit, the number of air battles, a summary of German and VVS losses, and an evaluation of VVS effectiveness. Through these summaries Stalin also learned about Luftwaffe deployment, air actions, and aircraft development. Two high-ranking air force officers prepared the reports after a systematic study of accumulated reports from the field. Gen. N. A. Zhuravlev, "who possessed the ability to say a great deal in a little space," wrote the final version of the briefing report for Stalin.[2]

Being assigned to Supreme Headquarters, the *Stavka*, involved hard work. Air Commander Novikov and a small group of senior commanders briefed Stalin on a regular schedule. All activity at the *Stavka* was subordinate to Stalin's will. He received detailed reports and made decisions, some all-encompassing in their impact, others touching only upon small matters. For the most part, Stalin preferred a limited coterie of talented subordinates around him. As Supreme Commander, he could be petty and vindictive, always exacting in his demands, but a quick learner of the military art. By the time of the Stalingrad crisis the *Stavka* had achieved a higher level of efficiency and demonstrated in its work the capacity to plan complex defensive and offensive operations.

For Novikov and other high-ranking officers who prepared the regular briefings there were the inevitable encounters with the Supreme Commander in the Kremlin, who maintained both an apartment and an office in a "little corner" near the Supreme Soviet. Col. Gen. S. M. Shtemenko, who worked at Supreme Headquarters, relates in his memoirs the context and procedure:

> We entered the small room of the chief of the personal guard through Poskrebyshev's office [Stalin's personal secretary] and from there into the Supreme Commander-in-Chief's suite. On the left side of the office, not far from the wall, stood a long, rectangular table. We used to roll out the maps on it and use them to make a report on each Army Group in detail, starting with the one where major action was taking place at that given moment. . . . At the end of the table, in the corner, there was a large globe on the floor. I must say that in the hundreds of times I visited the office, I never once saw the globe used during a discussion of operational questions.
>
> In addition to the Supreme Commander in Chief, as a rule, members of the Politburo and members of Supreme Headquarters were present at these briefing sessions. . . . Usually, all civilians present sat along the table against the wall facing us, the military, and the huge portraits of Suvorov and Kutuzov which hung

on the opposite wall of the office. Stalin used to pace up and down along the table on our side as he listened. From time to time, he would go over to his desk, which stood far back on the right, take two cigarettes, tear them open, and stuff his pipe with tobacco.[3]

During these sessions Stalin reviewed the overall situation and the various directives proposed to the *Stavka*. These directives, once corrected or supplemented, were signed by Stalin and the chief of the General Staff. In response to military emergencies, a directive fashioned by Supreme Head-quarters was transmitted immediately to the front from a nearby communications room. For Shtemenko, Novikov, and others, these sessions sometimes extended to 3:00 or 4:00 a.m., typifying the "rigid work schedule that Stalin had established and no one could change." Such a regimen, according to Shtemenko, required "enormous physical and moral resources . . . which not every man could take, the more so because, as a rule, men were dismissed from the General Staff for the slightest mistake with all the ensuing consequences."

Toward wartime aviation Stalin displayed an avid interest and, sometimes to the chagrin of aviation leaders, an exacting set of expectations. At the start of the war, he pressed for greater production of aircraft. Later, as the German threat diminished, he demanded qualitative improvements in Soviet aircraft. Aleksandr Yakovlev, aircraft designer and a deputy people's commissar of the Aviation Industry for Development and Research (1940–48), re-called in his memoirs being summoned along with P. V. Dement'yev, then in charge of aviation production, to Stalin's office in June 1943.[4] Upon entering, they noticed a piece of cracked wing-covering fabric on the table. Yakovlev saw the impending crisis immediately, and realized that "unpleasant talk lay ahead."

Stalin had been informed that wing coverings on Yak-9 fighters were cracking and tearing off in the stress of air combat. He pointed to the fabric on the table and asked: "Do you know anything about this?" Then he read aloud a report from the field and queried Yakovlev and Dement'yev in depth. Both men acknowledged that they were aware of the problem and reassured Stalin that steps were being taken to correct the situation. With each question, followed by nervous reply, Stalin grew more angry.

"Why did this happen?" he demanded, losing his composure more and more. "Why were several hundred airplanes produced with defective coverings? After all, you know that fighters at this point are as vital to us as the air we breathe! How could you permit such a thing? Why weren't countermeasures taken sooner?"

Yakovlev and Dement'yev explained that the glues and dyes used on the Yak-9 were hurriedly prepared substitutes to meet a crisis, that their defective character could only become apparent in frontline conditions when the fabric was exposed to the elements, and that wartime conditions at the plants made the discovery of such problems difficult since the aircraft were shipped immediately from the plant to the front.

Upon hearing that the problem had not been discovered at the plants, Stalin flew into a rage: "Do you know that only the most cunning enemy could do such a thing?! This is exactly what he would do—turn out airplanes in such a way that they would seem good at the plant and no good at the front. The enemy himself could do us no greater harm. He could have devised nothing worse. This is working for Hitler! . . . Do you know that you have put fighter aviation out of commission? Do you know what a service you have rendered Hitler? You Hitlerites!"

"It is difficult to imagine our condition at that moment," Yakovlev recalled. "I felt I was shivering. And Dement'yev stood there, completely flushed, nervously twirling a piece of the ill-fated covering in his fingers." After several moments of "tomblike silence" Stalin shifted from rage to problem solving, asking, "what are we going to do?" Dement'yev promised to repair the aircraft in two weeks, a promise he fulfilled, much to Yakovlev's surprise and relief.

Stalin's attention to detail required direct and accurate responses from subordinates responsible for aviation. The previous March, Stalin had met with Yakovlev and A. S. Shakurin, the organizer of the Soviet war industries. At this meeting Stalin queried both men on the Shvetsov M-82 engine, losing his temper at one point when Shakurin gave excuses for delays in the mass production of the air-cooled engine. Stalin also asked detailed questions about the effective range of Soviet fighters, comparing them unfavorably with British Spitfires and American Airacobras. Yakovlev quickly found himself the victim of Stalin's fury. He recalled: "When he quoted figures for the Spitfires, I understood that he was speaking of the Spitfire reconnaissance plane which had a range of over 1,250 miles, and I remarked that I carried no guns, that being a reconnaissance not a fighter plane. 'You're talking nonsense!' Stalin retorted. 'I'm not a child, am I? I am talking about the fighter, not the reconnaissance plane. Spitfires have a greater range than our fighters, and we must catch up in this respect without fail'"

From men such as Yakovlev, dealing with design and production, and Novikov, handling air-force planning and operations, Stalin demanded high performance. His prodding, sometimes marred by error and stubbornness, nevertheless played a key role in transforming the VVS into a formidable tactical air arm.[5]

The Yak and Lavochkin fighters, the object of Stalin's careful scrutiny, introduced a new level of performance at Stalingrad. This technological refinement coincided with a sudden display of combat skill by VVS fighter pilots. The ineffectual MiG-3 had gone out of production in favor of the Yak series. The LaGG-3, no less troublesome than the MiG-3, had been reprieved in a curious fashion by redesigning it to accommodate a radial engine, resulting in the highly successful La-5.

At Stalingrad the Yak-7b and Yak-9 provided the VVS with fast fighters known for their excellent maneuverability and range. The post-Stalingrad period of the war would see further development in these basic fighter types, culminating with the advanced La-7 and the Yak-3 models. Both Soviet and German accounts agree, more or less, that these newer versions of Soviet fighter aircraft achieved a rough parity with the Messerschmitt Bf 109G and with Fock-Wulf Fw 90, which was introduced on the Eastern front in 1943.

The Germans took a keen interest in Soviet fighter development. Early-model Yaks, LaGG-3s, and MiG-3s were captured and tested at the front. After 1943, when the Germans found themselves in strategic retreat except for local offensives, VVS aircraft become difficult to obtain. Hans-Werner Lerche, a Luftwaffe test pilot who flew an extraordinary number of captured

Allied aircraft, got an opportunity in September 1944 to test fly a captured La-5. Later he flew a Yak-3. His evaluation of both fighters provides an interesting enemy perspective on the evolving Soviet aviation technology.

Lerche traveled in the fall of 1944 to East Prussia, then under siege, to fly the La-5. Compared to the prewar I-16 Rata, Lerche reported, the La-5 had made a dramatic leap forward, being a more sophisticated machine than the I-16 and below 10,000 feet "an enemy to watch carefully." Despite bad weather and persistent VVS air raids, Lerche made several test flights, learning in each the mixed character of the La-5. He discovered that the airplane had excellent acceleration and was well adapted for low-level fighting. It could turn faster than the Fw 190 at sea level, although it could not outperform the Bf 109 in the same maneuver. Up to 10,000 feet the La-5 could outclimb its German radial-engine counterpart, the Fw 190. Overall, Lerche evaluated the La-5 just under the performance levels of both later model Bf 109s and Fw 190s. Lerche complained that the La-5 engine (ASH-82FN) was rough and loud, "leaving him almost deaf."

When a Yak-3 landed undamaged near Berlin (at Gross-Schimanen) in January 1945, Lerche gained access to the ultimate refinement in Soviet wartime fighter development. He was impressed. Lighter than the Yak-9, the Yak-3 possessed quick acceleration, light and responsive controls, and an excellent rate of climb. As did the La-5, the Yak-3 demonstrated prowess only at lower altitudes; once Lerche moved to medium altitudes and above, the Yak-3's superior qualities in power and performance diminished sharply. The German test pilot recorded that the Soviet fighter made "an exceptional impression" on him.

The problem with the wing fabric on the Yak-9—the crisis which had ushered Yakovlev and Dement'yev into the presence of an angry Stalin—was not evident in the Yak-3. In fact, Lerche admired the "faultlessly skinned plywood" of the wing, which was smooth and easily repaired in the field. Other aspects of the Yak-3 pleased Lerche: the sleek lines, the aerodynamic cleanliness, the wide landing gear, the spacious cockpit, and the buoyant character of the plane.

To fly such a "small fast beast," the German pilot noted, one must be alert on takeoff, otherwise a high-power setting and inattention might allow the aircraft to flip over. With its V-shaped, liquid-cooled engine (VK-107A), the visibility on the ground was poor, but in the air all was "in order." The engine ran flawlessly, which, Lerche said, gave him confidence to fly the aircraft at low altitudes. Lerche made several flights, including one to Oranienberg, where Hermann Goering himself inspected the aircraft with great interest. Lerche gave the Yak-3 high marks, asserting that in low-level dogfighting capabilities it could out perform the Bf 109 and the Fw 190.[6]

The Yak-7b and Yak-9 fighters, along with the new model La-5, were excellent additions to VVS fighter strength in 1943, but they were in short supply. The great length of the Stalingrad front, nearly 500 miles, meant that the VVS in the defensive stage could provide only token resistance. In his memoirs, Yakovlev asserted that this acute shortage of fighters extended into the fall of 1942. Meanwhile, the Luftwaffe continued to take a fearful toll of Soviet fighters. Stalin ordered a rapid increase in fighter production, to be achieved at breakneck speed and at whatever cost.[7] Moscow responded to this need by reorganizing its plants assigned to the manufacture of Yak fight-

Captured Allied Aircraft

A delegation of German industrialists and military officials view captured aircraft, including three Soviet airplanes, September 1943.

A P-39 and YAK-1 are visible in the foreground of this general view of captured aircraft. Two American bombers, a B-17 and a B-24, are in the rear.

Three captured Soviet airplanes: YAK-9, YAK-7b, and P-39.

This captured La-5, number "84," was from the Valeriy Chkalov squadron. Courtesy of National Archives via Jay Spenser.

ers on a mass-production basis. Various components were stockpiled. Plants began round-the-clock operations. Rather than build several variants, the Soviets shifted their production in mid-1942 exclusively to the most recent Yak model, the Yak-9.

Always faced with a shortage of aluminum, the Siberian aviation plants turned to indigenous resources to construct the Yak-9. Steel tubing, produced in local metallurgical plants, was used for the fuselage. Wooden wings, fashioned from abundant supplies of Siberian pine, replaced aluminum. Lend-Lease aid in the form of aluminum and other alloys remained at modest levels in 1942, necessitating self-sufficiency on the part of Soviet aircraft plants. For the Yak-9 production, various components—for example, electrical and radio equipment—were also manufactured in Siberia to avoid dependence on plants many miles away in the Soviet Union or abroad.[8]

At this stage in the war, there were acute problems with Soviet fighter operations at the front. General Rudenko complained that fighter cover for ground-attack aircraft lacked discipline. Inexperienced fighter pilots frequently abandoned their assigned positions in the heat of battle, making fighter protection occasional at best. When fighters and Shturmoviks broke formation singly, they exposed themselves to the ever-present danger of German fighters. Moreover, few of Rudenko's fighter pilots were prepared for the rigor of air combat, and they lacked technical knowledge about their new aircraft, since their brief transition training had afforded them little opportunity to learn the nuances of their fighter machines. Under the immense pressures of the German invasion, training had been abbreviated to meet the wartime emergency. Two-thirds of the pilots in the 220th Fighter Air Division, for example, arrived at Stalingrad with minimal flight experience in the newer Yak and Lavochkin fighter aircraft.[9] They also knew little of the geography of the region, giving them no particular advantage as defenders.

Given these concerns, Novikov endeavored to bring greater efficiency to VVS air operations. At the front, he gave considerable attention to better methods of air control, an area which improved dramatically with the use of radio. In the rear, Novikov saw clearly the need to improve training methods. His War Experience Analysis Section, providing detailed information on Luftwaffe strengths in equipment and tactics, was helpful in reshaping VVS training along more realistic lines.

Always energetic, Novikov visited frontline airfields and spoke at length with unit commanders and pilots. Many of these visits prompted him to order immediate changes to improve operational effectiveness. With typical Bolshevik rigor, Novikov always checked that the various levels of the air force command structure complied with his instructions.[10] Yakovlev observed in his memoirs that Novikov had a profound sense of duty and a singlemindedness about defeating the Luftwaffe.[11] He was animated as well by a pragmatism and willingness to learn. These qualities made him an effective air commander, one who never allowed himself to be trapped by the prewar operational modes which had brought the VVS to the point of extinction.

Novikov made his appearance at the Stalingrad front on August 23, 1942, as part of a special commission of high-ranking officials sent from the *Stavka* in Moscow. G. M. Malenkov, Stalin's wartime associate and member of the State Defense Committee, had arrived in the city on August 12 with Gen. A. M. Vasilevskiy, then chief of the General Staff. Already the Luftwaffe had

Italian fighter pilots, many of them veterans of the Spanish Civil War (1936–39), arrived in the east to assist the Luftwaffe. Two of the Italians are pictured in front of their Fiat G. 50 fighter aircraft. Courtesy of Glen Sweeting.

placed Stalingrad under bombardment, and German troops were moving forward across the Don.

During these critical days, the *Stavka* worked desperately to stem the German advance. By August 20, Gen. A. Ye. Golovanov had supervised the relocation of five of his ADD divisions from Moscow to the Stalingrad area. Between July 20 and August 17 Novikov reinforced the 8th and 16th air armies, along with 102d Fighter Aviation Division (PVO), with a steady flow of air regiments drawn from the Air Corps of the *Stavka* Reserve. The VVS, according to General Rudenko, had reached a level of 738 aircraft by September 4. This air flotilla could count on 150–200 bombers from ADD, but it was inadequate to meet the wide-ranging defensive requirements.[12] Overhead the Luftwaffe ruled supreme, and on the ground the Wehrmacht continued its advance.

As commander of the 16th Air Army, Rudenko faced critical problems at Stalingrad in the defensive stage. Various air units arrived at the front below full strength. The 228th Shturmovik Air Division (ShAD), for example, entered battle with one-third of its prescribed complement of combat aircraft. Most flight crews of the 16th Air Army were inexperienced. Quickly assigned to frontline airfields, VVS air units began their duties at once, flying reconnaissance, providing air support for the ground troops, and attacking enemy positions.

Confusion prevailed in this climate of emergency measures. There was little in the way of effective communication links between the arriving VVS air units and the army hierarchy. In the rear areas the logistics problems mounted as the Soviet Army attempted to stem the German advance. On September 4, the 16th Air Army, according to Rudenko, had three RAB, or logistical support units (23d, 35th, 80th), along with seventeen airfield-servicing battalions (BAO) and assorted depots for fuel and spare parts. Despite some aircraft reinforcements, supply problems remained to sharply curtail the combat effectiveness of the 16th Air Army.[13]

Air battles over the western approaches to Stalingrad arose suddenly in the fall of 1942. Only in rare instances did the VVS come away from these fierce encounters as the victor. Losses were great on both sides, but the Luftwaffe ruled the skies. The Soviet 434th Fighter Air Regiment, for example, flew 611 combat sorties in September (5,225 total for the 16th Air Army), participated in forty-eight air battles, and claimed eighty-two enemy aircraft downed. This level of air action reduced the serviceability of the 434th dramatically, and by the end of the month one-third of its combat aircraft were in serious disrepair.[14] With mounting losses in fighters, Rudenko ordered VVS fighter pilots in this defensive stage to avoid enemy fighters and strike at bombers and reconnaissance planes. The "*zasada*," or "ambush," became a new VVS technique to hit these more vulnerable enemy aircraft. Experienced VVS pilots, operating normally in the new *para* formation, awaited German bombers along their flight routes to Stalingrad.

Along with the piecemeal use of new tactics, VVS pilots continued to practice some old ones, namely ramming, which had proved successful in the first months of the war. The renewal of the ramming phenomenon, at the time of overall Luftwaffe air supremacy and devastating air raids on the city of Stalingrad, grew out of a mood of desperation.

On September 14 I. M. Chumbarev, a young pilot flying a Yak-1 with the 237th Fighter Air Regiment, was on an "ambush" sortie near his airfield. While patroling in his assigned zone, Chumbarev intercepted a Focke Wulf Fw 189 reconnaissance plane. The Fw 189 had arrived over the field undetected, and moved in and out of the heavy cloud cover to perform its mission. At around 3,500 feet Chumbarev drew in on the enemy aircraft, radio-assisted by observers on the ground. Chumbarev rammed the German aircraft from behind and below, sending it to its destruction. Wounded in the head, Chumbarev nevertheless maintained effective control of his plane and landed it in a field near some Soviet troops.[15]

On September 19 the VVS recorded two additional rammings, one by V. N. Chenskiye of the 283d Fighter Air Division (IAD), who managed to down one German aircraft and parachute to safety, and a second by L. I. Binov of the 291st Fighter Air Division, who downed an Me 110 and, like Chumbarev, guided his crippled aircraft safely to the ground.[16] For the Soviets, these men represented the highest expression of bravery. They had chosen not to abandon an unequal struggle, but to ram enemy aircraft. Despite such heroics, the VVS did not seriously challenge the Luftwaffe over Stalingrad in September–October, 1942. Beyond the Volga, however, the VVS moved resolutely to gather its resources for the anticipated winter offensive against the Germans.

The 8th Air Army, under Gen. T. T. Khryukin, assumed an active role in this period. Once the German Army had begun its crossings of the Don River on August 17, the 8th Air Army moved forward to help annihilate the enemy groupings. Attack groups of ten to thirty Pe-2s and Il-2 aircraft, covered by ten to fifteen Yak-1 or La-5 fighters, struck the advancing Germans. Between August 18 and 22 VVS pilots flew more than 1,000 sorties against enemy river crossings. Some ground-attack pilots flew as many as three sorties per day during these operations.

Such an intense level of air action slowed, but did not stop, the enemy. In fact, the Luftwaffe on August 23 attacked Stalingrad in a massive air strike by more than 400 aircraft. The Soviets describe this raid as particularly devastating. In twenty-five air battles above Stalingrad that day, the VVS as a whole claimed ninety enemy aircraft. On the same day the headquarters of the 8th Air Army was moved out of the city.[17]

The German push in late September had occupied much of the city of

German bomber crew with their Junkers Ju 88 bomber after completing 1,000 combat missions in the east. (SI 74–3030)

Stalingrad, now largely a vista of rubble and charred ruins. Named deputy supreme commander in chief, General Zhukov had assumed command of the crucial Stalingrad defense on August 29. As plans in Moscow went forward to organize a major counteroffensive, bitter fighting took place within the precincts of Stalingrad itself, as each side attacked and counterattacked with infantry, tanks, artillery, and air power.

In early September Zhukov attempted with little success to dislodge the Germans, who had positioned themselves at key points and along the high bluffs. Bitter fighting continued for weeks as the two sides fought for the rubble of factories, often floor by floor, room by room. On the Mamaya Heights, occupied by Gen. V. I. Chuikov's 62d Army, a fierce bloodletting unfolded in a maelstrom of sustained artillery fire. The Central Railroad Station changed hands three times. The Germans shelled Soviet reinforcements crossing from the east bank of the Volga around-the-clock; the Russians returned the artillery fire on German-held positions.

After taking the Stalingrad tractor plant, with a loss of over 3,000 men, the Germans cut Chuikov's sector in two, coming within 400 yards of the Volga. The climactic German drive against Chuikov's 62d Army took place on November 11, but failed. Chuikov and the Stalingrad defense managed to hold on.

VVS units, drawn from the 8th Air Army and ADD, supported the fierce defense of Stalingrad. Soviet air strikes hit one enemy sector after another with Il-2 Shturmoviks in low-level sweeps. Between September 27 and Octo-

German Ju 87D Stukas dive on Soviet targets during the summer of 1942. Courtesy of Glen Sweeting.

ber 8 the 8th Air Army flew nearly 4,000 sorties. Novikov also ordered an intensification of night attacks by the 8th and other participating air armies. In a directive issued on October 22, 1942, Novikov instructed each ground-attack and fighter air regiment to train five crews for night sorties. These same specially trained air crews were expected to fly in the difficult winter weather conditions which would soon descend on the region. During the defensive stage of the battle for Stalingrad, Il-2 Shturmoviks scored 406 night sorties.

The VVS experimented at this time with a radio guidance network. Air Commander Novikov put the system into operation along the Don front, using air units from the 16th Air Army. Earlier, as a frontal air force commander at Leningrad, Novikov had introduced a system of ground-based radio stations, a novelty at the time for the austerely equipped Soviet air units. Now in the crucible of Stalingrad, Novikov continued the effort in hopes of tightening the control of VVS air operations.

Such experimentation in the crisis period of late September required confidence on the part of Novikov in the efficacy of the system. To assure the proper use of the new radio technology, he sent two high-ranking officers to the 16th Air Army to set up the communications network, Gen. V. N. Zhdanov, deputy commander of the 13th Air Army (Leningrad front), and Gen. G. K. Gvozdkov, Air Force Headquarters Signal Directorate Chief. Both men, accompanied by specialists, helped the 16th Air Army command to prepare field instructions on the use of a radio-guidance system. Novikov monitored the program even as he attended to the pressing requirements for the air defense of Stalingrad.

Once the radio-guidance system had taken shape, it provided a new and powerful weapon. Fighter-guidance radio stations were placed adjacent to the front, about one to two miles from the forward line at intervals of five to six miles. Each station maintained contact with fighter pilots in the air, the various airfields, and the command posts of the 16th Air Army. The radio station network, which was subdivided into command and information stations, soon allowed the command of the 16th Air Army to receive situation reports quickly. Control and response became more effective, so much so that the radio stations expanded their operation to include ground-attack operations as well.

Novikov took advantage of the situation to exploit fully the training possibilities of the program. He called up twenty-five commanders and deputy commanders of reserve fighter air regiments to participate in the control and guidance operations. From this pivotal experiment, Air Force Headquarters in Moscow developed a field manual, *Instruktsiya dlya Voyenno-Vozdushnykh sil po upravleniyu, opoveshcheniyu i navedeniyu samoletov po radio* [Instructions to the Air Force on controlling, informing, and guiding airplanes by radio].[18]

As the defensive stage of the struggle for Stalingrad drew to a close, the VVS displayed an augmented strength. By November 1942 it had 4,544 aircraft, with around 1,400 committed to Stalingrad. Nearly three-quarters of all combat aircraft were now of modern design, a reflection of the growing productivity of the aviation industry. This augmented strength in modern aircraft made its impact at the fronts, where regiments now boasted three rather than two squadrons. The transition to new air tactics was well under way. The or-

Close-up of a burning oil-storage area and bombed-out factories at Stalingrad. Courtesy of Glen Sweeting.

ganization of the VVS command structure and the creation of the air armies gave promise that air power could assume a larger role in the projected Soviet offensive. [19]

Air Blockade

The Soviet Army opened the second phase of the Battle for Stalingrad on November 19, 1942, with a powerful counteroffensive. The strategy called for the troops of the Southwestern front to begin the attack on the northern perimeter of the German salient. The 5th Tank Army spearheaded the advance in close coordination with a massive artillery barrage. After five days, the troops of the Southwestern front reached Kalach, situated on the Don directly west and behind the German 6th Army. The Northern pincer had covered a distance of ninety-three miles. Moving off on November 20, troops of the Stalingrad front, as the southern pincer, had advanced seventy-one miles by the end of the fifth day. They captured the small town of Sovetskiy on November 23, closing the trap on the German 6th Army.

The role of the VVS in this first stage of the counteroffensive was limited, despite elaborate efforts to position Soviet airpower for a concentrated blow. [20] Poor weather—low clouds and fog—reduced VVS sorties to a mere 1,000 for the first four days of the offensive. [21] Once the weather improved, VVS air activity increased dramatically; 5,760 combat sorties were claimed by the 16th, 17th, and 8th air armies for the period of November 24 to 30. Against the Luftwaffe's 1,200 aircraft, the VVS had, by one estimate, a total of 1,414. [22]

While numerical parity had been achieved, 426 of the Soviet combat aircraft (Po-2s, R-5s, SB bombers) were obsolete and assigned to night operations. These machines, deployed around and adjacent to the German salient, were organized in the 2d, 16th, 17th, and 8th air armies, along with elements of ADD and PVO. [23] At the onset of the counteroffensive, however, these air units faced critical problems. Moved hastily to improvised airfields close to the breakthrough zones, they encountered enormous difficulties in sustaining air operations. The Soviet rear services in late 1942 still faced an acute shortage of trucks and air transport. Aviation fuel, ammunition, spare parts, and other supplies reached the frontline units only after considerable effort. Although denied an active role in the immediate breakthrough, the VVS quickly assumed a vital role in the Soviet drive to maintain the encirclement and destroy the 6th Army.

In a message to General Zhukov dated November 12, Stalin asserted that the VVS should be called upon to make a maximum effort. In fact, Stalin saw air power as a crucial component in achieving a breakthrough: "The experience of war . . . indicates that we can achieve a victory over the Germans only if we gain air supremacy." [24]

Novikov's report to Zhukov on the low state of preparedness of the VVS on the eve of the counteroffensive had prompted Stalin's statement on the role of Soviet air power. Despite concerted efforts to bolster the VVS in the Stalingrad region, there were persistent problems with a logistical system not yet fully capable of meeting the requirements of a major offensive. Novikov's report, for example, had indicated that the VVS in the second week of November was down to two rations of fuel, and faced an acute shortage in ammunition. Not only were there shortfalls in fuel and munitions, but General Rudenko claimed that the percent of inoperable aircraft remained quite high. The 16th Air Army on November 19, for example, had 343 aircraft, but 93 were grounded for repairs. This same situation prevailed in the other air armies. While the numbers of combat aircraft increased steadily, Rudenko and other commanders realized that the inadequate base for aircraft repairs, especially shortages in engines, slowed the tempo for rebuilding the VVS.[25]

Novikov played a key role in preparing the air armies for the counteroffensive, working closely with the *Stavka* representatives in Stalingrad—Zhukov, Vasilevskiy, and Voronov. With the major Soviet Army commanders, he prepared detailed battle plans, discussed the optimum uses of air power, and established procedures for the efficient interaction of air power with the ground forces. At the same time he planned specific air operations with his air army commanders at Stalingrad: Gen. S. A. Krasovskiy of the 17th Air Army (Southwestern front); Gen. S. I. Rudenko, 16th Air Army (Don front); and Gen. T. T. Khryukin, 8th Air Army (Stalingrad front).

Stalin had set forth, on November 12, the primary goals for the VVS at Stalingrad. The air force would first concentrate its actions in the breakthrough zones, clearing out enemy aircraft and providing effective air cover. With the advance of Soviet troops, the VVS would strafe and bomb German forces as part of a combined-arms effort to penetrate the tactical defense zone of the enemy. Once the German defenses had been shattered, the VVS air units would pursue retreating troops in a sustained fashion to prevent any enemy effort to reestablish a stable defensive line.[26] Such a blueprint for the offensive application of air power displayed boldness at a time when the VVS still remained inferior to the Luftwaffe in quality of machines and combat technique.

The Soviet plan rested first on the principle of concentrating air power at decisive points and then achieving the efficient coordination of air action with artillery, tanks, and infantry. The Red Army Field Manual, issued on November 9, 1942, gave definition to this emerging concept of an "air offensive," which consisted of two aspects, the preparatory and support phases. Aviation was to provide continuous support of the infantry with concentrated fire. At Stalingrad the 17th Air Army supported the 5th Tank Army and the 21st Army on the main axis of their advance. In like manner, the 16th Air Army flew in support of the 65th Army, and the 8th Air Army deployed 75 percent of its operational aircraft to assist the 50th Army.[27]

The 16th Air Army under Rudenko provides a representative profile of the VVS at the opening of the Stalingrad counteroffensive. Organized in August 1942, it consisted on November 19 of 125 fighters, 103 Shturmoviks, 93 night bombers, 7 reconnaissance and 14 liaison aircraft. Only 249 of 342 aircraft were operational, but Rudenko received a modest increment of ten Yak fighters just before the offensive began.[28] During November the 16th Air Army flew a total of 2,847 sorties. Rudenko targeted two-thirds of these sorties against German airfields, destroying a claimed sixty-three enemy aircraft. In thirty-two recorded air battles, the 16th Air Army claimed thirty-three German planes downed; Soviet losses were listed at thirty-five aircraft.[29]

The overall strength of the VVS at Stalingrad, according to Rudenko, was 1,350 combat aircraft, about equal to the Luftwaffe's 4th Air Fleet. While the Luftwaffe enjoyed "qualitative superiority," Rudenko pointed to the rapid transition by the VVS to newer types: the 16th Air Army, for example, had achieved at the time of the counteroffensive a 73 percent transition overall, nearly 97 percent within the fighter inventory. Among the 125 fighters, only nine were obsolete LaGG-3s. The Shturmovik units were almost completely reequipped with the modern Il-2s.[30] Moreover, the 16th Air Army obtained two divisions of Pe-2 bombers at the end of November, which greatly enhanced the striking power of Rudenko's force.[31]

The Soviet pincer movement had trapped more than 300,000 German troops within an area about the size of Connecticut.[32] To maintain the envelopment and systematically annihilate the German pocket, the *Stavka* ordered an increased level of VVS air operations. Consequently, the Soviet counteroffensive brought an inevitable clash with the Luftwaffe, which now had become a vital weapon for the relief and protection of Paulus's 6th Army. In the crucial days after November 19, Novikov remained at the forward control posts together with General Vasilevskiy.

The German High Command decided to mobilize the Luftwaffe for an airlift operation to sustain Paulus's trapped army. Historians debate the wisdom of this fateful decision, which was based in part on the apparent success of the Demyansk experience as much as Hermann Goering's bold assurances that the Luftwaffe could do the job. Many Luftwaffe commanders, including General Freiherr von Richthofen, questioned the Luftwaffe's capacity—even in warm weather—to meet the challenge. Richthofen and others argued forcefully against the airlift option, seeing Demyansk as a costly undertaking, not an analog for the salvation of the 6th Army.[33]

The option of ordering Paulus to attempt a breakout in the immediate aftermath of the encirclement appears to many today as wise counsel. Yet, it must be remembered that the Russians planned at Stalingrad not merely to trap Paulus, but to prevent any German action on the ground to liquidate the problem, either by Paulus's escaping west or by a relief force's breaking through the Soviet ring. When Field Marshal Erich von Manstein attempted the latter tactic on December 12, he was halted short of his goal. In fact, by the end of December the Russians had moved the Germans farther back toward the west, capturing the vital Morozovskaya and Tatsinskaya airfields used as major staging areas for the airlift. Standing in place at Stalingrad fitted into Hitler's peculiar mindset in 1942, which coincided with Stalin's own attitude of no retreat.

"Once a German soldier has taken his position," Hitler stated, "there is no power in the world strong enough to dislodge him."[34] To ask "what if" is essentially to abandon historical analysis for abstract war gaming. The German High Command, caught in a military crisis, moved ahead fatefully by necessity with the massive airlift. A more appropriate question—the only genuine historical question—is to ask why the airlift failed.

The German 6th Army required 750 tons of supplies per day. This level of support, given the winter conditions and the finite resources of the Luftwaffe, simply could not be achieved. To meet such a goal, 375 Ju 52 transports, each with a load of two tons, would have had to land daily in the pocket. With the normal operational readiness of 30 to 35 percent, the Luftwaffe would have had to deploy 1,050 Ju 52s.[35] No possibility existed that the Luftwaffe could mobilize such an enormous flotilla of air transports.

Beyond the question of numbers, there was the unpredictability of the Russian weather. Severe cold and heavy snow made any airlift difficult in November–December 1942. After further consultations, the Germans reduced the daily airlift goal to 300 tons per day, nearly half the total Paulus required.[36] Before even this goal could be achieved, the German airlift command for Stalingrad had to obtain additional transport aircraft. All available Ju 52s, He 111s, and Ju 90s were ordered to the east. From the Office of the Chief of Training, some of the most experienced flight instructors in the Luftwaffe were assigned on an emergency basis to the airlift. Even Ju 86s, used for training purposes, were deployed to airlift duty, along with small numbers of He 177s, Fw 200s, and Ju 290s.

A mood of desperation prevailed. This was evident in the fact that the Luftwaffe considered briefly the use of freight gliders—DFS 230 and GO 244 types. The idea proved impracticable because of the inadequate ground facilities.[37]

The formidable task of coordinating the Stalingrad airlift began to gain momentum after November 25, 1942, the first day weather permitted resupply by air to the 6th Army. At staging areas at Zaporozhe and Kirovograd, Ju 5 and other aircraft assigned for transport duty were converted for winter operations. Once completed, they were moved east toward Morozovskaya and Tatsinskaya airfields, which were 125 and 155 miles respectively from Stalingrad.

These fields, in time, became congested and quite inadequate for servicing the sudden increase of transports. Goods accumulated, and many Ju 52s proved to be inadequately prepared in advance for airlift duty. General von Richthofen observed the growing difficulties with alarm and requested that the 6th Army be ordered to break out. Hitler refused.[38]

The flight to the "Kessel," or pocket, normally took fifty minutes. The three-engine Ju 52s, later to be joined by a large number of the He 111s, on November 30 followed a radio beacon to Pitomnik airfield within the pocket. Upon landing, the transports were quickly unloaded. Wounded men were then taken on board for the flight back to Morozovskaya or Tatsinskaya. Gen. Martin Fiebig headed this airlift operation in an atmosphere of urgency and growing frustration.

Many of the Ju 52s were old, ill-suited for the cold-weather operations and lacking in armament and radios. Air crews with varying skills arrived from other fronts and training schools in Germany. Some were veterans, others had only minimal experience. Many faced the demanding airlift missions without winter clothing.[39] There were constant problems with sudden snow storms, which made the approach, landing, and departure from Pitomnik hazardous undertakings. The attrition in transports as a result of accidents grew with the onset of severe winter weather. Air traffic control faced daily the enormous challenge of directing the large number of transports in and out of the primitive airfield at Pitomnik.

The first flights there began on November 25, and after two days, the airlift had delivered 130 tons of materiel.[40] By December 17 the airlift had achieved an average level of 84.4 tons per day; the best day was when 289 tons were moved into the pocket with 154 transports.[41]

Problems grew with the airlift each day. The flight corridors quickly became aerial gauntlets, haunted by VVS fighters and swept by salvos of Soviet anti-aircraft fire. The rigors of the Russian winter once again frustrated the German will and resourcefulness. There were low clouds, fog, snow storms, ice damage, and numbing cold.

The Stalingrad airlift required German transports to operate under severe winter conditions. Courtesy of Glen Sweeting.

Interior view of a Junkers Ju 52 air transport. Courtesy of Glen Sweeting.

Ground crews at Pitomnik, often on reduced rations, worked long hours against formidable obstacles: the airstrip had to be cleared repeatedly of drifting snow; fingers froze to aircraft engine parts; and gas masks had to be worn to prevent frostbite. There were alarming increases in pilot error leading to frequent accidents. Goods piled up, adding to the congestion. Pressure from marauding VVS ground-attack aircraft and Soviet artillery increased with each passing day as the ring around the "Kessel" tightened. Shortages in medicine, ammunition, and food gradually sapped the encircled 6th Army of its fighting efficiency and morale.[42]

Soviet and German accounts of the Stalingrad airlift differ on the extent of Luftwaffe losses. Most Soviet sources list more than 1,000 German aircraft destroyed in the air and on the ground, about 80 percent being transports and bombers (see Table 2). Against the German airlift attempt, from November 19, 1942, to February 2, 1943, the VVS claimed 35,920 sorties flown, which, by their estimate, surpassed the number of German sorties by about two to one. Instead of 300 tons of supplies reaching the trapped German 6th Army, the Soviet air blockade allowed on the average fifty to eighty tons per day.[43]

VVS fighters hit the German transports both in the air and on the ground. On November 30, for example, fighters from the 283th Fighter Air Division, with Col. V. A. Kitayev in command, intercepted seventeen Ju 52s, escorted by four Bf 109s, over Gumrak airfield in the pocket. They destroyed five Ju 52s and one Bf 109. These *Okhotniki*, or free hunters, on some days destroyed up to half of the German transport "caravans." As fighter-bombers, these VVS aircraft showed equal skill. On December 2 they destroyed seventeen transports on the ground within the pocket, and between December 10 and 13 they claimed another eighty-seven transporting airplanes. The Il-2 Shturmoviks, being faster than the Ju 52, reversed their role on occasion and intercepted Ju 52s en route to the pocket.[44]

One German account acknowledges the loss of around 488 aircraft, along with 1,000 flight crew personnel: 266 Ju 52s, 42 Ju 86s, 165 He 111s, 9 Fw 200s, 5 He 177s, and 1 Ju 290. Besides the grievous loss of machines and personnel, the failure of the Stalingrad airlift resulted in a serious interruption of the Luftwaffe training program, for many experienced flight instructors were lost at Stalingrad.[45]

The German High Command made one serious effort to relieve the 6th Army at Stalingrad. Army Group Don, under Manstein, attempted to break the encirclement, on December 12, 1942, in the Kotelnikovo region southwest of the pocket. This drive pushed forward slowly until December 21, but

Table 2
Soviet Estimate of Luftwaffe Aircraft Destroyed in Air Blockade, December 1942–January 1943

Type	Numbers Destroyed	Percentage
Fighters		
Bf 109	148	13.9
Bf 110	14	1.3
Total Fighters	162	15.2
Bombers		
He 111	138	12.9
Ju 88	63	5.9
Others	26	2.5
Total Bombers	227	21.3
Transports		
Ju 52	676	63.5
Total Losses	1,065	100%

Source: I. V. Timokhovich, *Operativnoye iskusstvo Sovetskikh VVS v Velikoy Otechnestvennoy voyne* (Moscow: Voyenizdat, 1976), p. 177.

then faltered in the face of stiff Soviet resistance. The 8th Air Army alone flew 758 sorties between December 20 and 23, to help stop the relief effort. To stem Manstein's drive and simultaneously apply pressure on the pocket, the VVS had marshaled all available air units. Such an orchestration of airpower demonstrated again the growing efficiency of VVS command structure.

From Karpovka, within the pocket, the German 6th Army had prepared to move out to link up with Manstein, whose position at one point was a mere twenty-five to thirty miles away. VVS combat aircraft, drawn from the 8th and 16th air armies, then struck the enemy positions at Karpovka. On the morning of December 16, at the height of the battle, 100 VVS airplanes strafed the Germans.

To the south, the Soviets applied additional pressure to disrupt the German effort to liberate the 6th Army at Stalingrad. Here the *Stavka* activated the Southwestern front, hoping to strike at Manstein's rear. Part of this offensive operation included VVS air strikes at the Morozovskaya and Tatsinskaya airfields. Soviet air operations, by day and night, maintained constant pressure on the German positions. The tactical application of Soviet airpower became most apparent in the period of December 16–31, 1942, when the 2d and 17th air armies flew 4,177 sorties, 80 percent of them in support of ground troops.[46]

On Christmas eve, at the height of the Soviet counterattack, the Germans lost the Tatsinskaya airfield. No single event in the somber days of December brought greater dismay to General Fiebig, or more fateful consequences for the airlift operation. The Soviets signaled the attack on Tatsinskaya with an artillery barrage on the fog-shrouded morning of December 24. Fiebig, along with Richthofen, had appealed to Hitler to allow the evacuation of the airfield during the previous week. They had observed the Soviet build-up with alarm. Now the dreaded attack had materialized, threatening destruction to a massive number of Ju 52s crowded at the airfield.

After a few minutes of Soviet artillery fire, Fiebig ordered the immediate evacuation of the German transports, even as Soviet tanks and infantry approached. In an atmosphere of poor visibility and near panic, the Ju 52s took off. Two transports collided in mid-air and a large number of aircraft piled into each other on the ground. Fiebig himself narrowly escaped at the last moment as Soviet tanks overran the airfield. A total of fifty-six transports were lost. In the midst of this panorama of wrecked and burning aircraft, 124 transports escaped.[47]

In the air, Soviet fliers acquired a reputation for persistence and bravery during this period. One VVS sergeant, N. Abdirov of the 808th Ground-Attack Air Regiment (ShAP), flew his aircraft into a group of German tanks. He received the title of Hero of the Soviet Union posthumously. Soviet accounts of the air war at Stalingrad provide numerous examples of individual feats of bravery, and German recollections confirm the Soviet aggressiveness in the air. German troops respected the Shturmovik units, in particular for their courage and dogged determination. The spectacular deeds of Abdirov demonstrated in sharper focus the overall toughness of the Soviet ground-attack arm. Soviet sources provide impressive profiles of these proficient VVS units, many of which became elite guard units as a result of their combat action.

Capt. A. I. Molodchy, a two-time recipient of the gold star, Hero of the

Soviet anti-aircraft units quickly established a reputation for aggressiveness and accuracy. Here they score a near miss against a German He 111 bomber. Courtesy of Glen Sweeting.

Soviet Union, established a record for himself and his bomber regiment (748th Bomber Air Regiment, ADD). At the end of 1942, according to Soviet statistics, Molodchy's bomber crew had flown an average of two sorties per night for a total of 118,060 miles. They had dropped more than 200 tons of bombs on enemy targets, hitting supply and fuel-storage areas, railway cars, and other military targets. Such exploits—even with the occasional hyperbole of patriotic prose—represented the extraordinary intensity of the war on the Eastern front.[48]

At Zverevo, near the last staging airfields and still within the range of the Ju 52s, the Germans built another airstrip to supply Pitomnik. Zverevo was 2,000 feet long and 100 feet wide, and occupied a former cornfield. The runway consisted merely of hard-packed snow. For the construction of the Zverevo landing strip, there were no rollers available; everything had to be improvised. German troops, with the aid of the local population, managed to carve out this airfield under the most difficult circumstances. At first the ground crews lived in snow huts, later replaced by tents and crudely constructed wooden barracks.[49] Snow storms, constant companions, interrupted activity for days at a time. On occasion, heavy snow drifted over the Ju 52s, which had to be dug out by hand. Austere and storm-ridden, Zverevo became a makeshift emergency airfield, carved out of an icy wasteland.

The organization for the Soviet air blockade displayed careful planning and stewardship of resources. Four zones were defined, each with specific boundaries and functions. The first zone became the outer front of the encirclement. Here, along the periphery, were the German airfields—Morozovskaya, Tatsinskaya, Sal'sk, Novocherkassk, Rostov—used as stepping-off points for the airlift. The 17th and 8th air armies assumed air interdiction responsibilities for the first zone. The second zone, or ring zone, consisted of the area between the outer and inner fronts. Over this, the Germans established air corridors for the airlift. Depending on whether Germans fled out of Morozovskaya or Tatsinskaya, the flight to the pocket covered around 200 miles.

The VVS subdivided the second zone into five sectors, and the 16th and 8th air armies, along with the 102d PVO air division, deployed fighters to each. Thus, every VVS unit became thoroughly acquainted with its sector; yet the subdivision allowed for mobility and adaptation. The VVS command aimed to provide a powerful air-defense system, which would provide the maximum use of Soviet air power.

Ringing the pocket, the third zone encompassed a band varying in width up to nineteen miles.[50] Here the Soviets constructed a series of anti-aircraft positions along the anticipated flight paths of German transports. During the period of the air blockade these positions were strengthened and redeployed in order to maximize anti-aircraft fire. Already respected by the Luftwaffe, Soviet anti-aircraft gunners proved quite effective in establishing a curtain of fire which frequently caused German transports to veer to avoid intensive attack. At the same time, Soviet fighters, always close at hand, would often move in to attack these transports.

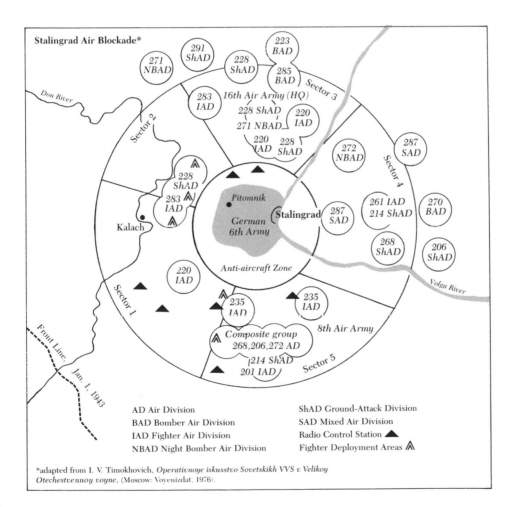

Stalingrad Air Blockade*

AD Air Division
BAD Bomber Air Division
IAD Fighter Air Division
NBAD Night Bomber Air Division

ShAD Ground-Attack Division
SAD Mixed Air Division
Radio Control Station ▲
Fighter Deployment Areas ⋀

*adapted from I. V. Timokhovich, *Operativnoye iskusstvo Sovetskikh VVS v Velikoy Otechestvennoy voyne*, (Moscow: Voyenizdat, 1976).

The fourth zone was the pocket itself. Besides Pitomnik, the Germans operated at the outset four other airstrips within the pocket—Gumrak, Basargino, Voroponovo, and Bol'shaya Rossoshka.[51] These airstrips, with their own fighter interceptors, maintained in a precarious way the vital lifeline of the 6th Army. On the ground, the Soviets moved relentlessly to reduce the area of encirclement and occupy these crucial airfields. Above, VVS fighters endeavored to destroy approaching and departing German transports. Constant pressure from VVS Shturmoviks and bombers made operations from the airstrips difficult at best.

Initially, the German airlift crossed over to the pocket singly or in small groups, and the transports approached Stalingrad from different directions and without fighter escort until they were over their destination. Within the pocket were forty fighters, mostly BF 109s, to provide a measure of air cover. The Luftwaffe air transport command mobilized sixty to seventy transports per day for airlift duty; once the operation was in full stride this level had been increased to 100 to 150. Between November 25 and 30 of 1942, the VVS applied significant pressure on the ever-increasing transports of the German airlift. Soviet fighters appeared along the air corridors, attacking the Ju 52s along the 200-mile pathway to Stalingrad. These attacks were sudden and, in the absence of German fighter escorts, very effective. Meantime, the VVS struck the German airfields within the pocket on a regular basis. On November 28 the Soviets destroyed twenty-nine enemy aircraft at Gumrak and Bol'shaya Rossoshka.[52]

The Germans then moved quickly to counteract the rising tempo of VVS air operations. Transports were now given fighter escort. To provide additional range, Bf 109s and Bf 110s were equipped with supplementary fuel tanks. Again the Russian environment of vast distances and extreme weather compelled adaptation. Each successive effort appeared more desperate and less effective.

Behind the organization of the Soviet air blockade was the imperative to use the full force of combat aircraft. At Demyansk, the VVS had used obsolete Po-2 aircraft for the night bombing of the encircled German troops. This tactic was embraced again at Stalingrad with great effectiveness. Bomber units, drawn from ADD, were deployed for raids at night, when the slow-moving Soviet aircraft operated in relative freedom, attacking German airfields at low altitudes. The VVS now had the capacity for sustained round-the-clock operations. Bomber units normally flew to their targets from airfields situated forty to sixty miles from the frontlines. Fighters, by contrast, were positioned much closer—twelve to thirty-one miles. Depending on the mission, Soviet bombers attacked their targets in regimental size units, anywhere from thirty to forty aircraft.[53]

The tempo of bomber attacks increased dramatically in the final month of the Stalingrad siege. To make the work of the Po-2s and the bombers more effective, the Soviets moved large numbers of artillery up to the frontlines, where they focused much of their attention on German airfields.[54] Once in place, Soviet firepower on the ground and in the air became a massive and sustained pressure on the enemy.

To maintain such pressure, the Soviets devised an elaborate and effective scheme for air-ground control. At Kotluban airfield, the 16th Air Army established its radio command post for the interdiction of the German transports.

This command post directed operations for the 16th Air Army and maintained regular contact with the corresponding command post for the 8th Air Army. Novikov vigorously pursued a goal of coordination that brought Kotluban into a larger scheme of guidance. Radio control stations, all linked to Novikov's headquarters, became a kind of a nervous system for the VVS air operations at Stalingrad.

In the four zones, these ground radio stations maintained contact with Soviet fighters, now equipped with radio sets for the first time, and later with ground-attack aircraft.[55] This enabled the Soviets to maintain radio guidance with their combat aircraft over the frontlines and with the rear airfields. They served the dual purposes of command and information gathering.

At Stalingrad, the Germans observed the general upgrading of the Soviet signal communications service. Where in 1941 there had been poor execution in most VVS air operations, all complicated by an absence of radios, the VVS now displayed greater effectiveness. Along with radio, the Soviets now employed radar, telephone, and teletype. Moreover, the VVS adapted various aircraft for liaison, courier, and command duties. The progress achieved at Stalingrad led to the decision that all fighters would be radio-equipped.[56]

In early January 1943 the Germans converted a primitive airstrip at Sal'sk into another major staging area for the airlift to Stalingrad. Sal'sk was little more than a frozen field, quickly cleared of snow for Luftwaffe air operations. It was rough, poorly equipped, but spacious. It was also vulnerable to Soviet air attack. The approach route to Stalingrad from Sal'sk was about 250 miles long, near the outer limit of the Ju 52s range.[57] On January 9, 1943, the hastily constructed airfield became the scene of one of the more spectacular raids by VVS Shturmoviks. By this date, the Germans had collected more than 300 aircraft at Sal'sk, about half of them transports.[58] These airplanes were parked in a congested fashion, and the whole operation, as reflected in its layout, had a disorderly, makeshift quality. Knowing the vulnerability of the airfield to attack, the Germans quickly assigned both fighters and flak units to Sal'sk.

On two occasions Soviet fliers from the 622d Ground-attack Division attempted to strafe the Sal'sk field, but were repulsed.[59] To hit his target, the VVS decided in early January to resort to a sudden, low-level attack by a small number of heavily armed Il-2s. On January 2 Capt. I. P. Baktin led 7 Il-2s, escorted by a squadron of Yak-1 fighters, toward Sal'sk. Once the Il-2s passed over the German lines, they descended to tree-top altitude at full speed, hoping to avoid enemy interceptors and detection by anti-aircraft units. Suddenly, Baktin and his group made one strafing run over the field out of the clouds, and then repeated it six times. The German defenses were caught off guard, and before a concerted response could be mustered, seventy-two German aircraft had been destroyed. The Soviets admitted the loss of only four aircraft in this raid.

The raid on Sal'sk symbolized the increased striking power of the VVS at Stalingrad, the impressive ability of VVS units to operate in marginal weather conditions, and the enlarged range of VVS air operations, which now included German rear areas. Baktin and three others received the gold star, Hero of the Soviet Union, for their bravery. Other attacks, by day and night, were made at Bol'shaya Rossoshka, Karpovka, and Gumrak.

When Erhard Milch, representing the German High Command, arrived at Taganrog on January 16, 1943, to inspect the airlift operations, he quickly saw the desperate state of the entire operation. By this date Sal'sk itself was in danger of being overrun on the ground and Paulus's capitulation was two weeks away.

The VVS, meanwhile, displayed improved skills at air interception over the pocket. Col. I. D. Podgorny, commanding eighteen fighters from the 235th Fighter Air Division, attacked sixteen Ju 52s en route to Pitomnik. During the initial encounter Podgorny's fighters shot down nine Ju 52s; five crashed in flames and the rest made emergency landings. Eight German airmen were taken prisoner. Seven Ju 52s turned back, but the Soviet fighters pursued them with relentless determination, shooting down all but one.

By January 1943 the VVS had made the German airlift extremely difficult. German fliers discovered that distance, severe weather, and primitive airfields were not the only hazards. The VVS had assumed an aggressive air-combat presence around Stalingrad. For the Luftwaffe, the attrition in aircraft and aircrews became a matter of deep concern.

From the beginning of the air blockade, Soviet fighters attacked German transports from "ambush." For example, the 16th Air Army in the northwest sector organized ambushes at Pichuga, Kotluban, and Kachalinskaya. At first these ambushes amounted to regular patrols by VVS fighters along the air corridors to Stalingrad. They attacked single planes, artillery positions, and moving targets on the ground. Once losses occurred, the Germans shifted their tactics. Fighter escorts were now provided, and transports were flown in larger groups for maximum protection against the marauding VVS fighters. Also, the number of night flights by German transports increased dramatically. The VVS countered by reassigning their fighters in pairs to the airspace adjacent to the German airfields within the pocket. This was done to catch the German transports at their most vulnerable moments—landing or taking-off—when their airspeed and defensive capability were sharply reduced.

In time, the Soviet radio-control stations acquired enough sophistication to provide accurate early warnings. As soon as the German transports were spotted crossing the belt separating the outer and inner frontlines, VVS fighter and Shturmovik units were alerted. Combat aircraft and aircrews were maintained on a constant alert status, to scramble quickly to intercept the enemy. The goal was to arrive over the German airfields or designated positions along the air corridor to Stalingrad at optimum times.

Speed was combined with a shrewd use of weather conditions. Soviet fliers, particularly the ground-attack pilots, took full advantage of clouds to effect sudden sweeps on unsuspecting German transports attempting to negotiate the difficult approaches to Pitomnik. Another favorite VVS tactic was to attack at dusk. These same conditions, of course, provided cover and protection for the German transports. The VVS, however, had the natural advantage of place, choice of time and target, and overwhelming numbers. By contrast, German aircrews faced the disadvantage of flying over enemy territory, in poor weather and with primitive maintenance facilities and only occasional fighter escort.

The VVS expanded the use of *Okhotniki*. Volunteers were accepted from among the most talented and experienced pilots to join these units. They had to possess consummate flying skills and excellent marksmanship, and demonstrate aggressiveness as fighter pilots. Now *Okhotniki* were created out of each fighter aviation division. In groups, most often in *para* or a *zveno*, they were deployed to specific regions to attack targets of opportunity. They roamed the air corridors to Stalingrad, attacking German transports and their fighter escorts with swiftness and efficiency. The pilots of each group became familiar with their area of patrol, and they flew the latest models of Soviet fighter aircraft—Yak-9s and La-5s—to allow the full exploitation of their skills.

These elite units quickly established a reputation for aggressiveness, persistence, and air-combat skill. In mid-December the Germans began to shift the majority of their flights to the night or periods when bad weather provided some cover without unduly increasing the dangers of landing in the pocket.

Having lost the airfields at Tatsinskaya and Morozovskaya in December 1942, the German High Command faced a grim situation at the beginning of 1943. For the Soviets, this was an occasion to push for the liquidation of the German 6th Army. The encirclement proved to be effective, despite Manstein's relief effort. The distance between the external and internal lines had been widened, deepening the geographical isolation of Paulus's troops and making the success of the airlift more problematical.

Events moved swiftly to force the capitulation of the German forces at Stalingrad. On the ground, the relentless pressure of the Soviet Army reduced the area of the pocket. Within the city, a brutal struggle continued as Paulus's weakened and poorly supplied troops attempted to hold out against the gathering weight of the Soviet Army. On January 9 the VVS again hit Sal'sk, an airstrike which further compromised the airlift by destroying over seventy aircraft at the Luftwaffe's last major staging field.

The VVS intensified the air blockade along the air corridors and struck repeatedly at the remaining airfields held by the Germans at Stalingrad. German airfields at Pitomnik, Bolshaya Rossoshka, Karpovka, and Gumrak faced an increasing tempo of VVS attacks by day and night. VVS fighters were moved up to airfields within fifteen to thirty miles (bombers and ground-attack aircraft, forty to sixty miles) of the pocket to allow sustained operations. At night Po-2s roamed over the beleaguered German airstrips, dropping bombs on transports unloading their cargoes. In January 1943 the superiority in numbers reached a level where the entire 16th Air Army with 610 combat aircraft was deployed for exclusive use of the 65th Army. The VVS was now able to send bombers in groups of forty to hit enemy positions.[60]

When the Germans rejected the demand for surrender, the Soviets launched their final drive on January 10, 1943. After furious fighting, Soviet troops occupied the western approaches to the city on January 12. A second offer to surrender was made and again was rejected. As the circle closed, the quantity of firepower from air and artillery units intensified. With radio guidance stations, the accuracy of Soviet fire improved even as it became more concentrated.

On January 24 Pitomnik itself fell. This sealed the fate of the German garrison. Pitomnik was the last working airfield after the January 10 offensive. Only Gumrak remained, and it lacked the size and operational status to continue the airlift. With the loss of Pitomnik, the Germans no longer had a link with the outside. The airlift had been reduced in the last two weeks of January to air drops by parachute, many of which fell into Soviet hands.

The assault on the reduced German pocket, now almost coextensive with

This Pe-8 (TB-7) flew V.M. Molotov, the Soviet foreign minister, to Dundee, Scotland, on May 20, 1942. The same aircraft flew Molotov on to Washington and then by the identical route back to the Soviet Union.

the city, began on January 22. Two days later the Soviets reached the western edge of Stalingrad. By January 25 they had linked up with the 62d Army under General Chuikov, cutting the enemy sector in half. Now the German units began to surrender. Finally, Field Marshal Paulus, in command of the northern group, capitulated on January 31. On February 2 the last remnants of the German 6th Army surrendered.

The Soviet use of air power had played a major role in deciding the outcome of the battle at Stalingrad. The Germans had made a valiant attempt to repeat the Demyansk airlift achievement. They failed. The consequences were profound. As events proved, the Luftwaffe survived Stalingrad, but emerged from that air war severely weakened overall, and with its transport operations in the east crippled. There was also the loss of that elusive factor of *esprit*, the high confidence which animated Luftwaffe operations in 1941–42. The vast German technological edge no longer existed.

Hitler had embraced a sort of positional warfare on the Volga in the fall of 1942, and then depended on the Luftwaffe for mobility. The highly vaunted Luftwaffe turned out to be inadequate for this task. It attempted in vain to overcome distance, weather, and the shrewd application of Soviet air power.

For the Soviets, Stalingrad provided a vehicle to implement Novikov's 1942 reforms. In their larger meaning, the Stalingrad air operations compelled the VVS for the first time to organize and coordinate large-scale efforts in support of several fronts. The air blockade was more than a token effort to intercept the German transports crossing to the pocket from Morozovskaya and Tatsinskaya airfields; it involved a complex system of fighter interception, ground assault, and bomber sorties in full coordination with ground operations. There had been four air armies, along with ADD and elements of PVO committed to the blockade, all enhanced by the use of a radio-control system. The logistical problems associated with the prolonged Stalingrad conflict had placed enormous strain on the Soviets. Ruthless mobilization measures, often under the aegis of the Communist Party, had made the difference.

Stalingrad demonstrated the elaborate requirements for the conduct of large-scale air operations—administrative centralization, the creation of large, mobile air armies for rapid deployment, close coordination and liaison with the ground forces, and the mobilization of logistical support. For the first time, the VVS command structure administered four air armies and five ADD divisions over a vast area in a five-month air campaign, shifting from strategic defensive to a coordinated "air offensive" and "air blockade."

For the VVS, the Stalingrad conflict brought honors and recognition. A total of nine air divisions were given the designation "guards." Seventeen pilots received the highest decoration for bravery, Hero of the Soviet Union. Another 1,000 medals were awarded to VVS personnel for their participation in the air war at Stalingrad. The official Soviet claim was 1,200 German aircraft downed, about 80 percent being transports (against the German admission of 488 aircraft). The VVS tally also included 35,920 sorties flown between November 19, 1942, to February 2, 1943, against 18,500 sorties credited to the Luftwaffe.

Among the experienced air army commanders to emerge out of the Stalingrad conflict were Generals S. A. Krasovskiy (17th Air Army), S. I. Rudenko (16th Air Army), G. G. Khryukin (8th Air Army), K. N. Smirnov (2nd Air Army) and A. Ye. Golovanov (ADD). These men, as events proved, became the leadership core for the postwar VVS high command.[61]

Chapter 5

Over the Kuban

The Kuban River in the North Caucasus became the remote locale in April–May 1943 for one of the most dramatic air battles of World War II. The Kuban air engagements fell chronologically between the siege of Stalingrad and the Battle of Kursk, and constitute a pivotal chapter in the Soviet struggle for air superiority.[1]

Yet, this intense two-month air war between the Luftwaffe and the Soviet Air Force (VVS) remains a shadowy episode for most Westerners. Over the Kuban, Aleksandr I. Pokryshkin scored twenty victories against the Luftwaffe, flying an American-made P-39 Airacobra. Pokryshkin's personal achievement attracted some attention at the time in the Allied press, but the larger combat role of the VVS in the Kuban sector, then and now, has remained obscure. The Kuban has been relegated to a sort of historical limbo in Western accounts of the war, being overshadowed by the dramatic "turning points" of Stalingrad and Kursk. Soviet chronicles of the air war in the east, however, have emphasized the Kuban in the same fashion as Americans have viewed the Battle of Midway as an important bench mark in the war against the Japanese in the Pacific.

Despite the fury of the Kuban air engagements, there were no major breakthroughs on the ground by either army. This fact explains in part the tendency of most Western histories to relegate the Kuban to a secondary place in the combat history of 1943. Compared to Stalingrad or Kursk, the entire Kuban conflict appears to lack the essential criteria for status as a "turning point"—there was no surrender of a German army nor the concrete achievement of shattering a major German offensive. From this perspective, the Kuban, at best, constituted an interlude, as transitional as the spring weather in which it was fought.

By contrast, Soviet accounts point out that the Kuban mirrored a subtle shift in the course of the air war—the crucial transition by the VVS from a defensive to an offensive posture. For the first time, the VVS displayed its rapidly evolving organizational efficiency, its numerical superiority and vast air reserves, its new equipment, and its revised tactical modes. All these components came together during the Kuban period, culminating two arduous years of development, adaptation, and piecemeal experimentation.[2] As Pokryshkin asserted in his memoirs, it was during the Kuban air war that the VVS articulated in theory and demonstrated in practice the isolated "lessons" learned in air combat tactics between 1941 and 1943.[3]

The Luftwaffe and the VVS engaged in a bitter struggle in the spring of 1943 for local air superiority over the so-called "Kuban bridgehead," which the German High Command had established in the aftermath of Stalingrad and the hasty retreat from the North Caucasus. Roughly coextensive with the Taman Peninsula and situated east of the Straits of Kerch, the bridgehead was the last German toehold in the Caucasus.[4] Here, the German 17th Army with a strength of fifteen divisions, along with some Romanian troops, established a network of powerful defensive positions in February–March 1943. The fortified line extended down from the marshy Kuban River delta on the northern shore of the Taman Peninsula, through the hill country just east of Krymskaya, to the seaport of Novorossisk on the Black Sea.

A secondary series of strongpoints, called the "Blue Line," provided further defensive capability against the anticipated Soviet superiority in infantry and tanks in the Krymskaya sector. The Germans viewed the creation of a defensive bastion in the Kuban as a necessary step to protect the eastern approaches to the Crimea. The Soviets, however, feared that the bridgehead would serve as a staging area for another offensive in the North Caucasus.[5] Consequently, the Kuban bridgehead had strategic importance for both sides, compelling the Luftwaffe and the VVS to deploy some of their best air units in this sector.

Gen. K. A. Vershinin, the overall Soviet air commander, described the Kuban conflict as prolonged and intense, sometimes involving several hundred aircraft aloft in combat at one time. On certain days up to a hundred air battles took place over the Kuban sector. In the airspace above the village of Abinskaya, where the VVS command post was located, Vershinin reported that he could see an aircraft fall every ten minutes.[6] Vershinin commanded two Soviet air armies during the most intense period of air combat—the 4th (under Gen. N. F. Naumenko) and the 5th (under Gen. S. K. Goryunov).[7] Included in the 4th Air Army were such elite units as the 16th Guards Fighter Air Regiment, commanded by Pokryshkin.[8]

Against the Soviets, the Luftwaffe deployed the 4th Air Fleet, which included the elite Udet, Molders, and Green Heart units. The Green Hearts had scored over 500 victories in the first two weeks of the war, and contained in its ranks some of the most experienced fighter pilots on the Eastern front. Moreover, the Luftwaffe introduced some of its latest aircraft during the Kuban air operations: the Messerschmitt Bf 109 G 2 and G-4, the Hs 129, and some experimental versions of the Ju 87 (the Ju 87G) and the Ju 88 (the Ju 88P).[9]

At the geographical heart of the Caucasus is the Soviet Republic of Georgia. In the 1940s Georgia had an enhanced political significance as the birth-

The Luftwaffe reaches the northern Caucasus in the summer of 1942. Junkers Ju 87 Stukas make a low-level sweep over the eastern shore of the Sea of Azov. Courtesy of Glen Sweeting.

place of Joseph Stalin. Scattered across the entire Caucasus region, at the time, were over fifty ethnic groups. This ethnographic patchwork surpassed even the Balkans in diversity. Mountain tribes, Christian or Moslem, often lived in isolation, speaking separate and mutually incomprehensible languages.

All groups lived restively under Soviet rule, and displayed varying degrees of loyalty to Moscow during the period of the German invasion. Many mountain tribes openly welcomed the German invaders. To add to Soviet anxiety in 1942–43, there was the fear of Turkish intervention in the wake of any dramatic reversal of Soviet military fortunes in the Caucasus.

The German thrust across the Don toward the Soviet oil fields in the summer of 1942 had forced both sides to conduct air and ground operations in the Caucasus Mountains, a remote and rugged environment of unusual diversity. At the center of the North Caucasus is the meandering, 563-mile-long Kuban River with all its changing aspects—the rapids near Mount Elbrus as the river descends through narrow rocky gorges; the long, winding movement through the Stavropol uplands, where the Kuban widens and slows to become a natural inland waterway; and the final passage through the lowland marshes on the northern shore of the Taman Peninsula into the Sea of Azov.

The vast Caucasus chain, the source of the Kuban, extends for more than 600 miles from the Black Sea to the Caspian Sea. Taller than the Alps, the

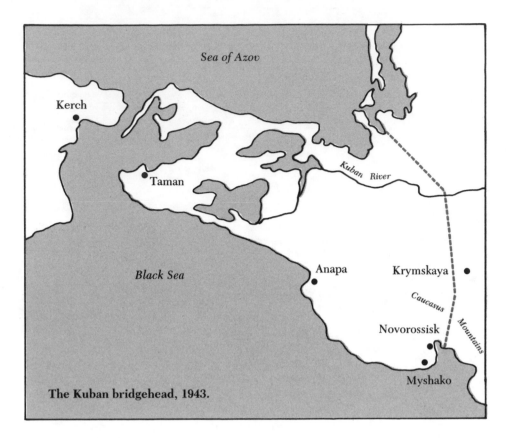

The Kuban bridgehead, 1943.

Yuri Shchipov of the 9th Fighter Air Regiment, Black Sea Fleet, in his LaGG-3 with a personal emblem, the "Lion's Heart." Eight stars indicate the number of air victories over the Luftwaffe. Courtesy of Carl-Fredrik Geust.

Caucasus provide a natural barrier between Europe and Asia on the Soviet Union's southern periphery. On the northern tier of this mountain range—at Maikop, Grozny, and Baku—were vital Soviet oil fields, first developed in the late-nineteenth century and once the setting for Stalin's revolutionary work. The Germans sought to control the strategic Caucasus oil reserves and gain access to other crucial raw materials, such as iron, copper, and natural gas.

For invader and defender alike, the Caucasian landscape provided few good highways. The formidable topography, always subject to the extremes of weather, made mobility difficult and logistical support a nightmare.

The Soviets fiercely defended the Kuban and the Caucasus for reasons beyond the obvious geopolitical factors. Going back to the sixteenth century, the Caucasus had occupied a special place in the national consciousness. Russians viewed the region with awe and profound attachment. Among all the Russian hinterlands, the Caucasus alone prompted positive images: a region of exotic beauty, of polyglot cultures, of fierce and independent mountain tribes—the locale of relative freedom beyond the grasp of bureaucratic Russia.

During the nineteenth century the Caucasus had entered Russian literature in the writings of Pushkin, Lermontov, and Tolstoy. Consequently, there were deep bonds, cultural as well as political, linking Russians to the Caucasus in the twentieth century. For many Soviet pilots, including Pokryshkin, the Kuban was inextricably a part of the Motherland (*Rodina*), to be defended with the same resolve as Moscow or Leningrad or Stalingrad.[10]

To defend the Kuban the VVS committed a substantial number of its combat aircraft. At the beginning of April 1943, the VVS had nearly 600 operational aircraft available for the North Caucasus front (250 aircraft from the 4th Air Army, another 200 from the 5th Air Army, seventy planes from the Black Sea Fleet, and fifty from ADD).[11] The VVS systematically reinforced its air armies during the course of the Kuban air operations, the tempo keeping pace with frontline requirements, thus providing the Soviets a decisive numerical superiority in the final stages of the conflict. The Luftwaffe found itself unable to match the ever-increasing numbers of VVS aircraft, and the high attrition in aircraft and air crews became a severe problem for the Germans toward the end of the Kuban fighting.

To correct the initial numerical inferiority of the VVS, the *Stavka* ordered reserve air units into the Kuban during the first three weeks of April, achieving a level of 800 aircraft by April 20 (270 fighters, 170 ground-attack planes, and 165 day and 195 night bombers). To acquire this level of operational strength, three air corps from the *Stavka* reserves moved into position in North Caucasus. Among these reinforcements were the 2d Bomber Air Corps (BAK), the 3d Fighter Air Corps (IAK), 2d Mixed Air Corps (SAK), and the 282d Fighter Air Division (IAD), plus the 50th and 52d bomber air divisions from ADD.[12] The transition to the newer model aircraft was nearly complete in the fighter units, and about 65 percent in the bomber units.[13]

Another significant reinforcement of the 4th Air Army took place at the end of April, giving the VVS a combat strength of more than 1,000 aircraft. During the most active phases of the Kuban air war, the VVS had available for combat duty anywhere from 800 to 1,150 airplanes, depending on the time, sector, and tactical requirements. For the final phase of the Kuban fighting, which began on May 26, the VVS, according to one Soviet estimate, had an operational strength of 924 aircraft.[14]

Other factors strengthened the VVS in its struggle with the Luftwaffe for air superiority over the Kuban. For the first time in the war the VVS possessed a substantial inventory of advanced-design aircraft of all types. From Soviet aircraft factories beyond the Urals, fighters in the Yak and Lavochkin series, along with Il-2 Shturmoviks and Pe-2 bombers, arrived in large numbers. In addition, there was a steady flow of Lend-Lease aircraft, as well as raw materials, equipment, and technical assistance, which provided an important stimulus to the expansion of Soviet air power.[15]

In the south, the VVS put P-39s, A-20s and even a small number of British Spitfires into frontline duty. Soviet accounts of Lend-Lease, however, consistently deemphasize its importance, pointing to the fact that it amounted to only 11 percent of the total Soviet aircraft inventory.[16] Sometimes Soviet historians have complained bitterly that the aid was not only marginal, but involved the shipment of obsolete aircraft to the Soviet Union. Pokryshkin, who ferried P-39s up from Iran into the Caucasus, echoed in his memoirs the frustration of Soviet pilots over the incessant delays in Lend-Lease operations.[17] Each delay or defect in equipment was typically viewed as treachery on the part of the Allies.

For the efficient transition of VVS pilots into combat operations, the 4th Air Army organized a realistic training program. During March and April experienced pilots instructed the new arrivals in air-combat techniques. The instruction was detailed, practical, and based on a careful analysis of Luftwaffe tactics. The VVS adoption of the *para*, a mirror copy of the Luftwaffe *Rotte* formation, had gone a long way toward providing Soviet fighter operations with flexibility. Along with the Soviet military in general, the VVS actively emulated the hated, but tactically and technologically superior enemy. The battle-experienced Luftwaffe remained in 1943 a formidable adversary. Although the new models of Soviet fighters and bombers had narrowed the technological gap considerably, air tactics persisted as a problem area for VVS air units, in particular for the fighter air arm. The Kuban became a singularly important sphere for the VVS to make the necessary adjustments in air-combat tactics, one of the final hurdles on the way to parity with the Luftwaffe.

Airfields in the Kuban were few in number and difficult to maintain once established. Most were grass airstrips with only rudimentary facilities for maintenance and storage. Housing for air crews and ground personnel remained primitive, often consisting of tents, dugouts, or temporary structures. Battlefield requirements dictated sites away from the few roads that existed in the area. Soviet commentators complain that the Luftwaffe, by contrast, had the advantage of occupying the few good airstrips in the Kuban sector. Once the Kuban bridgehead was established, the Soviets began to build a new network of airfields, an effort which was hampered by the spring rainy season. Some of these, as the Germans discovered later, turned out to be "dummy" fields.

The Soviet logistical services faced immense odds, even with the assistance of Lend-Lease. Distance, time, and the extremes of weather presented enormous obstacles. One of the great achievements of the Soviet Union in the war with Germany was its ability to mobilize and concentrate its massive air power. Airfield Servicing Battalions (BAO), along with other logistical ser-

vices, met the requirements in an impressive fashion.[18]

The strain on the Luftwaffe, so evident at Stalingrad, continued in the spring of 1943. According to Soviet accounts, the German 4th Air Fleet, which was given the responsibility for the Kuban operations, consisted of approximately 1,000 combat aircraft.[19] First-line aircraft probably numbered around 950, close to the Soviet estimate and representing just over 50 percent of the Luftwaffe combat aircraft in the east.[20] As of March 10, 1943, the Luftwaffe in the Kuban consisted of twenty-four combat groups and seventeen reconnaissance squadrons.[21]

During the previous fall (October–November) a significant number of Luftwaffe units had been withdrawn from the Eastern front to meet the Allied challenge in North Africa and the growing requirements for Reich defense.[22] By 1943 the overall condition of the Luftwaffe in the east had deteriorated sharply. The army's demands for air support during the 1942 offensive operations in the North Caucasus had not been fully met: German air units, often with meager reserves, were asked to cover a vast region—the frontage in the northern Caucasus alone was 800 miles. The immense distances prevented effective operations by fighter aircraft. Increasingly, the Luftwaffe assumed a defensive posture, largely restricting its air support to the bridgehead proper. There were occasional offensive thrusts—air raids on the seaport at Tuapse—but no attacks or even reconnaissance of other targets farther south along the Black Sea coast, such as the seaport at Bakumi.

"Death to Fascism!" appears on the fuselage of this Il-2 Shturmovik, belonging to the 8th Guards Fighter Air Regiment, Black Sea Fleet. This aircraft participated in the action over Novorossisk in 1943. Courtesy of Carl-Fredrik Geust.

For both the Luftwaffe and the Soviet Air Force there were few established airfields. Constant movement required improvised and often primitive facilities. Pictured here are German air personnel setting up tents on a grass strip. Courtesy of Glen Sweeting.

Luftwaffe transports continued their yeoman work, flying in fuel and supplies to forward units and flying out the wounded. These herculean efforts demonstrated the versatility of the German air arm, but the larger tactical requirements of the Wehrmacht were left unfulfilled. Defense, conservation, and improvisation, according to Asher Lee, were to dominate Luftwaffe operations for the remainder of the war.[23] The Kuban air war revealed in a dramatic fashion the reduced (and declining) operational strength of the Luftwaffe in the east.

Myskhako

The first obstacle to German plans to stabilize the Kuban bridgehead perimeter was the Soviet-held beachhead at Myskhako. On February 4, 1943, just two days after the surrender of Field Marshal Paulus at Stalingrad, a Soviet assault group landed southwest of the German-occupied port of Novorossisk. Once ashore, the small party established a nineteen-square-mile beachhead, which was quickly reinforced by troops from the Soviet 18th Army.

Called the "Little Land," the Soviet-held enclave became a serious problem for the Germans, threatening the port of Novorossisk, which secured the right flank of the Kuban bridgehead.[24] The seaborne assault had caught the Germans off guard, and their repeated efforts to overrun Myskhako met with fierce resistance. As long as the Soviet enclave survived, the Germans could not stabilize the right flank of the Kuban bridgehead.

The strategic port of Novorossisk was situated on the northern shore of the U-shaped Bay of Novorossisk. In their withdrawal from the northern Caucasus, the Germans had abandoned most of the coastline along the three-mile-long bay below the heavily fortified seaport. The Soviet assault group had landed on the German-held northern shore, just southwest of Novorossisk. This bold move enabled the Soviets to flank Novorossisk on two sides, to penetrate the Kuban bridgehead perimeter at a crucial point, and to challenge the Germans for effective control of the bay.

The landing site on the rocky shores at the foot of Mount Myskhako was a rugged terrain that offered the Soviets many excellent defensive positions. Steep foothills, covered by numerous clusters of woods, provided ideal cover. Once in place, the Soviet defenders were difficult to dislodge, even with sustained bombardment by air power and artillery; each Soviet bunker had to be taken one at a time.

After the initial February landing, the Germans had moved forcefully against the beachhead and cleared several pockets of Soviet resistance. But the reduced beachhead held on, compelling the Germans to break off their attack after heavy losses. The Soviets managed to reinforce the Myskhako beachhead on a regular basis in February–March by sea, mostly at night from the seaport of Gelendzhik.

Although the Luftwaffe 8th Air Corps flew repeated air strikes against Gelendzhik and the heavy volume of Soviet seaborne reinforcements crossing the Bay of Novorossisk to Myskhako, the results were mixed at best. Increased VVS air activity had made such attacks difficult and costly. Nevertheless, these raids applied enough pressure to compel the Soviets to resort to the nighttime reinforcement of Myskhako. During February–March the Germans assigned a number of Luftwaffe flak artillery units to Novorossisk, and these units, using parachute flares, directed heavy fire from their 88mm guns on the Soviet traffic crossing the bay at night. As a magnet Myskhako drew both sides into fierce combat in April 1943.[25]

The German offensive against Myskhako—operation Neptune—began on the morning of April 17, 1943, at 0630 hours. Anticipating fierce resistance, the German ground assault moved out only after an intense artillery and air preparation. The V Corps (4th Mountain, and 73d and 125th Infantry Divisions) were committed to overrun the entrenched Soviet positions. To assist these elements from the 17th Army, the Luftwaffe deployed two fighter groups (with Rumanian and Slovakian squadrons), two ground-attack groups, and a bomber wing of two groups—all drawn from 1st Air Corps.[26]

Soviet sources described the April 17 air bombardment at Myskhako as heavy, involving 450 bombers and around 200 fighters, flying more than 1,000 sorties.[27] The Soviet bastion, organized in depth, stood like a granite cliff against wave after wave of German air assaults.

To thwart the attack on Myskhako, the VVS deployed around 500 combat aircraft, about 100 of them bombers, but it faced enormous problems in maintaining a sustained air presence there. Not only were Soviet airfields hastily improvised, but many were quite remote from the scene. To reach the embattled air space around Novorossisk, many of these VVS air units had to fly over the northwestern spur of the Caucasus Mountains, sometimes from as far back as Krasnodar.

An unusual photograph of a Messerschmitt Bf 109 of the Green Hearts fighter wing, with an American-made 1940 Ford convertible, in Kerch, the Crimea, 1942. Courtesy of Uwe Feist.

By contrast, Luftwaffe fighter aircraft reached the battle zone quickly from their airfields at Anapa and Gostagayvskaya, which were a mere twenty-five to thirty miles away. More important, the German pilots could remain over Myskhako thirty to forty minutes as opposed to the brief ten-to-fifteen minute time frame allotted VVS fliers. To complicate matters, VVS aircraft frequently encountered fog and low clouds in the mountains.[28]

During the April 17 battle, the Luftwaffe conducted its air strikes with little interference from Soviet fighters. Only three Ju 87 Stukas, badly damaged from VVS fighter aircraft, crashed on landing after completing their attack runs, and a small number suffered damage from Soviet anti-aircraft fire.[29] If Luftwaffe losses were modest, the German 17th Army suffered heavy casualties in their abortive ground assault, which yielded an advance of half a mile.

On the second day of the Myskhako offensive, Ju 87s, in attack waves of twenty-five aircraft, flew repeated sorties against the beleaguered Soviet defenses. This daylong operation began at 0445 hours and ended at 1830 hours. The German air units encountered little interference from Soviet fighters and only sporadic anti-aircraft fire. The Ju 87s hit varied targets within the Soviet-held sphere—the southern part of Novorossisk, the railroad bend, the old fort, and the mud baths which had once been part of a Black Sea health spa. Despite the marginal weather, cloudy and overcast, the Germans scored a number of hits on Soviet infantry and artillery positions. These successes, however, were modest. After two days the Soviets retained a firm grip on the Myskhako beachhead.[30]

The battle continued on April 19, with negligible German gains on the ground and increasing difficulties for the Luftwaffe in the air. The Soviets had decided, beginning that day, to challenge the Luftwaffe over Myskhako in an aggressive fashion. With improving weather conditions, VVS air units moved boldly into the air space over Novorossisk to blunt the third day of German air assaults. A total of 294 Ju 87s, organized into fifteen attack groups, flew on April 19. These ground-attack sorties achieved some measure of success against Soviet artillery positions and troop concentrations, but the overall stalemate at Myskhako persisted. Unlike the day before, Soviet fighters seriously challenged the German air support for the 17th Army throughout the day. Large air battles now punctuated the daylight hours as both sides fought desperately for control of the air.

The mention of the word "Myskhako" prompts in Soviet historical memory an image of fierce determination and heroic sacrifice. At Brest, Sevastopol, and Stalingrad, Soviet troops had established a formidable reputation for resistance in the extreme—a willingness on occasion to fight to the last man. The VVS mirrored this ferocity and discipline in the *taran*, or aerial ramming tactic, which became commonplace in air combat between 1941 and 1943. In retrospect, Soviet historical accounts have portrayed this phenomenon as an expression of the patriotism which animated the Soviet Army throughout the war. Taking full advantage of this war-generated nationalism, the Communist Party conducted "party-political" work on all levels of the air force. Party control, although separated from operational command, remained pervasive. The political department of the VVS worked to instill high morale and discipline. Communists appear in postwar histories as selfless and courageous fighters, and the party as an institution is viewed as a special repository of authority and nationalistic fervor.[31] VVS pilots who had displayed extraordinary bravery were often given party membership.

When appeals to patriotic duty faltered and the impact of party indoctrination evaporated under the pressures of combat, political commissars resorted to coercion. At Stalingrad, for example, political officers armed with handguns stood in boats ferrying reinforcements across the Volga, to make sure that no one broke away from his assigned duty. As a group, VVS personnel were more highly motivated than other, nonelite components in the Soviet Army, but the ever-present party and police functionaries were a sobering reminder of the party's intention of retaining firm control.

Myskhako provided an opportunity for an important future leader of the Communist party to demonstrate his skills in "party-political" work. Col. Leonid I. Brezhnev headed the political department of the 18th Army during the time of that struggle. His work, perhaps somewhat exaggerated in retrospect, centered on maintaining "the high morale, steadfastness, and bravery" of the Myskhako defenders.[32]

The massive deployment of Soviet air power became a vital factor by April 20, the fourth day of the German offensive. On this day the Germans launched another major effort to overrun the Soviet defenses. On the ground, the 17th Army again suffered heavy losses, forcing it to break off the operation by the following day. In the air, the VVS appeared in considerable numbers. The *Stavka* had decided to transfer into the North Caucasus front—opposite the Kuban bridgehead—three air corps from the *Stavka* reserves. These units reinforced VVS operational strength by 300 aircraft. By April 20 there were 800 VVS combat aircraft available for frontal aviation duty: 270 fighters, 170 ground-attackers, 165 day bombers, and 195 night bombers.[33] Ample supplies of fuel and ammunition were also at hand, a testament to the growing efficiency of the Soviet logistical command.

The tenacious defense of Myskhako on the ground, and the escalating VVS presence above the beachhead, stalled the German drive in a decisive fashion on April 20. The German 17th Army had made no substantial progress after determined and costly assaults. In the air, the Luftwaffe employed nearly all of its available combat aircraft to turn the tide, attacking infantry and artillery positions, the Soviet headquarters command post, and landing areas along the beachhead. One night mission involved 165 Ju 87s attacking beachhead landing points in dive bombing runs from 10,000 feet.

In the course of the day, German fighters from the 1st Air Corps engaged in numerous dogfights with Soviet fighters. The Luftwaffe recorded some notable successes as units of the 1st Air Corps shot down ninety-one VVS aircraft, while German fighters operating on the right flank of 17th Army scored another fifty-six victories.[34]

Soviet accounts of Myskhako on April 20 also describe a decisive air battle. While these accounts confirm the intensity of the struggle suggested in German histories, they present a different chronicle of the events. The Soviet goal was to interrupt and neutralize German offensive operations on the ground and in the air. This Soviet aggressiveness became evident early in the morning of April 20, when sixty VVS bombers, escorted by thirty fighters, struck at German troop concentrations just beyond the periphery of the beachhead. This attack, by careful planning, occurred about thirty minutes before the anticipated time of the German ground assault on Myskhako. After a short interval, another wave of 100 Soviet aircraft struck the German staging area.[35]

To disrupt Luftwaffe operations over the entire Kuban bridgehead, a special group of fighter interceptors was organized (in close coordination with aviation units of the Black Sea Fleet) to attack German air traffic flying from airfields near Kerch. And in an effort to further confuse and weaken German air activity, long-range bombers from ADD were ordered to strike enemy airfields in the Crimea, including the major German base at Sarabuz. This raid, according to Soviet sources, was highly successful, with 100 German aircraft destroyed or damaged.[36] During this phase of the conflict, VVS aircrews were flying as many as three sorties per day.[37]

General Novikov visited a forward command post on April 21, and observed at close hand the intense air combat. While flying an Il-2 against German targets near Novikov's command post, pilot N. V. Rykhlin and his rear gunner, I. S. Yefremenko—both from the 805th Ground-Attack Air Regiment—discovered the perils of flying ground-attack sorties without fighter escort. In a sudden dive, four German fighters ambushed Rykhlin's Il-2. During the prolonged and unequal battle which followed, Rykhlin and Yefremenko shot down two of the German fighters. Before the engagement was broken off, Rykhlin was wounded and his Il-2 severely crippled. Despite his wound, Rykhlin managed to limp back across the lines to a nearby Soviet airfield and land safely. For their courage, both fliers were given battlefield promotions by Novikov—Rykhlin promoted to first lieutenant, Yefremenko to second lieutenant. Later, they were both awarded the gold star, Hero of the Soviet Union.[38]

Having seized the initiative at Myskhako, the VVS attempted to assert local air superiority over the Novorossisk sector. On April 21–22 the Soviets flew numerous sorties over Myskhako during daylight hours, actively seeking out enemy aircraft. They claimed the destruction of forty-five German aircraft during this period. The number of Luftwaffe sorties declined sharply, almost in an inverse proportion to VVS sorties: 1,248 sorties by the Luftwaffe on the first day of the offensive reduced to 281 sorties on April 24.[39]

At this juncture the Germans abandoned their effort to liquidate the Myskhako beachhead, although considerable air and ground action continued sporadically along the northern shore of the Bay of Novorossisk for several weeks. On April 24 the assault group at Myskhako, reinforced with fresh troops, counterattacked, and by April 30 had made some gains. According to Soviet sources, the Luftwaffe had lost 182 combat aircraft in air battles between April 17 and 24, with another 260 damaged or destroyed on the ground. VVS aircraft losses are not specified in Soviet sources beyond the vague statement that they were "considerably less" than the German losses.[40]

Whatever the actual figures for either side, the Soviets claimed an air victory in the first phase of the Kuban fighting over Myskhako. The reduced presence of the Luftwaffe after April 20 signaled to the Soviets that they had achieved a tenuous command of the air. According to one Soviet history, this fact compelled the Luftwaffe to withdraw much of its aviation to the rear, to the larger airfields, such as Sarabuz.[41]

Krymskaya
In late April the village of Krymskaya replaced Myskhako as the major arena

for the escalating air war over the Kuban. At Krymskaya, located near a railway junction northwest of Novorossisk, the Soviet 56th Army launched a major ground offensive on April 29. The goal was to establish a breakthrough corridor toward Anapa to the Black Sea Coast. The *Stavka* hoped to split the German Army groupings in the Taman Peninsula and destroy the Kuban bridgehead.

The Soviet offensive began at 0740 hours, following an intense artillery preparation. The Soviet planners anticipated victory, hoping again to catch the German defenders off guard. Having blunted the German effort to take the Myskhako beachhead, the Soviets were confident that the 17th Army was on the defensive, its strength depleted.

The VVS demonstrated its growing power and maturing skills as it supported the 56th Army at Krymskaya. On the night before the offensive, units drawn from the 4th Air Army and ADD flew air preparation missions against the German positions, dropping 210 tons of bombs. The 46th Night Bomber Regiment, a female guards unit under Maj. Ye. D. Bershanskaya, participated in these night bombing sorties in the area just outside of Krymskaya. Flying Po-2s, the women pilots made "precise attacks" against German ground forces.[42]

At 0700 hours on the morning of April 29, the VVS 4th Air Army made another massive raid to coincide with the ground offensive of the 56th Army. For three hours VVS aircraft—144 bombers, 82 ground-attack airplanes, and 265 fighters—pounded enemy positions. The Soviet goal was to administer a powerful preparatory air strike in the initial phase, and then provide sustained air support for the ground forces who were advancing on two sides of Krymskaya.[43]

Air units from the Luftwaffe's 1st Air Corps moved quickly to stem the Soviet breakthrough attempt. Bombers, ground-attack aircraft, and fighters flew repeated sorties against the advancing Soviet forces. The skies over Krymskaya on April 29 were filled with German and Soviet combat aircraft. In a narrow fifteen- to eighteen-mile sector, the Luftwaffe engaged the VVS in an intense air struggle, against a backdrop of fierce ground fighting. For the period leading up to May 12, huge air battles became a daily occurrence in this sector—up to forty clashes per day, involving fifty to one hundred aircraft from each side. The Luftwaffe, according to Soviet claims, lost eighteen fighters and twelve bombers daily, on the average.

During the April 29 air engagement Dimitriy Glinka, who ended the war as the fourth-ranking VVS ace with fifty victories, made his dramatic appearance over Krymskaya. Early in the morning a group of Ju 88 bombers crossed the village to intercept a large concentration of Soviet troops advancing toward the frontlines. Glinka, leading a group of six fighters, attacked the German bomber formation. He first downed the lead aircraft, and then in the ensuing combat shot down two more bombers. This bold attack disrupted a German raid by sixty aircraft. Despite the aggressive VVS air action, the advance of the 56th Army was slow, almost a mirror image of the German 17th Army's stalled progress at Myskhako. After extraordinary effort, the Soviets managed a forward progress of only slightly over a mile on the first day.

Georgiy Golubev, one-time wingman to Pokryshkin in the 16th Guards Fighter Air Regiment, described the Krymskaya engagements as fierce and all-consuming. For the individual fighter pilots, the dawn to dusk flying—averaging four to seven sorties and two to three dogfights per day—required extraordinary endurance. In the congested airspace above the Krymskaya sector dogfights arose with chilling suddenness, one following the other. Once a pilot entered this deadly environment, he found himself in a confusing vortex of air combat: "the flash of tracers, the rattle of machine gun fire, flak bursts, and the wild intermingling of aircraft at various altitudes." Often, Golubev observed, a single dogfight extended itself in an unpredictable fashion: "First a diving Bf 109 would trigger an attack by a Yak, which in turn drew into battle the intended victim's wingman. In a short time a LaGG appeared, quickly followed by a P-39 'Kobra.'" These fighters—at once hunters and hunted—"extended across the blue Kuban sky as if held together by an invisible thread."

On the ground, maintenance crews, according to Golubev, worked feverishly to maintain this high level of operational activity. Their role was crucial, and included a sequence of duties and gestures, which the fatigued fighter pilot remembered with appreciation: "They fastened you in the cockpit, started the engine, and shouted parting word of encouragement."[44]

The 298th Fighter Air Regiment on May 3 downed ten German planes and damaged two others. On the same day, Maj. V. G. Semenishin entered combat with eight Bf 109s, shot down one, and escaped unscathed. Writing many years later, Air Marshal Vershinin found Semenishin's success representative of the qualitative improvement in VVS operations in 1943. Although Semenishin, Vershinin notes, did not emerge from the Kuban with the reputation of Pokryshkin, his skills demonstrated the overall improvement in VVS fighter units. Semenishin began the war as a squadron commander, flying an I-16. At the start of the Kuban campaign, he was wounded. After a short stay in a hospital, he joined the 298th Fighter Air Regiment. Once he made the transition to the newer type aircraft, Semenishin showed exceptional flying skill, quickness, and a keen tactical sense. He adapted effectively to the *para* formation and other important changes in VVS fighter tactics introduced in 1943.[45]

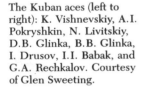

The Kuban aces (left to right): K. Vishnevskiy, A.I. Pokryshkin, N. Livitskiy, D.B. Glinka, B.B. Glinka, I. Drusov, I.I. Babak, and G.A. Rechkalov. Courtesy of Glen Sweeting.

Soviet bombers and ground-attack aircraft supported the advancing Soviet troops with growing effectiveness. On May 3, 162 aircraft from the 2d Bomber Air Corps (commanded by Gen. Maj. V. A. Ushakov) made sustained attacks on German artillery positions. These blows came at intervals of ten to

fifteen minutes, and were coordinated with Soviet Infantry and tank units which had penetrated German defensive positions south of Krymskaya.

Simultaneously, Shturmoviks from the 2d Mixed Air Corps, commanded by Gen.-Maj. I. T. Yeremenko, paved the way for Soviet tanks to assist in this breakthrough attempt. During a four-day period, bombers and Shturmoviks completed 2,243 sorties in support of this operation.[46] Such a display of massive air support revealed the growing prowess of VVS tactical air power. The 4th Air Army concentrated in this nineteen-mile-long zone (part of a 100-mile frontline) 90 percent of all its combat sorties. These large-scale air operations established a new bench mark for the VVS in the crucial year of 1943.

Against Soviet air power at Krymskaya, the Luftwaffe scored many successes, or what one German historian called "rich grazing": thirty-two Soviet aircraft downed on April 30, thirty-five on May 3, and another twenty-four on May 7. Despite these air victories (unconfirmed by Soviet sources), the Luftwaffe faced overwhelming odds as the VVS deployed massive concentrations of combat aircraft. Both Soviet and German accounts acknowledge the fact that during the first week in May the VVS, no doubt at considerable loss, achieved air superiority over the Krymskaya sector.[47]

The scale of these air engagements surpassed that of any previous VVS air operation in the south. From April 29 to May 10 the VVS 4th Air Army, in cooperation with Naval air units and ADD, flew 12,000 sorties.[48] Over half of these missions were against German ground positions along the frontlines and in the rear. VVS pilots participated in 285 air battles and downed 368 German aircraft.[49] The VVS action achieved momentary air control over the crucial Krymskaya sector. This difficult and costly achievement, however, did not alter the ground situation where the 56th Army had failed to break through to Anapa and the Black Sea.

A. L. Ivanov, of the 57th Guards Fighter Air Regiment, flew British Spitfires during April–June, 1943, in the Kuban sector. His memoirs suggest that the Spitfire, despite its heroics in the Battle of Britain, did not perform well on the Eastern front. "Our English birds," Ivanov lamented, "resemble too closely the Messerschmitt (Bf 109)." The confusion created dangers for the Spitfire-equipped 57th Guards. Ivanov himself was shot down twice by other VVS fighter pilots from neighboring air units, who mistook him for the enemy. Soviet anti-aircraft units showed the same tendency to fire, often with great accuracy, on the Soviet Spitfires. Several expedients were tried to make the Spitfire safe, including changes in unit markings on fuselage. None worked. For low-level sorties in support of the ground forces, a primary mission of the VVS, the Spitfire was not considered adequate by Ivanov and his fellow pilots. After a three-month stint, the VVS withdrew its Spitfires from the combat zones.[50]

The Soviet 56th Army finally captured Krymskaya on May 4, after an advance of only sixteen miles in width, 6 miles in depth. Otherwise, the German defenders held.

Throughout most of the Soviet offensive at Krymskaya, the VVS had challenged the Luftwaffe for air superiority with increasing numbers and aggressiveness. Generally, VVS air crews flew twice as many sorties per day as the Luftwaffe. With the claim by the Soviets of 368 downed German aircraft for the period April 20–May 10, Vershinin could assert that the Luftwaffe was losing an average of nine bombers and seventeen fighters every twenty-four

British Supermarine Spitfire MK V fighters being prepared for delivery to the Soviet Air Force in the Kuban in 1943. Courtesy of Carl-Fredrik Geust. (SI 81-2819)

hours. Soviet losses, again, were not listed by Vershinin, but from German sources one can speculate that they were substantial. By May 9–10, however, the Luftwaffe had reasserted itself over the Krymskaya sector, and once again had won local air superiority. Renewed German control of the air demonstrated the fact that the Luftwaffe remained powerful, despite the attrition of its ranks and the obvious gains of the VVS in the Kuban.

Over the Blue Line

After a lull of nearly two weeks, the Soviets resumed their offensive on May 26, against the German positions west of Krymskaya. Here the Germans had constructed the well-fortified "Blue Line," which secured the central sector of the Kuban bridgehead. The Soviet thrust aimed to establish a breakthrough zone between the villages of Kiyevskoye and Moldavanskoye. To spearhead this ambitious ground assault, the *Stavka* deployed the reinforced 56th Army. The recent Krymskaya action had weakened Wehrmacht strength in the sector, but the Blue Line afforded the German defenders the advantage of prepared defenses located on a series of elevated points. Also, the Luftwaffe was available to intervene if any serious Soviet breakthrough occurred.[51]

Soviet military planners anticipated an aggressive challenge from the Luftwaffe and moved substantial reserves to forward airfields adjacent to the Blue Line to reinforce the 4th Air Army. The Soviets constructed an elaborate network of command posts and radio guidance stations to assist in the coordination of air and ground operations against the Blue Line. For the initial stage of the Soviet offensive, the VVS was to play a major role, providing air preparation and intercepting the anticipated Luftwaffe response.

The VVS mounted its massive air preparation strike on the morning of May 26, preceded by night bombing raids and an artillery barrage. Committed to battle were 338 aircraft (84 bombers, 104 ground-attack planes, and 150 fighters), all pounding the narrow breakthrough sector. Once this strike was completed, the Soviets launched a powerful armored infantry thrust against the German lines. The coordinated air and ground assault brought some immediate success, but a determined German counterattack soon stalled the Soviet drive. There were frequent instances in which Soviet tanks managed to pierce the enemy lines in depth, only to find themselves separated from their infantry support. More than a hundred Soviet tanks were lost on the first day.[52]

The German response in the air was immediate. The ability of the Germans to hold the Blue Line depended in large measure on swift reaction. Within three hours after the start of the offensive, the Luftwaffe, by Soviet reckoning, had flown 1,500 sorties. This rapid German counterstroke hit Soviet positions along the frontlines and at some airfields as far back as Krasnodar. In the afternoon the Luftwaffe made another raid with 600 aircraft against the advancing Soviet troops. These alternating Soviet and German raids punctuated the hostilities on May 26. While Soviet sources are silent on impact of the concerted Luftwaffe action, the Germans in fact had regained local air superiority. One German source listed VVS losses for the first day at 350 combat aircraft. Whatever the tally of Soviet losses for May 26, the 4th Air Army had committed a substantial number of its aircraft to the offensive and had displayed an unprecedented aggressiveness.

From the first day of the Blue Line offensive, the VVS committed itself once more to a schedule of sustained ground support. The 4th Air Army had demonstrated its skills at tactical air support in the massive air strike on May 26. The coordination of 338 combat aircraft, mostly bombers and Shturmoviks, required no small amount of administrative effort. The air strike, which began at 0630 hours, fell on a narrow breakthrough corridor four miles wide and only a mile in depth. Covered by 150 fighters, the strike force approached the target zone in three echelons: the first wave consisted of eighty-four bombers; the second, thirty-six Shturmoviks; the third, forty-nine Shturmoviks. The higher-flying bombers served as the cutting edge, hitting the narrow sector with a concentrated blow. The Shturmoviks followed at nearly tree-top level with a series of close-in attacks on the beleaguered German defensive positions.

This phase of the Kuban air war also brought experimentation with new techniques for ground attack. For the first time, Il-2 Shturmoviks dropped a smoke screen in advance of the armored and infantry assault. Nineteen Il-2s in two groups flew this maneuver, approaching the target area at an altitude of thirty to sixty feet. The Il-2, with its formidable armor plating, was well suited for such a task, and Shturmovik pilots, already accustomed to the rigors of hedge-hopping sorties over enemy lines, performed their assignment effectively.[53] The smoke screen caught the German defenders by surprise, allowing the Soviet ground forces to pierce the enemy's first line of defense. Before a spirited German counterattack stymied the Soviet advance, a breakthrough corridor of two to three miles had been secured.

As the 4th Air Army sustained its ground attacks against German frontline positions, Il-2 losses mounted steadily. The airspace over the Blue Line was constricted, and the intensity of the ground fighting compelled both sides to commit air power on an ever-increasing scale. The Luftwaffe fighters remained a powerful foe, always capable of exacting a fearful toll of Soviet aircraft and air crews. German anti-aircraft units were ubiquitous and proficient. Despite these dangers, VVS Shturmovik units scored some notable successes in the two-week offensive over the Blue Line.

On June 2 Senior Lt. N. P. Dedov led thirty-six Il-2 "Il'yushas" against German artillery and infantry positions near Moldavanskaya. Knowing in advance the powerful enemy fighter and anti-aircraft defenses in the area,

Dedov experimented with a new technique of ground attack, hoping to reduce losses. With a fighter cover of thirty planes, Dedov directed the thirty-six Il-2s, separated into columns of six, against the predetermined enemy target at an approach altitude of 2,600 feet. An interval of 1,300–1,600 feet separated the attacking Shturmoviks. Once over the target area, the column formed into a "closed circle." This tactic allowed each Shturmovik pilot individually to descend in a deep dive toward the enemy position, drop his bombs close-in, bank to the left, and then return to the protected environs of the battle circle.

Dedov's air strike proved to be quite effective and losses were minimal. A group of four Bf 109s, according to Soviet records, had avoided the closed circle, with its considerable defensive firepower. Later, Air Commander Vershinin ordered Il-2 units to adopt this tactic as a standard procedure for ground attack.

The Luftwaffe also introduced some new tactics, aircraft types, and weapons. This effort represented a response by the Germans to the reality of improving Soviet military equipment in 1943 and the increasing threat from Soviet armor and artillery.[54] In 1941 the powerful Soviet T-34 tank had appeared in considerable numbers, along with the "Katyusha" artillery rockets. In the Kuban, and more dramatically at Kursk in July, the Germans faced the formidable challenge of coordinated thrusts by Soviet armor, artillery, and air power. The Kuban air campaign provided the Luftwaffe with a brief interlude to learn a great deal from the VVS, in particular the potential uses for "obsolete" aircraft.

In the Kuban, the Germans organized harassment bomber units and later night ground-attack units. These were equipped with He 46C, He 45C, and Ar 66 aircraft.[55] All along the vast Eastern front, the VVS had deployed their own vintage Po-2s, some flown by all-female units, to harass the German lines, to bomb airfields and communications centers, and to maintain links with partisan elements in the German rear areas. The endless expanse of the Russian front allowed for seemingly obsolete airplanes to perform vital combat roles. Unlike on the western fronts, the combatants in the Soviet Union found ample opportunities to experiment with myriad kinds of tactical aviation.

During the Kuban conflict, Col. Hans-Ulrich Rudel assumed command of a special anti-tank unit which tested a number of new ground-attack techniques and weapons. One of Germany's most decorated fliers, Rudel flew more than 2,500 combat missions during the war, sank the 26,000-ton Soviet battleship Marat, and became the acknowledged master of "tank-busting," with more than 500 Soviet tanks destroyed. Rudel's special unit studied in detail the silhouette patterns of Soviet tanks and their points of vulnerability, such as the engine, fuel tanks, and ammunition racks.[56]

After tests in Germany and Russia, Rudel's anti-tank command was ordered into the Crimea in the spring of 1943. For the first time the Germans deployed the Hs-129B equipped with 37mm cannon, a new type of aircraft in the east, which the Soviets observed with interest.[57] The major adaptations, however, occurred with older models—Ju 88s, Ju 87s, Bf 110s.[58] All were equipped with larger-caliber anti-tank weapons. In order to pierce the armor plate of Soviet tanks, the high-velocity ammunition was redesigned with tungsten-hardened cores. Rudel preferred the Ju 87D, which was fitted with a 37mm cannon beneath the wings and renamed the Ju 87G.

The slow-flying Ju 87 Stuka, already highly vulnerable to Soviet fighters, became in the Ju 87G even slower and less maneuverable. To accommodate the increased firepower, the Stuka's dive brakes were removed. Most of Rudel's pilots, despite their commander's enthusiasm, found the Ju 87G difficult to fly and extremely defenseless to Soviet forces.[59]

Air operations over the Kuban influenced the development of VVS bomber tactics and deployment. The *Stavka* had made the decision to place its primary emphasis on tactical air power. Fighter and ground-attack aviation expanded between 1941 and 1943 at an accelerated rate. Yet the VVS adopted a flexible approach in its building of a powerful tactical air force to include the use of light and medium bombers. The Il-4 and the Pe-2 provided the VVS with effective bombers, which could be used in a variety of air-support operations. In addition, Lend-Lease supplied the VVS with A-20 Havocs, allowing the Soviets to expand their bomber inventory in a short period of time.

The 4th Air Army began a systematic policy of attacking German rear areas during the Kuban fighting. This high profile of bomber raids paralleled a similar aggressiveness in the fighter and ground-attack units. VVS bombers hit not only German airfields, but bridges, port and supply installations at Taman and Kerch, seaborne traffic across the Straits of Kerch, and German naval bases on the southern coast of the Crimea. In contrast to earlier VVS bomber operations, these attacks were well organized and executed. Moreover, they struck areas hitherto immune from attack by Soviet air power. These deep raids caused considerable difficulty for the Germans, compelling them to adopt elaborate air-defense measures for rear-area installations and communications.

The ceaseless air war over the Kuban, especially in the final phase over the Blue Line, ushered Soviet fighter aviation into sudden prominence. An outstanding group of Soviet fighter aces emerged in the Kuban skies. One name—Aleksandr I. Pokryshkin—stands out in a singular fashion. Pokryshkin's skill as a fighter pilot (twenty victories in the Kuban air engagements) did not exhaust his contributions or influence. As a squadron commander, he forged in theory and practice a whole new set of fighter air tactics based on his own experiences in combat.

Grouped around him were other "heroes of the Kuban," fliers of impressive skill and bravery who did much in the spring of 1943 to redeem the tarnished reputation of VVS fighter aviation. There were the aforementioned Glinka brothers, Dmitriy and Boris, who scored twenty-one and ten victories respectively. G. E. Rechkalov, who later emerged as the Soviet Union's third-ranking ace (fifty-five total victories), shot down eleven German aircraft in the Kuban. Rechkalov survived the war as a two-time recipient of the gold star, Hero of the Soviet Union.

There were others: Vadim I. Fadeyev—nineteen victories in the Kuban; N. E. Lavitskiy—fifteen; A. L. Prukozchikov—twenty; N. K. Naumchik—sixteen; P. M. Berestnev—twelve; D. I. Koval'—thirteen; and V. I. Fedorenko—thirteen. Each of these elite fighters pilots scored ten or more victories during the two-month Kuban campaign.

Some of the fliers—Pokryshkin, the Glinka brothers, Rechkalov, and Fadeyev—went on to become the top-scoring Soviet aces of World War II. There were occasions when Pokryshkin and Rechkalov flew in the same

A.I. Pokryshkin emerges from his P-39 Airacobra. Pokryshkin shot down fifty-nine enemy aircraft during the war, including twenty over the Kuban in the spring of 1943. (SI 79-9499)

Another Kuban ace—G.A. Rechkalov, who ended the war with fifty-seven victories. During the Kuban campaign he flew as Pokryshkin's wingman on several occasions. Courtesy of Carl-Fredrik Geust.

zveno as part of the elite 16th Guards Fighter Regiment. Fighter pilots such as Koval' and Prukozchikov achieved aerial victories at a formidable pace—an average of one victory for every two air battles. "B. B." Glinka, sometimes flying missions with his older brother "D. B." Glinka, established the best average over the Kuban: ten victories in only fifteen air battles.[60]

While these more spectacular air feats dominated public attention, and continue today to command deserved recognition in Soviet historical accounts of the war, there were other Soviet fighter pilots of note. There was Maj. A. A. Doroshenkov of the 43d Fighter Air Regiment, who led a group of six Yak-7b fighters against Anapa air base, the primary Luftwaffe fighter base in the Kuban. Attacking at dawn on May 26, Doroshenkov's group destroyed a total of nine German aircraft. The raid was important because of its boldness and clear demonstration of the improved skills of VVS fighter aviation.[61]

Gone were the days when Soviet fighters avoided the Luftwaffe or, if compelled to fight, found themselves totally ill-equipped to contend with the enemy.

German evaluations of the VVS in 1943 confirmed the dramatic improvement of Soviet fighter aviation. During the first years of the war VVS fighter pilots, except in isolated instances, displayed little aggressiveness toward the Luftwaffe. The appalling VVS losses during the summer of 1941 conditioned in Soviet fighter pilots a profound sense of inferiority, a reflex reinforced by the objective circumstances of poor training, the confusion associated with outmoded tactics, and the transition to a new generation of fighter aircraft.

By 1943 Air Commander Novikov had guided the VVS to a higher level of flying proficiency. Luftwaffe fighter pilots and bomber crews could no longer operate freely and count on the passivity of the Soviet Air Force. German fighter pilots found the guard units (for example, Pokryshkin's 16th Guards Fighter Air Regiment) to be dangerous adversaries—aggressive, highly skilled in group tactics, and masters at individual combat. As German observers noted, VVS fighters began to concentrate along "points of major effort," to range across the frontlines into the German rear areas as fighter-bombers, and to display impressive discipline and coordination.[62] This more effective operational style contrasted sharply with the disorderly application of Soviet air power in the first stages of the war.

VVS fighter operations were enhanced by the timely arrival of the Lend-Lease P-39 Airacobra. Considered obsolete by the Allied air forces, the P-39 saw its moment of glory on the Eastern front in 1943, outperforming both the Spitfire and the P-40. Soviet pilots, with their tactical orientation, found the American aircraft to be an excellent, powerfully armed fighter-bomber. With Pokryshkin and other skilled fliers at the controls, P-39s proved to be effective interceptors, and were considered more robust fighting machines than Spitfires or P-40s. The placement of the powerplant behind the cockpit of the "Kobry" allowed Soviet pilots to fly their customary hedge-hopping sorties with abandon, making full use of the aircraft's 37mm cannon against ground targets.[63]

In the Kuban dogfights the Luftwaffe began to observe a mirror image of itself in the VVS attack formations. Soviet pilots had been trained in the 1930s to fly in a tight horizontal pattern, in groups of three, and according to fixed rules. As was the case with Britain's Royal Air Force, there was a belated recognition by the Russians that in combat with the Luftwaffe this type of formation was quite inflexible and dangerous. The Luftwaffe flew in the *Rotte* and *Schwarm* formations, the former an element leader with wingman, the latter a "finger four" formation. Such an organization allowed flexibility and maneuver, with all the advantages of attack and cover roles built into the basic two-man formation. With newer, high-performance aircraft and accumulating combat experience, Soviet fighter units began to break out of the straitjacket of the prewar air-combat tactics.

The *para* and *zveno* formations appeared in 1942–43 as copies of the *Rotte* and *Schwarm* to fully exploit the impressive maneuverability of Soviet fighter aircraft. The change was gradual and accomplished in a piecemeal fashion. German pilots reported in 1943 that VVS fighters still formed into defensive circles once they were attacked, but this maneuver, more often than not, was merely transitional. Rather than stay in a defensive formation,

Lend-Lease P-39s saw considerable action in the Kuban and along the entire Eastern front in 1943. Pictured here in the background are P-39s belonging to the 2d Guards Fighter Air Corps of the Leningrad Air Defense Troops, October 1943. Courtesy of Carl-Fredrik Geust.

VVS fighters began to attack as soon as a favorable opportunity appeared. Experienced Soviet pilots showed considerable initiative and flying skill in reaction to German attacks.[64]

All that was needed at the time of escalating air war over the Kuban was a synthesizer, a person who could forge the many isolated changes in Soviet fighter tactics into an integrated whole. This task fell in large measure to Pokryshkin, who was not an "air theorist" in the traditional sense, but a front-line combat pilot.

Aleksandr Pokryshkin had grown up in Siberia, where as a youth in the 1930s he became enamored of the aerial feats of Valeriy Chkalov. He made his first solo flight in a Po-2 biplane in 1937. In the late 1930s Pokryshkin flew I-15s and I-16s as a VVS fighter pilot, and made the transition to the MiG-3 just prior to the outbreak of war with Germany. Always a serious student of air-combat tactics, Pokryshkin was profoundly affected by the disaster that befell the VVS during Operation Barbarossa. At the air academies, the flight training schools, among flight instructors, and in the various manuals and printed instructions, Pokryshkin found a bewildering pattern of outmoded concepts about air combat.

His first encounter with the Luftwaffe took place on the second day of the war in an area near Jassy. At the time, Pokryshkin was flying a MiG-3, which he maneuvered skillfully to down an enemy airplane after his own was set aflame. This triumph and narrow escape exposed to Pokryshkin his own inadequacies, the technical inferiority of VVS fighter aviation, and the acute need to devise new air-combat tactics.[65]

Pokryshkin's role as a student and teacher of air-combat tactics began with that first combat experience. The frontlines, he said, made the study of combat tactics a "living necessity, a rule, a law." The requirements at the front differed markedly from the rehearsed skills acquired in flight training. As a senior pilot and squadron commander, he worked with newly assigned pilots, providing a crash course on the realities of air combat with the Luftwaffe. Always critical of "academic" or "theoretical" types who taught abstract concepts about flying, Pokryshkin forcefully asserted that combat was the best teacher. He displayed a willingness to learn and, if necessary, to adapt the superior methods of the enemy.[66]

Pokryshkin studied air combat in great detail, conversed with fellow pilots on the best tactics, and began the piecemeal adoption of proven techniques. "The effectiveness of every technique, formation, and calculation," according to Pokryshkin, "was tested in fire" and "conclusions rested on the lost lives of our comrades."[67]

"Altitude-speed-maneuver-fire"—this was Pokryshkin's formula. It was not original, and Allied fighter pilots at the time would have found his "discoveries" to be simplistic and derivative. Indeed they were, but for the VVS—operating for two years in isolation against the technically superior Luftwaffe—the Pokryshkin formula expressed in words a whole matrix of battle-tested knowledge.

For Pokryshkin, altitude was the primary element. Altitude gave the fighter pilot crucial advantages hitherto unexploited by Soviet airmen: freedom of maneuver, a vantage point to search for the enemy, and the option of selecting the best target. From altitude the Soviet pilot had the initiative. After a dive on the enemy, the acquired speed in the vertical axis gave the pilot the crucial factor of time, often just a few seconds, to make his attack. Together, altitude and speed translated into a set of flexible options of maneuver, either in the vertical or horizontal axes.

Finally, Pokryshkin emphasized the importance of close-in fire on enemy aircraft. Like Erich Hartman and all proficient fighter aces, Pokryshkin stressed the importance of firing at short range. The flying skill and patience required for this self-imposed discipline brought obvious rewards—greater accuracy and concentration of firepower.

Behind Pokryshkin's formula was the shift by VVS fighters to the tactic of "vertical maneuver." Deployed in two aircraft formations, or *para*, VVS fighters in 1943 flew in a more competent and aggressive posture, attacking from altitude and providing cover for each other. Victories mounted and losses diminished.

One practitioner of the formula, Col. N. Platonov of the 249th Fighter Air Regiment, added a Russian touch—the use of head-on attacks from altitude. In a battle over the Kuban, Platonov dived from altitude toward a German bomber, compelling the pilot to swerve at the last moment. Once removed from the formation by this threatened *taran*, or ramming, the German bomber became vulnerable to Platonov and other Soviet fighter pilots. In a postwar memoir, Platonov claimed three victories in this particular sortie.

During the war he completed 155 sorties, participated in twenty-six air battles, and downed six German aircraft. He received the gold star, Hero of the Soviet Union, on May 1, 1943.[68]

The study of air-combat techniques became more formal and systematic during the course of the Kuban fighting. Pokryshkin's pioneering study dealt with a variety of topics: *para* and *zveno* formations; the requirements for bomber escort, reconnaissance, and ground-attack operations; and the weapons and techniques of the Luftwaffe. All these crucial areas of reform acquired elaboration and broad application over time. Articles were published, various VVS units underwent new training, and "air tactics conferences" were held.

According to the VVS air commander in the Kuban, General Vershinin, the practical, hard-nosed approach of Pokryshkin prevailed. The best fighter pilots, including Pokryshkin, the Glinka brothers, Fadeyev, Rechkalov, and Semenishin, took part in numerous tactical seminars. VVS air units studied in depth each completed operation, identifying achievements and deficiencies. Concrete air-combat situations were defined and then discussed in terms of the most appropriate action or reaction to take.

Along with these tactical studies, Soviet pilots also attended "party-political" sessions where patriotic duty was stressed. This activity was coordinated by Vershinin's deputy, Gen. V. I. Verov. Finally, the army press supplied a continuous flow of pamphlets and articles on improving combat skills. All these factors enabled the VVS to make the gradual transition in 1943 to an offensive style.[69]

Among the VVS reforms in air-combat tactics, the "Kuban escalator" became one of the most important efforts at perfecting group-combat technique.[70] This innovation, as with so many VVS changes in tactics in 1943, was the result of Pokryshkin's emphasis on altitude and mutual support. It consisted of VVS fighters deployed in altitude, with each patrol separated by a vertical space of 2,600 to 3,200 feet. This arrangement allowed a larger formation to fly with the attack and cover roles. Such spacing, with the lower patrols extended forward, allowed greater visibility, defensive power, and flexibility. German sources acknowledged the change, but discounted the impact of the "Kuban escalator" as an effective tactic.[71] Such changes in tactical formations did not dramatically alter the air war, as German observers noted. Instead, the various piecemeal tactical adaptations by the VVS in 1943—as symbolized in the Kuban escalator—provided marginal improvements. When taken together and assessed in the context of a narrowing technological gap with the Luftwaffe, VVS tactical innovations sparked an important shift in the war. The VVS fighter air arm over the Kuban demonstrated a rough parity with the Luftwaffe for the first time.

The profile of VVS fighter aviation which took shape over the Kuban continued in its basic form through the remainder of the war.[72] The tactical units of the *para* and the *zveno* became standard. The largest tactical formation used by the VVS was the *gruppa*, which included a *zveno* and one independent *para*. On occasion, the *gruppa* consisted of two *zveno*, or eight aircraft. In time, the VVS learned to space their *para*, either horizontally or by altitude, with greater discipline and consistency. A typical *para* positioned the wingman out to the side at approximately 120 degrees. The wingman was "stacked up" a few feet (fifteen to sixty). In the *zveno*, the two *para* were

Lend-Lease aircraft became an important component in the Soviet war effort in 1942–43. Here Soviet pilots arrive at Abadan, Iran, to ferry Lend-Lease aircraft into the Caucasus. Courtesy of USAF.

widely separated horizontally, with the subordinate *para* echeloned from 600 to 900 feet above and to the rear of the lead *para*. For the typical *gruppa* formation an additional *para* was added, flying from 1,200 to 2,400 feet above the lead *zveno*. These formations were used for the extensive patrol and escort duties flown by VVS fighters during the war.

Over the Kuban, the VVS fighter units employed on a small scale the *Okhotniki*, or free hunter, tactic first used successfully at Stalingrad. Frequently, this meant the deployment of one *para*, always with skilled pilots, to the enemy rear to hit any targets of opportunity. Throughout the war the VVS emphasized in its fighter arm a flexible pattern of air-combat formations to meet shifting combat requirements.[73]

Sometimes the Soviet commanders complained that their fighters failed to provide this effective support for the army. This became a serious problem in the Kuban when the Luftwaffe conducted many ground-attack and bomber raids on Soviet positions at Myskhako, Krymskaya, and in the Blue Line sectors. Soviet fighters displayed poor target selection, and during enemy bombing raids they attacked the fighter escorts rather than the bombers. This pattern allowed German bombers to strike their targets with little interference from Soviet interceptors.[74]

As the air war over the Kuban progressed, the VVS fighter arm made a series of adjustments to provide more effective defense. Soon a pattern of fighter interception developed which proved to be more effective. When attacking bombers, VVS fighters approached from altitude in steep dives, ideally from the sun or clouds. Soviet fighters made every effort to break up the German bomber formations in order to give the *para* formations an opportunity to attack individual aircraft. Close coordination with command posts on the ground allowed Soviet fighters to meet urgent requests for air support more effectively. Once enemy bombers entered an anti-aircraft zone, the VVS fighters withdrew and flew parallel to the flight path of the enemy aircraft. If the enemy bombers approached in elements at different altitudes, the VVS fighters attacked the top-most group. To work in harmony with anti-aircraft batteries, VVS pilots were briefed in detail on the Soviet gun positions along the frontlines. On occasion, VVS fighters executed a closed-circle

Women pilots were used by the Soviet Union in numerous combat roles, the most famous being the night bombing missions with Po-2 aircraft.

The Po-2, designed in 1927, became legendary for its yeoman work on the Eastern front. With the vast dimensions of the landscape, the Soviets found many uses for older, slower aircraft such as the Po-2. Here a Po-2 has been adapted for use as a vehicle to evacuate the wounded. Courtesy of Carl-Fredrik Geust.

maneuver to tempt German fighters into a Soviet anti-aircraft zone.[75]

VVS fighter units acquired a new effectiveness in providing for ground-attack and bomber operations. This pattern evolved as the fighting continued. Toward the end of the war, the typical pattern for ground-attack escort included two elements: the immediate escort and the assault. The strength of escort element depended on a number of factors—distance, weather, fighter opposition—but the usual pattern was one escort fighter for each ground-attack plane.

Flying from 300 to 1,000 feet above and behind in a crisscrossing fashion, the immediate escort element protected the ground-attack aircraft close-in. Overarching the ground-attack aircraft and their immediate escort was an assault group which flew at an altitude of 1,500 to 3,000 feet. This element positioned itself directly above or ahead (one-half to three-quarters of a mile) of the ground-attack planes. Flying in a crisscross pattern, the assault formation sought to prevent enemy aircraft from penetrating into the protected airspace. On occasion, one *para* was placed in advance, as a point, to scout for enemy interceptors. Another *para*, if required, remained in reserve at a higher altitude.

After reaching the target, the assault formation assumed a patrol configuration at 10,000 feet until the ground-attack unit completed its mission. Escort for bombers followed the essentials of this two-element pattern, since Soviet bombers were frequently deployed for tactical missions.[76]

Although the Kuban conflict of 1943 ended in a bloody stalemate, broken off after both sides failed to achieve their purposes, it proved to be the largest air-combat encounter on the Eastern front to date. The VVS had challenged the Luftwaffe for local air superiority on a scale unprecedented in the war. For the first time, the German fighter air arm faced a spirited challenge from the VVS, and as German accounts testify, the VVS achieved a measure of air mastery during most phases of the Kuban fighting.

Such a triumph required high attrition in aircraft and personnel. Exact figures have not been published. While Soviet accounts of the Kuban air war record 35,000 VVS sorties flown and the destruction of 1,100 German aircraft (800 in air combat), they remain largely silent on Soviet personnel and aircraft losses.[77] German accounts, however, suggest a significant attrition of VVS aircraft during the entire Kuban operations—as high as 2,280 by October 1943, when the Germans evacuated the Kuban bridgehead.

By June 7, 1943, the Kuban air engagements had ceased. Two weeks later the Military Council of the North Caucasus front claimed victory in the air, noting that the VVS had compelled the Luftwaffe to abandon combat operations over the Kuban. On July 7 Air Commander Novikov issued a directive claiming that the VVS had emerged from the engagements with enhanced strength and control of the air. Both sides now turned their attention to the north, to a salient occupied by the Red Army around the town of Kursk. Here the Germans planned to launch their third summer offensive in Russia.

Soviet intelligence had intercepted the German plans well in advance, and the *Stavka* now prepared to mobilize its air and ground forces to blunt the anticipated German attack and then launch the first major Soviet summer offensive of the war. These events, already in motion at the time of the Blue Line engagements, quickly shifted the focus away from the Kuban sector.

The air action over the Kuban, however, had an important impact on the evolving capabilities and operational style of Soviet air power. As the official history of the Soviet Air Force has stated, the Kuban air operations were significant far beyond the immediate boundaries of the North Caucasus front: "They provided a school for the Soviet Air Force to perfect its skills."[78]

Chapter 6

Kursk

When Hitler and the German High Command planned their third summer offensive in 1943, they targeted the Soviet-held bastion centered around the small Ukrainian city of Kursk, 300 miles south of Moscow. In the aftermath of Stalingrad, the Kursk bulge measured 150 miles long and 100 miles wide. It occupied a crucial position in the middle of the long Russo-German front, which extended from Leningrad in the north through Novgorod, Smolensk, and Kharkov to Taganrog on the Sea of Azov. The German offensive, code-named Operation Citadel, called for a powerful pincer movement against the exposed Soviet position: the 9th Army was to advance southward from Orel, while the 4th Panzer Army was to spearhead a drive northward from the Belgorod-Kharkov sector.

Unlike previous summer campaigns, Operation Citadel pursued essentially limited objectives. For the Wehrmacht in 1943, there were no planned thrusts deep into Russian territory or grandiose ambitions of toppling the Soviet regime in a decisive offensive. By encircling the Kursk salient, the Germans hoped to knock out a powerful Soviet army grouping, to straighten out the forward line to allow better lateral communication, and to strengthen the overall strategic position of the German forces in the aftermath of Stalingrad.

Operation Citadel called for the mobilization of armor and airpower in large concentrations to establish breakthrough zones north and south of Kursk. To catch the Russians off balance, Field Marshals Erich von Manstein and Günther von Kluge, the German Army Group commanders, urged an early date for the offensive, at the beginning of May, to coincide with the end of the *rasputitsa*, or muddy season. Hitler, however, decided to postpone Operation Citadel to allow for the deployment of the latest Pzkw V Panther and Pzkw VI Tiger tanks.[1] The Luftwaffe component earmarked for the offen-

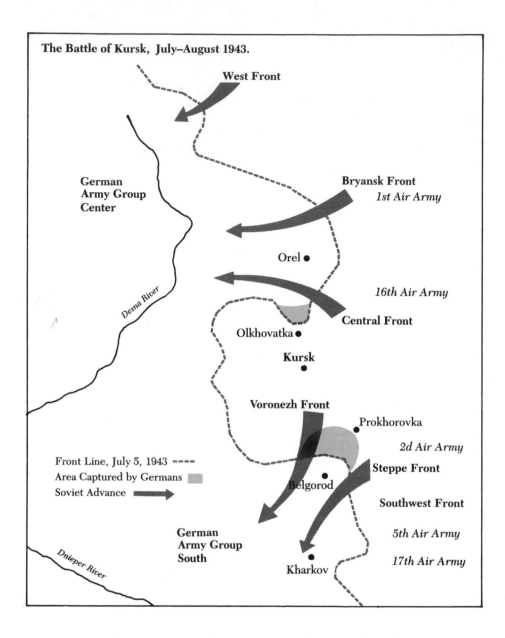

The Battle of Kursk, July–August 1943.

West Front

German
Army Group
Center

Bryansk Front
1st Air Army

Orel ●

16th Air Army

Central Front

Olkhovatka ●

Kursk
●

Voronezh Front

Prokhorovka
●

2d Air Army

Front Line, July 5, 1943 ----
Area Captured by Germans
Soviet Advance

Steppe Front

Belgorod ●

Southwest Front

German
Army Group
South

5th Air Army

17th Air Army

Kharkov ●

Desna River

Dnieper River

sive represented 70 percent of the German combat aircraft on the Eastern
front.[2]

From Germany, France, Norway, and other sectors of the Russian front,
the Luftwaffe ordered selected air units to move into forward airfields near
Kursk during the spring of 1943. Following an elaborate timetable, these reinforcements arrived in stages prior to July 5, the date selected for the
launching of the offensive. Two major Luftwaffe concentrations, the 6th Air
Fleet (Orel) and the 4th Air Fleet (Belgorod-Kharkov), took shape in May and
June with a combined strength of around 1,800 aircraft. Soviet sources list
the Luftwaffe strength for Operation Citadel at 2,050 planes (1,200 bombers,
600 fighters, 150 reconnaissance aircraft, and 100 of the new Henshel Hs 129
ground-attack planes).[3]

Gen. Hans Jeschonnek, Luftwaffe chief of staff, supervised the gradual build-up of air power for Operation Citadel. The deployment of German air units to the north and south of Kursk required a precise schedule and the construction of new airfields—all to be accomplished without giving telltale signs of German intentions. Already by June 1943 the Soviet partisan movement in the area had grown to formidable size. The German rear had become a second front in the east with countless disruptive actions by partisans against enemy supply lines. Logistical problems for the Luftwaffe arose at the same time, because of a dramatic increase in acts of sabotage. In 841 separate incidents the partisans had delivered a significant blow against the overstretched German supply lines. Fuel became the crucial part of the military equation since its availability governed the extent of air operations.[4]

A more fundamental consideration, however, was the fact that the Luftwaffe's 6th and 4th air fleets entered the Kursk air operations without substantial reserves. If Operation Citadel should be stalled and give way to a prolonged struggle, normal attrition would quickly weaken the Luftwaffe's striking power. Already German air units found it difficult to assert and maintain local air superiority and at the same time meet the increasing requirements of the German army for ground support.

The Soviet military leadership approached the forthcoming Battle of Kursk with confidence. There was no ignorance or uncertainty concerning the enemy's strategic planning. Rudolph Rossler and the "Lucy Ring," having penetrated the higher levels of the German High Command, provided the *Stavka* with accurate intelligence. With this foreknowledge of German intentions, Soviet military planners constructed elaborate and echeloned defensive fortifications within the Kursk salient. Hitler's fateful decision to delay the start of the offensive until July gave Moscow the fortuitous opportunity to mobilize thoroughly their growing air and ground forces to meet the German challenge.

At the core of the Soviet defenses at Kursk were two large army groupings: troops of the Central front under Gen. K. K. Rokossovskiy and the

This Shturmovik unit, the 281st Ground-Attack Division, received the Order of Suvorov at Tartu, Estonia, in October 1944. Courtesy of Carl-Fredrik Geust.

An Il-2 Shturmovik in flight over Stalingrad in 1943. The Il-2 symbolized the peculiar emphasis of Soviet air power, with its simple design, austere equipment, rugged construction, and tactical deployment. Courtesy of Carl-Fredrik Geust.

Voronezh front under Gen. N. F. Vatutin. To the southeast, in reserve, was the Steppe front, commanded by Gen. I. S. Konev. Within the bulge proper the *Stavka* placed two-thirds of its artillery and tanks in order to blunt the anticipated thrusts north and south of Kursk. Rokossovskiy and Vatutin together commanded a formidable military force: 1,300,000 troops, 20,000 guns and mortars, 3,600 tanks and self-propelled guns, and 2,900 combat aircraft.[5] For Kursk, the *Stavka* deployed the largest number of combat aircraft for frontline operations since the summer of 1941.[6]

The Soviets took pains to make the Kursk defenses impregnable. During June 1943 Moscow organized a *levée en masse*, a civilian labor force of 300,000 people, to build a succession of defensive lines to stop the German infantry and tanks.[7] Three fortified lines, positioned at intervals over a distance of twenty-five miles, stood in readiness to meet the full force of the German attack.[8] Three thousand miles of trench lines, numerous tank traps, and an elaborate system of fortified defensive positions fashioned from wood and earth protected Kursk in echelons along the anticipated breakthrough corridors. More than 400,000 mines were laid.

Forward Soviet airfields bristled with fighter and ground-attack aircraft, poised as a coiled spring to challenge the Luftwaffe for air superiority and to assist the ground forces in the destruction of German mechanized units. If these elaborate defenses failed, General Konev's Steppe front army stood prepared to intervene, along with additional infantry and tank reserves deployed in the Soviet rear. Once the defensive phase had achieved its purpose and Operation Citadel had been blunted, the *Stavka* planned to break out of the Kursk bastion. In the north, armies of the Western, Bryansk, and Central front armies would overwhelm Orel; farther to the south, the Voronezh, Steppe, and Southwestern front forces would advance against Belgorod and Kharkov. As at Moscow in 1942, the *Stavka* hoped to roll the Germans back, this time toward Kiev and the Dnieper River, in the first major summer offensive of the war. The counteroffensieve at Kursk would signal an end to the long and costly period of defensive warfare.

Soviet air preparations for the defense of Kursk began in mid-April 1943. VVS deployment within the Kursk salient consisted of two air armies: the 16th, under Gen. S. I. Rudenko, attached to the Central front below Orel, and the 2d under Gen. S. A. Krasovskiy, supporting the Voronezh front, on the Belgorod-Kharkov sector. Numbering together 1,880 combat aircraft, the 16th and 2d air armies equaled the total Luftwaffe air strength assigned to Operation Citadel. With assistance from the 5th Air Army (Steppe front) and the 17th Air Army (Southwestern front), VVS operational strength for the initial phase of the Battle of Kursk totaled 1,060 fighters, 940 ground-attack aircraft, 500 day bombers, and 400 night bombers.[9]

Such an air grouping was substantial, but not overwhelming, particularly in the category of fighters, where the Luftwaffe still excelled. The key to the Soviet Air Force's success rested with the *Stavka*'s capacity to maintain an effective flow of reinforcements.

Stalin had placed a strong emphasis on the creation of massive air reserves in rear areas, along with tank, artillery, and infantry concentrations, which could be thrown into battle at crucial moments in the war. By 1943 the Air Corps of the *Stavka* Reserve had grown into a vast reservoir of air power, fueling the various air armies with a seemingly endless flow of aircraft and air crews. On March 29, 1943, Air Commander Novikov ordered that these reserves be used only along the major axes of offensive operations. He wisely refused to permit his vital air reserves to be dispersed aimlessly into the various air armies. Such VVS reserve components, by order of the *Stavka*, moved back to the rear once a sector ceased to be an active combat zone.

During its apprenticeship in the first two years of the war, the air force high command had learned the advantages of centralization and mobility. As the VVS stepped up the tempo of its operations in 1943, Novikov had acquired additional experience in using reserves to achieve overwhelming local air superiority in offensive operations. At Kursk, he faced the challenge of orchestrating six air armies in joint operations.

The VVS made full use of the PVO fighter air units to bolster the frontal aviation units, along with 500 bombers from ADD to apply pressure on the German rear areas. These additional air units, if welcomed, did not constitute a decisive factor. Behind the forward air units there was the Soviet aircraft replacement capacity. The relocated aviation industry, with its impressive productivity, enabled the *Stavka* to augment its air strength in a dramatic fashion: 400 aircraft during the defensive stage (July 5–23) and 600 during the counteroffensive (July 12–August 23). During the crucial defensive stage Novikov would hold the 1st, 5th, and 15th air armies (2,750 aircraft) in reserve in order to release them for the decisive stage of the Soviet counteroffensive. For the entire Kursk campaign the VVS planned to deploy over 5,400 combat aircraft.[10]

The VVS entered the conflict at Kursk with updated aircraft and weapons systems. The war had accelerated the process of research and development. The Soviets, always alert to combat requirements, had modified the one-seater Il-2 Shturmovik into the Il-2M3. The new version possessed increased horsepower and a rear gunner armed with a 12.7mm machine gun designed by M. Ye. Berezin. The ShVAK (B. G. Shpital'nyy and S. V. Vladimirov) 20mm cannon had emerged at this juncture in the war as the standard armament for Soviet aircraft.

To enhance the firepower of VVS fighters and ground-attack planes, new weapons such as the NS-37 cannon now appeared in quantity. Designed by A. E. Nudelman and A. S. Suranov, the NS-37 was a 37mm anti-tank cannon which the Soviets fitted to the Il-2M3 Shturmovik during the summer fighting at Kursk. By 1943 the VVS also displayed as well a keen interest in rockets as anti-tank weapons, developing the RS-82 and the RS-132 projectiles.[11]

Another significant and timely innovation was the PTAB hollow-charge anti-tank bomb. The PTAB bomb, designed by I. A. Larionov, reflected the high priority given to tactical aviation by Soviet air planners. In contrast to the less dependable rocket projectiles, the PTAB ultimately proved to be an

The radial-engine La-5, a rival to the German Fw 190, made a dramatic appearance during the time of the Battle of Kursk. These La-5s belong to the 18th Guards Fighter Air Regiment of the 1st Air Army based at Tula (below Moscow) in 1944. Courtesy of Carl-Fredrik Geust.

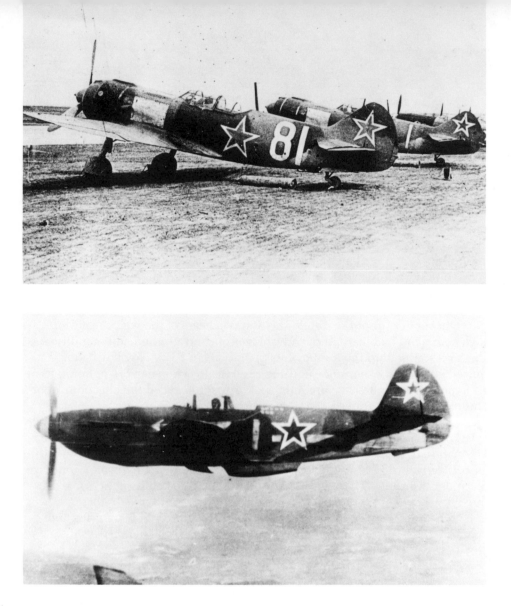

The Normandy-Nieman Regiment, a group of volunteer Free French pilots flying with the Soviet Air Force, made their air-combat debut at Kursk. This photograph, taken later in the war, shows a late-model YAK-3 fighter with the unit's markings. Note that the French pilot has eight air victories. Courtesy of Musée de l'Air, Paris.

This YAK-3 displays the Cross of Lorraine, the symbol of the Free French. Courtesy of Musée de l'Air, Paris.

A group of Soviet pilots receive instructions in front of their YAK-9 fighters. Courtesy of Carl-Fredrik Geust.

effective anti-tank weapon. Shturmovik pilots found this bomb to be a light-weight and highly effective weapon, even against the new Panther and Tiger tanks.

The VVS had made important strides in the tactical control of its air armies. Radio sets were now standard equipment for most frontal air units. The ZOS (ground aids to navigation) service, the use of Redut and Pegmatit radar, and the expansion of radio communications stations (from 180 to 420 in 1943) enabled local commanders to establish more efficient procedures.[12] The intensely fought Kuban air campaign had demonstrated to Novikov and the air force command the enormous effort required to coordinate several air armies in joint operations. During the Kuban period Novikov ordered adjacent air armies to maintain daily contact with each other. Along the vast sweep of the Eastern front, Novikov tightened his control and insisted on effective lateral communication between the staffs of the various air armies. As the VVS approached the Kursk air battle there was a keen awareness that in the sphere of organization the period of apprenticeship had passed. For the first time, the VVS could display its newly acquired skills in the coordinating of major air operations.

At the top, the *Stavka* continued to improve the air force command structure, promoting capable officers to key administrative and planning positions. In May 1943 Gen. S. A. Khudyakov assumed the post of air force chief of staff. In a subsequent appointment, the talented General Falaleyev became deputy commander of the air force. The Soviet Air Force Military Council expanded its role as the overall planning and mobilization center for Soviet air power, giving particular attention to improving the training programs for pilots, navigators, and air personnel. To be avoided at all costs were the aerial defeats of earlier campaigns, when hastily trained pilots and air crews entered combat, sometimes in units as large as squadrons or regiments, with no practical training.

Soviet air planners had learned that pilot training must embody the les-

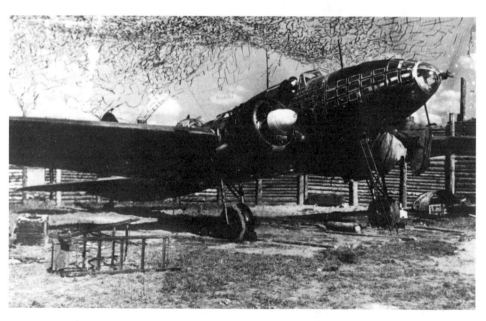

The Pe-2 dive bomber, known for its excellent speed, maneuverability, and firepower, played an important tactical role in Soviet air operations during the war. Courtesy of Carl-Fredrik Geust.

The Il-4 (DB-3F) bomber was the mainstay of Soviet bomber operations during the war. As the war progressed, the Il-4 was given largely tactical assignments, although the aircraft was designated a long-range bomber. Courtesy of Carl-Fredrik Geust.

sons of combat. Stalingrad had shown the requirements for conducting an effective air blockade, the Kuban had been the occasion to update fighter combat tactics, and now Kursk would be the crucible to forge new Shturmovik tactics against German armor. During 1943 Novikov wisely allowed the curricula for VVS combat tactics to be rewritten at the front. Once the gulf between operational reality and the rear training programs narrowed, the VVS began to demonstrate important qualitative improvements. These changes matched the growing quantitative edge of the VVS over the enemy.

The VVS monitored in great detail the German build-up for Operation Citadel. Alerted to German plans, the 4th Air Reconnaissance Regiment as early as May 14 had discovered a large concentration of enemy tanks near Orel, the first confirmation of Operation Citadel. In time, the systematic use of air reconnaissance revealed the details of the planned German summer offensive—troop groupings, a network of airfields, patterns of aircraft deployment, defensive fortifications, artillery positions, staging areas, and reserves. For the first time at Kursk, the VVS made full use of aerial photography as an aid to operational planning.

Air Commander Novikov, assisted by Generals Vorozheykin and Khudyakov, countered the German build-up by deploying six VVS air armies at forward airstrips in and around the Kursk salient. The elaborate Soviet battle plan dictated a precise application of air power for the defensive stage: the 17th Air Army to contribute 180 aircraft for an optimum 990 sorties during the first three days; the 2d Air Army, 170 aircraft for 990 sorties during the same time slot, and so on.[13] For the first time in the war the VVS would enter a major battle with a solid logistical base.

The VVS built a large network of airfields during the preparatory phase to accommodate the vast mobilization of air power. BAO units, assisted by civilian laborers, constructed 154 airfields for the 16th and 2d air armies alone, along with fifty "dummy" airstrips to confuse the enemy. At each airfield large quantities of munitions and fuel were stockpiled to sustain air operations for a minimum of ten to fifteen days. Frontal air armies were now at full strength. Moreover, the transition to modern types of aircraft (Soviet and Lend-Lease) had been completed. Only night bomber units, equipped with Po-2s, flew prewar models in the summer of 1943.[14]

Operation Citadel occurred then against a backdrop of overall Soviet military renewal. The earlier victories at Stalingrad and in the Kuban heralded the revived combat capabilities of Soviet air power. Novikov approached Kursk with confidence. The pendulum had swung in a dramatic way to the Soviets, as they claimed, although at the time German military planners viewed their recent losses as reversals, not decisive defeats. At Kursk, they planned to reassert the strategic initiative on the Eastern front.

Soviet technicians prepare "Molotov Breadbaskets" for bombing missions, with Il-4 bombers in the background. The whirling drop container of the bomb opened at a predetermined altitude, releasing a cluster of incendiary bombs.

Writing about the military situation on the eve of Kursk, modern-day Soviet historians point to a fundamental and irreversible shift of power to the Soviet Air Force. In the Kuban alone, the Soviets claimed to have destroyed 1,000 enemy aircraft. These losses by the Luftwaffe could not be easily replaced. Moreover, the Soviet aircraft production rate had increased threefold since December 1941, when aviation factories had resumed production beyond the Ural Mountains. Whereas in 1942 it took 20,000 man-hours to manufacture an Il-4 bomber, it now required only 12,500 man-hours.

With the quantity of production steadily increasing, the Soviets displayed improved skills at designing high-performance combat aircraft. At Kursk, the VVS introduced its La-5FN fighter to match the Luftwaffe's new Fw 190. As a radial-engine mutation of the ineffectual LaGG-3, the La-5 (later La-7) quickly achieved a rough parity with the FW 190. Between 6,500 and 13,000 feet, the Soviets claimed the La-5FN was 25 to 50 miles faster than the FW 190 in horizontal flight—and more maneuverable. In the savage air combat to come over Kursk, the VVS surpassed the Luftwaffe in total aircraft by 1.4 to 2.7 times, depending on the phase or circumstance of battle. The Soviets had twice as many fighters and enjoyed a superiority in absolute numbers in ground-attack planes. Only in day bombers did the Luftwaffe hold the advantage.[15]

The first test for the renewed Soviet Air Force came in May and June when the Luftwaffe launched a series of preparatory air strikes. German air units struck lines of communication, rail junctions, airfields, and supply depots. The first massed air raid on Kursk itself occurred on May 22, when the 170 German bombers attempted to knock out the rail terminal. This particular aerial incursion by the Luftwaffe did not go unchallenged. According to Soviet accounts, fighter aircraft from the 2d and 16th air armies, along with fighter aircraft from the 101st Fighter Air Division (PVO), intercepted the German bombers on the approaches to Kursk.[16]

Another raid by the Luftwaffe on June 2–3 again struck the Kursk rail terminal. More than 500 aircraft, including 424 bombers, participated in this mission, according to Soviet accounts. The combined day and night bombing raid prompted a spirited reaction by the VVS, which drew upon the 2d and 16th air armies for 280 fighters, along with air elements attached to the Kursk air defense zone. Coming in waves and from different directions, the Luftwaffe bombers successfully penetrated the Kursk air defenses and put the rail terminal out of action for twelve hours. Soviet historians list 145 German aircraft downed (104 by VVS fighters, forty-one by anti-aircraft fire) for the modest loss of twenty-seven fighters. They note that this massed air raid was an important bench mark, "the last major daytime raid by fascist aviation against Soviet rear facilities."[17]

During this same period six air armies (1st, 15th, 16th, 2d, 17th, and 8th) participated in one of the largest VVS air raids of the war, hitting between May 6 and 8 a number of German airfields situated along a 735-mile sector in the central part of the front opposite Kursk. Novikov aimed to disrupt the German air build-up for Operation Citadel, then in progress. A month later, the VVS again struck at German airfields—the Luftwaffe bomber air bases from which strategic bombing raids were being conducted against Soviet war industries at Gorki, Saratov, and Yaroslav.[18]

Such massive air raids were significant, for they demonstrated the growing strength and range of VVS operations. At best, the VVS bombers only weakened Luftwaffe air strength in the offensive zones (Soviet bomber units remained in 1943 the least effective branch of the now expanding VVS). Wherever attempted, bold daylight raids on Luftwaffe air bases proved costly in VVS aircraft, a fact concealed in Soviet histories of the air war in the east.

The Soviets, in fact, achieved greater success against the forward German airfields in their less spectacular night raids. The rapid increase in night bombing sorties on the eve of Kursk greatly alarmed the German command. Not only were airfields attacked, but the VVS night bombers, still largely the slow but nimble Po-2s, hit rail centers and supply depots filled with materiel earmarked for Operation Citadel. The Luftwaffe countered these attacks by deploying both light and heavy flak units at crucial points. The absence of Luftwaffe night fighters meant the VVS aircraft in large numbers could penetrate the combat zones. Among all the VVS wartime operations, the persistent and highly effective night bomber units have received the least attention.[19]

Over the Kursk salient the VVS continued the work of the *Okhotniki*, the "free hunters" first introduced into combat the previous winter at Stalingrad. Following the Stalingrad precedent, the VVS selected only its best fighter pilots to fly in *para* or *zveno* formations for this important work. The *Okhotniki* pilots displayed a uniform profile—experienced in combat and with demonstrated prowess as fliers, excellent marksmanship, and personal aggressiveness.[20] At Kursk, no flier joined such an elite unit without thorough schooling in the geography of the assigned combat zone.

While fighter pilots for the most part had been assigned as *Okhotniki* at Stalingrad, the VVS now broadened the scope of the free-hunt tactic at Kursk to include for the first time large numbers of Shturmovik pilots. By maintaining a continuous air presence in the enemy rear areas during the day—even in the extremes of weather—the *Okhotniki* applied enormous pressure on the Luftwaffe and the German anti-aircraft crews ordered to protect vital supply and communication lines. In groups of two to four aircraft, the *Okhotniki* roamed over their assigned zones as cunning and mobile predators, attacking trains, motorized columns, and infantry. Wherever they discovered a German train they hit the locomotive first, or if approaching a motorized column, the lead vehicle. The *Okhotniki*, in either fighter bombers or ground-attack planes, helped fill the acknowledged Soviet void in day bombers. Even so, they did not significantly interrupt the flow of German supplies and reserves. They did manage, however, to extend Soviet air power into the German rear and compel the hard-pressed Luftwaffe to diffuse its finite resources.

Operation Citadel, July 5–12, 1943

The script for Operation Citadel called for the German armies to begin their two-pronged drive on Kursk on the morning of July 5. Already alerted to the day and hour of the German offensive, the Soviets launched a bold predawn raid on five Luftwaffe airfields in the vicinity of Kharkov. More than 400 combat aircraft from the 2d and 17th air armies participated in this mission, which sought to catch the enemy bombers at the very moment they were assembling for their opening sorties against the Kursk salient. Soon after the large Soviet bomber formation was airborne, German radar detected the approaching aircraft. The Luftwaffe command quickly ordered fighters from the

Belgorod and Kharkov sectors—JG 3 "Udet" and JG 52 "Molders"—to meet the on-coming air armada. Just at the break of dawn the Soviet aircraft pierced the German-controlled airspace over Kharkov, to be met by waves of Bf 109s.

The resulting air engagement was one of the most spectacular of the war. More than 120 VVS aircraft were downed as Gen. Hans Jeschonnek, chief of the Luftwaffe General Staff, watched the air battle from a command post of the 8th Air Corps. German success came immediately as determined fighter pilots took a fearful toll of the attacking Soviet aircraft above 10,000 feet. When the Soviet bombers descended to begin their attack runs, German anti-aircraft units took their measure, scoring a series of dramatic hits. German losses were modest. The few Soviet attackers that survived the gauntlet of German fighters and ground fire failed to drop their bombs on the crowded German airfields. The failure of this preemptive strike in the south allowed the Luftwaffe a freer rein to assert local air superiority. A week passed before the VVS could reassert a strong air presence in the Belgorod-Kharkov sector.[21]

While Soviet historical sources remain vague about this air debacle, they describe in detail another air raid at Kharkov on the morning of July 5. According to this scenario, 132 VVS ground-attack planes, with an escort of 285 fighters, attacked eight German airfields. These Soviet air units, drawn from the 2d and 17th air armies, reported fifty enemy aircraft destroyed. The same Soviet accounts, however, admit that the raid failed to blunt the opening Luftwaffe air operations.[22] There is evidence that when the VVS aircraft arrived over the target zones, most of the German aircraft had already departed.

What happened over the skies of Kharkov during the first hours of Operation Citadel remains a murky episode in Soviet historical literature. Soviet silence on the abortive Kharkov raid has been largely unbroken. To deal with these events forthrightly and in detail would detract from the larger reputation for combat efficiency the VVS earned at Kursk. The Kharkov fiasco, then and now, has too many parallels with the devastating attrition of VVS bombers in the summer of 1941.[23]

Even as the air battle over Kharkov unfolded on July 5, two German spearheads moved forward on the ground, with close support by the Luftwaffe. The opening four days of Operation Citadel sparked intense air combat over the breakthrough corridors. During one phase of the battle—the advance of the 4th Panzer Army northward from Belgorod—an estimated 2,000 aircraft from both sides mingled in a fierce struggle for control of an airspace above a twelve-by-thirty-seven-mile sector. Sometimes as many as 150 aircraft tangled in fierce air combat. Farther north in the Orel sector, the Luftwaffe flew 2,800 sorties on the opening day in support of the German 9th Army in an area twenty-five miles wide and seven miles deep.[24]

Despite its foreknowledge of Operation Citadel and careful preparation, the VVS did not react swiftly to the Luftwaffe once the ground attack began. The initial setbacks over Kharkov in the south prompted confusion and hesitation. Heavy losses in Soviet aircraft—the Luftwaffe claimed 400 downed aircraft on the first day (the Germans claimed 400)—gave the Luftwaffe considerable flexibility and local air superiority in both attack zones. This freedom of action allowed German Stukas and the new Henshel He 129s to pro-

The Germans grew to respect the Soviets for their elaborate and effective efforts at camouflage. Here a "dummy" Stuka stands ready to confuse Soviet reconnaissance.

vide sustained air support, flying as many as five or six sorties during the course of the first day.[25]

Nevertheless, I. V. Timokhovich has described an active struggle on July 5 by VVS fighters in the Belgorod sector. In ninety-nine group air battles, Timokhovich claimed the VVS downed 175 enemy planes. The 8th Guards Fighter Division, commanded by Gen.-Maj. A. P. Galunov, scored seventy-six victories alone on July 5. Timokhovich also singled out three VVS fighter pilots of this elite air unit, who downed four planes each on the first day (Senior Lieutenants Belikov, Panin, and Bulayev).[26]

To the north in the Orel-Kursk axis, VVS fighters failed to challenge the Luftwaffe until the afternoon of July 5. This belated attempt to frustrate the large-scale German air operations over the Central front proved to be ineffectual, the Soviets losing as many as 110 aircraft by nightfall.[27] During the afternoon the VVS faced an augmented enemy air presence over the breakthrough corridor, which, according to one account included 300 German bombers, escorted by 100 fighters at one juncture. Against the Luftwaffe in this sector, the 16th Air Army flew 1,232 combat sorties, engaged in 76 group air battles, and by their own account scored 106 victories.[28] These Soviet claims have not been confirmed in German accounts. The air activity at Kursk on the first day of battle suggests that the VVS, despite its elaborate preparations, performed sluggishly against the determined Luftwaffe.

Once the VVS began to respond in force to the challenge of Operation Citadel there were many tactical errors. VVS fighters on occasion abandoned their primary targets—the German bombers and ground-attack planes—to engage enemy fighters. Tactical discipline frequently dissolved in a confusing spiral of overlapping air battles. The communications system failed at certain junctures, allowing German aircraft to deliver effective blows against Soviet defensive positions with no adequate alert or VVS response.[29]

Throughout the first day, Soviet air power showed little organization or capacity to direct concentrated air strikes against the Luftwaffe, even within the confined airspace over the breakthrough zones. The awkward debut of the VVS on July 5 had permitted the Luftwaffe to assert temporary air superiority.

On the second day of the battle, July 6, the VVS launched concentrated air strikes against the still-advancing German troops. This tactic corrected the opening day error of dissipating Soviet air power over the enemy's staging areas. On Rokossovskiy's Central front, the 16th Air Army, commanded by General Rudenko, made repeated assaults on German 9th Army units approaching the Ol'khovatka ridge, which was defended in depth by the Soviet 13th Army. The 6th Mixed Air Corps and the 2d Guards and 299th ground-attack divisions—a force of 450 airplanes—hit German infantry and tanks in the vicinity of Rodolyan and Soborovka.[30] Farther south, the 2d and 17th air armies made similar strikes in the Belgorod sector.

As the VVS applied more pressure on the German ground forces, front air commanders moved to a forward command post to assume direct control over air operations. For the first time the VVS units in both defensive zones began to perform their tasks with some discipline and in closer coordination with the ground forces. With improved air control and communications, VVS fighters managed to intercept enemy bombers and ground-attack planes more promptly. Furthermore, the VVS was able in these more organized circumstances to project Soviet air power into the German rear areas, frequently compelling the Luftwaffe fighters to abandon the ground-support role for air defense.[31]

Already by July 6 there were ominous signs for the German High Command of an impending defeat. The Soviet defensive system in the Central

German troops examine a downed Il-2 Shturmovik. The rugged construction of the "Il'yusha" is evident. (SI 80–18477)

and Voronezh fronts, organized with echelons of numerous anti-tank obstacles, frustrated the determined German advance at every point. These static defenses stood as effective barriers to Operation Citadel. In the air the VVS had recovered from its early setbacks and already had begun to apply significant pressure. Soviet losses remained high, but the VVS managed to apply intense pressure on the attacking enemy with its constant stream of replacement aircraft and air personnel.[32] Luftwaffe personnel at this point in the war retained their low opinion of the overall effectiveness of VVS units in training, tactics, and equipment, but the German air units soon found themselves struggling in vain against the growing VVS numbers.

Unable to sustain the level of the opening day's air operations, the Luftwaffe began to decline sharply in effectiveness. German fighters could achieve momentary air superiority only if concentrated and aggressive. The ubiquitous VVS squadrons at Kursk maintained a constant air pressure, and by sheer numbers asserted a measure of air ascendancy. An index of the Luftwaffe's decline was the steady decrease in the total number of combat sorties flown, down to only 2,100 on July 6, as opposed to 4,298 on the first day.[33]

During the intense air action over the Kursk on July 6, Ivan N. Kozhedub, later to be the Soviet Union's top ace, made his combat debut. Flying in Rudenko's 16th Air Army, Kozhedub had only recently joined his fighter regiment. Before Kursk, he had served as a flight instructor. Coming from a Ukrainian peasant background, Kozhedub at the age of twenty-three had the requisite humble origins to become an important Soviet war hero. His father had encouraged him to become an engineer, but as a youth Kozhedub's interest fixed on aviation.

Like Pokryshkin, Kozhedub followed with enthusiasm the prewar aerial feats of Soviet pilots, in particular the polar flights of Chkalov. After attending a technical school, Kozhedub received his pilot's license in 1940. On the eve of Barbarossa, he joined the Soviet Air Force and quickly displayed talent as a flier. Because of his flying skills, Kozhedub's superiors ordered him to remain as a flight instructor during the first year of the war. But Kozhedub was restive in this kind of duty in a rear area, and after repeated requests he finally received a combat assignment, joining a fighter unit near Moscow in November 1942. Here Kozhedub made the transition to the new Lavochkin La-5.

As with many great aces, Kozhedub's first encounter with the enemy nearly proved fatal. Flying a combat sortie north of Kursk, Kozhedub lost contact with his leader. Alone, he sighted a formation of German aircraft and recklessly dived toward them. His sweep, if unexpected, did little damage. Soon two Bf 109s pursued him aggressively, firing accurately and at close range. Kozhedub abruptly brought his damaged La-5 to lower altitudes to elude his pursuers, and then flew at tree-top level toward the Soviet lines. The damaged La-5, easily mistaken for its rival, the Fw 190, drew sporadic fire from Soviet anti-aircraft batteries, which shot away one of its wing tips. Kozhedub landed safely, but the experience dramatically illustrated the dangers of combat with the Luftwaffe, where boldness without flying technique usually proved fatal.

During the hectic days of Operation Citadel, Kozhedub repeatedly placed himself in dangerous situations, but his quick adaption to the rigors of air combat enabled him repeatedly to escape death. By the third day of Operation Citadel, he had destroyed two Ju 87s and two Bf 109s, receiving at the end of the Kursk hostilities the Order of the Red Banner and a promotion to the command of his own fighter squadron. During the subsequent Soviet campaign to cross the Dnieper River, Kozhedub in a burst of energy and skill scored eleven victories in ten days in some of the most bitter air combat of the war. His most impressive display of combat skill came in 1944 over Rumania, where he downed eight German planes in one week. On February 15, 1945, he shot down an Me 262. He ended the war with sixty-two victories, becoming the top-scoring Allied ace.[34]

By July 7 Operation Citadel faced an increasing tempo of Soviet air and ground resistance in both attack zones. Because of the high attrition rate, the Luftwaffe managed only 1,152 sorties on this day in the Orel sector. During the next two days the drop in this zone was more precipitous, being reduced to a mere 350 sorties on July 9. By contrast, the VVS 15th Air Army in this same sector flew 1,070 sorties on July 8, and at the end of the defensive stage of the Kursk fighting, on July 12, had flown a total of 7,600.[35]

By July 9 the 16th Air Army had launched an air strike of its own—a massed sweep of 150 ground-attack aircraft and bombers against the German 9th Panzer Division in the area of Soborovki. German air operations continued, but now in inverse proportion to the Soviet air action. On July 10 the Soviets observed that the German Army had been effectively stalled, particularly in its effort to overrun the Ol'khovatka ridge in the Orel-Kursk sector.

As the German offensive faltered in the north, the attention of both sides focused on the Prokhorovka sector to south of Kursk, where on July 12 the largest tank battle in history took place. Here, the Soviets chronicle a massive, overlapping battle of 1,200 tanks throughout the day. VVS ground-attack aircraft participated actively in the repeated armored clashes. Col. I. S. Polbin, commander of the 1st Bomber Air Corps and the Soviet equivalent of Hans-Udrich Rudel, led Soviet ground-attack and bomber units against the heavy concentration of German tanks and artillery, scoring a significant number of victories. Colonel Polbin's unit and Shturmoviks from the 1st Ground-Attack Air Corps and the 291st Ground-Attack Air Division fought a savage, day-long battle in support of P. A. Rotmistrov's 5th Guards Tank Army.

Waves of ground-attack aircraft from both sides appeared over the battlefield, fighting each other and attacking ground targets. At the end of the Prokhorovka battle the Germans still held the field, but they had lost over 300 tanks. Soviet losses equaled the German, but the muscular Soviet replacement capacity meant an immediate resupply of equipment for the VVS air units. For the Germans, on the ground and in the air, there was no way to match the quantitative edge held by the Soviets. After two years of war, Kursk exposed a grim reality for the Germans. They lacked the striking power, reserves, and mobility to crush the Soviets, even in a summer offensive.

At the end of the defensive period of the Battle of Kursk, on July 12, the VVS had a tenuous control of the airspace over Kursk.[36] The Luftwaffe still held a decided edge in qualitative categories, in particular in training and air-combat tactics, but these attributes were not sufficient to deny the VVS local air superiority. If properly mobilized and concentrated, German air units could still assert momentary air domination over a small sector of the front. They would do so in the weeks to come. But as the first phase of the Battle of

Kursk revealed, the Luftwaffe could not sustain a powerful air presence over the entire front. After July 6 the ability of the Luftwaffe to suppress VVS air operations, even in the narrow combat sectors, declined sharply.

Conversely, VVS fighters and Shturmoviks roamed over the battle zones and into the German rear with alarming boldness and frequency. For the entire defensive stage, July 5–12, the VVS averaged 1,500 sorties per day, a figure far higher than in any previous period of VVS air operations.[37]

Soviet sources state that the VVS destroyed around 1,400 German aircraft during the German offensive at Kursk (517 on the Orel-Kursk axis, 899 on the Belgorod-Kursk axis).[38] While these histories abound in statistics on VVS air armies, the types of aircraft deployed, totals of sorties flown, and the variety of air missions completed, there is a conspicuous absence of data on VVS aircraft losses.

One Soviet writer, M. N. Kozhevnikov, *Komandovaniye i shtab VVS Sovetskoy Armii v Velikoy Otechestvennoy voyne 1941–1945 g.g.*, has provided a rare, if oblique, glimpse into this shadowy aspect of Soviet war statistics. Kozhevnikov's coverage of the first four days of Operation Citadel (July 5–8) records fragmentary data on Soviet air losses.[39] By combining these scattered references one obtains a portrait of intense air combat during the opening phases of the Battle of Kursk (Table 3).

The Soviet acknowledgement of more than 500 aircraft losses suggests in a dramatic way the attrition endured by the VVS in its aggressive effort to challenge the Luftwaffe for local superiority at Kursk. These admitted air losses by the VVS, apart from the debate about their precise accuracy, breaks unwittingly an official silence on Soviet attrition. Kozhevnikov's fragmentary data confirm that German air power, if on the decline in the east, remained viable and potent in 1943. The Kozhevnikov claim of 854 Luftwaffe aircraft downed for the same four-day period over Kursk appears to be an exaggeration, a convenient counterpoint to make the Soviet losses seem less devastating. Yet the overall Luftwaffe attrition rate on the Eastern front remained high in the summer of 1943, much higher than normally assumed: a loss of 487 combat aircraft over Kursk and 785 in August during the Soviet counteroffensive.[40]

The Soviet Counteroffensive at Kursk (July–August, 1943)

The *Stavka*'s elaborate blueprint for the defense of Kursk was linked to a bold plan for a major counteroffensive. With the Germans weakened and seriously off-balance at Kursk, the Soviets launched their first strategic summer offensive of the war. The immediate goals were the German positions above and

Table 3
Aircraft Losses at Kursk (July 5–8, 1943)

Date (July)	Luftwaffe	VVS
5	260	176
6	217	171
7	211	122
8	166	97
Total	854	566

below Kursk, at Orel and Kharkov. Once these cities had been secured, the Soviet forces moved westward in late August toward the Dnieper River. This counteroffensive extended along a broad front and resulted in December in a dramatic series of victories, which included the liberation of Kiev and the sealing off of the German forces in the Crimean Peninsula. By the end of 1943 the Soviets had reasserted their control over 386,000 square miles of territory.

The collapse of the German offensive at Kursk had been evident before Hitler ordered the cancellation of Operation Citadel on July 17. Even as the epic tank battle at Prokhorovka unfolded on July 12, the Soviets launched a major attack in the Orel sector. This strategic counteroffensive coincided with the Allied invasion of Sicily. Soviet troops of the Central, Bryansk, and Western fronts overwhelmed stubborn German opposition, occupying Orel on July 19. By August 3 the *Stavka* ordered the Voronezh and Steppe fronts to take the offensive in the Belgorod-Kharkov sector. After bitter street fighting, Kharkov fell again, and for the last time, to Soviet troops.

The *Stavka* gave its formidable air armada a prominent place in this Kursk counteroffensive: first to establish air control over the battle zones to protect the advancing Soviet troops and armored units; and then to provide sustained air support along the breakthrough corridors. The Soviet use of air power at Kursk called for concentrated air strikes in cooperation with ground forces, to be followed by graduated air sorties into the enemy's rear areas.[41]

To blunt the growing Soviet air power, the Luftwaffe exercised a tight stewardship over its waning air strength. Such control dictated the application of air power only in those decisive combat sectors, abandoning for the most part the crucial Soviet rear areas. The Luftwaffe faced the unrelenting task of supporting the hard-pressed German frontline troops. These wide-ranging assignments nearly exhausted its remaining operational strength. No diversified, large-scale air operations typical of 1941 could be sustained for any length of time. The number of Luftwaffe aircraft was fewer in 1943 than in 1941. Moreover, the loss rate was particularly high in the contested air-space over the frontlines, ample logistical support was rarely in place, and the low serviceability of many air units now reached alarming proportions.

While these negative factors shaped Luftwaffe air operations at Kursk, the VVS steadily increased its operational range. Soviet air power began to extend as far as fifteen miles into the German rear. Such Soviet combat sorties hit German supply routes, storage areas, and airfields. The VVS's night bombing also increased dramatically at the time of Kursk, providing another serious problem for the hard-pressed German air-defense units. The Luftwaffe continued to maintain its technical superiority over the VVS, but the impact of superior Soviet numbers was evident. Persistent attacks by the Soviets made an impression, and with each passing month the improvement in VVS air tactics became clearer. German observers found the ground-attack units especially hard-hitting and effective.[42]

For the Orel counteroffensive, the VVS entered combat with more than 3,000 aircraft against an estimated 1,100 German aircraft. Three Soviet air armies attacked on three sides of German-occupied Orel: the 1st Air Army of the West front (Gen.-Lt. M. M. Gromov); the 15th Air Army of the Bryansk front (Gen.-Lt. N. F. Naumenko); and the 16th Air Army of the Central front (General Rudenko). From the Air Corps of the *Stavka* Reserve, selected air

A downed Soviet pilot (right) is questioned by German pilots. Note that he is wearing the gold star, Hero of the Soviet Union. Courtesy of Prentice-Hall, Inc.

units moved to the frontline airfields to augment Soviet air strength. The 1st Air Army, for example, expanded its operational strength with the addition of the 2d Bomber, 2d Ground-Attack, and 8th Fighter Air Corps units. The other participating air armies received similar reinforcements. Only in day bombers did the VVS display any inferiority in numbers to the Luftwaffe in the Orel sector. These timely reinforcements made the Luftwaffe's position extremely difficult at the very moment that German troops in the Orel sector faced the dangers of encirclement.[43]

At Orel the VVS assumed a combat role consistent with its size and capability. In the preliminary phases, the VVS made full use of its air-reconnaissance squadrons, which by 1943 had achieved a new level of maturity. Prior to the actual launching of the offensive, the VVS directed its air activity into the enemy's rear areas with steady blows from its night bombers. Coordination and communication with partisan units reached a new level of efficiency at Kursk.

Against the Luftwaffe's 6th Air Fleet and the entrenched German defenses around Orel, the VVS assumed an aggressive posture. The weight of VVS air power fell on narrow breakthrough corridors of the Soviet offensive. The enemy conceded ground at Orel only after considerable Soviet effort and sacrifice. Along the Bryansk breakthrough sector the Luftwaffe opposition turned out to be aggressive, even in the face of overwhelming VVS numbers. At Bolkhovsk, north of Orel, the VVS played an important role helping the Western and Bryansk armies break the stubborn German ground opposition.

The VVS maintained considerable pressure on the stubborn German defenders by deploying bombers in concentrated attacks. These bombing missions began on July 11, when ADD and bomber units from the 15th Air Army hit German defenses near Novosil (east of Orel). Another attack followed on July 12, which included bomber and ground-attack aircraft. As the bomber and ground-attack sorties increased in tempo in the weeks leading up to the fall of Orel, the VVS achieved a smoother coordination with other components of the Soviet armed forces. Along the breakthrough corridors, Soviet accounts describe a devastating combination of air and ground forces hurled against the retreating Germans.[44]

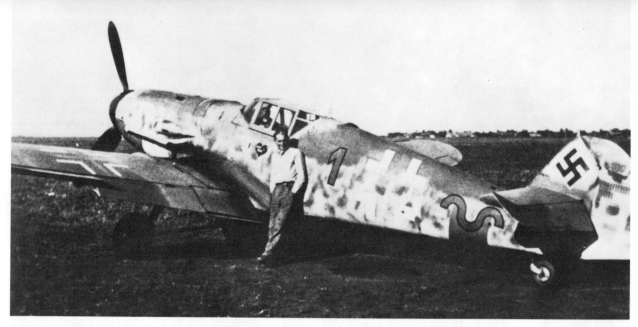

Erich Hartman, top-scoring German ace (352 victories), stands beside his Messerschmitt Bf 109 fighter. Courtesy of Prentice-Hall, Inc.

Ground crew greets Erich Hartman as he makes a sweep over the field after another air victory. Courtesy of Prentice-Hall, Inc.

Soviet infantry and tanks moved forward with powerful air support. The Soviets claimed a sharp reduction in Luftwaffe sorties over Orel in the last week of July, a clear indication that the VVS had achieved superiority in the air. Domination of the skies allowed the VVS to turn back German bombers and to strike at retreating German troops with Shturmovik and Pe-2 bombers. By August 8 Soviet troops had cleared the Orel sector of enemy forces. The Soviets claimed that they had destroyed twenty-one German divisions. The VVS had flown 60,995 sorties in the counteroffensive at Orel.

Over Kharkov the VVS achieved similar successes. Kharkov occupied a strategic place in the designs of both armies. In the aftermath of Stalingrad the Soviets had retaken the city, only to lose it to the German troops under Manstein in February 1943. Now in ruins, the city remained a key to German hopes of stabilizing the Eastern front.

The Soviet attack, via Belgorod, began in earnest on August 3, just on the eve of the fall of Orel. Again, the VVS applied its growing tactical air power in close cooperation with the advancing ground forces. On the night before the Belgorod counteroffensive, bomber units from ADD flew a total of 370 sorties against German defensive positions. This air preparation strike signaled a more extensive series of raids, which followed the next day. VVS ground-attack planes and bombers from the 2d and 5th air armies flew repeated missions to provide close air support of the Soviet Army during the crucial first twenty-four hours of the counter-offensive.[45] At the same time, the *Stavka* ordered the VVS fighter arm, which now enjoyed a three to one edge, to move in force over the battle zone and clear it of all enemy aircraft.

Careful planning, according to the Soviets, preceded the application of VVS tactical air power at Kharkov. Between July 26 and 30 the staffs of the two Soviet air armies met with infantry and tank commanders to elaborate precise plans for mutual cooperation. Special command posts of the 2d and 5th air armies were established a mere four to five miles from the front and tied into the network of command.[46]

By August 11–17 the VVS had achieved a powerful momentum in the south. With Generals Vorozheykin and Khudyakov serving as liaison officers for the *Stavka*, the VVS air armies launched an air offensive of unparalleled magnitude. VVS air pressure appeared not only on the forward edge of the Soviet advance, but in the German rear, where enemy reserves moved forward to plug holes in the lines.[47] When German troops withdrew, by choice or under fire, the VVS attempted to pin them down. At the height of the Soviet offensive, the VVS committed anywhere from 50 to 80 percent of its daily sorties to close air support, covering Soviet tank corps movements in particular.[48]

During the drive on Kharkov the VVS hit German rear airfields to weaken enemy opposition. On August 4 a group of twelve Il-2s escorted by eight Yak-1s attacked one German airfield in the Mikoyanovsk region, destroying fifteen enemy planes and a fuel-storage area. Backed by careful air reconnaissance, the raid took place at dusk and involved selected pilots who had been thoroughly briefed on the terrain. Again, on August 10, the VVS with 24 Il-2s and 15 Yak-1s struck at two other airfields. According to Soviet records, another twenty enemy aircraft were destroyed. The VVS displayed considerable discipline during the actual attack phase—some Il-2s bombing the anti-aircraft facilities, others strafing and bombing the parked aircraft. Both attacks were conducted at low altitudes to achieve surprise and the maximum concentration of firepower.[49]

The Il'yushin Il-2 Shturmovik emerged at Kursk as the potent wartime symbol of Soviet air power, much like the Zero for Japan and the Spitfire for the Royal Air Force. With its simple design and rugged construction, the Il-2 adapted well to the rigorous requirements on the Eastern front. The Soviets would produce 36,000 of these aircraft during the war.[50] Called affectionately the "Il'yusha" by the Shturmovik pilots, the Il-2 made a significant contribution to the Soviet victory at Kursk, flying countless sorties against German troops and tanks. Against the German 9th Panzer Division, Shturmoviks had destroyed seventy tanks in twenty minutes on July 7, 1943. In a four-hour assault on the 17th Panzer Division, Il-2s destroyed 240 tanks out of an approximate strength of 300, according to the Soviets. Shturmovik units flew with inordinate bravery and suffered enormous casualties. The heavily armored Il-2, called the "flying tank" by its designer, S. V. Il'yushin, proved to be a ubiquitous tactical weapon. Joseph Stalin, in a letter to the aviation factory workers early in the war, stated poignantly the value of the Il'yusha: "They are as essential to the Red Army as air and bread."[51]

Even while the Battle of Kursk raged, Il'yushin, in an article in *Pravda* (August 18, 1943), explained to the Soviet public the genesis of the Il-2 Shturmovik. He asserted that Soviet air doctrine had rejected Douhet's notion that an air force, acting independently, could decide the outcome of a future war. "It was clear to us that air forces would primarily be used in joint operations with land armies and the navy. Therefore, our design ideas were directed toward aircraft that would render the most effective assistance to the ground forces of Red Army."[52]

Il'yushin and his design team had begun work in 1938 on the TsKB-55, the Il-2 prototype, a low-wing, single-engine monoplane, powered by a liquid-cooled 12-cyclinder engine designed by A. Mikulin (the AM-38). For Il'yushin the targets for the future Il-2 would be enemy tanks, motor vehicles, artillery, and infantry. This meant combat sorties conducted at low level—at altitudes of 30 to 6,000 feet—with a diverse set of weapons: machine guns, cannon, bombs, and rockets.

The word "Shturmovik" in the broader sense applied to all ground-attack types, but with time it became associated with the Il-2, a merger of aircraft type and model in popular nomenclature comparable to the German use of "Stuka" for the Junkers 87.[53] Il'yushin viewed his creation as "a new type of aircraft," an air-combat weapon uniquely suited to ground support for a large continental army operating in the vast geographical expanse of the Soviet Union.[54]

Central to the design of the Il-2 as an assault aircraft (*bronirovannyy shturmovik*) was its armored shell (*bronekorpus*), which enclosed the engine and cockpit. The armored shell (the AB-2), developed at the All-Union Institute for Aviation Materials, combined toughness with relative lightness. Shturmovik pilots found the cockpit within the armored shell a secure environment. "In it," A. N. Yefimov wrote, "you felt protected against all dangers during operations under enemy fire. This was especially important, as I learned later, not so much for the wingman as for the element leader. The wingman had to do what the leader did and follow him. The leader, who had to break through to the target and lead the entire formation to it, had to overcome a psychological barrier at a certain moment and exert a serious effort of will power in order to swoop down, head-on into the fatal danger, through the dense shroud of anti-aircraft bursts. . . . But, it was not easy to force a pilot out of the attack. The Il-2 was well disposed to combat. It invited you to attack."[55]

The first Il-2, called the "hunchback" by Soviet pilots, was a one-seater which appeared in the Battle for Moscow in the fall of 1941.[56] This version demonstrated considerable potential, but Shturmovik pilots complained that it was underpowered, insufficiently armed, and difficult to maneuver.[57] At Tula, south of Moscow, the Il-2 regiments made their first large-scale appearance in November 1941. While immune from light ground fire, the Il-2, with its slow speeds and sluggish maneuvering characteristics, became vulnerable to Luftwaffe fighters. German fighter pilots discovered that the most effective

Il-2 Shturmoviks on the attack. These photographs, taken by a German cameraman, demonstrate the typical low-level sweeps made by Shturmovik pilots. Courtesy of Prentice-Hall, Inc.

approach was to fire on the one-seater Il-2 at close range from above and behind.

The Il-2M3 eventually succeeded the Il-2 and embodied a series of refinements which dramatically increased the effectiveness of Il'yushin's initial design. It was a two-seater with a rear gunner armed with a 12.7mm Berezin machine gun. To enhance its firepower as an anti-tank weapon the Soviets fitted a 23mm cannon (VYa-23) to the Il-2M3, later to be replaced by a 37mm cannon (NS-37). The AM-38 engine had not been effective, since it lacked sufficient horsepower. Without the requisite power, the Il-2 required long take-off runs from the rough grass strips. In the air, it displayed little maneu-

Rear view of an Il-2 with
ground crew. Courtesy of
Carl-Fredrik Geust.

verability with this engine. The augmented AM-38F provided a solution to
these problems with its take-off rating of 1,750 horsepower.[58] Certain refinements were also made in the outer wing panels to give the Il-2M3 cleaner
lines and greater stability.[59]

By the time of Kursk the Il-2M3 had evolved into a powerful weapons
platform. With 37mm cannon, rockets, and the new PTAB 2.5 hollow-charge
anti-tank bombs, the Shturmovik units became the main tactical attack force
of the VVS. They not only performed ground-attack duties, but assumed the
additional role of short-range daylight bombers.[60] Shturmoviks could hit German positions with impressive striking power—7mm cannon, 1,000-pound
bomb loads, and eight rockets.

Over time, Shturmovik air crews developed flying techniques to maximize the Il-2's combat effectiveness against individual enemy targets. VVS pilots preferred to make sudden strikes at targets right on the deck, sometimes
at no more than fifteen feet, firing cannon and rockets at close range. This
tactic, executed in small groups, a *para* or *zveno*, worked well against infantry and motorized columns. When attacking a fixed position or a target requiring pin-point accuracy, the Il-2 pilot entered a shallow dive from around
2,625 feet.

The circle method, or "circle of death," became the third—and the most
lethal—tactic employed by VVS Shturmovik units in 1943. In this, the Il-2s
approached a target in line astern, diving sequentially with the first plane
forming a loop. The circle would then be maintained until the objective was
destroyed or the ammunition ran out. Such a circle could be formed with one
zveno or a *gruppa* combination. As a closed loop, the circle provided effective
defensive fire against enemy fighters. Always wary of the effective German
anti-aircraft fire, each Shturmovik pilot maneuvered within the formation to

his best advantage—he could change altitude above or below the flight leader, reduce or increase the spacing between aircraft, and even turn slightly away if he continued to hold course.[61]

Shturmovik pilot Yefimov found the low-altitude surprise attacks on German airfields to be effective. In one raid his squadron struck at dawn: "The Hitlerites were not expecting our raid. The airfield was just beginning to stir. There were aircraft packed close together on hardstands. Evidently, the enemy anti-aircraft gunners would "sleep through" our arrival. They did not fire a single shot while we were making our passes on the target . . . the first formation had dropped delayed-action bombs directly on the fascist bombers, which was followed in a few seconds by a powerful explosion. The enemy aircraft were burning. The airfield was shrouded in black smoke."

A second sweep of the German field stoked the fires, transforming the airfield into a large pocket of fire—"The fascists were not able to save a single aircraft." The image of closely packed planes burning in place after repeated strafing evoked not too distant memories of Barbarossa, when the VVS had suffered similar depredations.[62]

Soviet pilots such as Yefimov admired the simplicity of the Il-2. "The process of flying it was not difficult when operating over the target or in air combat, the pilots' attention was not distracted by any difficult manipulations of instruments or equipment in the cockpit."[63] Moreover, Soviet estimates of the Il-2 have consistently pointed to its maneuverability, its easy control, and its forgiving character. From this perspective the Il-2, or more specifically the Il-2M3, allowed inexperienced Shturmovik pilots to enter abrupt maneuvers or even commit serious flying errors without fear of spins or loss of control.

Some western assessments of the Il-2 have been less favorable, seeing the aircraft as too slow, too heavy, and lacking in responsive controls. The Germans tested some captured early models of the Il-2 (not the Il-2M3) and gave them low marks for their handling characteristics, but they expressed considerable admiration for the bravery of the air crews. And as the number of Il-2 Shturmoviks mushroomed in 1943, the Luftwaffe acknowledged the growing effectiveness and striking power of the Soviet ground-attack air arm.[64]

Both German and Soviet combatants grew to appreciate the Il-2's durability. Lt. N. I. Dolzhanskiy's experience at Kursk was typical. Flying as a wingman, he was hit repeatedly by fire from German fighters, which damaged his engine. With an abrupt loss of power, Dolzhanskiy had no choice but to fly his plane into a thick woods. The armored shell protected the pilot and rear gunner despite the violence of the forced landing into a cluster of large trees. Both men returned to their regiment.[65]

Damaged Il-2s had to be repaired under primitive conditions: a bent propeller straightened out with a sledge hammer; wings and tail sections, if severely damaged, replaced in open-air revetments; or an engine removed and a new one installed in the course of a "single cold night." With its strong landing gear, the Il-2 withstood the formidable challenges of primitive VVS airfields. The landing gear survived the worst treatment of man and nature: crude landings, punctured wheels, belly-in maneuvers, and the ravages of snow, mud, and dust. Shturmovik pilots joked, "You can begin taxiing the Il-2 at an altitude of 50 meters."[66]

During the war few outsiders gained access to frontline Soviet airfields to observe firsthand the operational life of a VVS air unit. One rare glimpse came on the eve of Kursk, June 5, 1943, when a group of Royal Air Force officers inspected a Shturmovik regiment near Kaluga. Their impressions, later to be contained in an air intelligence report to the British Joint Staff Mission in Washington, D.C., gave confirmation to the growing power of Soviet ground-attack aviation; also, their reactions to VVS personnel, equipment, and combat tactics suggested that the VVS, circa 1943, embodied an amalgam of strengths and weaknesses.[67]

The one-day visit by the British began with a fifty-minute flight in a Lend-Lease DC-3 from Moscow to an area south of Kaluga, about 118 miles distant from the Soviet capital. One of the British observers found the Soviet attention to camouflage impressive. "The steps taken to conceal this aerodrome are most effective. The DC-3 approached the aerodrome in conditions of perfect visibility, but even after the pilot throttled back to land it was impossible to identify the aerodrome until a landing T had been put out."

Called a "field aerodrome," it was situated just south of a cluster of woods with a "very rough and undulating" grass strip some 2,000 yards in length. There were no buildings or service roads to suggest its presence. All the aircraft—a Shturmovik regiment of thirty to forty airplanes—were concealed in the neighboring woods. Despite its makeshift character, the Soviet divisional commander told his British guests that the airfield was new, one of the best in the sector, and he would have no hesitation using the field for a-1 medium bombers, including Bostons (A-20 Havocs), and all fighters except Airacobras. At the time, the Shturmovik regiment stationed at the field was attached to the 1st Air Army (Western front), which a month later would participate in the Soviet counteroffensive against Orel.

The British delegation spent the entire day talking to VVS officers and pilots, inspecting the Il-2 Shturmoviks and asking questions about VVS ground-attack operations. The regimental commander explained that he received his operational orders by telephone or R/T transmission from divisional headquarters. Further questioning revealed that the Shturmovik unit and the forward command posts used a single frequency, which created considerable confusion and compromised the regimental commander's effort to maintain air control during combat missions. For the Shturmovik pilots, who operated within a range of ninety-three miles of the Kaluga airfield, there were also significant navigational problems over the vast terrain. The hedge-hopping fliers overcame these problems by thoroughly learning the details of the terrain in their sector, studying maps and reconnaissance photographs, and making use of the radio compass, which had been recently installed as standard equipment in all Shturmovik aircraft. Crews remained in one area as long as possible, the British visitors were told, to take full advantage of their growing familiarity with the landscape.

While at the Kaluga airfield, the British officers watched a demonstration of an Il-2 Shturmovik attacking a line of wooden frames constructed at one end of the airstrip. The results were mixed. The author of the intelligence report found the demonstration not very convincing: "none of the aircraft took any avoiding action after making their attacks, some bombs were dropped from about 100 feet and failed to explode and one aircraft had engine failure during takeoff and had to force land with the undercarriage retracted."

There were some direct hits and near misses. None of the 82mm and

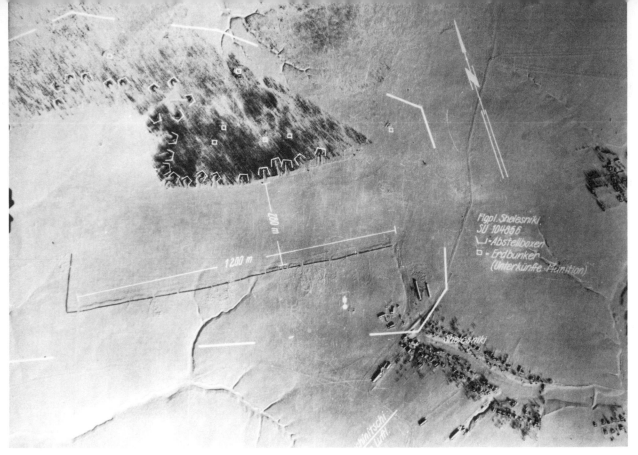

A German aerial reconnaissance photograph of a Soviet airfield. Taken in the winter of 1943, this photo reveals clearly the typical layout of a Soviet airbase. The woods adjacent to the town of Shelesniki housed revetments (Abstellboxen) for the aircraft and earthen bunkers (Erdbunker) for billets and munitions. The nearby village of Shelesniki no doubt provided housing for some of the air personnel. Courtesy of National Archives via Jay Spenser.

132mm rockets hit their targets, although some came close. The British observers noted the absence of dive breaks on the Il-2s, which dictated shallow dives from 800 feet at no more than 30 degrees or level attacks. The Il-2 aircraft itself, upon closer examination, prompted considerable interest on the part of the British, who used the occasion to gather detailed information on its armament and flying characteristics. The 7mm armor plating of the Il-2, along with 12mm armor plating at the rear of the cockpit and 52mm bullet-proof glass windscreen, gave substance to the Shturmovik pilot's faith in the ability of the aircraft to withstand punishment. Each aircraft was housed in an open, blast-proof shelter made of earth and wood. The maintenance crews lived in adjacent dugouts, while aircraft crews lived in a nearby village.

Such a visit, as brief as it was controlled in its scope, prompted considerable curiosity on the part of the British visitors, but answers, they discovered, were not always forthcoming from their Soviet hosts. One area—the attrition rate of the Il-2 in battle—was not available from the divisional commander despite persistent inquiries.

Toward their erstwhile Russian allies the British in their report displayed the appropriate wartime deference: "The Red General Staff have been asked to supply casualty figures for the Il-2, so that a more comprehensive picture of the value of this class of aircraft could be obtained." It is doubtful such a query was ever answered. Despite a floodtide of Soviet memoirs and histories in recent decades, many based on archival research, such questions remain unanswered.

While it is difficult to establish precise norms about the operational style of Shturmoviks, one can point to the Soviet preference for low-level attacks.

This approach allowed greater surprise and concentration of firepower. Shturmovik pilots learned to exploit shrewdly the natural advantages of sun, clouds, and terrain. German anti-aircraft fire, if intense and accurate, could force ground-attack formations to abandon their hedgehopping bravado and assume higher altitude for their attack runs. But the acquisition of altitude remained modest, normally 2,000 feet—4,000 feet being the upper limit.

In making their attacks, Shturmovik formations deployed a portion of their number to suppress enemy anti-aircraft fire. Sometimes in the absence of precise reconnaissance data, certain aircraft flew behind the main formation to observe the enemy defensive fire. Once determined, they moved aggressively against these anti-aircraft positions. If the enemy batteries were clearly known, this special unit would strike them in advance of the attack by the main formation. VVS fighter escorts, always an important component in Soviet ground-attack operations, attacked enemy ground fire if no opposition materialized.

Soviet ground-attack aviation flew against the enemy in all kinds of weather. One of the most impressive attributes of Shturmovik crews was their ability to fly in extremely low clouds, fog, bitter cold, and snow storms.

A Turning Point

In the Soviet counteroffensive at Kursk, the VVS had executed its first large-scale "air offensive." Massed attacks by Il-2s became a familiar scene in the Soviet script. The Soviets sought to make tactical air power complementary, either a protective panoply or part of the cutting edge along the main avenues of attack. During artillery preparations, Shturmoviks attacked targets just beyond the range of the guns. Such attacks extended the Soviet fire to the immediate rear of the enemy's frontlines. The constant strafing, bombing, and rocket barrages—often at low altitude—created confusion and prevented the enemy from making the necessary counterstrikes to halt a breakthrough by Soviet troops. Ground-attack units also moved with designated tank for-

An La-7 fighter. This updated version of the Lavochkin became an important Soviet fighter in the last two years of the war. Ivan Kozhedub, the top-scoring Soviet ace (sixty-two victories), downed a Messerschmitt Me 262 jet fighter in an La-7 in April 1945. (SI 81-2804)

American Lend-Lease A-20 Havocs were used extensively by the Soviets. At a command post on the Karelian front, A-20s are dispatched for a combat mission. The flag is the banner of the Soviet Air Force. Courtesy of USAF.

mations as they broke into the enemy's rear area. Shturmoviks assisted the advance on the ground, protected the flanks, and, at Kursk, participated in a major way in the destruction of enemy tanks and armored vehicles.[68]

At Orel and Kharkov the VVS demonstrated with its Shturmoviks the lethal power of a Soviet air offensive. For the first time, the air force high command put the air offensive concept into operational practice on a large scale. Wherever Soviet troops advanced, the VVS appeared in strength, attacking enemy tanks, artillery, and defensive positions. Along the attack corridors, and in depth behind the enemy lines, Soviet bombers and ground-attack aircraft swept down on their targets. Overhead, VVS fighter squadrons, providing a protective panoply, aggressively challenged the Luftwaffe for local air superiority. When Soviet forces penetrated the enemy's tactical defense zone, the VVS, always deployed along the cutting edge, provided cover for tanks and infantry, suppressed enemy artillery, and attempted to isolate forward German troops from their reserves. Such aggressive and sustained air operations at Kursk were costly in men and machines. The VVS effort, if exacting in attrition, achieved the strategic initiative in the air.

The intense struggle for the air continued after the dramatic Soviet air victories at Orel and Kharkov. Three VVS air armies, the 16th, 2d, and 5th, supported the efforts of the Central, Voronezh, and Steppe fronts in the general Soviet offensive to cross the Dnieper River and capture Kiev. Together these air armies had a force of 1,450 aircraft against a Soviet estimate of 900 German aircraft. From late August to December 1943, the VVS assisted the army in a series of fast-moving drives to outflank the enemy, to establish river bridgeheads, and to destroy pockets of resistance.

The 16th Air Army, supporting the Central front, engaged in a number of fierce duels with the Luftwaffe. At Nezhin, at the Desna River, and at the Dnieper north of Kiev, VVS units from the 16th Air Army provided support for advancing Soviet troops. Farther south, the VVS performed a similar role, often without established airfields or sure logistical support. Even as these air operations unfolded, the 17th and 8th air armies participated in the concurrent Soviet drive to liberate the Don Basin below Kursk. At Taganrog, Shturmovik units played an important part in breaking German defenses. Soviet air power became an important weapon in this sector, harassing retreating German columns.

When Soviet troops successfully crossed the right (western) bank of the Dnieper River at several points in October, German air attacks increased in tempo. The VVS again faced the challenge of maintaining control of the air—in this case over the Dnieper bridgeheads. During this period, Lt. K. A. Yevstigneyev, squadron commander of the 240th Fighter Air Regiment, displayed his skills in the contested air space over the Dnieper, shooting down twelve enemy aircraft in nine air battles. Yevstigneyev, a two-time recipient of the gold star, Hero of the Soviet Union, ended the war as the fourth-ranking VVS ace (fifty-six victories).

The fall of Kiev on November 6 and the subsequent consolidation of the Soviet Dnieper bridgehead provided a triumphal conclusion to the epic battle of Kursk. The ability of the VVS to maintain active operations in the general offensive following the intense Kursk fighting clearly indicated the maturing operational skills of the air armies, the ability of the *Stavka* and air force planners to mobilize and deploy air power effectively, and the capacity of rear services to sustain air operations over vast distances. This experience, of course, would be important for the final period of the war beginning in 1944.

Among all the factors explaining Soviet success at the Dnieper was the decided numerical advantage the VVS enjoyed over the Luftwaffe. With this vast quantitative edge, at times ten to one, the VVS could choose the time to assert air superiority. German air personnel learned the grim truth that the VVS in 1943 had acquired a new competence born of battle experience and upgraded air tactics. After Kursk, the Luftwaffe no longer possessed the means to win any sustained air battle with the Soviets.

For Soviet historiography the Battle of Kursk concluded the second period of the Great Patriotic War. From the launching of the Soviet counteroffensive at Stalingrad on November 19, 1942, to the end of December 1943, the Soviet Union had fought and seized the strategic initiative from the Germans. The VVS, with its expanding inventory of aircraft and new combat tactics, had flown with renewed confidence against the technologically superior enemy. As each month passed, the VVS asserted its increasing numerical superiority, compelling the Luftwaffe after Kursk to go over on the defensive.[69]

Along with a display of its maturing operational art at Kursk, the VVS leadership forged a more efficient pattern of coordination with the army. Most of these dramatic improvements grew out of Air Commander Novikov's reorganization of 1942. Novikov had stressed centralization and the close interaction of air power with the ground forces. At Kursk this imperative dominated Soviet Air Force operational planning. Front commanders met with the staffs of the air armies to establish unified procedures. VVS air corps and air division commanders assumed positions at command posts of the ground forces during battle to achieve more effective air-ground interaction. Air reconnaissance now played a more crucial role in supplying essential information on the enemy's deployment and movement. The increased scope of air force operations in 1943, to meet the shifting defensive and offensive requirements of the Soviet Army, called for the constant perfection of operational planning skills.

Squadrons of VVS fighter aircraft had flown over the Kursk battle zones with greater discipline, providing cover and assuming the additional tactical role of fighter-bombers. The improved combat discipline came as a result of the broad use of radio control. VVS command posts, now fully integrated into the larger army network of communication, became a vital factor at Kursk, calling VVS fighters into action quickly to meet the shifting requirements of the front.

Pokryshkin's reforms, in particular the *para* formation and vertical maneuver, found large-scale application in the air combat over the Kursk salient. Echeloned flight, group air battles, and the free-hunt techniques became a part of the VVS combat experience from the numerous fighter squadrons of the six air armies engaged in the Kursk air operations. These reforms prepared VVS fighter aviation for the large offensive operations of the third period of the war.

Always intent on learning lessons, the VVS high command did not let the Battle of Kursk pass without adapting the rich experience to air operations planning. In December 1943 the VVS Military Council convened a special meeting of military district air force commanders, commanders of reserve air brigades, and representatives from the front-line air armies. They met to consider ways of improving training in the reserve air regiments. Out of this conclave a series of new combat training courses for fighter, ground-attack, and bomber aviation were developed. As the final period of the war approached, the VVS prepared to take the strategic initiative for the first time. The conference helped forge a new training procedure to meet the demands of offensive air operations in 1944.

One practical expression of this approach came during December when the 17th Air Army, then committed to the projected campaign to liberate the right bank of the Ukraine, held a conference of commanders of air divisions, regiments, squadrons, and flights to discuss the need to improve air-combat skills for offensive operations. Gen. V. A. Sudets, commander of the 17th Air Army, joined with Gen. R. Ya. Malinovskiy, the front commander, and the two *Stavka* liaison representatives (Marshal Vasilevskiy and General Falaleyev) to plan for the new offensive. Already at work in the frontal air armies were personnel from the Main Directorate of Combat Training for Frontal Aviation (established in January 1943 and headed by Gen. D. F. Kondratyuk), who conducted lectures, war games, group exercises, and demonstration flights on various aspects of individual and group tactics. Together those programs were narrowing the qualitative gap with the better-trained Luftwaffe.[70]

At the end of the Battle of Kursk the VVS possessed a decided numerical superiority over the Luftwaffe, an edge to be magnified in the last year and a half of the war. The coming campaign to liberate Soviet territory and to drive toward Berlin would reveal how well the VVS had improved the quality of its equipment, tactics, and training.

Chapter 7

At Full Stride

The year 1944 signaled the start of the final period of the Great Patriotic War (January 1, 1944–May 9, 1945). By the beginning of 1944 the strategic initiative in the air, along with the war itself, had shifted to the Soviet Union. Two and a half years of bitter struggle had passed. Despite extraordinary materiel losses in 1941, the Soviet military had blunted successive German offensives in 1942–43 at Moscow, Stalingrad, and Kursk.

Behind the dramatic reversal in the military fortunes of the Soviet Union was the latent force of Soviet war industries, which by 1944 had achieved a formidable level of productivity. The Soviet Army's fighting strength in January 1944 was 6,165,000 men, 88,900 guns and mortars, 2,167 rocket launchers, nearly 5,000 tanks and self-propelled guns, and 8,500 aircraft.[1]

As this climactic phase of the war began, the Germans still occupied Estonia, Latvia, and Lithuania, most of Belorussia, Moldavia, a large slice of the Ukraine, and the Crimea. According to Soviet historians, Germany deployed 4,906,000 men on the Eastern front, along with a substantial arsenal of 54,000 guns and mortars, 5,400 tanks and assault guns, and 3,000 aircraft.[2] In the air, the Luftwaffe could muster on occasion 1,000 sorties per day. But Germany's 3,000 aircraft in the east were not all first-line; by 1944 the Luftwaffe possessed in operational terms around 2,000 aircraft at best, and many of these were obsolete prewar biplanes sent east to help stem the Soviet advance.

The Luftwaffe had survived as a fighting force in Russia in large part because of Soviet air doctrine, which dictated that the VVS operate as an integral part of the combined-arms operations of the Soviet Army. If the VVS had been released for extensive and sustained operations as an independent air arm, the attrition in German aircraft would have been higher.[3]

In September 1943 Allied pressure in the west had compelled Germany

V.A. Matiyevich, commander of the 26th Guards Fighter Air Regiment, Leningrad Air Defense (PVO), reads Stalin's order of the day in April 1945. Behind the regiment staff are Spitfire L.F. IX fighters (low-altitude versions), with guards emblem to the rear of the cockpit. Courtesy of Carl-Fredrik Geust.

Soviet air crewmen prepare for a combat mission with their Pe-2 bomber. Throughout the war the Soviet Air Force demonstrated impressive capacity to maintain air operations in the most severe weather conditions. (SI 79-9501)

to withdraw air units, particularly fighters, from the Eastern front for Reich defense duties. In 1944 the Luftwaffe—about half its 1941 strength—fought on bravely to maintain an effective air presence in the east. With their army now in retreat and the Soviets shrewdly applying pressure at shifting points, the German air units were stretched to the limit. Constant movement, high attrition, meager reinforcements, and the growing effectiveness of VVS air power required the Luftwaffe to abandon any goal of air superiority and seek

The Soviet Air Force flew missions around the clock. Here a Soviet ground crew prepares a bomber for a night mission. (SI 12356)

instead to plug holes wherever possible. As a result, Luftwaffe commanders exercised a careful stewardship over their ever-diminishing resources in order to maintain operations: they preserved essential equipment and parts, adapted bombers as air transports to supply encircled German troops, and kept a small, but viable, fighter arm over the battle zones as necessary air cover.

In time, the steady attrition not only meant a decline in operational aircraft, but, more important, the loss of highly trained pilots and air crews. These human resources could not be replaced. The Luftwaffe fighter strength at the close of 1943 numbered 385 aircraft (305 operational).[4] Such a small cluster of fighters could not meet even the minimum requirements of the German Army. Soviet aircraft production for the year 1944 would reach a total of 40,300 planes, mostly fighters and ground-attack aircraft. The sobering reality facing the Luftwaffe can best be illustrated by the fact that the VVS air armies would receive 4,848 high-performance, late-model Yak-3s alone during 1943–45. For the entire war more than 33,000 Yak fighters and 22,000 Lavochkin fighters entered frontal air armies, the Navy, and PVO units. Against such an air armada, the Luftwaffe committed its highly skilled flight personnel and excellent aircraft, but in 1944 these were in short supply.[5]

During the final phase of the war, the Eastern front became an arena for the Soviets to apply their developing offensive skills and for the Germans to strive in vain to stabilize a defensive line. In the aftermath of Kursk, the Soviets had driven across the Dnieper River and liberated Kiev, the ancient capital of Russia, on November 6, 1943. The Soviet winter campaign of 1944 quickly followed on the successes of this remarkable year in which the Soviet Army had advanced 808 miles in the south alone.

In the prolonged struggle for the western Ukraine, the VVS played an active role, particularly during the Korsun-Shevchenkovskiy operation of January–February, 1944, which ended with the Soviets reaching the borders of Rumania. To the north in January, the Soviets lifted the siege of Leningrad and pushed the German Army Group North back into the Baltic states. The Crimea was retaken in April and May. Again, the VVS assumed the crucial tasks of establishing air superiority over the breakthrough zones and of providing air support for the ground forces.

The summer-fall campaign of 1944 opened with the Soviet offensive in Belorussia against the German Army Group Center. The Belorussian campaign in short order destroyed the German pocket, containing a force of over 300,000 men. This dramatic Soviet victory followed the Normandy invasion and set the stage for the conquest of Poland. During July–August 1944 the Soviet Army expelled the Germans from most of the Baltic area. In the south, two campaigns, the L'vov-Sandomir Operation (July 13–August 29) and the Jassy-Kishinev Operation (August–September), catapulted Soviet forces into Rumania, Bulgaria, Poland, and Czechoslovakia. By autumn, Soviet troops had reached Hungary and Yugoslavia. At the end of 1944, only a small portion of Latvia still remained in German hands. For the first time in this prolonged struggle, the Soviet Army was poised to strike a blow at German territory.

The Finnish sector became another locale in June 1944 for the Soviets to display their growing air might. Here the *Stavka* ordered the 13th Air Army, naval aviation from the Red Banner Baltic Fleet, and 2d Guards Air Corps PVO to make a coordinated blow against Finnish defenses in the Karelian Peninsula. The Soviet air operations fitted into a larger scheme of the Leningrad front to shatter enemy defenses northwest of Leningrad and capture Vyborg.

Air Commander Novikov arrived on June 6, as the *Stavka* representative, to supervise the joint air operations. Even with the large number of aircraft earmarked by the Belorussian offensive, he had an air flotilla of 757 planes: 249 bombers; 200 ground-attack aircraft; 268 fighters; plus reconnaissance and liaison aircraft. Naval aviation contributed another 220 aircraft.

Over Finland, as elsewhere along the front, Soviet air units flew the latest bombers (Tu-2s, Il-4s, Pe-2s), the updated versions of the Il-2 Shturmovik, and Yak-9 and La-5 fighters. Beginning on June 9, 215 VVS bombers flying in long columns hit enemy targets from 3,300 to 9,900 feet. Shturmoviks followed in divisional strength to maintain constant pressure on enemy defenses, railroad and communication centers, and reserves. By June 20, the Soviets had taken Vyborg.[6]

On the eve of the Yalta Conference (February 4–11, 1945), the Soviets launched the Vistula-Oder operation. This offensive began on January 12. It was followed one day later by the Soviet drive on East Prussia, a bitterly contested campaign destined to last until April 25. The final storming of Berlin began on April 16, when General Zhukov's 1st Belorussian front, joined by General Konev's 1st Ukrainian front and General Rokossovskiy's 2d Belorussian front, attacked from three sides.

Soviet troops met American troops at the Elbe River on April 25, and captured the Reichstag on April 30, 1945. As the width of the Eastern front had shrunk with each Soviet offensive, the concentration of Soviet air power had become overwhelming.

The Korsun'-Shevchenkovskiy Operation

The Soviet effort to expel the Germans from the Ukraine during the winter of 1943–44 had led to a series of dramatic victories. German moves to stabilize their positions in the Ukraine had faltered under constant Soviet pressure at shifting points along the ill-defined frontlines. Breakthroughs by Soviet

troops became commonplace, and with each puncture of the lines the danger of encirclement beset the hardpressed units of the German Army.

One such encirclement in the Korsun'-Shevchenkovskiy sector brought the competing air forces into fierce combat between January 24 and February 17, 1944. Two Soviet air armies, the 2d and the 5th, supported the determined Soviet drive to destroy the German pocket. The entire operation was played out against a backdrop of difficult weather conditions, in particular an unexpected winter thaw in late January, which transformed the few VVS airfields into muddy quicksand.

The two participating air armies began their operations with 997 aircraft (772 operational). The weather, however, had reduced the VVS to three operational airfields with approximately fifty to one hundred aircraft each. In spite of these frustrations the Soviets managed to fly 3,800 sorties against the Germans at Korsun'-Shevchenkovskiy between January 29 and February 3, 1944.[7] As part of the air action, the VVS attempted to maintain a round-the-clock schedule of bombing and strafing. Soviet air commanders made extensive use of Il-2 Shturmoviks and Po-2 night bombers.

On February 4 the Germans made a serious effort to relieve their trapped army group. In response, the Soviet 2d Air Army carried out concen-

A Soviet DB-3 bomber is being loaded with a torpedo for a mission against enemy shipping in the Baltic Sea. Courtesy of Carl-Fredrik Geust.

A Tupolev Tu-2 bomber. This Soviet-designed aircraft saw considerable action during the war. Courtesy of Carl-Fredrik Geust. (SI 77-7754)

Pe-2 bombers, 13th Air Army, Estonia, September 1944. Courtesy of Carl-Fredrik Geust.

trated air strikes against the advancing relief column. The Soviets worked simultaneously to prevent a breakout to the west by the troops in the pocket and to blunt the efforts of the relief force to establish an escape corridor. Despite fierce fighting, punctuated by VVS air strikes, the German forces moved within seven miles of each other.

For the Korsun'-Shevchenkovskiy operations, the VVS set up an air blockade on the model of the Stalingrad experience of the previous year. Novikov organized four zones to interdict the German transports supplying the encircled troops. Gen. S. A. Krasovskiy of the 2d Air Army worked with Gen. L. G. Rybkin, commander of the 19th Fighter Air Corps (PVO), to deploy the maximum number of fighters to destroy the on-coming German transports. VVS ground-attack units struck at enemy forward airfields at Uman', Vinnitsa, and Novo-Ukrainka.[8] The 5th Air Army also deployed its available strength for direct air support of Soviet ground troops attempting to liquidate the German pocket.

The Soviets claimed a significant victory in the air blockade of Korsun-Shevchenkovskiy pocket. Between January 31 and February 15, for example, the VVS recorded 257 air victories, including thirty-one downed German transport aircraft. For the entire period of the air blockade the Soviets, by their own reckoning, destroyed 457 "fascist German aircraft" in the air and at the staging airfields for the airlift. These figures appear exaggerated, given the reduced aircraft inventory of the Luftwaffe in 1944. Whatever the actual German losses, the level of VVS air activity remained high during this period. Moreover, the Soviet air blockade played an important role in the ultimate destruction of the Korsun'-Shevchenkovskiy pocket by denying the trapped Germans the requisite materiel to hold out. According to Soviet statistics, this victory yielded more than 18,000 German prisoners, with the count of enemy dead and wounded put at 55,000 men.[9]

The German struggle to supply the pocket by air had begun on January 29, in difficult weather. Fog and snow kept most of the German planes grounded during the initial phase of the airlift. Luftwaffe losses, according to one Western account, totaled forty-four aircraft during the first five days of the airlift. On February 9 the Germans improvised a new airstrip within the pocket, allowing German transports to carry anywhere from 100 to 185 tons of ammunition daily.[10] If true, these figures suggest that the Germans had succeeded in escaping a minor Stalingrad at Korsun'-Shevchenkovskiy. By contrast, Soviet sources remain silent about the successful German breakout on February 16. More than 30,000 German troops broke out of the encirclement, but their narrow escape required the abandonment of most of the wounded, around 1,500 men, and their equipment.[11]

The Korsun'-Shevchenkovskiy air operations occupied a prominent place in the chronicle of VVS offensive operations in 1944. Once again, the VVS had demonstrated its ability, even in difficult winter conditions, to organize an air blockade of encircled German forces. At the conclusion of this phase of the winter campaign the Presidium of Supreme Soviet of the USSR awarded General Novikov the highest rank in military aviation—Chief Marshal of Aviation. By February 1944 Novikov had established an exemplary record as an air commander. The ability of the VVS to seize the offensive in 1944 rested in large measure on his effective leadership.

During the spring thaw of 1944, the VVS gave the Luftwaffe no reprieve. The 2d, 5th, 17th, and 8th air armies flew more than 66,000 sorties in the effort to help the army liberate the western Ukraine. The VVS claimed 1,400 German aircraft destroyed in the first four months of 1944. The sustained character of these operations, however, apart from their real or imagined impact on the Luftwaffe, had stretched the VVS resupply capacity to the limit. Also, there were obvious signs of strain among VVS air personnel and ground crews.

By mid-April the Soviets had reached the Dniester River and liberated Odessa. At this time Soviet air operations slowed as the *Stavka* shifted its attention to the Crimea. Throughout the spring of 1944, Hitler refused to order the evacuation of the Crimea, where the German 17th Army and the Luftwaffe's 1st Air Corps now found themselves in a perilous situation. The Soviet campaign to isolate the Germans there had begun the previous fall when the 4th Ukrainian front occupied the Perekop Isthmus blocking the escape route to the north into the Ukraine. Earlier, the Germans had evacuated the Kuban bridgehead, the site of dramatic air battles during the spring of 1943, for more defensible positions on the Crimean side of the Straits of Kerch. The VVS 8th and 4th air armies applied considerable pressure on the Germans during the winter of 1943–44, flying more than 50,000 sorties against enemy defenses and shipping in the Black Sea.

The severe Russian winter and primitive field conditions made flying a difficult undertaking, particularly for the Germans, who lacked experience in cold-weather operations. Here a Dornier 17Z is being readied for a mission. (SI 74-3293)

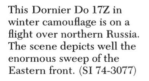

This Dornier Do 17Z in winter camouflage is on a flight over northern Russia. The scene depicts well the enormous sweep of the Eastern front. (SI 74-3077)

This German bomber crew has survived the crash of their Dornier Do 17Z bomber in severe winter conditions. (SI 74-3267)

The final Soviet campaign in the Crimea began on April 8. During the following week the Soviets advanced from the Perekop Isthmus and the Kerch Straits toward the Sevastopol fortress on the southwestern coast of the peninsula. The Soviet offensive moved forward rapidly as a result of the German decision to evacuate the Crimea. By May 12 the Germans had removed over 150,000 troops, but at the cost of equipment and an estimated loss of 80,000 men.

Throughout the Crimean campaign, the VVS faced modest air opposition from the Luftwaffe, a sharp contrast to the intense Kuban air battles of the previous year. General Falalayev served as the *Stavka* representative to coordinate the 2,255 aircraft drawn from two air units from the Black Sea Fleet, ADD, and PVO. He worked closely with Generals Khryukin and Vershinin, commanders of the 8th and 4th air armies respectively, to administer a joint operation of 35,000 sorties.

The once-determined defense of the Crimea by the Germans in 1943 had given way in 1944 to retreat, and with the collapse of enemy power there, the *Stavka* turned toward Belorussia for its next major summer offensive.

The Belorussian Campaign

The Anglo-American landings at Normandy on June 6, 1944, launched the long-awaited second front against Nazi Germany. This pivotal escalation of Allied pressure in the west (albeit a belated effort from the Soviet perspective) marked a turning point in the war.

No less spectacular was the Soviet offensive in Belorussia in June–July, which crushed Army Group Center, liberated the last vestiges of German-occupied Soviet territory, and paved the way for the invasion of Poland and the conquest of Berlin. This massive application of Soviet power in the Belorussian campaign, according to General Rudenko, demonstrated the enlarged role given to the VVS in the major army offensive during the third period of the war. The Belorussian air offensive in both its preparatory and attack phases revealed the VVS at full stride—5,683 operational aircraft from five air armies, supplemented by 1,000 bombers drawn from eight bomber air corps of ADD.[12]

Called Operation "Bagration" after a Russian national hero in the struggle against Napoleon, the Belorussian summer offensive aimed to annihilate Field Marshal Ernst Busch's Army Group Center.[13] In June 1944 Army Group Center occupied a salient, more or less coextensive with Belorussia, which extended eastward along the upper reaches of the Dnieper River toward Moscow. This bulge covered a vast area with a 650-mile-long front, a region of marshy lowlands, forests, and lakes situated between the Baltic states and the Ukraine.

While the area had remained under German occupation since 1941, the Soviet offensives north and south of the salient in 1943 had left the flanks of Group Center dangerously exposed. The German High Command, anticipating a Soviet summer offensive in the south, had stripped Field Marshal Busch of a significant amount of his infantry, tanks, and artillery, a move which made the German position in the center extremely vulnerable. The reduced strength of the Army Group Center on the eve of the Soviet attack consisted of approximately 400,000 men.

Operation Bagration became the most carefully planned Soviet offensive

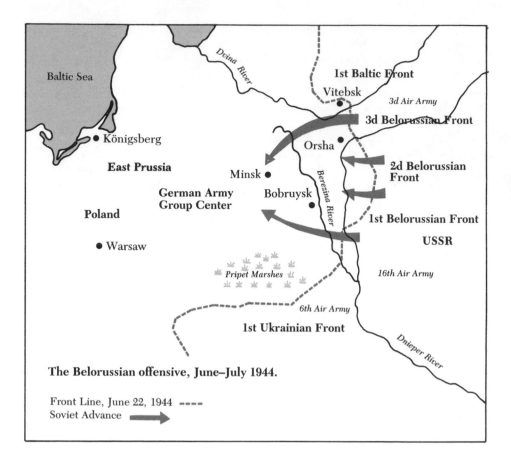

The Belorussian offensive, June–July 1944.

Front Line, June 22, 1944 ----
Soviet Advance ➡

in the war to date. The *Stavka* had elaborated a blueprint for a two-phase offensive in mid-May, which called for the extensive use of air power in all phases. Novikov himself played a prominent role in the *Stavka* planning sessions held on May 22–23 with Generals Zhukov and Vasilevskiy and the participating front commanders. The first phase of the Belorussian offensive, scheduled to begin on June 22, called for four Soviet fronts to break through the German-held salient at six points. With overwhelming forces concentrated on the narrow breakthrough sectors, the Soviets planned to envelop Army Group Center.

Partisan activity, already a serious challenge to German forces in Belorussia, was to increase concurrently, destroying vital supplies and creating havoc in the enemy rear. Once German opposition had been crushed, a second phase, to start on July 15, would carry the Soviet drive westward into Poland, the Baltic states, and East Prussia.[14]

According to Earl Ziemke, Operation Bagration proved in practice to be a worthy Soviet counterpart to Operation Barbarossa, which had been launched on the same date three years before. "In executing the breakthrough," he wrote, "the Russians showed elegance in their tactical conceptions, economy of force, and control that did not fall short of the Germans' own performance in the early war years."[15] As with Barbarossa, air power—in this case the Soviet Air Force—played a crucial role, hitting German positions with overwhelming firepower. The VVS assigned 2,000 ground-attack airplanes alone from five air armies. The depleted ranks of the Luftwaffe, always short of fuel and aircraft replacements, could not muster even token resistance. The German 6th Air Fleet, by one German account, had only forty fighters in operational condition on June 22, with critical shortages in aviation fuel.[16]

The lethal power of the VVS air offensive in Belorussia can be understood only if examined against the backdrop of the Soviet aviation industry. During the first months of 1944, Soviet aircraft production made a phenomenal leap, allowing the *Stavka* to assign nearly 6,000 combat aircraft to its frontal air armies, ADD, the naval air arm, and the Air Corps of the *Stavka* Reserve. By June 1 Soviet air power (including ADD and Naval Aviation) consisted of 13,428 planes.[17] Total production for the first half of 1944 reached 16,000 airplanes, which permitted the VVS to replenish fully its air armies, which had suffered high attrition during the winter months.[18]

The Soviets claim that the Luftwaffe's 6th Air Fleet, deployed at airfields at Minsk, Baranovichi, and Bobruysk, possessed 1,342 aircraft on the eve of the offensive. While German aircraft production in 1944 had increased, the Luftwaffe's replacement capacity could not keep pace with that of the Soviets. Against the growing VVS juggernaut, the Luftwaffe found itself outnumbered seven to one in total aircraft, around six to one in operational combat aircraft, and more than ten to one in the crucial category of fighters.[19]

On the eve of Operation Bagration, Air Commander Novikov again sought to improve the effectiveness of VVS air operations. In a directive to all the frontal air armies in early June 1944, Novikov summarized the results of the winter air operations, pointing out shortcomings and ordering corrective measures to be taken by division commanders. He reaffirmed in his directive the tactical character of VVS air operations: the various air staffs were to work

This LaG-5, number 15, belonged to Capt. Georgi D. Kostylev, who ended the war with eleven personal victories. Note the gold star, Hero of the Soviet Union, on the tail. Courtesy of Carl-Fredrik Geust.

diligently to improve the interaction of aviation with tank and mechanized formations.

In July Novikov ordered all fighter division commanders and their air staffs to tighten up radio air control procedures, an area still presenting difficulties. Air control for both fighters and ground-attack aircraft became more problematical in 1943–44 with the expanded inventory of aircraft and the aggressive posture assumed by the VVS. Novikov found that his stress on centralized control of air operations had been too rigidly applied, to the point where the VVS had lost flexibility and the capacity for quick response. Consequently, he prohibited air army commanders from controlling the actions of individual groups of VVS aircraft; instead, they were to give general instructions to the various air corps and division commanders, who would then direct the frontline sorties as circumstances dictated.

Novikov also ordered the chiefs of staff of the air armies to visit their subordinate staffs in a systematic fashion in order to sharpen overall control and efficient interaction. As reinforcements arrived at front-line airfields, Novikov himself, along with the *Stavka* air liaison officers, such as General Falaleyev, visited the headquarters of the various army front commanders to plan and coordinate air operations. Such activities were administrative as well. Novikov oversaw the construction of seventy new airfields to accommodate the ten VVS air corps and eight air divisions sent to the Belorussian front in the first half of June.[20]

The planning for the Belorussian air operations—deployment, basing, command and control, logistical support—required considerable effort. Novikov's centralized structure made these time-consuming tasks much easier for the various air armies. General Zhukov, representing the *Stavka*, arrived at the front on June 5. His overall leadership, along with that of General Vasilevskiy, encouraged the effective use of the combined-arms concept.[21] Zhukov worked with Novikov and other air force commanders (Golovanov, Rudenko, and Vershinin) in planning the operations for frontal aviation and ADD. At one point the tough-minded Zhukov required the troop commander of the 1st Belorussian front with his army subordinates to rehearse the forthcoming offensive in a remote forest. Here in a scaled-down simulation, the army, division, and regiment commanders acted out the script for the offensive, working out the details for interaction and answering Zhukov's questions.

Zhukov took particular pains to involve the various air commanders in these elaborate preparations. Novikov suggested, and Zhukov approved, the idea of massive bombing sweeps by ADD in the preparatory phases of Operation Bagration. For ten days leading up to the offensive, VVS bomber units attacked the various airfields of the Luftwaffe's 6th Air Fleet, a total of 1,472 sorties by these Soviet bombers.[22]

Night bombing missions by women pilots, flying the open-cockpit Po-2 biplanes, also applied pressure on enemy positions opposite the Soviet 2d Belorussian front. The 46th Guards Night Bomber Air Regiment (GvNBAP), commanded by Maj. Ye. D. Bershanskaya, demonstrated dramatically the willingness of the Soviet military throughout the war to allow women to engage in actual combat. Night bombing, in particular, was dangerous, and involved numerous flights through heavy enemy anti-aircraft fire. Other women, such as Col. V. S. Grizodubova, Hero of the Soviet Union and commander of 31st Guards Bomber Air Regiment (GvBAP), and Maj. Marina Raskova, killed in action and later buried in the Kremlin wall, became prominent war heroines. There was also a prominent woman ace, Lilya Litvyak, who flew with the 7th Fighter Air Regiment and, before her death in 1943, downed twelve German planes.

German airmen were always surprised to encounter VVS women pilots in active combat roles. One Luftwaffe pilot, Maj. D. B. Meyer, remembered being attacked near Orel by a group of Yak fighters. During the ensuing air duel the jettisoned canopy of Meyer's fighter struck the propeller of one of the pursuing Yaks, forcing it to crash. Upon landing Meyer found his dead adversary to be a woman—without rank insignia or parachute. On another occasion, over the Gulf of Finland on May 5, 1943, when the Luftwaffe downed a Lend-Lease A-20 Havoc, the Germans were considerably shocked to discover that the three-member crew included a woman—a gunner. In all, VVS women pilots flew more than 24,000 sorties during the war.

While the pilots of Major Bershanskaya's regiment acquired fame for their work in the Belorussian campaign, they were not the only women in active or auxiliary military service. In the Soviet Army's medical service women constituted 41 percent of the doctors, 43 percent of the medical assistants, and 100 percent of the nurses. In the Moscow Air Defense (PVO) force, 30.5 percent of the personnel were women. Women also served as liaison pilots to the partisans, always a vital combat assignment; snipers (as at Stalingrad); tank crew members; administrative support workers; and, of course, laborers in the war plants. A total of eighty-six women received the gold star, Hero of the Soviet Union award.[23]

The Soviets unleashed the Belorussian campaign over a three-day period in a series of bold strokes which brought immediate and devastating results. Troops attacked the German northern flank on June 22, the central sector on June 23, and the southern area of the German salient just above the Pripyat marshes on June 24. Each of these attacks fell on Army Group Center much like successive tidal waves crashing on a beach; they were overwhelming in their effect, forcing German units to fall back in confusion. Soviet air power, applied on the cutting edge of the offensive, had a powerful impact. Never before had Soviet aircraft appeared in such numbers and force. Gen. I. Kh. Bagramyan's 1st Baltic front and General I. D. Chernyakhovskiy's 3d Belorussian front—supported by the 3d and 1st air armies—pushed forward rapidly, shattering Col. Gen. Georg-Hans Reinhardt's 3d Panzer Army and isolating German-held Vitebsk.

By June 25 the German 53d Corps, under Maj.-Gen. Friedrich Gollwitzer, had been encircled at Vitebsk. During the next two days the 53d Corps fought desperately to free itself from the Soviet pincers. VVS units flew repeated sorties against the encircled enemy troops in coordination with the Soviet ground forces, a steady application of pressure which forced Gollwitzer to surrender on June 27. For this phase of the operation, the 3d and 1st air armies had a total of 2,881 aircraft.[24]

In the center—against German positions along the line east of the Dnieper River between Orsha and Mogilev—forces of Gen. G. F. Zakharov's 2d Belorussian front struck. Here the 4th Air Army under General Vershinin, with 528 aircraft, hit artillery positions and strafed retreating infantry and mechanized units with great effectiveness. Once the Orsha and Mogilev positions were shattered, the Germans retreated westward toward the Berezina River. Near the city of Berezino the VVS, drawing on the resources of the 4th Air Army and the adjacent 16th Air Army, attacked the German river crossings.

Between June 28 and 30 the VVS flew 3,000 sorties in a systematic effort to halt the German retreat. Waves of Shturmoviks made strikes against German troops clustered on the east bank of the Berezina River. From June 29 to July 3 the 4th and 16th air armies continued the air pressure, which slowed the enemy withdrawal across the river toward Minsk. This entire air operation played into the larger Soviet goal of closing the pincer movement, advancing from the north and south, at Minsk.

In the center, the VVS had established local air superiority quickly, which enabled Soviet aviation to hamper German withdrawal. By late June the Germans were fighting desperately to prevent encirclement at Minsk.[25] The Belorussian offensive in the center witnessed a successful coordination of three-strike forces: Soviet tank formations encircling a large concentration of German troops (German 4th Army) east of Minsk by advancing from the north and the south; infantry assaults on the German frontline positions; and the VVS blocking the enemy retreat to Minsk.

To the south, General Rokossovskiy led a two-pronged attack by the 1st Belorussian front against Bobryusk, a heavily fortified German position protecting Army Group Center along the Berezina River above the Pripyat marshes. Here Lt. Gen. Hans Jordan's powerful 9th Army occupied both sides of the river. Air Commander Novikov deployed the 16th Air Army, a force of 2,096 aircraft under General Rudenko, to support Rokossovskiy's assault. The 6th Air Army, under Gen. F. P. Polynin, reinforced Rudenko's air armada with 178 planes. Because the Soviets anticipated powerful German resistance in the Bobryusk sector, the *Stavka* delayed Rokossovskiy's main attack until June 24, to allow ADD units to participate fully in the opening strikes and then shift their power southward in time to assist in the drive on Bobryusk.[26]

The Bobryusk operation allowed the VVS to apply the full fury of an air offensive in both preparatory and attack phases. Over three hundred bombers participated in the night preparatory air strikes. After the artillery barrage on the morning of June 24, VVS bombers and ground-attack planes made two massed attacks on German defensive positions. With more than 3,200 sorties completed on the first day, the VVS appeared like a locust storm over the narrow Bobryusk breakthrough zones.

V. S. Grossman, a Soviet reporter, observed that "the sky was in tumult" as the 16th Air Army descended on enemy fortified positions, "with the rhythmic roaring of the dive bombers, the hard, metallic voices of the attack planes, the piercing whine of Yakovlev fighters. Fields and meadows were splashed with the darting outlines of hundreds of planes."[27]

Despite fierce German opposition, the Soviets surrounded Bobryusk on June 27, trapping elements of the 9th Army. Some 30,000 troops managed to breach the Soviet ring of encirclement on June 29, but the entire southern sector of Army Group Center had been ripped open. Once the town of Bobryusk fell, Soviet mechanized units continued to advance from two sides on Minsk. On July 3 the forces of Generals Rokossovskiy and Chernyakhovskiy closed the pincer west of Minsk.

On to Berlin! Il-2 Shturmovik at captured Luftwaffe airfield at Tartu, Estonia, August, 1944. A wrecked German aircraft is in the foreground. Courtesy of Carl-Fredrik Geust.

Throughout this offensive the VVS maintained an aggressive posture, attacking along the breakthrough corridors and applying pressure on the German rear areas. VVS bombers and Shturmoviks struck repeatedly at the enemy on crowded highways and bridges, on airfields and at supply depots. Soviet aviation strafed enemy reserves moving forward. With its defenses breached at six points, Army Group Center had been shattered, forcing the Wehrmacht into a chaotic retreat, a catastrophe of major proportions which could not be reversed by Hitler's appointment of Field Marshal Walther Model on June 28.

By July 4 the Soviet Belorussian offensive had achieved its objectives: Army Group Center ceased to exist as a military entity. The German High Command had lost nearly 300,000 men in less than two weeks. As a component in this dramatic victory, the VVS had flown 55,011 sorties from June 22 to July 4, an average of 4,500 sorties per day. Over Belorussia, Soviet tactical air might flew into combat on an unprecedented scale, giving the VVS absolute air superiority during the entire offensive.

Among the important Soviet innovations during Operation Bagration was the skillful use of ADD, the Soviet "long-range" bombers. Gen. A. E. Golovanov and his deputy, Gen. N. S. Skripko, had played a vital part in the planning for the Belorussian air operations. The tactical employment of long-range bombers—in actuality a force consisting largely of medium bombers (Il-4s, B-25 Mitchells, some A-20 Havocs, and Li-2s converted for night bombing)—represented a shrewd stewardship of the growing VVS inventory. These aircraft had little range or the striking power to operate as strategic bombers. Moreover, Soviet air doctrine had abandoned any notion of strategic bombing prior to the war in favor of building a strong tactical air arm.

Golovanov's ADD units, later to be reorganized as the 18th Air Army, provided a powerful striking force in the breakthrough zones and against the immediate German rear areas during Operation Bagration. By 1944 day and night bombing of German rear area installations had become commonplace, and in Soviet offensive operations VVS bombers had assumed an enlarged role in blunting German withdrawal movements.[28]

For individual Soviet pilots, there were frequent occasions to engage enemy aircraft in air-combat duels. Fighter pilot G. Lobov, later a lieutenant general in the VVS and recipient of the gold star, Hero of the Soviet Union, found the return to the skies over Belorussia in the summer of 1944 a matter of personal vindication. Lobov's fighter regiment had endured bitter defeat during Operation Barbarossa. Now, three years later, Lobov returned to the same area, flying a modern La-5 fighter, first over Vitebsk and Orsha in fighter-escort duty for bombers and ground-attack planes and then in fighter sweeps against various targets of opportunity in the German withdrawal.

Over Bogushevsk, Lobov escorted bombers in a series of air strikes. Before the attack VVS fighters cleared the target zone of enemy aircraft. The main force of bombers followed in groups of nine with a *para* of fighters proceeding to either side of each bomber column (the fighter *para* alternating to the left and to the right with successive groups). Above, and one to two miles to the rear, a larger striking group of fighters provided cover, Lobov reported.

On one "free hunt" mission near Orsha, on June 23, Lobov flew an La-5 in a *para* formation against four Focke-Wulfe Fw 190s. The combat that followed involved alternating upward and downward spirals. Lobov's *para* claimed two Fw 190s. Knowing the superiority of the Fw 190 to La-5 in dives, and the reverse in climbing speed, VVS fighter pilots, according to Lobov, found that the Germans willingly accepted combat in tight turns, and if the engagement proved disappointing, they quickly withdrew with a roll and steep bank. To destroy the enemy, Lobov and others avoided combat in diving maneuvers, if possible, and strove instead to catch the Fw 190s at the moment they recovered from a dive.

Through air-combat experience, Lobov and his fellow fighter pilots learned to increase the distances and intervals between *pary* (pairs). "The 'stacks' used in aerial combat in the Kuban had to be modernized slightly. Because the main enemy forces acted from low altitudes up to 9,900 feet, and the combat qualities of our aircraft enabled us to conduct combat successfully even without an initial altitude advantage over the enemy, we began to concentrate our forces at altitudes up to 13,000 feet. This immediately increased the number of encounters with fascist aircraft."

Lobov observed that the VVS fighter formations sharply increased the practice of operating in small groups, a *para* or *zveno*, rather than in squadrons. During the Belorussian air operations VVS fighters also expanded their sorties against enemy ground targets. Some VVS fighters were equipped with bomb racks and armed with two bombs. These changes required new training.[29]

By the end of August 1944 the Soviet offensive in Belorussia had ended: Army Group Center had been crushed, Belorussia liberated, and Soviet troops had marched 373 miles westward, reaching Lithuania and Poland.

From July to November 1944, the Soviet Army cleared Moldavia, captured the Ploesti oil fields and Bucharest, and invaded Bulgaria; in the north, troops swept through the Baltic states and reached the Vistula River at Warsaw. The rapid pace of the Soviet advance during this period again stretched the capacity of the various VVS air armies to keep pace. Logistical support became an acute problem. On July 23 the 16th Air Army, which had participated in the Bobryusk-Minsk fighting in support of Rokossovskiy's 1st Belorussian front, found itself with just enough aviation fuel for one refueling of its operational aircraft. The rapid push forward did not always provide adequate airfields for the redeployment of VVS units.[30]

With its air triumphs over Germany in 1943–44, the *Stavka* moved to make VVS air operations more international in scope. This new internationalism took two forms: the expansion of foreign volunteer air regiments to include nationalities soon to fall under the domination of the Soviet Army—Poles, Czechs, Rumanians, and Bulgarians—and an awkward collaboration with the Americans in the "shuttle raids." Neither of these experiments grew out of any pressing combat requirements of the Russo-German war: the VVS did not lack pilots or aircraft in 1944 and the *Stavka* was confident that victory over Nazi Germany was merely a matter of time. Soviet motivations, always opaque and self-serving, grew out of political considerations vis-à-vis Eastern Europe on the eve of "liberation" and a reluctant acquiescence to an important ally's repeated requests for assistance in the strategic bombing campaign against Germany.

The use of foreign pilots originated in 1942 when the Normandy Fighter Air Regiment was organized.[31] This regiment, consisting of French volunteers, participated in air battles at Moscow and later at Kursk. While the Luftwaffe considered the French unit a minor irritant at best, the Soviet propaganda organs portrayed their combat role in heroic terms, as an expression of international solidarity against "fascist aggression." Several French aces received the gold star, Hero of the Soviet Union, and the unit itself in October 1944 would be renamed the "Normandy-Nieman" regiment in recognition of its contribution in covering Soviet troops crossing the Nieman River.

According to Soviet sources, the Normandy regiment fought 78 air battles and scored 129 victories in the summer and fall of 1944. Soon the French fliers were not alone. As early as July 1944 Polish pilots had been recruited to fight along with Soviet air crews. As the Soviet Army approached Poland, new Polish units took shape—1st Warsaw Fighter Air Regiment, equipped with Yak-1s and the 2d Cracow Night Bomber Air Regiment, flying Po-2s. By the end of the year, Polish regiments were numerous enough to organize into divisions—the Polish 4th Mixed Air Division, consisting of the 1st fighter, the 2d light bomber, and 3d ground-attack regiments.[32]

Such efforts persisted into 1945 when the Polish I Mixed Air Corps, consisting of a fighter, bomber, and ground-attack divisions, took form under the command of Gen. F. A. Agal'tsov. From these Soviet-equipped air units a new "Polish Air Force" emerged in 1945. The Soviet-created Polish Air Force flew more than 5,000 sorties from August 1944 to the end of the war.

Other Eastern European nationalities found their place in the expanded Soviet air operations during 1944–45. Czech pilots were organized into a fighter air regiment in July 1944, a unit later to be expanded into the 1st Mixed Air Division. As did the Poles, the Czechs at first flew with VVS air units. Typically, the Czech units flew combat missions over their homeland once the Soviet Army itself had advanced to Czechoslovakia. The Rumanians, erstwhile allies of Germany, withdrew from the Axis and joined in alliance with the Soviet Union in 1944. Accordingly, the Soviets organized the Rumanian 1st Air Corps to assist the 2d Ukrainian front in its conquest of Bucharest and the Soviet advance into Transylvania.

To assist Tito's partisans in Yugoslavia, at the time genuine allies of the Soviet Union, the VVS first assigned a special air group, commanded by Gen. A. N. Vitruk. It included the 10th Guards Ground-Attack Air Division and the 236th Fighter Air Division. In 1945 the Yugoslav 1st Fighter Air Regiment and the 2d Ground-Attack Air Regiment were formed for the final campaign to liberate Yugoslavia. No less important was the recruitment of a token number of Bulgarian pilots in September 1944 to fly with the 17th Air Army in support of the 3d Ukrainian front's invasion of Bulgaria.

Soviet Air Force cooperation with the United States Army Air Force in 1944 proved to be difficult despite the highly vaunted "Grand Alliance" against Nazi Germany. The organization of air regiments filled with sympathetic foreigners, always under VVS control, served the larger military and political purposes of the Soviet state. Working jointly with a powerful ally such as the United States, however, did not fit smoothly into Soviet plans, expecially in 1944 when military collaboration brought few rewards and considerable trouble for Moscow.

In 1943 the United States first pressured the Soviet Union to allow American bombers to use Russian bases as eastern terminals for bombing raids conducted from Great Britain and Italy. Further discussions at the Teheran Conference gave the projected operation an important impetus. Called Operation Frantic, the plan aimed to conduct "shuttle" bombing from widely separated bases in the west and the east, bringing the entire matrix of German war industries within range of Allied strategic bombing. Such a move on the part of the Allies, it was argued by the Americans, would compel the Germans to spread their fighter defenses even thinner. Moreover, shuttle bombing from the American perspective might reduce the strain already evident in United States-Soviet relations by providing a concrete avenue for military cooperation in their common struggle.

While the Soviets had appealed for direct military involvement by the Western Allies on the Eastern front in the desperate context of 1941, there was little interest in allowing Anglo-American military units on Russian soil in 1944, when the crisis of the German invasion had passed. The Soviets, as events had proved, displayed little enthusiasm for the pieties of wartime cooperation so evident in the West. Yet, the steady flow of American Lend-Lease materiel—weapons, equipment, and raw materials for the Soviet war industries—compelled the Soviets to make periodic concessions to the Americans. One reluctant move was the acquiesence to Operation Frantic, which was approved by Stalin in February 1944.

By April 1944 the specifics of the shuttle bombing had been negotiated with the Russians. In a report by Maj. Gen. F. L. Anderson, Deputy Commanding General for Operations, to the Commanding General, 15th Air Force, dated April 28, the operational plans were outlined. Three air bases (not six as originally requested) were made available to the Americans at Poltava, Mirgorod, and Piryatin. The 15th Air Force would plan for 800

The shuttle raids brought the American and Soviet air forces into a period of awkward cooperation in a combat zone. Despite the many difficulties, friendships did develop among pilots at Poltava and Mirgorod. Lt. Thompson Highfill of California stands between two Soviet airmen. Courtesy of USAF.

Lt. Gen. Ira C. Eaker, commander-in-chief, Mediterranean Allied Air Forces, talks to an American fighter pilot after the first shuttle raid from Italy to the Ukraine. Looking on are Maj. Gen. Robert Walsh and Maj. Gen. A.R. Perminov, the local Soviet air commander for the Poltava-Mirgorod air bases. Courtesy of USAF.

bomber sorties per month, with supervising personnel, supplies, and equipment to be dispatched during April-May, 1944. For aircraft maintenance the Americans planned to use Russian personnel as airplane and engine mechanics, assistant crew chiefs, sheet-metal workers, fabric workers, and propeller specialists.

General Anderson promised an ample supply of highly explosive bombs, incendiary bombs, and ammunition for air operations covering thirty days. Elaborate signal services were required, as well as 12,000 tons of steel planks to reinforce the runways, portable housing and storage buildings, and a 100-bed field hospital. Much depended on Russian assistance. The Soviets, according to Anderson, would supply part of the ordnance (highly explosive bombs and .50-caliber ammunition), deploy 400 support personnel, and complete the construction of the runways and airfield facilities under the supervision of American engineers.[33]

From the Soviet side, Novikov organized a special section (later an air force directorate) under Gen. A. V. Nikitin, the VVS deputy commander, to coordinate combat activities with all Allied air units on Soviet soil. The 169th Special Air Base took shape to assist the American air group at Poltava. To provide air cover for an estimated 360 B-17 and B-24 bombers, the VVS assigned the 210th Fighter Air Division (PVO). Each of the three American airfields was provided with Soviet air defense units.

The first shuttle raid took place on June 2, 1944, when 750 airplanes from Italy struck targets in Germany. Out of this strike force, 128 B-17 bombers, escorted by sixty-four P-51 Mustangs, flew from the target zone to the Poltava airfield complex. Lt. Gen. Ira Eaker commanded the first group to fly into Russia. According to General Nikitin, a warm welcome greeted the

The Poltava shuttle raids, 1944. A B-17 Flying Fortress, *Patches*, is escorted by two P-51 Mustangs on a shuttle raid to Russia. American bombers of the 8th and 15th air forces made bombing runs deep into the Axis heartland, flew on to Poltava or Mirgorod airfields in the Ukraine, and then bombed Germany again on the return trip. Courtesy of USAF.

Two aerial views of Mirgorod airfield, used for the shuttle raids, taken from a P-38 on an approach to landing. Close-up shows B-17 bombers at Mirgorod. Courtesy of USAF.

B-17 Flying Fortresses take off from a Soviet air base for a shuttle raid against Germany. Courtesy of USAF.

American air crews on their arrival. Other raids followed on June 6 and 11. On June 21, the eve of Operation Bagration—and the eve of the third anniversary of Operation Barbarossa—the U.S. 8th Air Force conducted a shuttle raid over Berlin to Russia. It ended in disaster.

After bombing their targets over Berlin, the American strike force of B-17s and P-51 escorts flew on to Poltava, monitored the entire time by a German Ju 88 reconnaissance plane. Brig. Gen. Benjamin Kelsey (Ret.), then flying a P-51 escort, was anxious to chase and down the trailing enemy aircraft. Upon landing, however, the VVS commander refused the American request to pursue it.[34] At sunset another German reconnaissance airplane, an He 177, flew boldly over Poltava, photographing the American B-17 bombers now lined up neatly on the crowded airfields. After studying these photographs at Minsk, Luftwaffe Col. Wilhelm Antrup quickly ordered eighty Ju 88s and He 111s from the 4th Air Corps to strike the Poltava complex. The German strike, which took place shortly after midnight, turned out to be one of the most destructive air raids of the war.

Against a backdrop of illumination flares, the Luftwaffe bombers made repeated sweeps for over an hour and a half against the Poltava and Mirgorod airfields. No VVS night fighters appeared to challenge the enemy bombers. Soviet anti-aircraft batteries also failed to provide a spirited defense of the American airfields, firing only sporadically and inaccurately at the roaming German aircraft. On the ground the American personnel observed the unfolding tragedy from slit trenches. The "Damage and Casualty Summary" issued by the Eastern Command, U.S. Army Air Force, listed forty-seven B-17s destroyed or damaged beyond repair, plus the loss of ordnance and 200,000 gallons of high-octane fuel. This dramatic Luftwaffe strike seriously compromised the shuttle bombing operation for weeks.[35]

For the Germans, the Poltava raid was a much-needed boost in a year of military reversals. Karl Stein, then a Luftwaffe ground-attack pilot ferrying a new aircraft to Vitebsk, arrived at the Minsk airfield just at the time Antrup's bombers returned from Poltava. "Not since Barbarossa," one bomber crew member told him ecstatically, "have we done so well. It reminded me of the old days."[36]

The Poltava affair helped to fuel the growing tension between the Americans and Russians associated with Operation Frantic. The shuttle flights continued, but only at the price of Lt. Gen. Carl Spaatz's having to order American officers to abstain from criticizing the Soviet air defenses at Poltava. For the Americans there, the failure of VVS "night fighters" to appear suggested at a minimum gross incompetence.[37]

The Soviet commander, Gen. A. R. Perminov, explained to astonished American officers that the VVS fighters had been ordered to attack enemy airfields. Such an explanation seemed ludicrous to American personnel who had watched German bombers in the bright light of marker flares pound the base for nearly two hours. Washington's commitment to Operation Frantic, however, compelled the Americans connected with the shuttle raids to remain silent about the incident, and the use of the Poltava airfield complex continued into September 1944.

Soviet histories treat the Poltava affair with a mixture of disdain and distortion. For the VVS, these bombing raids played a marginal role in the war. The German air triumph at the Poltava and Mirgorod airfields, by one Soviet

This is a dramatic photograph of the German bombing raid of June 22, 1944, on the Poltava and Mirgorod air bases. Flares and anti-aircraft fire are clearly visible. Courtesy of USAF.

The morning after the Poltava raid—a destroyed B-17 bomber of the 8th Air Force. Courtesy of USAF.

account, resulted in the destruction of forty-four American and fifteen Soviet aircraft, "despite intense anti-aircraft fire and the actions of night fighters protecting these airfields."

Regarding the larger question of responsibility, the Soviets claim that General Perminov suggested to the Americans on June 21 that they disperse their aircraft before dark. "This suggestion was rejected. By evening the Soviet command had ordered the American planes dispersed along the edge of the airfields. . . .All anti-aircraft defenses were made combat ready. These measures helped to decrease the American losses, but they failed to prevent them completely."[38]

One curious episode, again from the Soviet perspective, occurred on June 5, 1944, shortly before the Poltava disaster. Air Commander Novikov, on the eve of his departure from Moscow to supervise the aforementioned VVS air raids on Finland, met with United States Ambassador W. Averell Harriman. Earlier, Novikov asserts, Harriman had promised the VVS a contingent of B-29 heavy bombers. Novikov admired the speed and payload of the B-29; he was also anxious to use the aircraft to bomb Finnish defenses in the Karelian Peninsula. At the meeting with the American ambassador, however, Novikov found little encouragement. Harriman told Novikov that the United States would not supply the "promised" B-29s. Implicit in Novikov's reference to Harriman's alleged promise was the Soviet expectation in June 1944 that shuttle bombers, in this case the most advanced American long-range bomber, would be used against enemy targets on the Eastern front.[39]

On to Berlin, January–May 1945

The year 1945 found Nazi Germany at the edge of total collapse. The Belorussian offense of the previous summer had destroyed Army Group Center. This victory paved the way for continued Soviet pressure in the second half of 1944. The subsequent L'vov-Sandomir offensive pushed the Germans out of the Ukraine. Finland dropped out of the war. The Soviet invasion of the Balkans in August–September prompted similar moves by Rumania and Bulgaria. As reversal followed reversal, the Germans evacuated Greece and Yugoslavia. By the end of the year Soviet troops had reached Hungary as far west as Lake Balaton.

Even as Soviet forces advanced from the east to the Vistula River and from the Balkans into Hungary, Hitler unleashed the Ardennes offensive against the British and the Americans in December 1944. Rather than weaken the Anglo-American drive and free Germany for a renewed offensive against the Soviet armies in the east, the Ardennes drive recklessly consumed the limited reservoir of German fighting strength. An effort in early January to retake Budapest only deepened the crisis. All of these events placed Germany in a position of strategic weakness in 1945. The great Soviet offensive followed, first the Vistula-Oder operation and finally the capture of Berlin.

The air equation in 1945 strongly favored the Soviet Union. The Luftwaffe had 1,875 aircraft (360 fighters) in the east, covering a broad front from the Baltic to Czechoslovakia. Facing the Soviet Army at the Vistula was the Luftwaffe's 6th Air Fleet, which in January 1945 consisted of 1,060 airplanes (190 fighters). These air resources were quite inadequate to meet the anticipated Soviet offensive in the Vistula-Oder sector facing Berlin. At this late date in the war the Luftwaffe confronted the problem of acute fuel shortages, a consequence of the loss of the Rumanian oil fields and Anglo-American bombing of German refineries. Whatever residual punch the Luftwaffe could muster in 1945 came through improvisation, desperate effort, and the maximum use of existing resources.

Adolf Galland, then commanding general of Luftwaffe fighter operations, found a context of unreality at Hitler's headquarters. During one visit, Galland remembers Hitler seated at a table before a large-scale map of Russia. As aides looked on, he moved battalions around in a manner inconsistent with their actual deployment and possibility for maneuver. Some units, Galland noted, were as far away as 250 miles from where they appeared on Hitler's map. Everyone realized the "planning" bore no resemblance to actual conditions at the front, but no one spoke or attempted to correct the Fueh-rer. The whole meeting assumed the character of game playing—chilling, un-real, and foreboding in its implications.

Galland had been assigned in the course of the war to various posts in the west, but he had observed the gradual transformation of Soviet air power. "The technical quality of the Soviet Air Force," Galland has noted, "improved considerably, and by the end of the war Soviet personnel and equipment was roughly equal to the Luftwaffe." As did most Luftwaffe fliers, Galland praised the Il-2 Shturmovik as a singularly effective warplane.[40]

In contrast to the German situation, the VVS possessed an unprece-dented combat strength in 1945 of 15,815 aircraft; the strategic initiative in the air, which allowed maximum maneuver; and a breathtaking capacity for replacing losses in aircraft and air crews. Ten VVS air armies now challenged the Luftwaffe. The Soviet aviation industry had increased production by 15.6 percent in 1944. In VVS frontal aviation, there were 14,500 new combat air-craft. This meant VVS operational units flew the latest-model aircraft, includ-ing the Yak-3 and La-7 fighters, and some Il-10 Shturmoviks.

On December 6, 1944, the VVS organized its long-range aviation, for-merly ADD, into the 18th Air Army. This decision reflected a belated effort on the part of the VVS to organize a strategic bomber force. With the end of the war just a few months away, the VVS would not engage in any strategic bombing campaigns, although Königsberg, Budapest, and Berlin were hit by Soviet bombers in a systematic fashion. Soviet historians, in retrospect, give exaggerated emphasis to VVS wartime strategic aviation operations. VVS bomber units in 1944–45 continued to be used largely for tactical operations. One of the postwar period tasks for the Soviet Union would be the design and production of heavy bombers for its strategic air arm, which in January 1945 existed more on paper than in reality (see Appendix 7 on 18th Air Army).[41] In the crucial category of operational fighters and ground-attack planes, the VVS showed on January 1945 a dramatic upsurge over January 1, 1944—fighters, 2,478 to 5,184; ground-attack aircraft, 1,858 to 3,845.[42]

The Vistula-Oder Campaign, the first Soviet blow in 1945, called for the army to move across the Vistula on two axes toward Poznan and Breslau.[43] By crossing to the Oder River, the Soviet Army planned to move into Germany from Poland and set the stage for the climactic assault on Berlin. The *Stavka* assigned General Zhukov as commander of the 1st Belorussian front to spear-head the strategic Vistula-Oder offensive in cooperation with the 1st Ukrainian front. These two fronts were systematically built up in advance of the offensive to 163 divisions and 2,200,000 men, with 6,460 tanks and self-propelled guns.[44]

The *Stavka* deployed two air armies to support the advancing ground troops, the 16th Air Army commanded by General Rudenko and the 2d Air Army led by General Krasovskiy. Rudenko's 16th, consisting of more than 2,200 combat aircraft (excluding the Po-2 night bombers), provided air sup-port for Zhukov's main drive along the Warsaw-Berlin axis. While Soviet sources vary slightly on the actual number of VVS aircraft participating in the offensive, a reasonable estimate would fall between 4,700 and 5,000 planes, divided about equally between the two air armies. Counting Vershinin's 4th Air Army supporting Rokossovskiy's 2d Belorussian front and Khryukin's 1st Air Army attached to Chernyakovskiy's 3d Belorussian front facing East Prus-

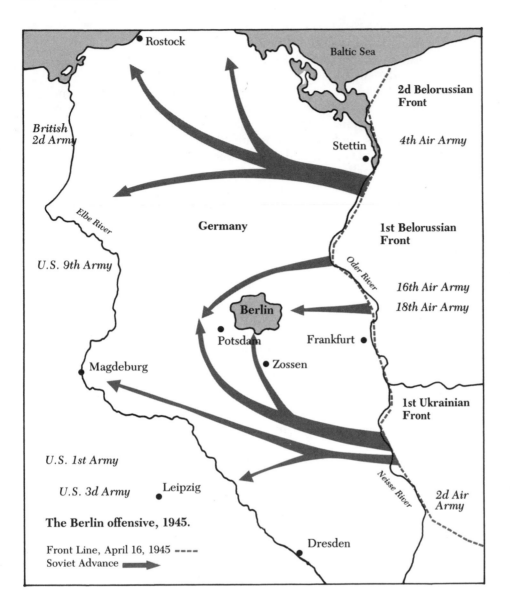

The Berlin offensive, 1945.

Front Line, April 16, 1945 ----
Soviet Advance ➡️

sia, the VVS had over 8,000 combat aircraft.[45]

Soviet sources indicate that the VVS took pains to conceal the huge air armada earmarked for the Vistula-Oder operations. Air units flew in stages to their forward positions with elaborate precautions taken to keep their numbers and location secret. Within the sector of the 16th Air Army Soviet laborers skillfully constructed fifty-five "dummy airfields" with 818 full-scale models of Soviet aircraft. To add authenticity, the VVS maintained flights into and out of these dummy installations. The VVS recorded successes in attracting German air strikes to these bogus airfields, while their carefully camouflaged operational airfields were spared. Such meticulous preparations extended to air reconnaissance as well, where VVS air crews photographed the German defenses in great depth. Few crucial points escaped the Soviet air reconnaissance—enemy defensive lines, anti-tank ditches, river crossings, airfields, artillery positions, deployment of reserves.[46]

Stalin had planned to launch the Vistula-Oder offensive on January 20, but moved the date up to January 12, to counter the German pressure in the Ardennes. The Soviet advance began in the southern sector, where General Konev's 1st Ukrainian front moved out from its bridgeheads toward Cracow and German Silesia. Konev's operation was followed on January 14 by Zhukov's 1st Belorussian front. During the 2d Air Army's operations in support of the 4th and 3d Guards tank armies, more than 400 Shturmoviks and bombers flying in small groups made continuous blows against enemy defensive positions. These air-support units gave valuable assistance to the tank spearheads by hitting German reserves moving forward to blunt the Soviet breakthrough. Bad weather, however, prevented any large-scale application of Soviet air power in this sector until January 16.

The German 4th Panzer Army found itself woefully incapable of resisting the massive onslaught of Soviet infantry, artillery, and tanks. The 2d Air Army's contribution of 4,000 sorties on January 16–17 only accelerated a Soviet combined-arms operation well on its way to victory. Konev's troops found VVS air cover helpful at the the Mysa, Pilica, and Warta river crossings. Cracow fell on January 19, and, by the end of the month, the 1st Ukrainian front had advanced across the Oder into Silesia.

Zhukov moved forward north and south of Warsaw on January 14, one day after Soviet troops had launched an assault on the enemy in East Prussia. As with Konev's operation, bad weather on the opening day precluded any large-scale Soviet air operations. The 6th Ground-Attack Air Corps, flying in support of the 2d Guards Tank Army, managed only 272 sorties, the 2d and 11th Guards Ground-Attack Air Divisions a mere 345 sorties in support of the 1st Guards Tank Army. No Luftwaffe opposition, according to the Soviets, appeared on the first day because of the severe weather. For those VVS pilots who ventured out, the weather became a constant threat with snowstorms, low clouds, and minimum visibility. Only the most experienced VVS squadrons flew these dangerous missions, which were conducted at altitudes of only 160–650 feet. On the second day the VVS faced similar weather conditions, but Soviet pilots flew 181 sorties, mostly by Shturmoviks and Okhotniki.[47]

By January 16 the weather had improved sufficiently to allow the 16th Air Army to participate fully in the ground offensive now under way. The third day coincided with Soviet efforts to capture Warsaw, and Rudenko's air units registered a total of 3,431 sorties in support of the advancing Soviet troops.[48] With the acceleration in VVS air operations, the Soviets could apply greater pressure on the retreating Germans at bridges and river crossings and along the rail and road arteries.

The roaming VVS air units played a key role in this phase of the campaign by supplying a constant stream of reconnaissance information on the enemy withdrawal. With this information the various VVS command posts could more intelligently direct Shturmoviks in hot pursuit of the enemy. The improved weather allowed the Luftwaffe to challenge the VVS once again. Air combat took place along the entire sweep of the Soviet advance. The Soviets claimed eighteen victories in twenty-two air battles. The 176th Guards Fighter Air Regiment (GvIAP), an elite unit which included top Soviet ace Major Kozhedub, participated in the combat encounters.[49]

At the time of the Soviet assault on Warsaw, the 16th Air Army assigned the Polish 4th Mixed Air Division to assist in the capture of the city. This division flew a reported 400 missions against the German defenders. Even as these events unfolded, the 16th Air Army airlifted a large quantity of mortars, anti-tank rifles, automatic weapons, ammunition, food, and medicines to "the patriots of the Warsaw underground."[50]

Such a gesture of air support to the Polish underground appeared to flow from political rather than military realities. When the Poles desperately required resupply the previous summer during the Warsaw uprising, the VVS had failed to appear. At that time the Soviet Army had advanced to the Vistula River. General Bor (Tadeusz Komorowski) of the Home Army then ordered the Polish underground forces in Warsaw to rise up against the Germans on August 1. For more than two months the Poles fought alone and heroically, being compelled finally to surrender on October 9 to overwhelming German force.

During this entire uprising, as Poles bitterly complained, the VVS air units on the east bank of the Vistula made no effort to intervene on behalf of the Home Army. Meeting only occasional Soviet anti-aircraft fire, German Ju 87 Stukas operated freely over the Polish-held sections of Warsaw, making pin-point dives at angles of 45 degrees against buildings (and sometimes rooms) occupied by the Polish insurgents. The belated appearance of VVS air support in January 1945 coincided with arrival of the Soviet army—not with Polish national aspirations. Warsaw was now in ruins and the Home Army crushed. The Soviet-sponsored Lublin Government assumed political authority over the war-shattered Polish capital.

The fall of Warsaw on January 17 led to additional victories as the Soviet Army moved across Poland to Germany: Lodz on January 19, Poznan invested on January 25 (to surrender on February 23), and the crossing of the German border on January 29. By the beginning of February these advances by Zhukov's 1st Belorussian front had cleared most of central and western Poland of German forces. Now Soviet armies occupied positions on the Oder, only thirty-eight miles from Berlin. The speed of these ground movements, fifteen to twenty miles per day, created enormous problems for the Soviet logistical command.

Lend-Lease P-39 Airacobras, lined up for shipment at Ladd Field, Alaska. Courtesy of National Archives via Jay Spenser.

Unable to keep pace with the advance of the Soviet Army, the VVS improvised by using German autobahns as temporary airstrips, an emergency measure already adopted by the hard-pressed Luftwaffe. The construction of new airfields or the renovation of old ones required time and considerable effort. Frequently, the rapid advance of the Soviet Army placed these on-line airfields too far back of the frontlines to be effective operational bases. The freeways provided an ideal airstrip for Soviet fighter units. Colonel Pokryshkin, then commander of the 9th Guards Fighter Air Division (GvIAD), was the first to utilize German freeways during the Soviet Vistula-Oder offensive.[51] For the entire drive to the Oder River during January, the 16th and 2d air armies flew 54,000 sorties and claimed 908 enemy aircraft.

While the Vistula-Oder offensive unfolded, the Soviet armed forces concluded another hard-fought campaign, the conquest of East Prussia.[52] Concurrent VVS air operations over Königsberg served as a dress rehearsal for the assault on Berlin. The VVS 1st and 4th air armies, commanded by Generals Khryukin and Vershinin respectively, deployed over 3,000 aircraft for the

East Prussian sector. The Luftwaffe, according to Soviet sources, had around 775 aircraft from the 6th Air Fleet. The VVS took the same pains to conceal the East Prussian air build-up as they had along the Vistula, building dummy airfields and taking extraordinary steps to achieve camouflage and deception. For the dummy airfields the VVS built models of one hundred ground-attack planes and sixty fighters. Radio stations simulating the work of an air army headquarters, a ground-attack air corps, and three bomber divisions began operation in the vicinity of the dummy airstrips on the eve of the offensive.

On the morning of January 13, 1945, the 3d Belorussian front went on the offensive, to be followed the next day by troops of the 2d Belorussian front. Just prior to the assault, the 1st Air Army conducted a series of preparatory strikes against the German defenses. By January 15 the two air armies, operating in joint strikes, filled the airspace over Königsberg and its environs with 1,320 combat aircraft. As in the Vistula-Oder operation, the VVS command planned on using bombers for tactical air support. On the fourth day, for example, 342 Soviet bombers made a massed air strike against German defenses in support of the 2d Tank Corps. After the tanks had advanced on the ground to the next line of German defenses, the VVS sent another 284 bombers to assist in the second assault. Air support for the tank corps came from five bomber divisions, three ground-attack divisions, and one fighter air division. Between January 19 and February 9, the VVS claimed that its 4th Air Army flew 8,130 sorties and the 1st Air Army 9,740 sorties, helping Soviet troops storm German fortified positions and surround Königsberg on three sides.

The importance attached to the East Prussian campaign, the first German territory captured by the Soviet Army, was evident when Air Commander Novikov arrived at the headquarters of the 3d Belorussian front on February 23, to command personally the VVS air armies over East Prussia. Soon the German garrison of Königsberg, defined by Hitler in 1945 as a fortress city, became a formidable defensive grouping blocking the *Stavka*'s goal of quickly liquidating enemy resistance in East Prussia. The assault on Königsberg unfolded as a carefully planned combined-arms operation. Artillery and aviation, in particular, helped to destroy both the enemy's will and capacity to resist.

The heavy stress placed by the VVS on bombing can be seen in the breakdown of operational aircraft—the 1,124 bombers made up nearly half of the aircraft deployed against Königsberg.[53] The Soviets attempted to block German sea traffic in and out of the city, a goal which not only brought the Baltic Fleet air arm into action, but allowed the VVS to experiment further with torpedo bombing.[54] For the first time in the war Soviet naval aviation, from the Red Banner Baltic Fleet (commanded by Gen. M. I. Samokhin) participated with the VVS in an offensive. More important, however, the VVS command acquired additional experience in administrating large concentrations of combat aircraft in diverse operational roles over a narrow sector of the front.

Soviet bombers over Königsberg encountered fierce resistance from the Germans, who were now defending their homeland. VVS operational plans, worked out at the headquarters of the 1st Air Army, called for an initial two days of preparatory air strikes, beginning on April 1, 1945. These strikes called for 5,316 sorties to drop 2,620 tons of bombs on defensive strong points around the city and the surviving Luftwaffe airfields. During this final phase of the war, the VVS aimed to destroy "fascist aviation" on an entire front, not merely to subdue German air resistance as part of a Soviet Army offensive.

On the first day of the operation, the VVS scheduled 539 aircraft (406 TU-2 and Pe-2 bombers with 133 fighter-bombers) for a concentrated attack on German positions. Once the bomber sweep had been completed, a second attack by Shturmoviks was to follow in close support of advancing tanks and infantry. Three fighter divisions (129th, 240th, and 330th), with supplementary air units from the 11th Fighter Air Corps, were assigned to Königsberg for fighter-cover duty over the battle zone. Other fighter air units were deployed in a larger air space to intercept any enemy fighters. On this first day alone, as events proved, there were more than 4,000 sorties, one of the strongest air strikes yet organized. In subsequent days six ground-attack divisions flew against fortress Königsberg.

Fighter aviation, along with Soviet bomber units, found itself charged with enlarged responsibility for ground-attack missions. The entire 130th Fighter Air Division (Col. F. I. Shinkarenko) flew the specially equipped Yak-9 fighter-bombers with a bomb capacity of 800 pounds. The large number of VVS aircraft operating over a narrow battle zone required all divisions to fly in assigned corridors at defined altitudes. Three days before the offensive, the air reconnaissance command had prepared detailed photographs of Königsberg, along with large-scale maps and diagrams outlining specific targets. Forward command posts with portable radios again played an important role in guiding VVS ground-attack aircraft to frontline targets.

A powerful VVS air assault on Königsberg came on April 7–8, after poor weather conditions had reduced dramatically the number of VVS sorties. This raid coincided with penetration of the city's defenses by Soviet troops and involved the first massed daytime raid by the 18th Air Army. Over 500 VVS bombers, escorted by 108 fighters, struck the forts of Königsberg for about an hour, leaving, according to one Soviet commentator, "the city engulfed in smoke." The VVS 18th Air Army claimed 550 tons of explosives dropped on the German fortress-city on April 7, and after four days a total of 4,440 tons.

The East Prussian campaign illustrated the improved skills of the VVS in coordinating several air armies, long-range aviation, and naval aviation. Soviet air historians are quick to point out that the VVS had been a vital force in bringing about the swift and decisive defeat of the enemy in East Prussia. Königsberg fell to four Soviet armies on April 9, 1945.[55]

Within a week Zhukov's 1st Belorussian front, then situated along the Oder River in the center of the shortened Eastern front, launched the final assault on Berlin. The Soviet sweep through Pomerania, and Konev's drive through Upper and Lower Silesia, had placed Soviet forces to the east and south of Berlin. Now the German capital awaited the final assault. Stalin's decision to permit Zhukov's armies to storm the symbol of Nazi power meant an important air-support role for Rudenko's veteran 16th Air Army. As a spearhead, the 16th was reinforced from the Air Corps of *Stavka* Reserve to reach an unprecedented level of 3,188 combat aircraft.[56] With the adjoining frontal aviation, the 4th Air Army (2d Belorussian front), the 2d Air Army (1st Ukrainian front), the 18th Air Army (long-range bombers), and the recently deployed Polish air arm, Soviet air power for the final Berlin offensive achieved the muscular level of 7,500 combat planes. All the wartime momen-

Three Soviet Pilots

Flight leader Senior Lt. Peter G. Sgibnev, 78th Fighter Air Regiment, Northern Fleet, is shown with his Hurricane MK IIB in 1942. Sgibnev received the gold star, Hero of the Soviet Union, on October 23, 1942. He was killed in action on May 3, 1943, ending a combat career of 318 missions, 38 aerial combats, and 19 personal victories.

Capt. Vladimir I. Popkov in front of his Lavochkin La-5 fighter with thirty-three air victory markings. Awarded the gold star, Hero of the Soviet Union, twice, Popkov flew with the elite 5th Guards Fighter Air Regiment. He survived more than 300 missions and 117 air battles to score forty-one air victories at the conclusion of the war.

tum of the resurgent Soviet Air Force came to a peak over Berlin—the vast numbers, the improved operational skills, and the immense tactical firepower.

The Soviet Army's difficult but irresistible advance into the ruined precincts of the German capital coincided with the VVS's clearing the skies of the last vestiges of the once-powerful Luftwaffe. On the cutting edge of Soviet advance, Shturmoviks made low-level attacks on German tanks and crumbling defenses. Soviet bombers—now free to cross German airspace at will—hit exposed tactical objectives within the Berlin defense perimeter. The average density of Soviet aviation per mile along the frontline was nearly fifty combat aircraft, reaching over 200 aircraft per mile within the breakthrough zone of the 5th Strike Army and the 8th Guards Army of the 1st Belorussian front.[57]

In retrospect, most Soviet accounts of the VVS in the Berlin operation focus more on the enhanced VVS organizational and operational skills than on the impressive number of combat aircraft. No previous Soviet offensive during the war had involved the numbers deployed on three fronts at Berlin—and the task of forging them, unit by unit, into a coordinated, effective air arm required considerable skill. The air operations at Berlin evolved out of careful preparation and attention to detail, mobilization, and timing.

Air Commander Novikov was at the front, working with the commanders to assure VVS participation in the entire sweep of the offensive to capture Berlin. The VVS faced the challenge of meeting effectively a diverse set of goals—the achievement of air superiority, effective support of the ground forces in breakthrough operations, reconnaissance, air cover for river crossings (Oder, Niesse, Spree rivers), and combat sorties against enemy reserves. The bulk of the aviation of the 16th and 2d air armies—75 percent—was assigned to move forward with the tank armies, again affirming the tactical character of VVS air action. For the vast concentration of air units (209 air regiments in nineteen air corps and sixty-five divisions of the three air armies) the VVS organized twenty-three air base regions (RAB) and 163 air maintenance battalions (BAO) with large stockpiles of ammunition and fuel.[58]

The Soviets list Luftwaffe air strength in April 1945 at 3,300 aircraft in the east, a figure which included 123 Me-262 jets. German air power, including Hitler's defensive bastion at Berlin, has been portrayed by the Soviets as formidable in its final hours. Most Western accounts have been decidedly more conservative, estimating Luftwaffe strength around Berlin in March at 2,200 aircraft.[59] During the final month of the war the Luftwaffe disintegrated quickly in the face of the converging Allied offensives. High attrition, loss of airfields, acute fuel shortages, and the collapse of the command structure reduced the once-powerful Luftwaffe to impotency. Whatever paper strength the Luftwaffe possessed on the eve of the Berlin offensive, it did not translate, as in the past, into any effective air operations. Even the long-standing German edge in skilled crews had been largely dissipated in the prolonged air war with the VVS.

The final assault on Berlin began in the early morning hours of April 16, 1945, when 150 night bombers from the 16th and 4th air armies hit German positions in a coordinated attack with artillery and mortar. The Oder River valley became a stormy vortex of artillery fire, explosions, and advancing tanks. A low fog in the morning delayed the arrival of the 16th Air Army's major strike force until the afternoon. But by 1500 hours, there were 647 combat aircraft in the air. The appearance of the VVS units sparked a swift response by the Luftwaffe, and during the afternoon a number of air battles raged over the battle zone. Despite the German air resistance the bulk of the VVS aircraft remained close to the breakthrough corridors, providing air cover and support for Soviet tanks. The first day ended, by Soviet reckoning, with 5,300 combat sorties, flown mostly against enemy tanks, artillery batteries, and defensive lines. VVS fighter pilots, by their own account, fought 151 air battles, downing 131 Luftwaffe planes, but losing 87 aircraft of their own.

To the south, General Konev's 1st Ukrainian front had moved forward quickly, crossing the Niese River and penetrating deeply into German defenses. Along the way, Krasovskiy's 2d Air Army provided substantial air support. During this combined-arms operation, the VVS air army delivered concentrated blows by ground-attack and bomber aircraft. Out of 3,546 combat sorties recorded, 2,380 were in direct support of the main offensive axis.[60] By April 19 Konev's troops had crossed north of Spremberg and threatened Berlin from the south and southwest.

Zhukov's advance from the east on April 17–19 had been slowed by fierce German resistance—in particular around the Seelow Heights—and difficult weather conditions. The *Stavka* then ordered the 2d Belorussian front to go over to the offensive on April 20, a planned Soviet thrust which bypassed Berlin on the north. By April 21 Zhukov's 1st Belorussian front had reached Berlin, as German resistance began to collapse under the weight of these successive blows. Soviet troops linked up west of Berlin, just northwest of Potsdam, on April 25. With the Soviet armies encircling the German capital, the Luftwaffe lost most of its airfields—and its air activity lessoned dramatically.

On the night of April 26, 563 bombers of the 18th Air Army, flying from western Poland, struck Berlin in a massive raid. As Soviet tank formations captured German airfields, the VVS moved immediately to occupy them, as they did at Tempelhof Airport, on April 28. VVS air units, drawn largely from the 16th, 2d and 18th air armies, concentrated much of their striking power for this final push. Bombers of the 18th Air Army, according to the Soviets, played a significant role in the entire Berlin operation, flying a total of 91,000 sorties in support of the three fronts. In these last hours the Soviets acknowledged the loss of 527 aircraft to air combat and anti-aircraft batteries. At the same time, the VVS claimed the destruction of 1,132 enemy planes.[61]

Hitler committed suicide on April 30, and German resistance within the ruined capital quickly collapsed as Soviet troops advanced, street by street, toward the Reichstag and the chancellery. On May 1 fighter pilots of the 2d Air Army dropped red banners by parachute over the Reichstag, which had fallen to troops of the 3d Shock Army the previous evening. Gen. Helmuth Weidling, commander of the Berlin garrison, surrendered to the Soviet general, V. I. Chuikov. On the following day, May 9, 1945, Germany signed the unconditional surrender.

Capt. P. I Chepinoga, a squadron commander with the 508th Fighter Air Regiment, in front of his P-39Q with twenty-four air victory stars. Along with his gold star, Hero of the Soviet Union (awarded October 26, 1944), Chepinoga proudly displays his decorations: Order of Suvorov and the Guards emblem (on his right) and the gold star (HSU), the Order of Lenin, two Orders of the Red Banner, and the Medal for Bravery (on his left). Courtesy of Carl-Fredrik Geust.

Chapter 8

Barbarossa to Berlin: A Summing Up

Alexander A. Novikov
1900–1976

Alexander A. Novikov assumed command of the Soviet Air Force in 1942. As overall commander of the air force and the People's Commissar of Defense for Aviation, Novikov displayed considerable skill and energy. He was the first recipient of the new rank of Marshal of Aviation in 1943 and also the first to be promoted to Chief Marshal of Aviation in February, 1944. Despite his brilliant wartime career Novikov fell victim to a purge of the air force, ordered by Stalin, in 1946. After Stalin's death in March 1953, Novikov was released from prison and given command of Long-Range Aviation. In 1956 he became commandant of the Higher Civil Aviation School in Leningrad. Novikov died in retirement in 1976.

The Soviet Air Force, targeted as the first victim of Operation Barbarossa on June 22, 1941, emerged at the conclusion of World War II as the most powerful tactical air arm in the world. Flying low-level sorties in support of the Soviet Army, the VVS deployed more than 7,500 combat aircraft for the Berlin offensive, an air juggernaut which overwhelmed the last vestiges of the once-powerful Luftwaffe.

No less impressive was the commitment of three air armies—nearly 4,000 combat aircraft—against the Japanese in August 1945. Now at full strength, the VVS controlled the airspace on the periphery of the Soviet Union's vast borders. No air force had suffered greater losses, endured more hardships, or experienced such a dramatic rebirth from the ashes of defeat as had the VVS between 1941 and 1945. This phoenixlike transformation signaled as well the advent of the Soviet Air Force as a formidable component in the post-1945 Soviet military establishment. For the VVS, the difficult war years had proved a rapid transition to modernization and first-rank status as an air power.

During the prolonged war with Nazi Germany, the Soviet Air Force served as flying artillery, linked organically with the army, moving into action when the ground forces required air support, and only occasionally striking the enemy's rear areas. Soviet doctrine compelled air units to function in close synchronization with the army in its shifting defensive and offensive modes of operation. Backed by the relocated and resuscitated Soviet aviation industry, the VVS grew dramatically in size between 1942 and 1945, making its tactical striking power an awesome component in the drive to victory. The VVS was never allowed independent status, nor used extensively as a strategic air power.

Soviet frontal aviation in combat operated under the direct control of the army front commanders. Rather than allow this relationship to be a mere pro forma link, the Soviet military planners took considerable pains between 1941 and 1945 to perfect air-ground coordination. Close cooperation between the VVS and the ground forces emerged as an operational imperative and, from the Soviet perspective, an ongoing measure of the maturing skills of the VVS. For the large-scale offensives between 1943 and 1945, the smooth interaction of the VVS and advancing Soviet Army spearheads became an absolute necessity to sustain breakthroughs in the enemy's tactical defense zones.

Western historians have displayed little interest in the dramatic air war between the Luftwaffe and the VVS between 1941 and 1945. The unparalleled success of the Luftwaffe in Operation Barbarossa in 1941 fixed in Western historical consciousness a vivid image of an oversized, poorly equipped, and ineffectual air force destroyed in one preemptive strike. From that moment forward the vertical dimension of the war in the east receded into the background for many Westerners. The floodtide of Soviet histories and memoirs since 1960 on the air war has not altered Western perceptions. Ground action by Soviet infantry, tanks, and artillery continues to overshadow the wartime contributions of Soviet air power.

For Soviet military historians, however, the dark outlines of Operation Barbarossa do not exhaust the history of their air force. The more remarkable story unfolded after the illusory Luftwaffe triumphs, when the VVS made its dramatic recovery. Despite staggering losses, the Soviet Air Force in 1941–42 survived the worst onslaughts of the Luftwaffe. The acquisition of the strategic initiative in the air by 1943 set the stage for the reorganized VVS to apply overwhelming air power against the enemy in a series of decisive campaigns. To ignore this image would be analogous to persisting with an image of the United States Navy as it appeared in the immediate aftermath of Pearl Harbor: by the end of 1942 the United States possessed a mere three aircraft carriers! This same navy, however, concluded the war with 99 carriers of all types, and deployed a naval flotilla of 1,500 warships off Japan in 1945.[1] As in the case of the United States Navy, the VVS should be evaluated in terms of its mature aspect, not in the first but in the final weeks of the war.

Soviet Air Force High Command and air army commanders, 1945 (first row, left to right): S.D Rybal'chenko, A.V. Nikitin, G.A. Vorozheykin, A.I Shakurin, A.A. Novikov, N.S. Shimanov, F. Ya. Falaleyev, A.K. Repin; (second row, left to right): N.F. Papivin, N.F. Naumenko, V.A. Sudets, S.I. Rudenko, T.T. Khryukin, V.N. Zhdanov, K.A. Vershinin, S.A. Krasovskiy, S.K. Goryunov, and I.P. Zhuravlev.

The Limits of German Air Power

By the end of 1941 the Luftwaffe in the east found itself in deep trouble. Despite the early successes, longterm prospects looked bleak. Overall air superiority remained in German hands, but the grasp appeared weak and uncertain. The decision of the German High Command in December 1941 to withdraw Kesselring's 2d Air Fleet from the Moscow sector to the Mediterranean weakened Luftwaffe air strength in the east. This move, however, could not explain by itself the precipitous decline of the Luftwaffe; nor could Soviet airpower alone explain it. Certainly, the VVS persisted into 1942 as a viable force, but in its anemic state it could merely frustrate the Luftwaffe.

The actual challenge from the VVS came a year later, particularly in the Kuban and Kursk air battles. The Luftwaffe's difficulties grew out of its Russian mandate, the nearly impossible requirement of providing air support for three major army groupings on a front which by 1942 extended over 2,300 miles. Brilliant tactical victories in the opening stages concealed from a view a steady decline in fighting efficiency, the high rate of attrition (a surprise), and constant problems with logistics.

German air power, with its finite resources, failed in a gallant effort to contend with Russian geography. Stretching from the Arctic to the Caucasus, the Eastern front crossed tundra, forests, swamps, steppes, meandering rivers, mountains and lakes. There were few roads, even fewer established airfields, and incomparable distances to traverse. Weather in its sporadic violence, as the winter of 1941–42, could almost freeze men and machines in place. But it was the sweep of the Russian geography which sapped Luftwaffe strength. Only a vast air fleet, superbly equipped and lavishly maintained, could begin to meet the challenge of the Russian front. Nazi Germany, belated in its response to the demands of total war, could not muster such airpower, particularly in 1942, when German strategic commitments embraced several fronts. In fact, no substantial air reinforcements reached the east after 1943 to bolster the Luftwaffe's waning strength. Decline became inevitable, retarded only by the superior Luftwaffe equipment and flying technique.[2]

One American fighter pilot, Benjamin S. Kelsey, observed this battle-front first hand when flying escort duty for B-17s during the "shuttle" raids of 1944. "While flying over the Ukraine," Kelsey observed, "it became evident to me that there was no continuous line of contact between the Soviets and the Germans. There was plenty of evidence of concentrated action in isolated areas. It appeared that by concentrating force it was hoped to seize the initiative in local areas. Since either side could use the tactic, flanking action was always possible. The defender was always at the disadvantage."[3] Given these circumstances, the Luftwaffe did well at first with its modest numbers and uncertain supply lines. But the larger task of providing sustained air support for the German Army could not be met.

At times, German air units operated in primitive conditions from grass fields adjacent to rail lines, or from air bases hastily set up near the frontlines. Constant rebasing of air operations, along with the rugged terrain, took a fearful toll in equipment. Low serviceability of aircraft and air crew fatigue appeared early, only to deepen in seriousness as the VVS became more aggressive and numerically superior. As Kelsey observed, "The defender was always at a disadvantage," a somber reality for the Luftwaffe after 1942. Individual exploits by German pilots—Erich Hartman (352 victories), Gerd Barkhorn (302 victories), and Hans-Ulrich Rudel (over 500 tanks and a Soviet battleship)—suggested exceptional flying skill, but these heroics, as well as many others, could not stem the tide.

It should be understood that the VVS endured the same hardships as the Luftwaffe. The geography, except for its familiarity, offered few advantages to the Soviets, whose aircraft also had limited range, flew from primitive airfields, and broke down frequently under constant movement. After Operation Barbarossa, the VVS not only struggled on with few modern aircraft, but faced a crisis of confidence within its own ranks. Occasional displays of bravery and aggressiveness did not compensate for the obvious gap between the VVS and the Luftwaffe in equipment, technique, and battle experience. Until 1943 the VVS counted few victories over the Luftwaffe. Not until the last year of the war did the Soviets themselves possess the adequate numbers of aircraft to overcome the natural disadvantages of the vast Russian geography.

The Soviet Air Force rebuilt its command structure and deployed its numerous aircraft into mobile strike forces (the air armies) in order to effectively operate in this vast arena of war. The Soviet aircraft industry and (to a lesser degree) Lend-Lease provided the means to assert the strategic initiative in the air. It should be remembered, however, that the Soviets had adequate numbers of aircraft only in the last year of the war. The Air Corps of the *Stavka* Reserve, often holding 50–55 percent of all Soviet combat aircraft, became the great reservoir to replenish VVS frontal aviation. The *Stavka* used these reserves shrewdly, responding to the shifting requirements for offensive operations. Soviet air losses, never officially disclosed, were no doubt high, consistently high, to maintain the strategic initiative after 1943.

High attrition in VVS aircraft and air crews, even after the Soviets had produced flying machines equal to the Luftwaffe, became a necessary price to pay to achieve air supremacy. As events illustrated, Moscow was prepared to meet these inordinate demands of the war largely because the Soviet Union had the means to wage a prolonged war of attrition: While the *Stavka* counted reserves of eighteen air corps at the end of 1943, the same reservoir of air power had mushroomed to thirty by 1945.

The Luftwaffe served a teacher, not merely a fierce adversary, for the Soviet Air Force. Here the role of the Luftwaffe proved to be less limited by time and circumstance. Technical exchanges between the two air forces went back to the early 1920s. Hitler had abandoned the contacts in the 1930s, but the influence of German air power on the VVS persisted. Soviet air planners, even prior to World War II, had endorsed the German emphasis on the tactical uses of airpower.

The Soviet shift in 1940 toward fighter-bombers and ground-attack aircraft at the expense of bombers mirrored German priorities. The emergence of the Il-2 Shturmovik symbolized fully the VVS commitment to tactical aviation. Other patterns of emulation followed. A. A. Novikov, the VVS air commander, urged his pilots to emulate German fighter tactics, as Western air forces had done earlier. This pivotal change, accomplished in isolation, allowed the VVS with its modern-type fighters—the Yak and Lavochkin series—to assert air superiority. As events proved, the Luftwaffe ultimately became the victim of VVS skill and numbers, and, ironically, of its own tactics.

Contradictions in Soviet Air Operations

Anyone attempting to evaluate the combat performance of the Soviet Air Force in World War II encounters a cluster of contradictory images. Neither side of the "Iron Curtain" provides a congenial atmosphere for dispassionate enquiry. Soviet historical materials have improved in recent decades, but they are for the most part secondary accounts, keyed in tone and content to official interpretations and designed to accentuate Soviet achievements. Deficiencies or failures are noted, but only in passing, being overshadowed by the larger panorama of the Soviet victory in the Great Patriotic War. From the West, the reflex for a more objective treatment is apparent, but the vantage point is not always ideal. Too often, the postwar German recollections have been accepted uncritically. The result has been to view the VVS largely through the prism of the German experience, admittedly a valuable perspective, but often one riddled by bias and self-justification.

The problem, however, is more basic than historical perspective, the contrast between official Soviet accounts and Western perceptions (or, as the Soviets call them, "bourgeois falsifications"). The conduct of the air war itself revealed the VVS to be an air force with many guises depending on time and place. Soviet airmen in the first two years of the war proved to be courageous and cowardly, aggressive and docile, competent and inept. Fighter air units in the opening phases of the war, except for those in the south, were extremely cautious and ineffectual. Bomber air crews, as evidenced in the summer of 1941, displayed a singlemindedness of purpose which bordered on the suicidal. Shturmovik units appeared to be uniformly aggressive and competent.

Soviet pilots, as a group, possessed mediocre flying skills at the start of the war, a harsh estimate which Luftwaffe airmen only grudgingly revised after 1943. The use of the aerial ramming tactic, or *taran*, by many Soviet pilots in the first years of the war astounded Luftwaffe air crews. The VVS prowess in cold-weather flying genuinely impressed the Germans, who soon adapted these proven methods in their own air operations. The Luftwaffe also copied the Soviet practice of using obsolete biplanes for night bombing. As the war progressed, the Luftwaffe observed with consternation the steady improvement in VVS aircraft and fighting techniques. At the end of the war, the VVS differed markedly from the air force the Luftwaffe had encountered in 1941, and it had regained once again its numerical edge.

Soviet bombers, once a marvel of technological achievement in the prewar years, played a confusing role in the war. The long-range bomber command, ADD (reorganized as the 18th Air Army after December 1944), had only a handful of modern four-engined bombers, a mere seventy-nine Pe-8 types. The remainder of the bomber fleet, consisting of Lend-Lease and indigenous designs, were in reality medium bombers thrown into a tactical air support role. Except for occasional forays into the enemy rear, these bomber units flew air support sorties in or close to the tactical battle zones. During the entire war, Soviet long-range bombers flew only 215,000 sorties (about 4 percent of all VVS combat flights) against targets in the enemy's rear.[4]

In 1945 the 18th Air Army made a belated and feeble effort to hit German economic and urban centers, but this bombing campaign had little effect on the course of the war. The overall failure of Soviet air power to strike Ger-

Russian planes

taxi strip (same as runway)

Lend-Lease A-20's

Soviet airfield at Tashkent, October 1943. Capt. W. E. Johnson flew Averell Harriman to the Soviet Union, via Teheran, in 1943. On the way back he stopped at Tashkent, which had Soviet SB-2bis bombers and Lend-Lease A-20s, en route to the front. This photograph shows labels from the original U.S. intelligence report. Courtesy of USAF.

man rear installations, reserves, and retreating columns stands as one of the major criticisms of Soviet air operations.

Another inexplicable feature of Soviet combat operations was the use of airborne troops. Before the war the Soviet Union ostentatiously displayed the mobility and striking power of its large airborne force (*Vozdushno-desantnyye voyska*). During Red Army maneuvers in 1936, for example, 3,000 airborne troops parachuted into the Belorussian countryside in a highly rehearsed operation to impress foreign military observers. Once the war with Nazi Germany began, however, Soviet airborne troops did not perform the combat role anticipated for them in the maneuvers of the mid-1930s. The near-collapse of the Soviet Air Force, the acute shortage in air transports, and the menace of Luftwaffe interceptors may have influenced this decision. Airborne troops did see considerable action early in the war, however, as infantry units at Kiev, Odessa, and in the Black Sea area, performing special missions in coordination with the front armies.

One major Soviet airborne assault took place in January–February, 1942, at Vyazma. As part of the Soviet winter counteroffensive, this complex operation was designed to assist Soviet forces attempting to encircle the German 4th Army. Over 10,000 Soviet troops, arriving by parachute or air landing, participated in the operation at Vyazma in an environment of deep snow and subzero temperatures. Although the Soviets displayed skill in landing men and equipment, and threatened the German 4th Army for weeks, they failed ultimately in their overall purpose. Airborne assaults ceased for the most part after the abortive Vyazma effort, except for minor operations along the Dnieper River in 1943 and against the Japanese in Manchuria in 1945. Airborne troops, as did the long-range bomber units, functioned in ways unforeseen in the prewar years.[5]

The Soviet understanding of "air supremacy," as defined in the peculiar context of the Eastern front, differed sharply from the Anglo-American operational practice. Forged in the difficult middle period of the war, Soviet-style air supremacy meant the capacity to apply at will overwhelming air power in close support of the ground forces. Air supremacy was measured as leverage, largely in the tactical zones, not as a commanding air presence coextensive with the Eastern front. The crucial Novikov reforms of 1942 sought to adapt VVS organization to the exigencies of the Eastern front and to provide the basis for offensive air operations; by design, they created an air force to meet the priorities of centralized control, mobility, and concentration of firepower.

To defeat the Germans, the Soviets embraced the concept of mass, the application of enormous firepower at selected points to establish break-throughs and encirclements. The Soviet Air Force—along with tanks, artillery, and rockets—served as one component in this mode of operation. There was never a clear-cut, one-on-one air struggle between the VVS and the Luftwaffe.

Rather than attempt to destroy the Luftwaffe as a fighting force, the VVS stayed close to the cutting edge of Soviet offensives. This fact allowed the Luftwaffe a curious reprieve in the east, the ability to maintain diverse air operations until the final weeks of the war. There were occasions after 1943 when a concentration of German air power, properly applied, could still assert temporary local air superiority. In the more constricted airspace in the west, such options were not open to the Luftwaffe.

Through the prism of the Anglo-American wartime experience, the Soviet Air Force may appear to have been deficient in many respects, or even "unaggressive." Permitting the Luftwaffe to conduct air operations, more-or-less freely, from rear airfields stands out as one primary error. To explain this behavior, Chief Marshal of Aviation P. Kutakhov has written that the Soviet Air Force in 1944 began a more systematic attack on German rear targets.[6] At this juncture, the time of the Belorussian offensive, the VVS had the requisite aircraft to extend its power beyond the tactical zone deep into the enemy's rear. More important, the combat zone had shrunk dramatically, making the breadth of the Eastern front in the second half of 1944 comparable in size to the frontlines in the west.

During this final stage of the war, the VVS, according to Kutakhov, realized the good results of applying the steady pressure of air power along the entire front and at considerable depth. At no time, however, did the VVS belatedly embrace a concept of strategic bombing. Long-range bomber aviation (later the 18th Air Army) lacked the aircraft and training to complete the task. More typically, Soviet bombers (Il-4s and Tu-2s combined with 2,908 A-20 Havocs and 862 B-25 Mitchells from Lend-Lease) engaged in tactical low-altitude bombing attacks. The reduced dimensions of the Eastern front allowed deeper penetration and a more diversified target selection in 1944–45.

Soviet accounts of the air war in the east—histories, memoirs, interpretive articles—have not been indifferent to VVS operational deficiencies. Many echo the criticisms of Allied and German commentators. Looking at the role of the VVS in Soviet offensive operations, Kutakhov acknowledged in 1977 the oft-mentioned failure of Soviet air units to attack the enemy rear. He cited the Orel, Belgorod-Kharkov, and Smolensk offensives of 1943 as prime examples. In the struggle for control of the air during this same period, Kutakhov accused the frontal air armies of sloppy coordination; in particular, he cited their failure to properly inform neighboring air armies of their plans.[7] Soviet historians, however, have treated these matters as shortlived in nature, as aberrations in organization, the kind of deficiencies to be expected in an air force rebounding from the severe losses of 1941.

By the end of the war, the VVS had come a long way: quantitative growth in combat aircraft and vast reserves; air army commanders with valuable battle experience; and the impact of the Novikov-led reforms stressing the centralized control of air power. The VVS learned to maneuver its huge air armies quickly in order to support the shifting requirements of the Soviet Army. The same Kutakhov who criticized the VVS in 1943 for its slow reflexes

Lend-Lease and the Soviet Air Force

While Lend-Lease aircraft amounted to less than 12 percent of Soviet combat aircraft, the shipment of more than 14,000 aircraft made a significant, if not decisive, contribution to the Soviet war effort. Pictured here are wartime photographs from the Ladd Field, Alaska, Lend-Lease operations.

Group of American and Russian officers at Nome base, Alaska, July 8, 1944. Courtesy of USAF.

Russian and American enlisted men celebrate the second anniversary of the Alaska Lend-Lease operations, October 3, 1944. Courtesy of USAF.

A Soviet pilot prepares to depart from Ladd Field, Alaska, in a Lend-Lease P-40 in 1942. Courtesy of USAF.

This battered DC-3 brought the first Soviet military mission from Siberia to Alaska on September 4, 1942. On the last leg of the journey (over 500 miles), the passage from Nome to Fairbanks, the plane reportedly used eighty quarts of oil. Courtesy of USAF.

A-20 Havocs and a B-25 Mitchell in front of the Operations Building at Ladd Field, Alaska, February 1944. The temperature was at minus 35 degrees F. Courtesy of USAF.

Soviet personnel make a final check on an A-20 before a flight to Siberia. Courtesy of USAF.

A Soviet pilot relaxes with American air personnel at Ladd Field. Courtesy of National Archives via Jay Spenser.

points with pride to the Berlin operation in 1945 as an illustration of the mature skills of the air force. In this campaign it took General Vershinin's 4th Air Army a mere thirty minutes to rush to the Oder River in overwhelming force to answer General Rokossovskiy's call to assist the 65th Army.[8]

The Evolution of Soviet Air Operations

In the costly struggle with Nazi Germany, Soviet military planners found new operational modes for the employment of their reborn air force. The "air offensive," first used at Stalingrad, became a major wartime Soviet innovation.[9]

It enlarged on the proven Luftwaffe techniques of air-ground coordination, and provided an effective vehicle to exploit fully the potential of Soviet frontal aviation. In simple terms, the air offensive called for powerful and sustained air support for advancing troops in breakthrough operations. Air offensives were divided into two phases: aerial preparation attacks (preliminary and immediate) and air support (accompaniment) of troops. During the rapid advance of the Soviet Army along the entire Eastern front in 1944–45, the VVS deployed as much as 90–95 percent of frontal aviation in the various air offensives. VVS air army commanders, for example, concentrated as many as 1,500–2,500 combat aircraft in the major breakthrough zones during the L'vov-Sandomir, Vistula-Oder, and Berlin operations.

The air offensive, articulated as a concept by the People's Commissariat of Defense on November 9, 1942, did not become an effective type of operation until the Battle of Kursk in July–August 1943.[10] Because of the lack of aircraft, the air offensive made little impact until mid-war, when the Soviet aviation industry attained full productivity and the Soviets had achieved the strategic initiative. Only combat experience, frequently accompanied by high costs in men and machines, provided the necessary skills for maneuvering large numbers of VVS aircraft. The use of radio, the development of mobile networks of command posts, and the improved methods for control and interaction brought success. Air Commander Novikov or his deputies moved up and down the vast Eastern front, providing liaison with army commanders and maintaining centralized control of VVS formations.

Being a tactical air force, the VVS operated in close coordination with artillery, mechanized units, and tank armies. Ground-attack air units, at the end of the war in air-corps strength, performed a diverse role: air-preparation strikes, close air support of tank armies in breakthrough phases, and the engagement of enemy reserves and retreating troops. Overhead, fighter units provided air cover for frontal troops. On the average, two fighter divisions covered a tank army. By the end of the war these fighter units displayed aggressiveness and confidence toward the Luftwaffe. New machines, best symbolized in the fast and maneuverable Yak 3, had narrowed dramatically the technological edge German fighter aircraft enjoyed in 1941. More important, the Soviet fighter pilots had acquired tactical skills and discipline.

The qualitative transformation of Soviet air power, telescoped in the time frame of 1942–43, remains one of the most remarkable turnabouts of World War II. Recognition of this fact is crucial for any historical analysis of Soviet air operations. Moreover, attention to this feature of VVS development provides a necessary counterweight to the oft-repeated and simplistic conclusion that the Soviet air victory over the Luftwaffe resulted merely from the brutish application of overwhelming numbers.

The Eastern front, with its alternating offensives and encirclements, gave birth to another tactical innovation, the "air blockade." Devised as a combined arms operation of VVS frontal aviation and air defense units, the air blockade endeavored to deny encircled enemy troops reinforcement by air and to assist the ground forces in blunting enemy breakout maneuvers. As theory, the Soviets claim the concept of the air blockade appeared in their military art in the 1930s.[11]

Whatever its origins, the air blockade became an operational mode early in the war, at Demyansk and Kholm in 1942–43, when the VVS attempted to

halt a Luftwaffe airlift to an encircled force of 100,000 men. Early Soviet efforts at air blockade, at Demyansk, for example, proved to be quite ineffectual, reflecting their ad hoc character. But the VVS did elaborate a highly effective air blockade technique as the war progressed, most memorably at
Stalingrad from November 23, 1942, to February 2, 1943. The VVS participated in successful air blockades in the Korsun'-Shevchenkovskiy,
Belorussian, Königsberg, Budapest, and Breslau operations.

Wherever the Soviet Army managed to encircle large pockets of German
troops, the resulting air blockade sparked a violent air struggle. On these occasions, the VVS appeared in force to challenge the Luftwaffe for local air superiority, to attack German transports attempting to airlift supplies, and to assist the ground forces in the liquidation of the enemy pocket. Since the
requirements and location for an air blockade could never be fully anticipated, the VVS placed a high premium on quick response and the requisite
force levels to conduct sustained air operations.

During air blockades, considerable organizational effort went into coordinating the various air-ground components. Zones were organized between
the outer and inner lines under a single warning system. Centralized control
of participating air armies and PVO fighter interceptor units became a complex undertaking. Air blockades demanded precise organization and enormous effort. At Stalingrad, there was the formidable task of coordinating the
actions of three air armies, the air defense forces (fighter interceptors and
anti-aircraft units), and the ground forces positioned along the inner and
outer lines. Later at Breslau (February 23–May 6, 1945), an air blockade took
shape in more constricted space and on enemy territory. Both operations followed a similar pattern of multizonal organization, a single warning system,
centralized control, and around-the-clock coordination of air-ground action.
The air blockade taxed the logistical capabilities of the Soviets to the extreme,
compelling the perpetually overextended system to meet sudden demands
for fuel, maintenance, and airfield construction.

The Soviet air blockades have no exact parallel in the air war in the west.
They should not be dismissed as curiosities or as peripheral episodes. On the
contrary, the air blockades provided moments for intense air force effort, occasions to gauge the maturing offensive skills of the VVS after 1942.

Air operations in support of the partisan movements constitute another
important chapter in the history of the Soviet Air Force. From the beginning
of the war to late 1944, partisans played a crucial role in the struggle against
Nazi Germany. Operating from forests and swamps in the hinterland of Russia, these groups depended on VVS units for supply and liaison with the Soviet Army. During the war the *Stavka* had more than 6,200 partisan detachments operating against the Germans. To assure their success, the VVS
airlifted an enormous quantity of arms, ammunition, signal equipment, food
and clothing, as well as agents, training personnel, and party cadres.

Soviet pilots, many of them women, flew a regular schedule of flights
into the enemy rear. Depending on the mission, the VVS used the dependable, slow-flying Po-2 or Li-2 (C-47) cargo aircraft. The Germans took concerted measures on the ground and in the air to halt the airlift, but to no
avail.[12] In the Bryansk forests, for example, one air regiment, flying Li-2s to
the Saltanovka-Borki and Smelizh landing fields, delivered in the course of
five months 300 tons of cargo and 240 personnel. Over 1,000 wounded and

civilians were evacuated. In the course of the airlift this air regiment chalked up 250 flights, making sixty landings. This clandestine air war consumed a considerable amount of VVS energy. Through the airlift, the VVS made a vital contribution to the Soviet war effort.

The story of the VVS in World War II is one of shrewd adaptation and efficient stewardship of expanding air power. Always pragmatic in approach, the VVS made full use of seemingly obsolete aircraft—mobilizing Po-2 biplanes for effective night bombing operations and enlisting antiquated behemoths such as TB-3s for air transport duty. Soviet night bombing became a vehicle to apply steady pressure on the enemy in the combat zones. The vastness of the Eastern front allowed the VVS to use obsolete aircraft such as the Po-2 for specialized missions—bombing, harassment raids, liaison with the partisans.[13]

Soviet ground crews, not always respected by the Germans or Western Allies for their expertise, kept VVS aircraft in the air, sometimes performing remarkable feats in the most primitive conditions. They could improvise solutions, often lacking in aesthetic appeal, which worked in their own curious way—as evidenced in German rear areas when Po-2s, fitted with grappling irons on long cords, made low-level sweeps over German telephone lines, ripping them asunder. This pervasive pragmatism gave birth to countless field modifications of VVS combat aircraft throughout the war.

The VVS displayed impressive skills at camouflage. No other air force during the war went to the considerable lengths of the VVS to construct "dummy airfields" in order to confuse the enemy. Going back to the dark days of July 1941, the VVS air force command issued a directive to camouflage airfields. A strict discipline on concealment pervaded air operations throughout the war. No effort was spared to make camouflage and the building of bogus airfields a systematic program.[14] Special teams working with each air army constructed these dummy airstrips largely to misdirect Luftwaffe bombing raids. The practice became so widespread that Luftwaffe aerial reconnaissance personnel took particular pains to locate dummy installations, even making a Russian instruction manual on building of these "airfields" available to photo-interpreters.

As the war progressed, the Soviets devoted great effort to simulating air operations: in July 1943 special teams erected in the district of Voroshilovgrad a whole network of fake airfields. On one such installation they fashioned 183 dummy aircraft, with all the apparent personnel and air support services of a typical VVS airfield. As a consequence, one of these dummy bases was bombed seven times by the Luftwaffe.[15] The clever use of camouflage and concealment techniques by the VVS stands as an impressive achievement. It reflects as well the high seriousness of the Soviet military toward techniques of deception.

The recovery of the Soviet Air Force from the disasters of 1941 had been remarkable, perhaps the most dramatic reversal by any armed service during the war. The VVS had perfected its organizational structure, had built huge air armies, had shrewdly adapted its operational art to serve the Soviet Army in combined arms operations (as well as to meet the peculiar demands of Russian geography), and had narrowed, if not closed, the technological gap with the Luftwaffe. Yet these achievements alone could not guarantee parity with Western air forces in the postwar period. Among the victorious Allied air forces, the VVS had done the least in jet aviation research and development. Unlike the British or Americans, the VVS had no operational jet fighters. With the advent of the nuclear age, the VVS also found itself without a large, long-range bomber force.

To help close the technological gaps in jet aviation, the Soviets made systematic use of German technology to build its first jet fighters—the MiG-9 and YAK-15. When four B-29s made emergency landings on Soviet soil in 1945, after a bombing raid on Japan, the Soviets fortuitously acquired the most advanced American strategic bomber. Within a year the highly derivative Tu-14, almost a carbon copy of the B-29, entered service on the Soviet Air Force. Despite these efforts in the immediate aftermath of World War II, the VVS still faced serious problems in modernizing its aircraft, not to speak of adjusting its air doctrine, to meet the requirements of the nuclear age.

In retrospect, the VVS—along with the Soviet military as a whole—had narrowly escaped defeat. Without the immense productivity of the Soviet aircraft industry, the VVS could not have made its remarkable recovery. Production lines, retooled in 1940 to manufacture a new generation of combat aircraft, turned out more than 125,000 aircraft during the war. This immense outpouring of modern-type aircraft allowed the VVS to recoup its massive losses in 1941 and, as the war continued, keep pace with the high attrition at the front. The herculean effort in 1941 to evacuate war industries beyond the Ural Mountains, a massive display of mobilization, preserved the vast warmaking power of the Soviet Union.

Since the VVS relied ultimately on its quantitative edge to achieve air supremacy, the evacuation of the aircraft industry in 1941 was a necessary prelude to victory. Having preserved these plants, the Soviets after 1942 emphasized the mass production of a few basic aircraft designs, all subject to constant refinement in powerplant and armament. No radical changes in aircraft design were permitted. Wherever possible, the VVS incorporated the technological breakthroughs by the Germans or the Anglo-American air forces.

Today, the epic conflict with Nazi Germany remains a powerful conditioning and limiting factor on developments in the Soviet Air Force. Advances in technology and weapons, as Soviet commentators remind us, have not erased the strategic lessons learned in that war. As recently as the mid-1970s, VVS Commander P. Kutakhov pointed to the Great Patriotic War as a mighty reservoir of strategic wisdom, particularly for air commanders dealing with the application of air power in the contemporary context.[17]

Notes

Chapter 1—The Arduous Beginning

1. I. V. Timokhovich, *Operativnoye iskusstvo Sovetskikh VVS v Velikoy Otechestvennoy voyne* (Moscow: Voyenizdat, 1976), pp. 21–22.
2. M. N. Kozhevnikov, *Komandovaniye i shtab VVS Sovetskoy Armii v Velikoy Otechestvennoy voyne, 1941–1945 g.g.* (Moscow: Nauka, 1977), p. 37.
3. Robert Jackson, *The Red Falcons: The Soviet Air Force in Action, 1916–1969* (London: Clifton Books, 1970), p. 92; Timokhovich, p. 22. The Soviets acknowledged 1,136 aircraft destroyed on June 22, of which 800 were on the ground.
4. See Herman Plocher, *The German Air Force Versus Russia, 1941*, USAF Historical Study, no. 153. (New York: Arno Press, 1965).
5. Timokhovich, p. 26.
6. K. A. Vershinin, *Chetvertaya vozdushnaya* (Moscow: Voyenizdat, 1975), p. 99.
7. Plocher, pp. 41–42.
8. Jackson, p. 85.
9. Barry A. Leach, *German Strategy Against Russia, 1939–1941* (Oxford: Clarendon Press), pp. 193, 202.
10. John Toland, *Adolf Hitler* (New York: Ballantine Books, 1976), p. 924.
11. See A. Yeremenko, *V nachale voyny* (Moscow, 1966.) (Translated into English as the *Arduous Beginning*, Moscow, 1966.) This Soviet work provides ample evidence of Luftwaffe air superiority during the opening months of the war.
12. Leach, p. 193.
13. Toland, pp. 888–89.
14. John Erickson, *The Road to Stalingrad* (New York: Harper and Row, 1975), p. 8.
15. Toland, p. 889.
16. *Ibid.*, pp. 915, 925.
17. Harrison Salisbury, *900 Days: The Siege of Leningrad* (New York: Avon Books, 1970), p. 97.
18. Toland, p. 96.
19. Erickson, p. 65.
20. Gen. K. A. Vershinin, author of *Chetvertaya vozdushnaya*, commanded the 4th Air Army during the war. His memoirs echo the feelings of many Soviet air commanders who claimed in the postwar years that they understood the threat posed by the German overflights, but were unable to act.
21. Alexander Boyd, *The Soviet Air Force Since 1918* (Briarcliff Manor: Stein and Day, 1977), p. 105.
22. Plocher, p. 33.
23. Harriet F. Scott and William F. Scott, *The Armed Forces of the Soviet Union* (Boulder, Colo.: Westview Press, 1979), p. 22; Vershinin, p. 211.
24. Boyd, p. 109; Richard C. Lukas, *Eagles East: The Army Air Force and the Soviet Union, 1941–1945* (Tallahassee: Florida State University Press), p. 9.
25. Alexander Werth, *Russia at War 1941–1945* (New York: Avon Books, 1964), pp. 141–53.
26. Plocher, p. 18; Vershinin, p. 76. Soviet sources claim that the conversion program was 20 percent complete at the time of the German invasion.
27. John Erickson, "The Soviet Responses to Surprise Attack: Three Directives, 22 June, 1941," *Soviet Studies* 23, no. 4 (April 1972): 537.
28. *Ibid.*, pp. 533–34.
29. *Ibid.*
30. *Ibid.*, p. 540; Kozhevnikov, p. 39.
31. Erickson, "The Soviet Responses to Surprise Attack," p. 548.
32. Kozhevnikov, pp. 37–38.
33. See *Aviatsiya i kosmonavtika*, no. 6 (1967): 128.
34. Boyd, pp. 120ff.
35. A. I. Pokryshkin, *Nebo voyny* (Moscow: Voyenizdat, 1975), pp. 7–8.

36. *Ibid.*, p. 15.

37. *Ibid.*, pp. 31–32.

38. *Ibid.*, p. 34.

39. Vershinin, p. 99.

40. Timokhovich, p. 43.

41. A. Ya. Kutepov, ed., *Uchenyy i konstruktor S. V. Il' yushin* (Moscow: Nauka 1978), pp. 178ff; "To Berlin by Night—the Yermolayev Bomber," *Air Enthusiast* 3, no. 4 (October 1972): 181ff; Carl-Fredrik Geust, *Red Stars*, vol. II (Helsinki: Tietoteos, 1982), p. 41.

42. There has been some debate among Soviet historians about who should receive the honor as the first Soviet pilot to perform a *taran*. Some credit Lt. D. V. Kokorev, not Ivanov, as the first, at approximately 4:15 a.m., on June 22, 1941. See A. Zaitsev, "V pervyy den' voiny," *Aviatsiya i kosmonavtika*, no. 6 (1971), and S. Smirnov, "Taran' nad Brestom," *Voyenno-istoricheskiy zhurnal*, no. 1 (1963). For an American wartime reaction to the phenomenon of ramming, see Robert B. Hotz, "The Ramming Russians," *Flying* (October 1942): 32, 100.

43. Kozhevnikov, p. 39; Boyd, pp. 116ff.

44. Kozhevnikov, p. 117. One Soviet pilot, N. Gastello, deliberately flew his aircraft into an advancing enemy column. The "ground *taran*", unlike the aerial *taran*, was an act of suicide. There is speculation, too, that the Finns first employed the ramming tactic during the Winter War, 1939–1940 (anonymous Finnish pilot to author, November 16, 1981).

45. Ray Wagner, ed., *The Soviet Air Force in World War II* (Garden City N.Y.: Doubleday and Co., 1973), p. 101. This work is an English translation of the official history of the Soviet Air Force in World War II.

46. A. Tolstoy and others, *Ram Them!* (Moscow: Foreign Language Publishing House, 1943), p. 18.

47. Lukas, p. 12; Werth, pp. 213–23; "Samoletostroiteli—frontu," *Aviatsiya i kosmonavtika* 8 (1977): 46–47; I. Shakurin, "Aviatsionnaya promyshlennost' nakanune Velikoy Otechestvennoy voyny," *Voprosy istorii* 2 (February 1974): 83ff.

Chapter 2—Where Was Our Air Force?

1. S. A. Krasovskiy, ed., *Aviatsiya i kosmonavtika SSSR* (Moscow: Voyenizdat, 1968), pp. 25–28. A. V. Mozhayev, a former military pilot with the Imperial Russian Air Force, coordinated aviation affairs in the first weeks of Bolshevik rule. For a brief historical account of the first Bolshevik-led air unit see *Vestnik vozdushnogo flota*, no. 7 (1952): 70–74.

2. See *Vestnik letchikov i aviatsionnykh motoristov obnovlennoy Rossii*, no. 1 (May 1917) and no. 2–3 (June 1917).

3. Asher Lee, *The Soviet Air Force* (London: Duckworth, 1952), p. 23; Robert A. Kilmarx, *A History of Soviet Air Power* (New York: Frederick A. Praeger, 1962), p. 44.

4. Istoriya *Voyenno-vozdushnykh sil Sovetskoy Armii* (Moscow: Voyenizdat, 1954), p. 159. A total of 307 of this number were in operational squadrons, 350 in air parks, 112 in storage, and 211 at the factories.

5. Kilmarx, p. 36.

6. Krasovskiy, p. 29.

7. Lee, p. 24.

8. *Ibid*, p. 25; Kilmarx, p. 45–46.

9. Lee, p. 26; Kilmarx, p. 49; Krasovskiy, p. 50.

10. Kilmarx, p. 51.

11. Krasovskiy, p. 42.

12. *Ibid*, p. 53.

13. Lee, pp. 27–28; Kilmarx, p. 63.

14. Krasovskiy, p. 54.

15. "Russia," from *L'Illustration—Paris*, published as a translation in *Aeronautical Digest* 3, no. 2 (August 1923): 87.

16. Krasovskiy, p. 54.

17. *Ibid.*, pp. 54–55; Lee, p. 29.

18. Neil M. Heyman, "NEP and Industrialization to 1928," *Soviet Aviation and Air Power: A Historical View*, ed. Robin Higham and Jacob W. Kipp (Boulder, Colo.: Westview Press, 1978), pp. 39ff.

19. Alexander Boyd, *The Soviet Air Force Since 1918* (New York: Stein and Day, 1977), p. 24; Richard E. Stockwell, *Soviet Air Power* (New York: Pageant Press, 1956), p. 6.

20. Heyman, p. 40; Kilmarx, p. 73, lists a total of 400 German engineers.

21. Heyman, p. 40.

22. Kilmarx, p. 103.

23. Boyd, p. 19. Baranov succeeded A. P. Rozengol'ts. He served as air commander until 1931, when he was succeeded by Ya. I. Alksnis.

24. Heyman, pp. 42–43.

25. Krasovskiy, p. 62.

26. Kilmarx, p. 103.

27. Richard C. Lukas, *Eagles East: The Army Air Forces and the Soviet Union, 1941–1945* (Tallahassee: Florida State University Press, 1970), p. 7; Kenneth R. Whiting, "Soviet Aviation and Air Power under Stalin, 1928–1941," in *Soviet Aviation and Air Power: A Historical View*, p. 66, quotes Shakurin, who claimed that the Soviet Union by the second half of 1940 had twenty-eight aircraft, fourteen engine and thirty-two aircraft-component factories, which, according to Marshal Zhukov in his memoirs, produced 17,745 combat planes, 3,719 of the newer types, between January 1939 and June 22, 1941. See also A. I. Shakurin, "Aviatsionnaya promyshlennost v gody Velikoy Otechestvennoy voyny," *Voprosi istorii*, no. 3 (March 1975): 134–54, and no. 4 (April 1975): 91–103; A. I. Shakurin, "Aviatsionnaya promyshlennost' nakanune Velikoy Otechestrvennoy voyny," *Voprosi istorii*, no. 2 (February 1974): 83.

28. Lukas, p. 7.

29. Kilmarx, p. 105.

30. See Lucas, p. 7. Lukas quotes the "Preliminary Report," 8A-3, of the U.S. War Department, and a second set of estimates from the Institute for Research in Social Science, *The Soviet Aircraft Industry* (Chapel Hill: University of North Carolina, 1955), p. 90.

31. Kilmarx, p. 103.

32. Ray Wagner, ed., *The Soviet Air Force in World War II* (Garden City, N.Y.: Doubleday and Co., 1973), p. 7.

33. The contemporary German MG-17 7.02 MM had a rate-of-fire of 1,000 sychronized, 1,100 unsynchronized.

34. Krasovskiy, p. 63.

35. See K. E. Bailes, "Technology and Legitimacy: Soviet Aviation and Stalinism in the 1930s," *Technology and Culture* 17, no. 1 (January 1976): 24–54.

36. Whiting, p. 53.

37. Bailes, p. 66.

38. Krasovskiy, p. 68, says the contingent consisted of 141 pilots.

39. Derek Wood and Derek Dempster, *The Narrow Margin, the Battle of Britain and the Rise of Air Power, 1930–1940* (London: Arrow Books, 1961), pp. 107ff.

40. Whiting, p. 57, records a total of 1,500 aircraft, about one-third being operational, with 500 to 600 I-15, I-153, I-16 fighters included; Bailes, p. 69, records 500 I-15 and 475 I-16 fighters sent to Spain. The Soviet Military Encyclopedia lists a lower figure of 648 aircraft.

41. Kilmarx, p. 146; Bailes, p. 74. Many of the Soviet pilots who returned from the Spanish war became victims of the Stalinist purges.

42. Whiting, p. 60.

43. Krasovskiy, p. 70.

44. *Ibid.*, p. 71.

45. *Ibid.*, pp. 72–73; Kilmarx, p. 307, fn., lists one source which recorded 600 Japanese aircraft lost to 143 Soviet; Bailes, p. 76, records data from Japanese classified documents listing 1,252 Soviet losses to only 149 Japanese planes.

46. Kilmarx, p. 64.

47. *Ibid.*, p. 151; Whiting, p. 65. According to Carl-Fredrik Geust, Finnish aviation historian, 118 of this total were operational aircraft.

48. Whiting, p. 65.

49. *Ibid.*; Kilmarx, p. 151; Robert Jackson, *The Red Falcons* (London: Clifton Books, 1970), p. 66.

50. Jackson, p. 65.

51. Kalevi Keshinen, *Havittaja-Assat* (Helsinki: Tretoreor, 1977), pp. 150–51. Geust estimates Soviet aircraft losses fell between 620 and 696 for all causes. Finnish losses were sixty-two aircraft and seventy-five pilots.

52. Alexander Boyd, *The Soviet Air Force Since 1918* (New York: Stein and Day, 1977), pp. 37 and 57.

53. *Ibid.*, p. 89.
54. *Ibid.*, p. 90; Scott and Scott, p. 32 fn.
55. See G. A. Ozerov, *Tupolevskaya sharaga* (Frankfurt, 1971).
56. *Ibid.*, quoted in Boyd, *The Soviet Air Force Since 1918*, p. 99; Bailes, p. 71.
57. *Ibid.*
58. Scott and Scott, p. 18.
59. A. M. Nekrich, *June 22, 1941, Soviet Historians and the German Invasion*, trans. Vladimir Petrov (Columbia: University of South Carolina Press, 1968), pp. 134–36.
60. Scott and Scott, p. 20.
61. *Ibid.*, p. 21; Bailes, p. 72.
62. Scott and Scott, p. 21. Among those appointed were: N. G. Kuznetsov, senior naval officer and Deputy People's Commissar of the Navy; Marshal of the Soviet Union S. M. Budyenny, Deputy People's Commissar, and in charge of supplies; A. I. Zaporozhets, Deputy People's Commissar and Chief of the Main Administration of Propaganda for Red Army; Marshal of the Soviet Union G. I. Kulik, Deputy People's Commissar for artillery; Marshal of the Soviet Union B. M. Shaposhnikov, Military Engineers administration; and Gen. K. A. Meretskov, combat training.
63. Bailes, p. 72.
64. Kilmarx, p. 157; Carl-Fredrik Geust et al., *Red Stars in the Sky, the Soviet Air Force in World War Two* (Tietoteos, Finland, 1979), p. 41.
65. Long-range Bomber Command (DBA) replaced *Aviatsiya osobogo naznacheniya* (AON), or "Aviation of Special Assignment."
66. M. N. Kozhevnikov, *Komandovaniye i shtab VVS Sovetskoy Armii v Velikoy Otechestvennoy Voyne 1941–1945 gg.* (Moscow: Nanka, 1977).
67. *Ibid.*
68. Krasovskiy, p. 79.
69. *Ibid.*
70. *Ibid.*, p. 81.
71. Kozhevnikov, pp. 34 ff.
72. Scott and Scott, p. 72 fn.
73. Wagner, p. 7. A. M. Nekrich, *June 22, 1941*, provides an interesting example of how Operation Barbarossa still haunts Soviet historiography of the war. Nekrich, writing in 1965, attacked Stalin for not preparing the Soviet Union adequately for war. Nekrich also criticized Soviet military theory for its failure to deal with a surprise mass attack, the army for its failure to provide realistic training to thwart Nazi aggression, and Stalin for the destruction of the Soviet officer corps on the eve of the invasion. As soon as Nekrich's book appeared, the "de-Stalinization" period gave way to a shift towards Communist orthodoxy. In July 1967 the Control Commission of the Communist party ousted Nekrich from the party ranks, and his work as a historian ended. The debate, however, continues.

Chapter 3—Battle for Moscow

1. Michael T. Florinsky, *Russia: A History and an Interpretation*, vol. 2 (New York, 1965), p. 675.
2. S. A. Krasovskiy, ed., *Aviatsiya i kosmonavtika SSSR* (Moscow: Voyenizdat, 1968), p. 105. See also the official history of the Soviet Air Force edited by Ray Wagner, *The Soviet Air Force in World War II* (Garden City, N.Y.: Doubleday and Company, 1973), p. 65, which lists 364 aircraft. Alexander Boyd, *The Soviet Air Force Since 1918* (New York: Stein and Day, 1977), p. 132, indicates that 373 aircraft were available.
3. Krasovskiy, p. 105. See also "Moskovskaya bitva v tsifrakh (period oborony)," *Voyenno-istoricheskiy zhurnal*, no. 3 (1967): 70–72, which lists a total of 936 aircraft, including 285 fighters. On the Western front, the VVS had 145 fighters as part of a total of 272 aircraft. For an overview of the battle for Moscow, see *Bitva za Moskvu* (Moscow: Moskovskiy robochiy, 1966). This anthology contains accounts of the battle by many important participants, including contributions by N. A. Sbytov and D. A. Zhuravlev on air defense. N. N. Dmitrevskiy, *Zaschitniki neba stolitsy* (Moscow: Voyenizdat, 1962) provides a brief survey of air action over Moscow during the summer of 1941. The most detailed air history is A. B. Fedorov's *Aviatsiya v bitve pod Moskvoy* (Moscow: Nauka, 1971).
4. Fedorov, p. 76.
5. Boyd, p. 130. See also, A. Pervov, "Maneuvr aviatsionnymi reservami stavki VGK,"

Voyenno-istoricheskiy zhurnal, no. 2 (1977): 94–100, and M. Kozhevnikov, "Sozdaniye i ispol'zovaniye aviatsionnykh reservov stavki VGK," *Voyenno-istoricheskiy zhurnal*, no. 10 (1976): 28–35.

6. Fedorov, p. 76. See Konev's own account in "Nachalo Moskovsky bitvy," *Voyenno-istoricheskiy zhurnal*, no. 10 (1966): pp. 65 ff.

7. Fedorov, pp. 77–78.

8. W. Schwabedissen, *The Russian Air Force in the Eyes of German Commanders*, USAF Historical Study, no. 175 (New York: Arno Press, 1960), pp. 138–39.

9. A. A. Yakovlev, *Sovetskiye samolety. Kratkiy ocherk* (Moscow: Nauka, 1979), p. 205.

10. Schwabedissen, pp. 138–39. See also memoirs of Soviet women pilots: R. Ye. Aronova, *Nochnyye ved'my* (Moscow: Sovetskaya Rossiya, 1969 and 1980); M. P. Chechneva, *Samolety ukhodyat v noch* (Moscow: Voyenizdat, 1962); and *Boyevyye podrugi moi* (Moscow: DOSAAF, 1967 and 1975).

11. Wagner, p. 69.

12. *Ibid* pp. 70–71; Fedorov, p. 80.

13. *Ibid*.

14. H. Plocher, *The German Air Force versus Russia, 1941*, USAF Historical Study, no. 153 (New York: Arno Press, 1965), p. 228.

15. M. N. Kozhevnikov, *Komandovaniye i shtab VVS Sovetskoy Armii v Velikoy Otechestvennoy voyne 1941–1945 gg* (Moscow: Nauka, 1977), p. 60.

16. *Ibid*., p. 62; N. Dmitrevskiy, *Zashchitniki neba stolitsy* (Moscow: Boyenizdat, 1962), pp. 13–14.

17. *Ibid*.; Fedorov, pp. 79–96.

18. Seweryn Bialer, ed., *Stalin and His Generals, Soviet Military Memoirs of World War II* (New York: Pegasus, 1969), p. 265; see also Zhukov, "Vospominaniya komanduyushchego frontom," *Bitva za Moskvu*, pp. 55–77.

19. Alexander Werth, *Russia At War, 1941–1945* (New York: Avon Books, 1964), p. 238.

20. *Ibid*., pp. 230–45.

21. Plocher, *The German Air Force Versus Russia, 1941*, pp. 233ff.

22. Plocher, *German Air Force Versus Russia, 1941*, pp. 104–7. For Soviet cold-weather operations, see *Samolet*, no. 1 (1941): 29–30; *Sovetskaya arktika*, no. 12 (1940), pp. 67–69.

23. Wagner, p. 78.

24. General Halder estimated the total losses on the Eastern front as of February 28, 1942, to be 1,005,000 killed, wounded, and missing. See Bialer, p. 596, and Plocher, *German Air Force Versus Russia, 1942*, USAF Historical Study, no. 154, (New York: Arno Press, 1966), p. 113. Alexander Werth, *Russia At War*, p. 225, notes that German losses in the west in 1940 amounted to 156,000 casualties, around 30,000 being killed.

25. Albert Seaton, *The Russo-German War 1941–1945* (New York: Praeger Publishers, 1970), pp. 187–88.

26. Asher Lee, *The German Air Force* (New York: Harper and Brothers Publishers, 1945), pp. 113–14.

27. *Ibid*., p. 115.

28. *Ibid*., p. 114.

29. Kozhevnikov, p. 63–67.

30. Harrison E. Salisbury, *The Unknown War* (New York: Bantam Books, 1978), p. 91. For a detailed account of the Soviet counteroffensive, see Erickson, pp. 297–342.

31. Bialer, p. 594; Kozhevnikov, p. 69. Kozhevnikov states that the VVS had 1,200 aircraft to the Luftwaffe's 700.

32. Werth, pp. 257–59; Salisbury, pp. 107–9.

33. Plocher, *German Air Force Versus Russia, 1941*, pp. 239, 243.

34. The 22d, 39th, 29th, 30th, and 31st armies.

35. See S. I. Rudenko, *Kril'ya pobedy* (Moscow: Voyenizdat, 1976).

36. Fedorov, pp. 175, 176; Boyd, pp. 136–37.

37. *Ibid*., p. 169; Kozhevnikov, pp. 70–73. L. Mikryukov and G. Bryukhovskiy in their recent article, "Opyt boyevogo primeneniya aviatsii pri proryve oborony protivnika," *Voyenno-istoricheskiy zhurnal*, no. 2 (1981), p. 29, indicate that 90 percent of available VVS aircraft were assigned to the Western front, a total of 1,000 warplanes. Among these aircraft, 75 percent supported the right flank of the Western front.

38. Fedorov, pp. 178, 190; Krasovskiy, p. 105. See also I. Mikhaylenko, "Iz opyta upravleniya voyskami protivovozdushnoy oborony Moskvy," *Voyenno-istoricheskiy zhurnal* 12 (1977):

27–34; N. A. Svetlishin, *Voyska PVO strany v Velikoy Otechestvennoy voyne* (Moscow: Nauka, 1979).

39. Fedorov, p. 190; Svetlishin, p. 55, claims the destruction of 952 enemy planes by PVO up to December 5, 1941.

40. Svetlishlin, p. 61.

41. Krasovskiy, p. 119; see also "Protivovozdushnaya oborona Moskvy 1941–1942," *Sovetskaya voyennaya entsiklopediya*, vol. 6, p. 584. Talalikhin belonged to the 177 IAP. Katrich, decorated Hero of the Soviet Union in October 1941, belonged to the 120th IAP, PVO; Katrich's unit was made the 12th Guards Fighter Air Regiment (GvIAP), on March 7, 1942.

42. Krasovskiy, pp. 110–11, 118–20.

43. Kozhevnikov, p. 62.

44. Fedorov, p. 203. The Soviets had forty-nine infantry, fourteen tank, and eight motorized divisions, plus smaller support units.

45. Wagner, p. 88.

46. Fedorov, p. 207.

47. *Ibid.*, p. 208.

48. *Ibid.*, p. 211.

49. Plocher, *German Air Force Versus Russia, 1942*, p. 126; see also Schwabedissen, p. 211.

50. *Ibid.*, pp. 215, 288.

51. Fedorov, p. 211.

52. Plocher, *The German Air Force Versus Russia, 1942*, p. 16.

53. *Ibid.*, p. 69.

54. *Ibid.*, pp. 75–77. The Luftwaffe used the DFS 230 (or LS 230), towed by Ju 52s. They also used the larger GO 242 gliders for the transport of heavier loads, which were towed by He 111 bombers.

55. *Ibid.*, p. 79.

56. *Ibid.*, p. 150; Fritz Morzik, *German Air Force Airlift Operations*, USAF Historical Study, no. 167 (Maxwell AFB, Ala.: Air University, 1961), p. 145.

57. *Ibid.*, p. 172.

58. Plocher, *The German Air Force Versus Russia, 1942*, p. 82. For a description of Soviet anti-aircraft weapons used at Moscow, see V. Prokhorov, "Soviet Anti-aircraft Guns," *Soviet Military Review*, no. 4 (April, 1972): 38–40.

59. *Ibid.*, p. 85; Morzik, p. 158. Morzik indicates that air transport losses to Soviet fighters were slight.

60. F. A. Kostenko, *Korpus krylatoy gvardii* (Moscow: Voyenizdat, 1974), pp. 77–78. Early in the war the Soviet military introduced the "guards" designation, a term drawn from the tsarist past, to honor various air and ground units which had distinguished themselves in battle.

61. I. V. Timokhovich, *Operativnoye iskusstvo Sovetskikh VVS v Velikoy Otechestvennoy voyne* (Moscow: Voyenizdat, 1976), pp. 174–75; V. A. Zhelanov, "Iz opyta pervoy operatsii no okruzheniye," *Voyenno-istoricheskiy zhurnal* (1964, no. 12).

62. Kozhevnikov, p. 83. By spring the Soviet aviation industry had achieved a high level of output, going from 693 planes produced in December 1941, to 976 in January 1942, 882 in February, 1,532 in March, and 1,432 in April. For the first quarter of 1942, 3,301 aircraft were produced; for the entire year, the number was 21,681.

63. Rudenko, *Kril'ya pobedy*, pp. 86–87.

64. Lecture by Adolf Galland, delivered on February 5, 1981, at the National Air and Space Museum, Smithsonian Institution.

65. Boyd, p. 141. See also P. S. Kutakhov, "Glavniy marshal aviatsii A. A. Novikov," *Voyenno-istoricheskiy zhurnal*, no. 11 (November 1970): 62ff.

66. The Berlin raids were planned and conducted under the overall command of Major General Zhvoronkov of the naval air arm of the Red Banner Baltic Fleet (VVS-KBF). A joint task force, drawn from the Baltic Fleet and DA, flying DB-3s and DB-3Fs, operated from Saarema (Osel) Island. There was also an independent air strike made with P3-8 (TB-7) bombers.

67. There is conjecture that only three B-29s were interned by the Soviet Union. One B-29 (with tail number "358") was repaired and test flown. The Soviets copied the B-29 in detail, producing their own version known as the Tu-4.

68. Kozhevnikov, p. 82.

69. *Ibid.*, pp. 83–86.

70. A decree issued by the People's Commissariat of Defense on August 26, 1942.
71. See S. I. Rudenko, "Birth of the Air Armies," *Aerospace Historian* 22, no. 2 (June 1975): 73–76. (Translated by John T. Greenwood.)
72. Wagner, p. 91.
73. Bialer, p. 596.
74. A total of 1,350 large plants were removed, along with 10 million workers and 1.5 million tons of freight by the end of December 1941. See *Istoriya Velikoy Otechestvennoy voyny Sovetskogo Soyuza, 1941–1945*, vol. 6 (Moscow: Voyenizday, 1960–65), pp. 45ff.
75. K. A. Vershinin, *Chetvertaya vozdushnaya* (Moscow: Boyenizdat, 1975), pp. 214–15.
76. Schwabedissen, p. 172.
77. Klaus Uebe, *Russian Reactions to German Airpower in World War II*, USAF Historical Studies, no. 176 (New York: Arno Press, 1964), p. 97.
78. A. I. Yeremenko, *The Arduous Beginning* (Moscow: Progress Publishers, 1966), p. 281.
79. Lee, p. 118.
80. Florinsky, p. 675.

Chapter 4—Stalingrad

1. Ray Wagner, ed., *The Soviet Air Force in World War II* (Garden City, N.Y.: Doubleday and Company, 1973), p. 116, records the following figures: 1941—15,735 aircraft; 1942—25,436 aircraft. By 1942 the MIG-3, Yak-4, and Su-2 types were out of production. The La-5 replaced the LaGG-3, and the Yak-1 gave way to the Yak-76 and the Yak-9. Il-2 ground-attack planes moved through a series of modifications, with the Il-2M3 version (with rear gunner) given high priority. The highly successful Pe-2 dive bomber continued in production, along with the Il-4 bomber. M. N. Kozhevnikov, *Komandovaniye i shtab VVS Sovetskoy Armii v Velkoy Otechestvennoy Voyne 1941–1945 g.g.* (Moscow: Nauka, 1978), p. 83, states that the aircraft production for 1942 was 21,681. See also *Istoriya vtoroy mirovoy voyny 1939–1945*, vol. 5 (Moscow: Voyenizdat, 1974), p. 48.
2. Kozhevnikov, p. 96.
3. Seweryn Bialer, ed., *Stalin and His Generals, Soviet Military Memoirs of World War II* (New York: Pegasus, 1969), p. 354. Shtemenko's reference to the globe is an indirect defense of Stalin. Nikita Khrushchev in his "secret speech" during the Twentieth Party Congress (1956) denounced Stalin and accused him of using the globe to make strategic military plans. See Harrison Salisbury, *The 900 Days: The Siege of Leningrad* (New York: Avon Books, 1968), p. 253.
4. Dement'yev was the first Deputy People's Commissar of the Aviation Industry; Yakovlev, only one of the numerous Deputy People's Commissars. Yakovlev's recollections must be read with caution. For a less complimentary view of Yakovlev see the recollections of A. I. Shakurin in *Voprosy istorii* 6, nos. 4 and 5 (1975).
5. Bialer, pp. 381–82, See also Aleksandr Yakovlev, *Tsel' zhizni zapiski aviakonstruktora* (Moscow: Politizdat, 1972), pp. 317–32; English translation: Alexander Yakovlev, *The Aim of a Lifetime, The Story of Alexander Yakovlev, Designer of the Yak Fighter Plane* (Moscow, Progress Publishers, 1972).
6. Hans-Werner Lerche, *Testpilot auf Beuteflugzeugen Motorbuch* (Verlag Stuttgart, 1977), pp. 213–24.
7. Yakovlev, *The Aim of a Lifetime*, pp. 194–95.
8. During World War II, 35,732 Yak fighters were manufactured: Yak-1, 8,721; Yak-7, 6,399; Yak-9, 16,769; and Yak-3, 4,484. Nearly half were built at Factory No. 153 at Novosibirsk. See Jean Alexander, *Russian Aircraft Since 1940* (London: Putnam, 1975), p. 436.
9. G. K. Prussakov, *16-ya vozdushnaya Voyenno-istoricheskiy ocherk o boyevom puti 16-y vozdushnoy armii, 1942–1945* (Moscow: Voyenizdat, 1973), p. 28. The 220th IAD became the 1st GvIAD (Guards) on January 31, 1943.
10. Kozhevnikov, p. 109.
11. Yakovlev, *The Aim of a Lifetime*, p. 207.
12. Prussakov, p. 11. The 102d IAD PVO became the 2d GvIAD PVO (Guards) on February 10, 1943.
13. *Ibid.*, pp. 13–15; See also S. I. Rudenko, "Aviatsiya v bitve za Stalingrad (Oboronitelniy period-iul-novyabr 1942 goda) *Voyenno-istoricheskiy zhurnal*, no. 7 (July, 1972): 32ff.
14. Prussakov, pp. 31–32. The 434th IAP became the 32d GvIAP (Guards) on November 21, 1942.
15. *Ibid.*, pp. 32–33.

16. *Ibid.*, pp. 29. The 237th IAD became the 54th GvIAP on January 31, 1943. Chenskiye's regiment was the 563d IAP, later 116th GvIAP (September 2, 1943).

17. Kozhevnikov, p. 109.

18. *Ibid.*, p. 104.

19. *Ibid.*, pp. 105ff; See also I. V. Timokhovich, *Operativnoye iskusstvo Sovetskikh VVS v Velikoy Otechestvennoy voyne* (Moscow: Voyenizdat, 1976), p. 35.

20. *Ibid.*, p. 138.

21. S. A. Krasovskiy, ed., *Aviatsiya i kosmonavtika SSSR* (Moscow: Voyenizdat, 1968), pp. 136–37.

22. S. I. Rudenko, "Aviatsiya v kontrnastuplenii," *Voyenno-istoricheskiy zhurnal* 11 (1972): 48. Rudenko gives the total number of Soviet aircraft as 1,350.

23. Wagner, p. 135.

24. Rudenko, "Aviatsiya v. kontrnastuplennii," p. 47.

25. *Ibid.*, p. 48.

26. *Ibid.*

27. See *Polevoy ustav Krasnoy Armii, 1942: Proyekt* (Moscow, 1942), cited in Kozhevnikov, p. 109.

28. Prussakov, p. 44.

29. *Ibid.*, p. 48.

30. Rudenko, "Aviatsiya v kontrnastuplenii," p. 48.

31. Prussakov, p. 44.

32. Wolfgang Pickert, "The Stalingrad Airlift: An Eyewitness Commentary" *Aerospace Historian* 18 (December 1971): 183–86. Pickert states that there were 230,000 German troops encircled. See also Timokhovich, pp. 171ff.

33. Fritz Morzik; *German Air Force Airlift Operations*, USAF Historical Study, no. 167 (Air University, Maxwell AFB, 1961), p. 180.

34. *Ibid.*, p. 181.

35. *Ibid.*, p. 184.

36. *Ibid.*, p. 185.

37. *Ibid.*, p. 186.

38. William Craig, *Enemy at the Gates, The Battle for Stalingrad* (New York: Readers Digest Press, 1973), p. 220.

39. *Ibid.*, p. 216.

40. *Ibid.*, p. 217.

41. Richard Suchenwirth, *Historical Turning Points in the German Air Force War Effort*, USAF Historical Study, no. 189 (Air University, Maxwell AFB, 1959), p. 104.

42. Craig, p. 308.

43. Kozhevnikov, p. 114.

44. S. I. Rudenko, *Kril'ya pobedy* (Moscow: Voyenizdat, 1976), p. 138.

45. Suchenwirth, p. 104, for the German figures; Timokhovich, p. 177, for the Soviet claims.

46. Wagner, pp. 135, 141.

47. Craig, pp. 280–81.

48. Wagner, p. 140. Abdirov's regiment was the 808th ShAP, later the 93d GvShAP (Guards). He was made a Hero of the Soviet Union on March 31, 1943. Molodchy's 748th AP ADD became 2d GvAP (Guards) August 18, 1943.

49. Morzik, p. 191.

50. Rudenko, "Aviatsiya v kontrnastuplenii," p. 52. Rudenko states that the ring was somewhat smaller, five to six miles; see also Timokhovich, pp. 175–79 and Kozhevnikov, pp. 112–13.

51. Prussakov, p. 51.

52. Rudenko, "Aviatsiya v kontrnastuplenii," p. 49.

53. *Ibid.*, p. 59.

54. *Ibid.*, p. 45, 54; See also A. A. Novikov, *V nebe Leningrada, Zapiski komanduyushchego aviatsey* (Moscow: Nauka, 1970), p. 266. Novikov praises the Il-2 units for their day and night, cold-weather operations at Stalingrad.

55. *Ibid.*, pp. 276–77.

56. Schwabedissen, *The Russian Air Force in the Eyes of German Commanders*, pp. 254–55.

57. Morzik, p. 191.

58. Wagner, p. 142; Krasovskiy, p. 139.

59. Prussakov, p. 59.

60. N. M. Skomorokhov, *17-7a Vozdushnaya armiya v boyakh ot Stalingrada do Veny*, (Moscow: Voyenizdat, 1977), p. 31.

61. Kozhevnikov, pp. 117–18.

Chapter 5—Over the Kuban

1. See M. N. Kozhevnikov, *Komandovaniye i shtab v Velikoy Otechestvennoy voyne 1941–1945 gg.* (Moscow: Nauka, 1977).
2. See S. A. Krasovskiy, ed., *Aviatsiya i kosmonavtika SSSR* (Moscow: Voyenizdat, 1968); I. V. Timokhovich, *Operativnoye iskusstvo Sovetskikh VVS v Velikoy Otechestvennoy voyne* (Moscow: Voyenizdat, 1976); and M. V. Zakharov, ed., *50 let Vooruzhennykh Sil SSSR* (Moscow: Voyenizdat, 1968).
3. Aleksandr I. Pokryshkin, *Nebo voyny* (Moscow: Voyenizdat, 1975), pp. 244–53; K. A. Vershinin, *Chetvertaya vozdushnaya* (Moscow: Voyenizdat, 1975), pp. 258–61.
4. H. Plocher, *The German Air Force Versus Russia, 1943*, USAF Historical Study, no. 155 (New York: Arns Press, 1967), pp. 36–50. This defensive bastion of the German 17th Army was called the "Gotenkopf position."
5. Krasovskiy, p. 143; Kozhevnikov, p. 164, states that the Soviet troops of the North Caucasus front were superior to the Germans in infantry and tanks by a factor of 1.5 and in artillery by a smaller amount. But the Luftwaffe (4th Air Fleet) remained dominant at the start of the conflict with 510 bombers, 250 fighters, 60 reconnaissance planes, and 170 transport aircraft. Prior to April 23, 1943, VVS strength consisted of the 4th Air Army (250 airplanes), 5th Air Army (200 airplanes), 70 aircraft from the Black Sea Fleet, and one bomber division (60 aircraft) from Long-Range Aviation (ADD). For defense of the Kuban bridgehead, Kozhevnikov said the Germans placed primary emphasis on the Luftwaffe, which enjoyed a numerical advantage at the outset of hostilities.
6. "The 4th Air Army in Combat for the Motherland," *Aviatsiya i kosmonavtika*, no. 5 (1965): 9.
7. The command structure of the 5th Air Army was attached to the Steppe front on April 24, 1943. Gen. K. A. Vershinin assumed command of the 4th Air Army. See Krasovskiy, p. 147; Vershinin, p. 234.
8. The 16th GvIAP was made a Guards Unit on March 7, 1942 (formerly the 55IAP).
9. Christopher Shores, *Ground Attack Aircraft of World War II* (London: Macdonald and Jane's, 1978), pp. 81–100; Hans-Ulrich Rudel, *Stuka Pilot* (London: Vale and Oakley, 1952), pp 81–93.
10. N. Denisov, *Boyevaya slava sovetskoy aviatsii* (Moscow: Voyenizdat, 1953), p. 145.
11. Vershinin, p. 216.
12. Kozhevnikov, p. 166. See also Vershinin, p. 231. These reinforcements, according to Vershinin, consisted of the 3d Air Corps (Gen. Ye Ya Sovitskiy); 2d Bomber (Gen. V. A. Ushakov); 2d Mixed Air Corps (Gen. I. I. Yeremenko); and 287th Fighter Division (Col. S. P. Danilov).
13. *Ibid.*, p. 231; see also Golubev, *V pare s "sotym"* (Moscow: DOSAAF, 1978), pp. 88–89.
14. *Ibid.*, p. 234. The removal of the 5th Air Army command to the Steppe front (near Kursk) on April 23 released the 287th and 236th Fighter Air Divisions and 132d Night Bomber Division—256 aircraft in all—to the 4th Air Army.
15. Robert A. Kilmarx. *A History of Soviet Air Power* (New York: Frederick A. Praeger, 1962), pp. 174, 200, 207. See also Richard C. Lukas, *Eagles East: The Army Air Forces and the Soviet Union, 1941–1945* (Tallahassee: Florida State University Press, 1970).
16. Vershinin, p. 231. For the growth of the Soviet aviation production, see Alexander Boyd, *The Soviet Air Force Since 1918* (New York: Stein and Day, 1977), pp. 187–204.
17. Pokryshkin, *Nebo voyny*, pp. 235ff.
18. For an account of Soviet frontline airfields, see Ye V. Ovcharenko, *Na frontovykh aerodromakh* (Moscow: Voyenizdat, 1975).
19. Krasovskiy, p. 145. Denisov, p. 145, claimed an overall Luftwaffe strength in Kerch, the Kuban, and the Donbas of 2,000 combat aircraft, about half of them fighters.
20. Earl F. Ziemke, *Stalingrad to Berlin: The German Defeat in the East*, Army Historical Series (Washington: Office of the Chief of Military History, 1968), p. 93. Ziemke lists the strength of Luftwaffe at 4,950 aircraft.
21. Ray Wagner, ed., *The Soviet Air Force in World War II* (official history by the Ministry of Defense of the USSR), translated by Leland Fetzer (Garden City, N.Y.: Doubleday and Company, 1973), p. 148fn.
22. Asher Lee, *The Soviet Air Force* (London: Duckworth, 1952), p. 126.
23. Ibid., p. 127.
24. Zakharov, p. 353. The Myskhako landing group consisted of the 83rd and 255th marine

brigades, the 165th infantry brigade, and a single paratroop regiment. See Leonid
Brezhnev's own account, *Malaya Zemlya* (Moscow: Izdatel'stvo politicheskoy literatury), 1979.

25. Plocher, *The German Air Force Versus Russia, 1943*, pp. 25–26.

26. *Ibid.*, p. 35. The 8th Air Corps had been withdrawn.

27. Kozhevnikov, p. 168.

28. *Ibid.*, p. 168; Vershinin, p. 230. For an account of the VVS role at Myskhako, see A. P. Kalinin, *Istrebiteli nad "goluboy linily"* (Moscow: Voyenizdat), pp. 3–22.

29. Plocher, p. 36.

30. Vershinin, p. 230; Plocher, p. 37.

31. Kalinin, pp. 23 and 53ff, provides a typical interpretation of the role of the Communist party.

32. Kozhevnikov, p. 169.

33. Vershinin, p. 231.

34. Plocher, pp. 37–38.

35. Kozhevnikov, p. 169; Vershinin, p. 232.

36. See Plocher, p. 167, on the importance of the Sarabuz air base for German operations.

37. Krasovskiy, p. 145.

38. *Ibid.*, p. 145; Kozhevnikov, p. 170.

39. Vershinin, p. 233.

40. *Ibid.*, p. 234.

41. Krasovskiy, p. 146.

42. *Ibid.*

43. Kozhevnikov, pp. 171–72; Kalinin, pp. 23–42.

44. Golubev, pp. 90–91.

45. Vershinin, p. 245; Kalinin, pp. 29ff.

46. Vershinin, p. 240. The 2d BAK became the 1st GvBAK (Guards) on September 2, 1943.

47. Plocher, p. 38; Wagner, p. 156.

48. Kozhevnikov, p. 173, records 10,000 sorties flown.

49. Wagner, p. 158.

50. A. L. Ivanov, *Skorost', Manevr', Ogon'* (Moscow: DOSAAF, 1974), pp. 190–219.

51. Plocher, p. 38.

52. *Ibid.*, p. 39; Kozhevnikov, p. 173.

53. Vershinin, p. 252.

54. Shores, p. 73.

55. *Ibid.*, p. 90.

56. Plocher, p. 40.

57. Pokryshkin, p. 243.

58. Shores, p. 85.

59. *Ibid.*, pp. 83–84; Plocher, p. 40.

60. Golubev, pp. 93–94. See Kalinin, pp. 45–54, for a discussion of Kuban air-combat innovations.

61. Vershinin, p. 255.

62. W. Schwabedissen, *The Russian Air Force in the Eyes of German Commanders*, USAF Historical Study, no. 175 (New York: Arno Press, 1960), pp. 36–50.

63. *Ibid.*, p. 197. See also Military Attache Report (Russia), "Information on Russian Fighter Planes," Military Intelligence Division W.D.G.S., dated March 18, 1943. Major Mirles, French volunteer fighter pilot with the VVS, reported that the Soviets assigned their best pilots to the P-39. According to Mirles, many Soviet pilots referred to British Hurricanes as "flying graveyards," but considered the P-51 Mustang the best fighter aircraft in existence.

64. Schwabedissen, p. 198. For a Soviet view of VVS fighter tactics, see V. Myagkov, "Razvitiye taktiki istrebitelnoy aviatsii," *Voyenno-istoricheskiy zhurnal*, no. 6 (June, 1973): 25ff.

65. Pokryshkin, pp. 3–36.

66. Ibid., p. 246–47; Denisov, p. 150.

67. A. I. Pokryshkin, "Nebo voyny," *Aviatsiya i kosmonavtika* 10 (1964): 111. The article is an excerpt from his book *Nebo voyny*.

68. N. Platonov, "V Groznom nebe," *Aviatsiya i kosmonavtika* 9 (1968): 8.

69. Pokryshkin, p. 111.

70. Pokryshkin, *Nebo voyny*, pp. 248–49; Denisov, p. 151.

71. Schwabedissen, p. 196. Schwabedissin pointed out that the technique achieved "no outstanding success." Moreover, it had the disadvantage of committing all fighter units at

once, thereby removing fighter cover at certain times.

72. See *Handbook on USSR Military Forces*, War Department Technical Manual, TM-430, War Department, November 1945, Xl-29-40.

73. *Ibid*.

74. See Wagner, p. 160; Denisov, p. 152.

75. *Handbook on USSR Military Forces*, TM-430, Xl-34.

76. *Ibid*., Xl-37.

77. Krasovskiy, p. 148; Wagner, p. 162. The Krasovskiy account asserts that the VVS suffered "substantially fewer losses," and these were quickly replaced by the increased flow of well-trained flight crews and new types of aircraft. Also, the Krasovskiy history claimed that the Luftwaffe in the spring of 1943 lost 3,700 aircraft (p. 152), an estimate which is wildly exaggerated. In their official history, *The Soviet Air Force in World War II*, edited by Ray Wagner, the Soviet claim is more modest—900 German aircraft destroyed in air combat by VVS air units. (p. 162).

78. *Ibid*., p. 163.

Chapter 6—Kursk

1. Herman Plocher, *The German Air Force Versus Russia, 1943*, USAF Historical Study, no. 155 (New York: Arno Press, 1976), pp. 72–74.

2. Ray Wagner, ed., *The Soviet Air Force in World War II* (Garden City, N.Y.: Doubleday and Co.), p. 165.

3. M. N. Kozhevnikov, *Komandovaniye i shtab VVS Sovetskoy Armii v Velikoy Otechestvennoy voyne, 1941–1945 g.g.* (Moscow: Nauka, 1977), p. 141.

4. Plocher, pp. 80–81.

5. Harriet F. Scott and William F. Scott, *The Armed Forces of the Soviet Union* (Boulder, Colo.: Westview Press, 1979), p. 26, indicates there were 2,800 combat aircraft; most Soviet sources give the figure as 2,900 planes.

6. M. V. Zakharov, ed., *50 let Vooruzhennykh Sil SSSR* (Moscow: Voyenizdat, 1966), pp. 362, 365. At the beginning of July, this Soviet source lists a total VVS inventory of 8,293 aircraft with only 467 classified as older types. The Central and Voronezh fronts together had 3,130 combat aircraft along with the ADD long-range bombers.

7. *Ibid*., p. 363.

8. Earl F. Ziemke, *Stalingrad to Berlin: The German Defeat in the East*, Army Historical Series (Washington: Office of the Chief of Military History, 1968), pp. 134–35.

9. Kozhevnikov, p. 142.

10. Ivan Parotkin, ed., *Battle of Kursk* (Moscow: Progress Press, 1974), pp. 348–50. These estimates are contained in an article by S. I. Rudenko, commander of the 16th Air Army.

11. The RS rockets were first used in 1939 in Khalkhin-Gol.

12. Kozhevnikov, pp. 192–93; see John Erickson, "Radio-location and Air Defense Problem: The Design and Development of Soviet Radar, 1934–1940," *Science Studies* 2 (1972): 241–63.

13. I. V. Timokhovich, *Sovetskaya aviatsiya v bitve pod Kurskom* (Moscow: Voyenizdat, 1959), p. 14. See also Alexander Boyd, *The Soviet Air Force Since 1918* (Briarcliff Manor, N.Y.: Stein and Day, 1977), pp. 172–73; Parotkin, *Battle of Kursk*, p. 194, Albert Seaton, *The Russo-German War* (New York: Praeger Publishers, 1970), p. 358; and Zakharov, p. 361.

14. Timokhovich, pp. 5–7.

15. *Ibid*., p. 15.

16. Kozhevnikov, pp. 148–49.

17. *Ibid*., p. 149.

18. Wagner, p. 167.

19. Timokhovich; p. 39; Plocher, p. 82. Timokhovich claims that the VVS night bomber units flew 42,000 sorties on the eve of the Battle of Kursk.

20. A. V. Vorozheikin, *Nad Kurskoy dugoy* (Moscow: Vozenizdat, 1962), pp. 196ff; Timokhovich, p. 34.

21. Plocher, pp. 84–85; S. Luganskiy, *Na glubokikh virazhakh*, Alma-Ata: Izdatel'stvo "Zhazushy" (1966), pp. 128–30. See also Julius R. Goal, "The Karov Massacre" (*sic*), *Air Combat* 7, no. 4 (July 1979): 75–81.

22. Timokhovich, pp. 51–52.

23. Wagner, pp. 172–73, Kozhevnikov, pp. 149–50; Plocher, p. 84; and Timokhovich, p. 50.

24. *Ibid*., p. 40; Wagner, p . 174.

25. Plocher, p. 85; Wagner, p. 173.
26. Timokhovich, p. 52. The 8th GvIAD was the former 217th IAD. This air division had been transferred to guards status on May 1, 1943.
27. Plocher, pp. 85–86.
28. Kozhevnikov, p. 151.
29. *Ibid.*, pp. 151–52; Timokhovich, pp. 50–56.
30. Kozhevnikov, p. 152; Parotkin, pp. 191–93. See also G. K. Prussakov, *16-ya vozdushnaya. Voyenno-istoricheskiy ocherk o boyevom puti 16-y vozdushnoy armii, 1942–1945* (Moscow: Voyenizdat, 1973), pp. 95–98.
31. Plocher, p. 86.
32. *Ibid.*, p. 87.
33. Kozhevnikov, p. 152; Prussakov, p. 98, claims that the Luftwaffe air sorties over the Central front had been reduced to 870 by July 8.
34. Timokhovich, pp. 57–59; Robert Jackson, *Fighter Pilots of World War II* (New York: St. Martin Press, 1976), pp. 163–76.
35. Wagner, p. 172.
36. Kozhevnikov, pp. 155ff. During the defensive phase of the Battle of Kursk the Soviets claimed 28,00 sorties, 1,000 air battles, 1,400 enemy aircraft destroyed (517 in the Orel sector; 899 in the Belgorod-Kharkov sector).
37. Timokhovich, p. 71.
38. Kozhevnikov, p. 155; Timokhovich, p. 72, claims a figure of 1,500 enemy aircraft destroyed.
39. Kozhevnikov, pp. 151–55.
40. T. Wood and B. Gunston, *Hitler's Luftwaffe. A Pictorial History and Technical Encyclopedia of Hitler's Air Power in World War II* (New York: Crescent Books, 1978), p. 80.
41. See Plocher, pp. 82 and 86.
42. *Ibid.*, p. 87.
43. Timokhovich, p. 76. The West and the Bryansk fronts were under the military command of V. D. Sokolovskiy and M. M. Popov respectively. See also Prussakov, pp. 106–15. The 2d BAK became the 1st GvBAK on September 2, 1943. The 2d ShAK was designated the 3d GvShAK on October 27, 1944.
44. *Ibid.*, p. 180.
45. *Ibid.*, pp. 182; Timokhovich, p. 101.
46. Ibid., pp. 104–5; Kozhevnikov, pp. 159–63.
47. Timokhovich, pp. 100–101.
48. Kozhevnikov, pp. 158ff; Timokhovich, p. 109; Wagner, p. 184.
49. Timokhovich pp. 113–14.
50. A total of 41,000 Shturmoviks if you count the Il-10, an updated version of the Il-2 and Il-8 introduced in 1944.
51. Sergei Il'yushin, "ily na sluzhbe-roding," *Aviatsiya i Kosmonavtika* (May, 5, 1968): 9.
52. A. Ya. Kutepov et al., eds., *S. V. Il'yushin; Scientist and Designer* (*Uchenyy i konstruktor S. V. Il'yushin*) (Moscow: Nauka, 1978), p. 260.
53. Ibid., pp. 261–62; Witold Liss, "The Ilushin Il-2," *Aircraft in Profile*, vol. 4 (1970), p. 188.
54. Kutepov, p. 262. See also S. Chepelyuk, "Razvitiye taktiki shturmovoy aviatsii v Velikoy Otechestvennoy voyne," *Voyenno-istoricheskiy zhurnal*, no. 1 (January 1970): 23–33.
55. "The Annals of Ilyusha . . . Ilyushin's Proliferous Shturmovik," "*Air Enthusiast* 12 (1980): 2; Kutepov, pp. 68, 111.
56. "Annals of the Ilyusha," p. 4.
57. Kutepov, p. 119 (Minayev article). For a description of Soviet armament for both flights and ground-attack aircraft, see George J. Geiger, "Russia's Flying Cannon," *Air Combat* 4, no. 3 (May 1975): 48–61.
58. *Ibid.*
59. "Annals of the Ilyusha," p. 10.
60. Kutepov, p. 112–113 (Minayev article).
61. Kutepov, p. 86 (Yefimov article). For a discussion of Shturmovik tactics and the interaction of Shturmoviks with tanks and artillery, see L. Mikryukov and G. Bryukhivskiy, "Opyt boyevogo primeneniya aviatsii pri proryve oborony protivnika," *Voyenno-istoricheskiy zhurnal*, no. 2 (1981): 30. This same article refers to another source of information on the Kursk battle and the role of aviation: B.A. Ageyev and I.V. Timokhovich, *Bitva pod Kurskom. Deystviya Voyenno-vozdushnykh sil (iyul'-avgust 1943 g.)*, Monino, 1955.

62. *Ibid.*, p. 84.

63. *Ibid.*, p. 86; Sergei Il'yushin, "Na shuzhbe rodiny," p. 6.

64. "Annals of the Ilyusha," p. 5.

65. Kutepov, pp. 74, 82.

66. *Ibid.*, p. 82.

67. Air Intelligence Report, British Joint Staff Mission, Washington, D.C., August 1943; see also George D. Ray, "I Saw Russia's Air Power," *Aviation* (May 1944): pp. 121ff. Ray was an aeronautical engineer who served as a member of a technical mission sent to the Soviet Union in August 1943. His article provides information on the P-39 and Il-2 aircraft.

68. Christopher Shores, *Ground-Attack Aircraft of World War II* (London: Macdonald and Jane's, 1978), pp. 71–73. For a Soviet perspective on Shturmovik tactics, see S. Chelpelyuk, "Razvitiye taktiki shturmovoy aviatsii v Velikoy Otechestvennoy voyny," *Voyenno-istoricheskiy zhurnal* 7 (1970): 23–33.

69. See John T. Greenwood, "The Great Patriotic War, 1941–1945," in R. Higham and J. Kipp, eds., *Soviet Aviation and Air Power, A Historical View* (Boulder, Colo.: Westview Press, 1977), pp. 102–11.

70. Kozhevnikov, pp. 162–63.

Chapter 7—At Full Stride

1. M. N. Kozhevnikov, *Komandovaniye i shtab VVS Sovetskoy Armii v Velikoy Otechestvennoy voyne 1941–1945 g.g.* (Moscow: Nauka, 1977), p. 164.

2. Harriet F. Scott and William F. Scott, *The Armed Forces of the U.S.S.R.* (Boulder, Colo.: Westview Press, 1979), p. 27.

3. H. Plocher, *The German Air Force Versus Russia, 1943* USAF Historical Study, no. 155 (New York: Arno Press, 1967), p. 270. This final section of the Plocher study was written by Harry R. Fletcher. The British Air Ministry's *Rise and Fall of the German Air Force, 1933–1945* (London, 1948) states 1,710 aircraft on the Eastern front, as quoted in John T. Greenwood, "The Great Patriotic War, 1941–1945," unpublished manuscript, which has appeared in an abbreviated form in R. Higham and J. Kipp, *Soviet Aviation and Air Power, A Historical View* (Boulder, Colo.: Westview Press, 1979), pp. 69–136. (Hereafter J. T. Greenwood, unpublished manuscript.)

4. J. T. Greenwood, unpublished manuscript, p. 51.

5. *Ibid.*, p. 56.

6. I. G. Inozemtsev. *Pod krylom-Leningrad* (Moscow: Voyenizdat, 1978), pp. 208–33; A. A. Novikov, *V nebe Leningrada* (Moscow: Nauka, 1970), pp. 273–303.

7. Kozhevnikov, p. 168; "Korsun'-Shevchenkovskaya operatsiya, 1944," Sovetskaya voyennaya entsiklopediya, vol. 4 (Moscow: Voyenizdat, 1977), p. 377, states that the VVS flew 2,800 combat sorties; N. Tereshchenko, "Korsun'-Shevchenkovskaya operatsiya v tsifrakh," *Voyenno-istoricheskiy zhurnal* 11, no. 7 (1962): 49; J. T. Greenwood, unpublished manuscript, p. 98. The 5th Air Army had 754 planes (573 operational), the 2d Army, 243 planes (199 operational). Farther south on the Dnieper River, the 17th Air Army had 552 planes and the 8th Air Army, 811 planes. These two air armies supported the 3d and 4th Ukrainian fronts respectively. Averaging around 500–700 aircraft each, they underwent a rapid expansion during 1944.

8. Kozhevnikov, p. 170; see also N. A. Svetlishin, *Voiska PVO strany v Velikoy Otechestvennoy voyne* (Moscow: Nauka, 1979), pp. 163–80.

9. Kozhevnikov, pp. 170–71.

10. Earl F. Ziemke, *Stalingrad to Berlin: The German Defeat in the East*, Army Historical Series (Washington: Office of the Chief of Military History, 1968), p. 231.

11. *Ibid.*, p. 231–38; *Sovetskaya voyennaya entsiklopediya*, vol. 4, p. 377; *Istoriya Velikoy Otechestvennoy voyne Sovetskogo Soyuza, 1941–1945*, vol. 4 (Moscow: Voyenizdat, 1960–65), pp. 62–69.

12. S. I. Rudenko, "Osobennosti boyevykh deystviy aviatsii v Belorusskoy operatsii," *Voyenno-istoricheskiy zhurnal* 20, no. 2 (1971): 22.

13. For general reference to the Belorussian campaign and the role of Soviet air power, see N. Denisov, *Boyevaya slava sovetskoy aviatsii* (Moscow: Voyenizdat, 1953), pp. 193–201; Kozhevnikov, pp. 171–92; S. A. Krasovskiy et al, *Aviatsiya i Kosmonavtika SSSR* (Moscow: Voyenizdat, 1968), pp. 187–204; G. K. Prussakov et al., *16-ya Vozdushnaya, Voyenno-istoricheskiy ocherk o boyevom puti 16-y vozdushnoy armii (1942–1945)* (Moscow:

Voyenizdat, 1973), pp. 140–85; S. I. Rudenko, *Kryl'ya pobedy* (Moscow: Voyenizdat, 1976), pp. 196–232; S. I. Rudenko, editor, *Sovetskiye voyenno-vozdushnyye sily v Velikoy Otechestvennoy voyne, 1941–1945 g.g.* (Moscow: Voyenizdat, 1968), pp. 290–311 (see English version: Ray Wagner, ed., *The Soviet Air Force in World War II* [Garden City, N.Y: Doubleday and Co., 1973], pp. 269–83). See also S. I. Rudenko, "Osobennosti boyevykh deystviy aviatsii v Belorusskoy operatsii," pp. 22–31 (an English version of this article by S. I. Rudenko has been published with an introduction by John T. Greenwood, "The Belorussian Air Offensive (June–August, 1944)," *Aerospace Historian* [March 1973], pp. 17–26): "Belorusskaya operatsiya, 1944," *Sovetskaya voyennaya ensiklopediya*, vol. 1, pp. 431–34; "Belorusskaya operatsiya v tsifrakh," *Voyenno-istorisheskiy zhurnal* 13, no. 6 (1964).

14. Kozhevnikov, p. 173.

15. Ziemke, p. 321.

16. *Ibid*. Ziemke quotes K. Tippelskirch, *Geschichte des Zweiten Weltkrieges*, p. 462.

17. Quoted in J. T. Greenwood, unpublished manuscript, p. 199, N. N. Pospelov, *Istoriya Velikoy Otechestvennoy voyny Sovetskogo Soyuza, 1941–1945* vol. 4 (Moscow: Voyenizdat, 1960–65), pp. 20, 125.

18. Kozhevnikov, p. 172; Krasovskiy, pp. 185–86.

19. Greenwood, unpublished manuscript, p. 112.

20. Rudenko, *Kryl'ya pobedy*, p. 207; Kozhevnikov, p. 175.

21. General Zhukov commanded the 1st and 2d Belorussian fronts and General Vasilevskiy, the 1st Baltic and the 3d Belorussian fronts.

22. Kozhevnikov, p. 178.

23. V. Murmantseva, "Sovetskiyye zhenshchiny v Velikoy Otechestvennoy voyne 1941–1945 godov," *Voyenno-istoricheskiy zhurnal*, no. 2 (1968): 47–54. For reference to the Gulf of Finland incident, see Ossi Anttonen, *Luftwaffe Suomessa-in Finland 1941–1944*, vol. 2 (Helsinki, 1980), p. 94; V.S. Grisodubova is mentioned in A. M. Verkhosin, *Samolety letyat k partizanam. Zapiski nachal'nika shtaba*, 2d ed. (Moscow: Izdatel'stvo politicheskoy literatury, 1966). One English work, part of the Time-Life "Epic of Flight" series contains a brief, illustrated account of Soviet women fliers: Valerie Moolman, *Women Aloft* (Alexandria, Va.: Time-Life Books, Inc.), pp. 157–64. For the large role of the VVS in the partisan conflict, see Karl Drum, *Airpower and Russian Partisan Warfare*, USAF Historical Study, no. 177 (Research Studies Institute, Air University, 1962).

24. The 3d Air Army, commanded by Gen. N.F. Papivin, consisted of 876 aircraft. Gen. T.T. Khrykin's 1st Air Army had 2,005 airplanes.

25. Kozhevnikov, p. 182; Prussakov, pp. 157–85.

26. Greenwood, unpublished manuscript, p. 114.

27. V.S. Grossman, *With the Red Army in Poland and Byelorussia* (London: Hutchinson and Co., Publishers, 1945), p. 10. For another view of air combat, see A. Pokryshkin, "Letom sorok chetvertogo," *Aviatsiya i kosmonavtika* 8 (1971): 10–11. Pokryshkin commanded the 9th Guards Fighter Division, which flew in support of the 1st Ukrainian front.

28. Rudenko, "Osobennosti boyevykh deystviy aviatsii v Belorusskoy operatsii," p. 21.

29. *Aviatsiya i kosmonavtika* 8 (1964): 22–23.

30. See Ye. V. Ovcharenko, *Na frontovykh aerodronmakh* (Moscow: Voyenizdat, 1975); Denisov, p. 201; Greenwood, unpublished manuscript, p. 124.

31. Interview with Karl Stein, May 1979. Stein flew ground-attack planes with the Luftwaffe on the Eastern front during 1944–45. He states that the Luftwaffe pilots considered the French Normandy regiment to be "very aggressive." Four French pilots received the Hero of the Soviet Union decoration during the war.

32. Alexander Boyd, *The Soviet Air Force Since 1918* (New York: Stein and Day, 1977), p. 182. According to Jan Szczepanski, *Polish Society* (New York: Random House, 1970), pp. 33–42, there was a total of 230,000 Polish soldiers in Western Europe and 380,000 in the underground home army. The Soviets organized the Union of Polish Patriots who fought with the Soviet forces from October 1943 to the end of the war. There were two Polish governments, each with their own army.

33. "Shuttle Bombing Operations Utilizing Bases in Russia," special report by Maj. Gen. F.L. Anderson to commanding general, 15th Air Force, dated April 28, 1944, p. 3.

34. Brig. Gen. B.S. Kelsey (Ret.) to author, January 8, 1981.

35. Glenn B. Infield, *The Poltava Affair, A Russian Warning: An American Tragedy* (New York: Macmillan Publishing Co., 1973), p. 141.

36. Interview with Karl Stein, May 1977.
37. Infield, p. 171.
38. Kozhevnikov, p. 190–91.
39. Novikov, pp. 271–72. For a Soviet perspective on allied strategic bombing, see A. Orlov and N. Komarov," Flying Fortresses over the Third Reich," *Soviet Military Review*, no. 7 (July 1975): 51–52.
40. Adolf Galland to curators and staff, National Air and Space Museum, Smithsonian Institution, February 10, 1981.
41. Compared to the U.S. Army Air Force with its 5,334 heavy bombers in 1945, the VVS had only a handful of Pe-8s (perhaps 79!)—the Soviet Union's sole long-range bomber comparable in range and bomb load to the B-17.
42. Greenwood, unpublished manuscript, pp. 139–41.
43. For the Vistula-Oder campaign, see Denisov, pp. 230–37; Rudenko, *Kryl'ya pobedy*, pp. pp 258–325; Krasovskiy, pp 204–17; Kozhevnikov, pp. 193–98.
44. Greenwood, unpublished manuscript, p. 141.
45. *Ibid.*, p. 142.
46. Kozhevnikov, pp. 193–94.
47. Prussakov, p. 262–65.
48. Kozhevnikov, p. 197; Prussakov, p. 265–70.
49. Prussakov, p. 270. The 176th GvIAP was the former 19th IAP. This unit was elevated to guards status on August 19, 1944.
50. Kozhevnikov, p. 196–97; Prussakov, pp. 227–31, 276 P.; Rudenko, *Kryl'ya pobedy*, pp. 251–56, provides lengthy description and apologia for Soviet action toward Poland.
51. Kozhevnikov, pp. 197–98; Prussakov, pp. 281–91; Rudenko, *Kryl'ya pobedy*, pp. 285–87. The 216th IAD had been elevated to the 9th GvIAD on June 17, 1943.
52. Denisov, p. 232; Kozhevnikov, pp. 198–207.
53. *Ibid*, p. 201. The total amounted to 2,444 aircraft—500 long-range bombers, 470 ground-attack planes, 830 fighters, and 20 torpedo planes (Il-4s?).
54. The first joint naval-VVS air operation occurred on June 25, 1941, when 263 bombers, escorted by 224 fighters, hit targets in Finland and Norway. See Novikov, pp. 50–51.
55. Kozhevnikov, p. 207.
56. For Berlin offensive, see "Berlinskaya operatsiya, 1945," *Sovetskaya Voyennaya entsiklopediya*, vol. 1, pp. 456–61; "Berlinskaya operatsiya v tsifrakh", *Voyenno istoricheskiy zhurnal* 14, no. 4 (1965); Denisov, pp. 233–45; Krasovskiy, pp. 217–21; Prussakov, pp. 321–89; Rudenko, ed., *Sovetskiye voyenno-vozdushnyye sily v Velikoy Otechestvennoy Voyne, 1941–1945 g.g.*, pp. 388–414 (English version: Wagner, ed., pp. 345–60); Rudenko, *Kryl'ya pobedy*, pp. 325–72; A.A. Novikov, "Voyenno-vozdushnyye sily v Berlinskoy operatsii", *Voyenno-istoricheskiy zhurnal* 27 (1975): 89.
57. Kozhevnikov, p. 109. L. Mikryukov and G. Bryukhovskiy in "Opyt boyevogo primeneniya aviatsii pri proryve oborony protivnika," *Voyenno-istoricheskiy zhurnal*, no. 2 (1981), p. 32, point to the rapid increase of VVS aircraft and firepower in the final stages of the war. In 1942 an air army had around 300–400 aircraft; by mid-war, 650–1,000; for the concluding offensives, 1,800–2,500; and for critical operations over 3,000 combat aircraft. They list 3,188 aircraft assigned to the 16th Air Army for the Berlin operations. In 1943, they state, the Soviets dropped an average of 17–20 tons per square kilometer; by 1944 this average had reached 60–80 tons; in 1945, 100 tons or more. As the war progressed the VVS improved its skills at concentrating its air power: the 2d Air Army applied 88 percent of its aircraft in 1944 at one point to support the 1st Ukrainian front. Against major enemy targets, the VVS deployed in 1944–45 anywhere from 350–500 aircraft.
58. Greenwood, unpublished manuscript, p. 152.
59. Kozhevnikov, p. 277.
60. *Ibid.*, p. 286.
61. *Ibid.*, pp. 289–90.

Chapter 8—Barbarossa to Berlin: A Summing Up

1. See Norman Polmar, *Aircraft Carriers, A Graphic History of Carrier Aviation and its Influence on World Events* (Garden City, N.Y.: Doubleday and Co., 1969), pp. 140, 479.
2. Asher Lee, *The German Air Force* (New York: Harper and Brothers, Publishers, 1946), 19. Adolf Galland has written on the reasons for the overall defeat of the Luftwaffe in World

War II in "Defeat of the Luftwaffe: Fundamental Causes," *Air University Review* 6, no. 1 (Spring 1953): 32ff.

3. Interview with author, March 26, 1979.

4. "Dal'naya aviatsiya," *Sovetskaya voyennaya entsiklopediya*, vol. 3, pp. 91–92. See also A.D. Tsykin, *Ot "Il'i Muromtsa" do raketonostsa. Kratkiy ocherk istorii dal'ney aviatsii* (Moscow: 1975).

5. "Vyazemskaya vozdusho-desantnaya operatsiya, 1942," *Sovetskaya entsiklopeduja*, vol. 2, pp. 445–46. See also Hellmuth Reinhardt, "Encirclement at Yukhnov: A Soviet Airborne Operation in World War II," *Military Review* (May 1963): 61–75; *Istoriya Velikoy Otechestvennoy voyny Sovetskogo Soyuza 1941–1945*, vol. 2 (Moscow: Voyenizdat, 1963), pp. 271–362; *Velikaya Otechestvennaya voyna Sovetskogo Soyuza 1941–1945* (Moscow: Voyenizdat, 1970), pp. 114–54; I.I. Lisov, *Desantniki* (Moscow, 1968); and A.G. Fedorov, *Aviatsiya v bitve pod Moskoy* (Moscow: Nauka, 1971), pp. 230–44; I.I. Lisov. *Airborne Troops of the Soviet Army* (Moscow: Novosti Press, 1974) is available but provides only a brief historical background.

6. P. Kutakhov, "Primeneniye VVS po frontovykh nastupatel'nykh operatsiyakh," *Voyenno-istorisheskiy zhurnal* 6 (1977): 34

7. *Ibid*.

8. Ibid., p. 37.

9. See Y. Veraksa, "Air Offensive," *Soviet Military Review* 4 (April 1973): 38–41; I.V. Timokhovich, *Operativnoye iskusstvo Sovetskikh VVS v Velikoy Otechestvennoy voyne* (Moscow: Voyenizdat, 1976), pp. 101–94; K.A. Vershinin, *Chetvertaya vozdushnaya* (Moscow: Voyenizdat, 1975), pp. 214–15. For a wartime analysis of VVS tactics by an American observer, see Curtiss Fuller, "How the Red Air Force Fights," *Flying* (May 1945): 21ff.

10. Contained in *Boyevoy ustav pekhoty Krasnoy Armii* 41 (Moscow, 1942), p. 8, as quoted in M. Kozhevnikov, "Sovershenstvovaniye aviatsionnogo nastupleniya," *Voyenno-istoricheskiy zhurnal* 5 (1971): 16. For further analysis of the air offensive see the following: R.L. Garthoff, *How Russia Makes War* (London: George Allen and Unwin, Ltd., 1954), pp. 326ff; John T. Greenwood, "The Great Patriotic War, 1941–1945," in R. Higham and J.W. Kipp, *Soviet Aviation and Air Power, A Historical View* (Boulder, Colo.: Westview Press, 1977); I.V. Timokhovich, "Aviatsionnaya podderzhka i prikrytiye tankovykh armii po opytii nastupatelnykh operatsii," *Voyenno-istoricheskiy zhurnal* no. 5 (May 1974): 21–27; A. Silant'yev, "Upravleniye aviatsiya v nastupatel'nykh deystviyakh voysk," *Voyenno-istoricheskiy zhurnal*, no. 4 (April 1976): 29–38; and M.N. Kozhevnikov, "Vsaimodeystviye Voyenno-vozdushnykh sil s sukhoputnymi voyskami v nastuplenii," *Voyenno-istoricheskiy zhurnal*, no. 5 (May 1976): 30–38.

11. "Vozdushnaya blokada," *Sovetskaya voyennaya entsiklopediya*, vol. 2, p. 279.

12. Karl Drum, *Airpower and Russian Partisan Warfare*, USAF Historical Studies, no. 177 (Air University, Maxwell AFB, 1962).

13. Timokhovich, p. 325.

14. Ye. Simakov, "Operativnaya maskirovka VVS v nastupatel'nykh operatsiyakh," *Voyenno-istoricheskiy zhurnal* 12 (1977): 19–26; Klaus Uebe, *Russian Reactions to German Airpower in World War II*, USAF Historical Studies, no. 190 (New York: Arno Press, 1964), pp. 35–36; Vershinin, pp. 275ff.

15. Simakov, "Operativnaya maskirovka VVS v nastupatel'nykh operatsiyakh," p. 22.

16. Kutakhov, "Primeneniye VVS vo frontovykh nastupatel'nykh," pp. 30–39; A. Silant'yev, "Nekotoryye voprosy planirovaniya boyevykh deystviy aviatsii v nastupatel'nykh operatsiyakh," *Voyenno-istoricheskiy zhurnal* 12 (1975): 25.

Appendixes

Appendix 1

Combat Sorties, Imperial Russian Air Force, 1914–17*

Month	Year			
	1914	1915	1916	1917
January	—	487	627	1241
February	—	643	463	1264
March	—	650	944	—
April	—	1112	1036	—
May	—	1142	1563	—
June	—	1026	1441	—
July	—	1368	1374	—
August	1162	1099	2116	—
September	369	907	1954	—
October	506	675	1305	—
November	720	466	1098	—
December	472	418	1520	—
Total	3229	9993	15435	2505

* Total sorties for the war, 31,162. Adapted from *Istoriya Voyenno-vozdushnykh sil Sovetskoy Armii* (Moscow: Voyenizdat, 1954).

Appendix 2

Combat Record of Red Air Fleet, 1918–22*

Year	Sorties	Air Battles	Bombs Dropped (kg)	Leaflets Dropped (kg)
1918	1,756	6	2,868	240
1919	3,568	32	7,568	2,272
1920	7,265	93	42,304	5,952
1921	4,436	—	4,136	432
1922	352	—	2,912	—
Naval Aviation 1918–1922	2,000	13	34,720	104
Total	19,377	144	94,508	9,000

* Adapted from *Istoriya Voyenno-vozdushnykh sil Sovetskoy Armii* (Moscow: Voyenizdat, 1954).

Appendix 3

Composition of VVS on Eve of Operation Barbarossa, June 1941

Military District	Air Divisions				Air Regiments				
	BAD	IAD	SAD	Total	BAD	IAD	ShAP	Recon.	Total
1. Leningrad	1	3	4	8	9(1)	13(4)	1	1	24(5)
2. Baltic Special	—	1	4	5	8(1)	8(3)	2(1)	1	19(5)
3. Western Special	2	1	3	6	13(2)	12(5)	2(1)	2	29(8)
4. Kiev Special (June 1, 1941)	3	2	5	10	11(4)	17(5)	2(1)	2	32(10)
5. Odessa (June 1, 1941)	—	—	3	3	7(2)	7(4)	—	1	15(6)

Adapted from M. V. Zakharov, *50 let Vooruzhennykh Sil SSSR* (Moscow: Voyenizdat, 1968). Figures given in parentheses record number of air regiments undergoing transition training with new-model aircraft at the time of the German attack. Abbreviations: BAD—bomber air divisions; IAD—fighter air divisions; SAD—mixed air divisions; ShAP—ground-attack regiment; Recon.—reconnaissance regiments. (See also Glossary.)

Appendix 4

Soviet Air Force Commanders, 1921–45*

A. V. Sergeyev, 1921–22
A. A. Znamenskiy, 1922–23
A. P. Rozengol'ts, 1923–24
I. I. Baranov, 1924–31
Ya. I. Alksnis, 1931–37

A. D. Laktionov, 1937–39
Ya. V. Smushkevich, 1939–40
P. V. Rychagov, 1940–41
P. F. Zhigarev, 1941–42
A. A. Novikov, 1942–45

* The Soviet air arm originated as an organic part of the Red Army (Krasnaya Armiya), known as the Workers and Peasants Red Air Fleet (Raboche-Krest'yanskiy Krasnyy Vozdushnyy flot). After 1924, the Red Air Fleet became known as the Air Forces of the Workers and Peasants Red Army (VVS RKKA—Voyenno-vozdushnyye sily Raboche-Krest'yanskaya Krasnaya Armiya).

Appendix 5

Soviet Air Force High Command, 1941–45

Post	Name	Date
Air Force Commander *	Lt. Gen. P. F. Zhigarev Col. Gen. A. A. Novikov **	June 22, 1941–April, 1942 April 11, 1942–end of war
Deputy Chief, Air Force Main Directorate for Political Affairs	P. S. Stepanov N. S. Shimanov	June 29, 1941–August, 1942 March 17, 1943–end of war
Air Force Chief of Staff	Maj. Gen. P. S. Volodin Maj. Gen. G. A. Vorozheykin Maj. Gen. S. A. Khudyakov Col. Gen. F. Ya. Falaleyev Col. Gen. S. A. Khudyakov	June 22–29, 1941 August, 1941–April, 1942 April–July 1942 July, 1942–May, 1943 May, 1943–end of war
Long-Range Aviation, ADD, Commander	Lt. Gen. A. Ye. Golovanov ***	March 5, 1942–December 6, 1944

* As of June 29, 1941. Held post of USSR Deputy People's Commissariat of Defense.
** A. A. Novikov, as of March 1943 appointed Marshal of Aviation. He became Chief Marshal of Aviation in February 1944.
*** A. Ye. Golovanov was appointed Chief Marshal of Aviation in August 1944. In December 1944 he assumed command of the 18th Air Army, successor to ADD. During Golovanov's tenure as commander of long-range aviation G. G. Gur'yanov served as deputy commander for political affairs; Lt. Gen. M. I. Shevdev (March 1942–July 1944) and Lt. Gen. N. V. Perminov (July–December, 1944), respectively, as chief of staff.

Appendix 6

Air Force Organization, 1943

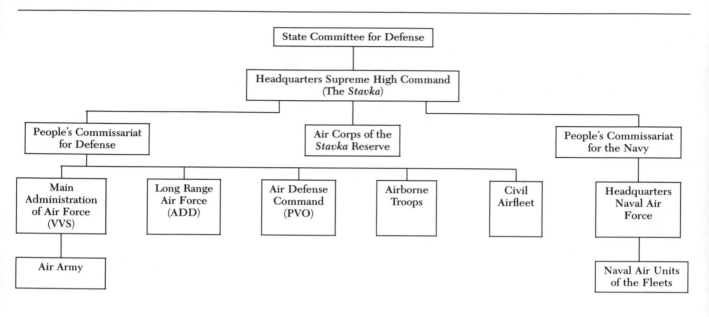

Appendix 7

The Air Armies, 1942–45

The air armies provided the Soviet Air Force (VVS) with a highly mobile air strike force during the Great Patriotic War. The Supreme High Command, the *Stavka*, created a total of eighteen air armies—seventeen from frontal aviation and one from long-range bomber aviation (the 18th Air Army). Except for isolated special units, the air armies became coextensive with Soviet frontal aviation for the period 1942–45. Highly centralized and carefully coordinated with the ground forces, the VVS air armies served as an effective tactical air weapon in both defensive and offensive operations.

Each front possessed its own operational air army. During major offensives, particularly in the last stages of the war, the *Stavka* frequently assigned more than one air army to an active front. Throughout the war the Air Corps of the *Stavka* Reserve systematically absorbed and/or reinforced the various air armies to meet the shifting combat requirements. On occasion, the *Stavka* subordinated one air army to a neighboring one to achieve a concentration of air strength for a combined-arms operation. Through the air armies, the Soviet high command achieved swift deployment of air power, mobility, and unified command.

Between 1942 and 1945 the average size of an air army grew dramatically. Beginning with a modest aggregate of 200 or so aircraft in 1942, it reached around 1,000 aircraft by 1943, and for the final Soviet offensives in 1944–45, it achieved the unprecedented level of 2,000–2,500 aircraft. Some air armies, for example the 16th, in the culminating assault on Berlin, exceeded 3,000 aircraft. Such an augmentation in air power allowed the Soviet military to assert overwhelming air supremacy at crucial points and times.

Abbreviations for Soviet air units: fighter air division—IAD; bomber air division—BAD; ground-attack air division—ShAD. (See also Glossary.)

1st AIR ARMY

Formed:

May 5, 1942. Five air divisions attached to the Western front served as the nucleus for the new air army. Later the 1st Air Army expanded to thirteen air divisions: 201, 202, 234, 235 IAD; 213 (night) BAD; 215 mixed air divisions; and 214, 224, 231, 232, 233 ShAD.

Combat Path:

Participated in a series of air operations from Moscow to Königsberg. Assigned initially to support the Western front near Moscow, the 1st Air Army went on to assist the Soviet Army in the Rzhev-Vyazma offensive (1943), the campaign around Smolensk (winter 1943–44), and the Belorussian-East Prussian campaigns during the concluding phases of the war. At Vitebsk, Orsha, and the Berezina and Nieman river crossings, the 1st Air Army played a significant role. The Normandy-Nieman regiment, a group of French volunteer pilots, served with this air army.

Total Sorties: 290,000

Command:

Gen. T. F. Kutsevalov, May–June, 1942
Maj. Gen. S. A. Khudyakov, June 1942–May 1943
Lt. Gen. M. M. Gromov, May 1943–July 1944
Col. Gen. T. T. Khrykin, July 1944–end of war

2d AIR ARMY

Formed:

May 1942 from air units of the Bryansk front. Eight air divisions: 205, 206, 207 IAD; 208 (night), 223 (short range) BAD; 225, 226, 227 ShAD; and two separate air regiments.

Combat Path:

The 2d Air Army flew diverse combat missions from Voronezh in 1941 to Berlin and Prague in 1945. During the Soviet counteroffensive at Stalingrad in November 1942, the 2d Air Army provided air support for the Southwestern front. Later it joined with the 8th, 16th, and 17th air armies to execute the successful air blockade at Stalingrad. At Kursk, the 2d Air Army flew more than 15,000 combat sorties in support of the Voronezh front, followed by air operations in support of the Soviet drive to cross the Dnieper River. During the final phases of the war the 2d participated in a number of difficult undertakings: The Korsun-Shevchenkovskiy and L'vov-Sandomir operations of 1944; and the campaigns in Czechoslovakia and at Berlin in 1945. Top VVS ace I. N. Kozhedub (62 victories) flew with the 2d Air Army.

Total Sorties: 300,000

Command:

Maj. Gen. S. A. Krasovskiy, May–July, 1942
Maj. Gen. K. N. Smirnov, July 1942–March 1943
Col. Gen. S. A. Krasovskiy, March 1943–end of war

3d AIR ARMY

Formed:

May 1942. Organized with air elements of the Kalinin front, consisting of six air divisions: 209, 210, 256 IAD; 212 and 264 ShAD; and 211 BAD.

Combat Path:

The 3d Air Army first entered combat in July 1942 in the Rzhev sector west of Moscow. In February 1943 it applied air pressure on trapped German army units at Demyansk. Later in the same year the 3d Air Army participated in the campaign to capture Smolensk. Attached to the 1st Baltic front in 1944, the 3d Air Army took part in the Belorussian campaign. In 1945, it flew numerous sorties in support of the East Prussian offensive, concluding the war on the Leningrad front in joint operation with the 15th Air Army. The 3d Air Army provided sustained air support and liaison with partisan units in Belorussian and Baltic areas.

Total Sorties: 200,000

Command:

Maj. Gen. M.M. Gromov, May 1942–May 1943

Col. Gen. N.F. Papavin, May 1943–end of war

4th AIR ARMY

Formed:

May 1942. Based on frontal aviation of the Southern front. Initial air strength consisted of six air divisions: 216, 217, 229 IAD; 218 (night), 219 BAD; 230 ShAD; and seven air regiments.

Combat Path:

The 4th Air Army, particularly its fighter air units, established its impressive combat record in the Caucasus in 1942. Having fought in defensive operations in the Donbas and North Caucasus, the 4th Air Army went on to engage in the intense air battles over Krasnodar, Kerch, the Kuban, and the Crimea in 1943. With the clearing of the Crimea of enemy troops in the spring of 1944, the 4th Air Army moved north to join 2d Belorussian front in June–July 1944 for the Belorussian offensive. In January 1945, the 4th Air Army supported the Soviet drive into East Prussia, to be followed by air operations over the Oder River and at Berlin.

Total Sorties: 300,000

Command:

Maj. Gen. K. A. Vershinin, May–September 1942

Maj. Gen. N. F. Naumenko, September 1942–May 1943

Col. Gen. K. A. Vershinin, May 1943–end of war

5th AIR ARMY

Formed:

May 1942. Based on the North Caucasus front. Composition at outset included five air divisions: 236, 237, 265 IAD; 132 BAD; 238 ShAD; and separate air regiments.

Combat Path:

The 5th Air Army entered combat in the summer of 1942, providing air support for retreating Soviet forces in the North Caucasus. With the 4th Air Army, it participated in the crucial Kuban air operations in the spring of 1943. At the time of Kursk, the 5th Air Army engaged in the Soviet offensive operations in the Belgorod-Kharkov sector. During the winter of 1943–44, it flew in support of the Dnieper River crossings and the capture of Kiev. Subsequent operations followed a combat path across the Ukraine into Rumania, Hungary, Czechoslovakia, and Austria.

Total Sorties: 180,000

Command:

Col. Gen. S. K. Goryunov, 1942–end of war

6th AIR ARMY

Formed:

June 1942. Organized with the frontal air units of the Northwestern front and composed of five air divisions: 239 and 240 IAD; 241, 242 (night) BAD; 243 ShAD, and seven mixed air regiments and three separate air squadrons.

Combat Path:

The 6th Air Army was relatively inactive in the first months of its existence. In 1943, however, it assisted in the air blockade of the Demyansk pocket and participated with an air group mobilized to support the Kalinin front. In November 1943, it was withdrawn into the Air Corps of the *Stavka* Reserve with selected air units transferred to the 15th Air Army. In February 1944, the 6th Air Army entered active status again in support of the 2d Belorussian front, to be reassigned in April to the 1st Belorussian front under the overall command of the 16th Air Army. During the summer of 1944, the 6th participated in the Belorussian offensive. Subsequent operations included the Soviet drive into Poland and the Vistula River crossing. Withdrawn into the Air Corps of the *Stavka* Reserve in September 1944. Command of 6th Air Army served as the basis for the new, Soviet-sponsored Polish Air Force.

Total Sorties: 120,000

Command:

Maj. Gen. D. F. Kondratyk, June 1942–January 1943

Col. Gen. F. P. Polynin, January 1943–October 1944

7th AIR ARMY

Formed:

November 1942. Karelian front. Initial composition consisted of four air divisions: 258, 259 IAD; 260 ShAD; and 261 BAD.

Combat Path:

Wartime air operations largely restricted to the Karelian front, although air units from the 7th Air Army did conduct joint operations with the naval air arm of the Northern Fleet. In the summer of 1944, the 7th Air Army provided air cover for Soviet troops crossing the Svir' River. In October 1944, it covered troops of the 14th in their offensive in the Petsamo-Kirkenes sector. By the end of 1944, the 7th Air Army entered the Air Corps of the *Stavka* Reserve.

Total Sorties: 60,000

Command:

Col. Gen. I. M. Sokolov

8th AIR ARMY

Formed:

June 1942. Organized on the Southwestern front with an initial air strength of ten air divisions: 206, 220, 235, 268, 269 IAD; 270, 271, 272 BAD; and 226, 228 ShAD.

Combat Path:

The 8th Air Army first entered combat in the summer of 1942, providing air cover in the defensive battles around Poltava and Stalingrad. Once the Soviet counteroffensive at Stalingrad began in November 1942, the 8th Air Army assumed a leading role in the Soviet air blockade of the encircled German 6th Army. After the Stalingrad air operations, the 8th Air Army supported Soviet offensives at Rostov, in the Donbas, and across the Dnieper River in 1943. During 1944, the 8th again played a major role in the south, assisting both the 1st and 4th Ukrainian fronts in wide-ranging air operations from the Crimea to the Carpathian Mountains. The 8th Air Army also participated in the crucial L'vov-Sandomir operation, July–August 1944. In the final Soviet offensives of 1945, the 8th Air Army provided air support for the Soviet Army's drive through southern Poland and Czechoslovakia, culminating in the capture of Prague.

Total Sorties: 220,000

Command:

Col. Gen. T. T. Khryukin, June 1942–July 1944

Lt. Gen. V. N. Zhdanov, August 1944–end of war

9th AIR ARMY

Formed:

August 1942. Based on the air units of the 1st, 25th, and 35th Combined-arms armies of the Far East front. Seven air divisions formed the air army: 32, 249, 250 IAD; 33, 34 BAD; and 251, 252 ShAD.

Combat Path:

Up to April 1945, the 9th Air Army helped to secure the airspace of the Soviet Far East. For the assault in August 1945 on the Japanese Kwantung Army, the 9th Air Army assisted the Soviet 1st Red Banner and 5th armies. Reinforced with the 19th Bomber Air Corps (BAK), from long-range aviation, the 9th Air Army hit the enemy rear at Harbin and other key points. It also aided Soviet airborne troops in landings at major Manchurian cities, such as Changchun, Mukden, and Harbin.

Total Sorties: 4,400

Command:

Maj. Gen. A. S. Senatorov, August–September 1944

Maj. Gen. V. A. Vinogradov, September 1944–June 1945

Col. Gen. I. M. Sokolov, June 2–September 1945

10th AIR ARMY

Formed:

August 1942. Based on the air force of the 25th Combined-Arms Army of the Far East front. A total of five air divisions: 29 IAD; 53, 83, 254 BAD; and 253 ShAD.

Combat Path:

In the war with Japan, the 10th Air Army was attached to the 2d Far East front. During this campaign the 10th devoted most of its resources to the Soviet 25th Army and the Red Banner Amur River Flotilla.

Total Sorties: 3,297

Command:

Maj. Gen. V. A. Vinogradov, August 1942–September 1944

Col. D. Ya. Slobozhan, September 1944–May 1945

Col. Gen. P. F. Zhigarev, June–September 1945

11th AIR ARMY

Formed:

August 1942. Based on air units of the 2d Red Banner Army of the Far East, the 11th Air Army consisted of three air divisions: 96 IAD; 82 BAD; and 206 SAD (mixed).

Combat Path:

On December 20, 1944, the *Stavka* reorganized the 11th Air Army into the 18th Mixed Air Corps. For the war with Japan, this air corps entered the 10th Air Army.

Command:

Maj. Gen. V. N. Bibikov

12th AIR ARMY

Formed:

August 1942. Attached to the Trans-Baikal front with an air strength of five air divisions: 245, 246 IAD; 30, 247 BAD; and 248 ShAD.

Combat Path:

Up to August 1945, the 12th Air Army helped to secure the border in the Far East, and to prepare pilots for combat. For the war with Japan, the 12th Air Army possessed thirteen air divisions. Along with its air support role for the advancing Soviet troops in Manchuria, the 12th Air Army also flew joint missions with the naval air arm of the Pacific Fleet, and landed assault troops at crucial points, such as Changchun and Mukden, and airlifted supplies to the 6th Tank Army.

Total Sorties: 5,000

Command:

Lt. Gen. T. F. Kutsevalov, August 1942–June 1945

Gen. S. A. Khudyakov, July–September 1945

13th AIR ARMY

Formed:

November 1942, Leningrad front. Consisted of three air divisions: 275 IAD, 276 BAD, and 277 ShAD.

Combat Path:

The 13th Air Army first participated with the 67th Army of the Leningrad front in January 1943, a total of 2,000 sorties, in an effort to break the siege of Leningrad. Subsequent air operations in 1943 centered in Krasnoborsk and Minsk sectors. At the beginning of 1944, the 13th Air Army played an active role in the Soviet offensive which lifted the Leningrad siege. During 1944, air units of 13th assisted in the capture of Vyborg, and, to the south, supported Soviet troops in their drive toward Tallinn. The 13th Air Army ended its active combat role with the clearing of Estonia of enemy forces in November 1944.

Total Sorties: 120,000

Command:

Col. Gen. S. D. Rybal'chenko

14th AIR ARMY

Formed:

June 1942. Organized with the aviation of the Volkhov front. Four air divisions: 278, 279 IAD; 280 BAD; and 281 ShAD.

Combat Path:

The 14th Air Army participated in the 1943 winter offensive in Leningrad sector. A year later, it flew against German defensive positions in the Leningrad-Novgorod sector, part of an offensive effort which lifted the siege of Leningrad. In April it joined the 3d Baltic front in the Pskov sector. In the fall of 1944, the 14th Air Army assisted in the clearing of enemy forces from the Baltic (Tartu and Riga operations). At the end of 1944, it entered the Air Corps of the *Stavka* Reserve with many of its air units reassigned to other air armies.

Total Sorties: 80,000

Command:

Lt. Gen. I. P. Zhigarev

15th AIR ARMY

Formed:

July 1942. Organized with three air divisions of the Bryansk front: 286 IAD, 284 BAD, 225 ShAD; and three separate air regiments.

Combat Path:

The 15th Air Army first entered combat in the defensive fighting around Voronezh in the fall of 1942. During the following winter (1942–43) it supported the troops of the Bryansk front. The 15th Air Army participated in the crucial Battle of Kursk in the summer of 1943. In October 1943, it moved to the 2d Baltic front at Vitebsk to conduct air operations against Army Group North. In 1944 it played an active role in the Soviet drive into Latvia, culminating in the capture of Riga. The 15th ended its combat activity in support of the 2d Baltic front in 1945.

Total Sorties: 160,000

Command:

Maj. Gen. I. G. Pyatykhin, July 1942–May 1943

Lt. Gen. N. F. Naumenko, May 1943–end of war

16th AIR ARMY

Formed:

August 1942. At the outset, consisted of four air divisions: 220, 283 IAD; 228, 291 ShAD; and two separate air regiments.

Combat Path:

The 16th, destined to be one of the major VVS air armies, began its operational life on September 4, 1942, in defense of the Stalingrad front. It then participated in the counteroffensive and air blockade at Stalingrad in the winter of 1942–43 (Don front). Switched to the Central front in spring 1943, the 16th contributed 56,350 combat sorties in the crucial battle of Kursk. In the winter of 1943–44, it assumed a pivotal role in the liberation of the Ukraine and eastern portions of Belorussia. Attached to the 1st Belorussian front in the summer of 1944, the veteran 16th Air Army contributed major blows in the destruction of Army Group Center, particularly in the Bobruysk and Minsk sectors. For the second half of 1944, units of this air army operated in eastern Poland. The *Stavka* deployed the 16th Air Army in 1945 for major responsibilities, again with the 1st Belorussian front: the Warsaw-Poznan operations in January–February; the East Pomeranian operations in February–March; and the culminating assault on Berlin in April–May. For the Berlin operations, the 16th Air Army possessed over 3,000 aircraft (eight air corps, plus separate air divisions and regiments).

Total Sorties: 280,000

Command:

Maj. Gen. P. S. Stepanov, August–October 1942

Col. Gen. S. I. Rudenko, October 1942–end of war

17th AIR ARMY

Formed:

November 1942. Based on frontal aviation of the Southwestern front. Initial composition of the air army consisted of the following: 282, 288 IAD; 221, 262 (night) BAD; and 208, 637 ShAD.

Combat Path:

The 17th Air Army first entered combat at Stalingrad in November 1942, supporting the Soviet counteroffensive to encircle the German 6th Army. It then participated in the subsequent air blockade of the encircled enemy troops. After Stalingrad, the 17th Air Army supported the Southwestern front in its offensive to reoccupy the Donbas. In July it took part in the defensive battles at Kursk in support of the Voronezh front. Once the Soviet counteroffensive had begun at Kursk, the 17th moved south, concentrating its air strength around Kharkov in late August 1943. From this sector, it moved westward across the southern Ukraine in the fall of 1943. During the winter of 1943–44, units of this air army played a major role in the Soviet drive to liberate the Ukraine. Other important air campaigns followed in late 1944 to the end of the war: the Jassy-Kishinev operation; the invasion of Hungary; the capture of Vienna; and concluding air operations in Czechoslovakia.

Total Sorties: 200,000

Command:

Lt. Gen. S. A. Krasovskiy, November 1942–March 1943

Col. Gen. V. A. Sudets, March 1943–end of war

18th AIR ARMY

Formed:

December 1944. Successor to ADD, or Long-Range Aviation. A total of five BAK, bomber air corps, made up the 18th Air Army: 1st Guards Smolenskiy, 2d Guards Bryansk, 3d Guards Stalingradskiy, 4th Guards Gomel'skiy, and 19th BAK; and four separate BAD. Together these units amounted to twenty-two air divisions. Administration remained in Moscow; command post moved to Brest toward the end of the war.

Combat Path:

The 18th Air Army, according to Soviet accounts, established an active combat role in the final campaigns of the war, first in the Vistula-Oder offensive and subsequently in East Prussia and at Berlin. Its bombing missions were coordinated with Soviet frontal aviation, hitting enemy cities, strong points, communications, and reserves. During the storming of Königsberg (April 7, 1945), the 18th Air Army launched a daytime raid by 516 bombers to assist troops of the 3d Belorussian front. A subsequent raid on the Oder River defenses consisted of 743 bombers. The 19th BAK participated in the campaign against the Japanese Kwantung army in August 1945.

Total Sorties: 19,164 (13,368 night) for the period January 1–May 8, 1945.

Command:

Marshal of Aviation A. E. Golovanov

Appendix 8

Combat Aircraft of Soviet Air Force, 1941–1945*

	General Data			Performance Data			Armament		Production
Type	Year	Engine type/hp	Gross Weight kg(lb.)	Speed km/hr(mph)	Range km(miles)	Ceiling m(ft.)	Guns mm	Bomb Load kg(lb.)	Totals
Fighters									
I-15	1933	M-25/715	1,373(3,020)	362(225)	725(450)	9,800(32,150)	4 × 7.62	100(220)	674
I-15bis	1936	M-25B/775	1,659(3657)	370(230)	770(478)	9,800(32,150)	4 × 7.62	150(331)	2,408
I-16	1933	M-25/715	1,422(3,135)	454(282)	820(510)	9,200(30,175)	4 × 7.62	100(220)	6,555
I-16 (Type 24)	1939	M-62/1000	1,912(4,215)	489(304)	600(373)	9,470(31,070)	2 × 7.62 2 × 20		
I-153	1938	M-62/1000	1,960(4,221)	444(280)	470(292)	10,700(35,105)	4 × 7.62	200(440)	3,437
LaGG-3	1940	M-105PF/1,210	3,150(6,944)	570(354)	556(345)	9,600(31,495)	2 × 7.62 1 × 12.7 1 × 20	200(440)	6,528
MiG-3	1940	AM-35A/1350	3,350(7,385)	640(398)	1,250(777)	12,000(39,360)	2 × 7.62 1 × 12.7	200(440)	3,322 (100 MiG-1)
Yak-1	1940	M-105P/1050	2,895(6,382)	585(364)	850(528)	9,500(31,170)	2 × 7.62 1 × 20	200(440)	8,721
Yak-7b	1942	VK-105PF/1,210	3,030(6,680)	615(382)	820(509)	10,000(32,810)	1 × 20 2 × 12.7	—	6,399
Yak-9D	1943	VK-105PF-3/1,360	3,080(6,790)	602(374)	1,410(876)	10,600(34,775)	2 × 12.7 1 × 37	—	16,769
Yak-3	1943	VK-105PF/1240	2,659(5,842)	660(410)	900(559)	10,800(35,425)	2 × 12.7 1 × 20	—	4,848
		VK-107A/1659	2,984(6,579)	720(447)	1,660(659)	11,800(38,350)	2 × 20		
La-5FN	1942	ASh-82FN/1850	3,230(7,121)	648(403)	765(475)	9,500(31,160)	2 × 20	—	10,000
La-7	1944	ASh-82FNV/1850	3,265(7,183)	665(413)	635(395)	9,900(32,470)	2 × 20	100(220)	5,754
Bombers									
DB-3	1937	2 × M-85/765	7,600(16,758)	408(254)	3,000(1,860) (max.)	8,400(27,560)	1 × 12.7 2 × 7.62	500(1102)	1,528
IL-4 (DB-3F)	1938	2 × M-88b/1100	10,055(22,167)	445(277)	3,800(2,361) (max.)	9,700(31,800)	1 × 12.7 2 × 7.62	1,000(2204)	5,256

Aircraft	Year	Powerplant	Weight kg(lb)	Speed km/h(mph)	Range/Ceiling	Ceiling m(ft)	Armament	Bomb load kg(lb)	Number built
Pe-2	1940	2 × M-105R/1100	8,520(18,783)	540(336)	1,200(746)	8,800(28,900)	3 × 12.7 / 2 × 7.62 (also 20)	600(1323)	11,427
Pe-8 (TB-7)	1939	4 × AM-35A/1350	32,000(70,548)	440(273)	4,700(2,920) (max.)	9,300(30,500)	2 × 20 / 2 × 7.62 / 2 × 12.7	2,000(4409) or 4,000(8818)	79
SB-2	1934	2 × M-100A/860	5,732(12,637)	424(263)	980(608)	9,560(31,350)	4 × 7.62	500(1102)	6,656
SB-2bis	1939	2 × M-103/960	6,380(14,036)	450(279)	1,200(745)	10,000(32,800) (max.)	4 × 7.62	600(1320)	
Su-2	1940	1 × M-82/1330	4,700(10,340) (max.)	486(302)	1,100(683)	8,400(27,550)	—	400(880)	—
TB-3	1930	4 × M-34RN/970	19,500(43,000)	288(179)	2,470(1,535)	7,740(25,390)	8 × 7.62	2,000(4,409)	818
Tu-2	1943	2 × ASh-82FN/1850	10,380(22,880)	547(340)	2,100(1,305) (max.)	9,500(31,170)	3 × 12.7	1,000(2,200)	2,527
Ground Attack									
Il-2	1939	1 × AM-38/1600	5,340(11,775)	470(292)	750(465) (max.)	4,000(13,120) (service)	2 × 23 / 2 × 7.62	400(880)	36,163
IL-2/M3	1942	1 × AM-38F/1760	5,873(12,950)	420(261)	765(475)	3,500(11,480) (service)	2 × 23 / 2 × 7.62 / 1 × 12.7 (rear)		
IL-10	1944	1 × AM-42/2000	6,336(13,979)	507(315)	1,000(620) (max.)	7,500(24,600) (max.)	2 × 23 / 2 × 7.62 / 1 × 12.7 (rear)	400(880)	4,966
Others									
Po-2 (U-2)	1927	1 × M-110/115	1,400(3,080)	131(81)	450(280)	1,500(4,920)	—	250(550)	20,000
MBR-2	1932	M-17B/680	4,182(9,220)	195(121)	1,500(932)	—	3 × 7.62	300(600)	
MBR-2bis	1935	M-34N/830	4,245(9,358)	243(151)	1,500(932)	5,000(16,404)	2 × 7.62		1,300

* The above data on powerplant, performance, and armament is approximate, suggesting typical variants of Soviet aircraft which participated in the Great Patriotic War. Throughout the war the Soviets made many design refinements, as well as field modifications, to update their basic fighter, bomber, and ground-attack aircraft. The transition to lighter, faster, and more heavily armed aircraft is apparent. Maximum speeds are calculated at varying altitudes, but normally below 16,000 feet, where Soviet aircraft operated. Bomb loads varied, and the total load often included both bombs and rockets. Soviet sources on aircraft data differ on occasion, but two authoritative reference books exist: B.V. Shavrov *Istoriya konstruktsiy samoletov v SSSR,* vol. I (up to 1938), vol. II (1938–1950) (Moscow: Mashinostoyeniye, 1969 and 1978); A.S. Yakovlev, *Sovetskiye samolety* (Moscow: Nauka, 1979). See also Bibliography.

Appendix 9

Soviet Aircraft Production

Production of Soviet Aircraft, 1931–37

Year	Bombers	Fighters	Total (All Types)
1931	100	120	860
1933	291	336	2,952
1935	59	776	2,529
1937	1,303	2,129	4,435

Productions of New Types, 1940–June 1941

Year 1940–1941	MiG-1	MiG-3	Yak-1	LaGG-3	IL-2	Pe-2	Total
(to June 22)	111	1,289	399	322	249	459	2,829

Production of Soviet Aircraft, 1941–45

Year	Total Aircraft	Average Per Month	Output in Percentage compared with 1940
1941 (second half)	9,777	1,630	—
1942	25,436	2,120	178
1943	34,884	2,907	223
1944	40,241	3,355	239
1945 (to May 10)	15,317	3,483	—
Total	125,655*		

* This figure includes approximately 54,000 fighters, 35,000 Shturmoviks and 16,000 bombers of various types. Tables are adapted from the *Sovetskaya voyennaya entsiklopediya*, vol. 1, pp. 28–29.

Appendix 10

Lend-Lease Aircraft Exports to USSR
June 22, 1941–September 20, 1945

Aircraft Types Delivered to Soviet Union

Type	Delivered at Destination
Fighters	
P-39	4,719
P-40	2,097
P-47	195
P-63	2,400
Total	9,438
Bombers	
A-20	2,908
B-25	862
B-24A	1
Total	3,771
Others	
C-46	1
C-47	707
O-52	19
AT-6	82
Total	809

Aircraft Shipments by Route

Alaskan-Siberian Ferry Route	7,925
South Atlantic Ferry Route	993
Water Route to North Russia	1,232
Water Route to Abadan, Iran	3,868
Total	14,018

Adapted from Richard C. Lukas, *Eagles East: The Army Air Force and the Soviet Union, 1941–1945* (Tallahassee: Florida State University Press, 1970). Lukas provides a detailed breakdown of Lend-Lease shipments by route and type, showing figures as well for aircraft lost enroute or diverted to other destinations. His figures, which include Lend-Lease shipments via the United Kingdom, are based on the *Report on War Aid Furnished by the United States to the USSR* (Office of Foreign Liquidation, Department of State, Washington, 1945). See also Ray Wagner, ed., *The Soviet Air Force in World War II.* (Garden City, N.Y.: Doubleday and Company, 1973), pp. 397–99.

Appendix 11

Soviet Naval Aviation

Soviet naval aviation, *Aviatsiya Voyenno-morskogo flota* (VVS-VMF), played only a peripheral role in the Great Patriotic War. At various times naval aviation joined with frontal aviation, normally adjacent air armies, to contribute valued assistance in defensive and offensive air operations. But these local air actions at best merely supplemented the larger-scale efforts of the VVS in support of the ground forces. Despite the limited nature of VVS-VMF air operations, a reflection of the overall restricted role of the Soviet Navy in the war, contemporary Soviet histories stress the crucial role of the naval air arm as part of a combined-arms effort against the Germans. While this appears exaggerated as history, it does reflect Soviet military doctrine, which explains victory in the war as a combined effort of all military branches.

Russian naval aviation first appeared in 1912–14, when the tsarist government organized seaplane squadrons for the Baltic and Black Sea fleets. During World War I, Russian naval aviators flying Curtiss and Grigorovich (M-1, M-4, M-5, and M-9) seaplanes conducted aerial reconnaissance and harassment raids. On the eve of the Bolshevik Revolution in 1917, there were 269 naval aircraft of various types. Once the Bolsheviks entered the prolonged Civil War, 1918–21, they organized naval air brigades to operate on the Baltic and Black seas, and to serve lake and river flotillas. These units, according to the Soviets, completed over 2,000 sorties.

Between the wars, Soviet aviation planners placed considerable stress on the development of seaplanes, beginning with the three-place Grigorovich M-24 (1922) and concluding with the MTB-2 (1936). At the start of the Great Patriotic War, the VVS-VMF possessed a substantial inventory of fighters (I-15bis, I-16, I-153), bombers (DB-3, DB-3F, AR-2, TB-3), and seaplanes (MBR-2, MDR-2, MTB-2). The Soviets also produced in the 1930s the six-engine flying boat, Mk-1 (ANT-22), and the Be-2 and Be-4 catapult-launched seaplanes. The entire VVS-VMF air inventory in 1941 amounted to 2,824 aircraft of all types.

The VVS-VMF, reorganized as a separate aviation component of the Soviet Navy in 1938, consisted of four individual fleet air arms: the Northern Fleet Air Force (VVS-SF); the Red Banner Baltic Fleet (VVS-KBF); the Black Sea Fleet Air Force (VVS-ChF); and the Pacific Fleet Air Force (VVS-TOF). Col. Gen. S. F. Zhavoronkov assumed command of the VVS-VMF in June 1939, a post he held to the end of the war. On June 22, 1941, the three western fleets deployed 1,445 aircraft: fighters, 45 percent; reconnaissance aircraft, 25 percent; bombers, 14 percent; and torpedo bombers, 10 percent; other, 6 percent. Among these aircraft were torpedo-equipped DB-3 and IL-4 (DB-3F) bombers; some Pe-2 dive bombers; and 72 new model fighters, Yak-1s, MiG-1s and MiG-3s.

The VVS-VMF suffered significant losses in the first year of the war. Naval air units from the Red Banner Baltic Fleet, however, did launch a bomber raid on Berlin in August 1941. At Odessa and Sevastopol, the Black Sea Fleet made a more impressive showing in the fall of 1941, providing needed air support for the Soviet defenders of these besieged ports. In the north, the VVS-VMF flew escort duty for the Allied convoys (assisted by the RAF 151 Fighter Wing), but these air operations prompted criticism from the Western Allies for their restricted and unaggressive character. The VVS-VMF, along with VVS frontal aviation, was slow to exploit opportunities to hit enemy rear areas throughout the war.

Between 1941 and 1945, the VVS-VMF expanded dramatically to achieve a level of 3,000 combat aircraft. Most of these were modern types—torpedo-equipped TU-2 bombers and Il-2 Shturmoviks, Pe-2 dive bombers, and the later model Yak and Lavochkin fighters. Tied closely to the combat operations of VVS frontal aviation, the VVS-VMF underwent an important transformation: fighters and bombers began to dominate the naval aviation inventory. By the end of the war, four-fifths of all VVS-VMF aircraft were land based. This shift allowed the VVS-VMF to participate more effectively in land offensives such as the campaigns to expel the Germans from Belorussia and the Crimea. The VVS-VMF also made important contributions in the war to the work of the various river flotillas and assault landings in the Black Sea theater. The Soviets claim 350,000 total sorties flown by the VVS-VMF during the war, leading to 5,500 enemy aircraft destroyed along with 792 warships sunk (another 700 ships damaged). Among VVS-VMF air units, a total of twenty-five achieved guards status, and 259 aviators earned the gold star, Hero of the Soviet Union (five of them twice).

Aircraft Deployed by VVS-VMF*

	1941 (June 22)	1943 (January 1)	1944 (January 1)	1945
Northern Fleet	114	284	298	400
Baltic Fleet	707	208	313	787
Black Sea	624	231	429	400
Pacific Ocean	—	—	—	1,495**
Total	1,445	723	1,040	3,082

* See S. A. Krasovskiy, ed., *Aviatsiya i kosmonavtika SSSR* (Moscow: Voyenizdat, 1968), pp. 259–301.

** Figure available for combined Pacific and North Pacific fleets against Japan, August 1945.

Appendix 12

Fighter Aviation—National Air Defense Forces (IA-PVO)

Air Defense Fighter Aviation, *Istrebitel'naya aviatsiya protivovozdushnoi oborony* (IA-PVO), can trace its origins back to 1916 when the Russian Army organized a separate air division consisting of three fighter detachments (six aircraft) for the air defense of Petrograd. By April 1918, the Bolsheviks had mobilized in the Red Army nearly 200 anti-aircraft batteries and twelve fighter detachments (six aircraft) for widely dispersed air-defense duties. No integrated structure for air-defense forces existed during the period of the Civil War, 1918–21. Only Petrograd possessed an air-defense "system," linking together sixteen anti-aircraft batteries and nineteen fighter aircraft.

As a component of the PVO *strany*, the National Air Defense Force, IA-PVO units underwent expansion in the interwar years. Air-defense zones, covering major industrial, urban, coastal, and military installations, took shape between 1921 and 1940. The Soviet aircraft design bureaus during this same period developed a series of fighter interceptors which enhanced the striking power of IA-PVO. In 1925 the IA-PVO had a number of fighter aircraft of Soviet design, including the I-5 with a speed of 200–240 kph (124–149 mph) and a ceiling of 6,000 meters (19,685 feet). During the 1930s the I-153 and I-16 models, equipped with heavier armament and rockets, dramatically surpassed the modest performance of the I-5. On the eve of the German invasion, IA-PVO units had initiated the transition program to Yak-1 and MiG-3 fighters, modern interceptors with speeds of 580–640 kph (360–398 mph) and the capability in the case of the Mig-3 of operating in an air space up to 12,000 meters (39,360 feet). Despite these steady improvements in aircraft performance, IA-PVO units proved to be ineffectual at the start of the Great Patriotic War. The German blitzkrieg exposed a whole matrix of deficiencies. The absence of an effective warning system, the failure to appreciate the value of radio communications and radar, poor coordination of fighter interceptors with anti-aircraft batteries, the paucity of night fighters, and deficient training compromised the air defense role of IA-PVO.

Beginning the war with around forty fighter air regiments, IA-PVO gradually enlarged its operations, reaching a level of ninety-seven regiments by 1945. At Moscow in 1941–42, IA-PVO units played an important role, contributing eleven air regiments (around 600 aircraft) and 26,000 sorties. One of the great heroes of the war, V. V. Talalikhin, performed the first night aerial ramming as a fighter pilot assigned to the Moscow Air Defense (PVO) zone. IA-PVO, re-equipped with La-5, La-7, Yak-9 and Yak-3 fighters, maintained an active, if not decisive role, in Soviet air operations from 1942 to the end of the war. The failure of IA-PVO units at Poltava in June 1944 to protect USAAF B-17s from a devastating night raid by Luftwaffe bombers remains a controversial subject even today. PVO night fighter squadrons, including those equipped with Pe-3 aircraft at Poltava, did not operate with advanced radar equipment. At this stage most air crews had not mastered instrument and blind-flying techniques.

During the war the Luftwaffe mounted no large-scale strategic air campaign against Soviet cities and industrial centers. For this reason, IA-PVO played a minor role. The postwar years, however, saw a rapid expansion of the air defense forces, including IA-PVO, to meet the dangers of the atomic age. By 1948 PVO *strany* had been organized as a separate service.

Appendix 13

Soviet Civil Aviation, 1941–45

The Civil War Fleet (*Grazhdanskiy vozdushniy flot*, or GVF) played an important role in the Great Patriotic War. At the outset of hostilities, the GVF performed emergency tasks, flying personnel and equipment to help the beleaguered Soviet defenses. The GVF, once mobilized for military service, also assisted in the evacuation of Soviet war industries from European Russia to rear areas east of the Ural Mountains. As the war progressed, the GVF faced acute shortages in transport aircraft, a problem relieved in part by the shipment of Douglas C-47s through Lend-Lease. The Soviet-built version of the C-47, the Li-2 continued to be manufactured during the war, joining the Po-2 and TB-3 to complete a diverse range of air transport duties.

The Soviet Civil Air Fleet, according to Soviet sources, flew 2,300,000 passengers and 400,000 tons of freight between 1941 and 1945. More than 40,000 flights were made into the enemy rear areas in support of the partisans. GVF aircraft helped to maintain regular contact between the various fronts throughout the war. Six GVF air units achieved guards status and twelve aviators earned the gold star, Hero of the Soviet Union.

Appendix 14

Soviet Aces and Air Victories

Kozhedub, I. N.	62 (1 Me-262)
Pokryshkin, A. I.	59
Rechkalov, G. A.	58
Gulaev, N. D.	57 (4 before June 1941)
Vorozheykin, A. V.	52 (6 in Mongolia)
Yevstigneyev, K. A.	52
Glinka, D. G.	50
Klubov, A. F.	50

The Soviets give considerable attention to P. N. Nesterov, who on August 26, 1914, executed the first aerial *taran*, or ramming, against an Austrian aircraft. For the period of World War I and the Civil War which followed, Soviet histories are selective in their emphasis, honoring K. K. Artseulov (eighteen victories) and Ye. N. Krumen' (fifteen victories), but ignoring Alexander Kazakov (seventeen victories), who opposed the Bolshevik Revolution.

During the Great Patriotic War, the Soviets claim that over 800 pilots achieved sixteen or more air victories. There were twenty-six fighter pilots who scored anywhere from twenty-two to fifty-seven air victories, earning twice the golden, five-pointed star *Geroi Sovetskogo Soyuza*, Hero of the Soviet Union (HSU), the highest award for bravery.

The HSU was first awarded in 1934 to the seven pilots who rescued the crew of the trapped research ship, *Chelyuskin*. In the late 1930s, 181 pilots received this award (four twice) in the assorted air battles in Spain, Khasan (Manchuria), and Khalkhin-Gol (Mongolia), and Finland (Winter War, 1939–40). A total of ninety pilots achieved this award after the war with Finland. During the Great Patriotic War, 2,420 pilots (895 fighter pilots) earned this coveted award. Of the ninety-eight double HSU orders, sixty-five were pilots. The HSU was awarded three times: Gen. G. Zhukov and two pilots, I. N. Kozhedub (sixty-two victories) and A. I. Pokryshkin (59 victories).

Certain air units achieved the honorary title of "guards," first established in September 1941. Guards air units received a special banner and members of the unit wore a guards insignia on their uniforms. The first guards air units were organized in December 1941. By the end of the war, 288 units had earned this high distinction. Other honorary titles and orders were awarded to many of these air units. A total of 708 units in the VVS were awarded honorary titles and/or orders during the course of the war.

Appendix 15
Composition of 16th Air Army on Eve of Major Air Campaigns, 1942–45

Campaign	Date mo/day/yr	Fighters	Ground Attack	Bombers (day)	Bombers (night)	Recon	Other	Total
Stalingrad (defensive)	9/04/42	42	79	31*	—	—	—	152
Stalingrad (offensive)	11/19/42	125	103	93*	—	7	14	342
Stalingrad (air blockade)	1/10/43	215	103	105	87	—	75	585
Kursk	6/05/43	455	341	260	74	22	—	1,052
Kiev	9/01/43	263	150	183	130	14	—	740
Belorussia	6/24/44	1,108	661	331	149	70	—	2,319
Vistula-Oder	1/01/45	1,116	710	330	174	91	—	2,421
Berlin	4/15/45	1,548	687	533	151	114	—	3,033

Adapted from G. K. Prussakov, ed., *16-ya vozdushnaya. Voyenno - istoricheskiy ocherk o boyevom puti 16-i voydushnoy armii, 1942–1945* (Moscow: Voyenizdat, 1973).
* These figures represent bomber aircraft of all types.

Appendix 16
Deployment of Soviet Frontal Aviation, January 1, 1945*

Air Army	Front	Units Assigned Corps	Divs	Regts	Operational Aircraft Fighter	Ground Attack	Bomber	Misc.	Total
13th	Leningrad	1	2	2	357	57	12	55	481
15th	2d Baltic	4	3	2	139	166	73	37	415
3d	1st Baltic	4	17	4	495	338	298	41	1,172
1st	3d Belorussian	0	12	5	500	456	220	110	1,286
4th	2d Belorussian	3	14	3	640	543	199	99	1,481
16th	1st Belorussian	6	21	4	1,172	750	388	86	2,396
2d	1st Ukrainian	8	21	3	990	771	419	93	2,273
8th	4th Ukrainian	2	5	2	194	184	80	41	499
5th	2d Ukrainian	3	11	2	316	227	66	36	645
17th	3d Ukrainian	1	10	2	381	353	102	46	882
Total		29	121	29	5,184	3,845	1,857	644	11,530

* Adapted from *Voyenno-istoricheskiy zhurnal*, no. 7 (July 1975): 77.

Appendix 17
Composition of Soviet Air Force in Far East, August 1945

Air Army	Air Corps	Air Divisions Bomber	Ground Attack	Fighter	Mixed	Transport	Separate Regiments	Combat Aircraft
9th	1 bomber	3	2	3	—	—	4	1,137
10th	1 mixed	1	2	3	2	—	2	1,260
12th	2 bomber	6	2	3	—	2	2	1,324
Total		10	6	9	2	2	8	3,721

Adapted from *Voyenno-istoricheskiy zhurnal*, no. 8 (1975): 66.

Glossary

ADD	*Aviatsiya dal'nego deystviya* [Long-Range Aviation]
AK-RVGK	*Aviatsionnyy korpus reserva Glavnogo Komandovaniya* [Air Corps of the *Stavka* Reserve]
AM	Alexander Mikulin
ANT	Andrei Nikolayevich Tupolev
AON	*Aviatsiya osobogo naznacheniya* [Special-Purpose Aviation]
BAD	Bombardirovochnaya aviatsionnaya diviziya [Bomber Air Division]
BAO	*Batal'on aerodromnogo obsluzhivaniya* [Airfield Servicing Battalion]
DA	*Dal'naya aviatsiya* [Long-Range Aviation]
DB	*Dal'niy bombardirovshchik* [Long-Range Bomber]
DOSAAF	*Dobrovol'noye obshchestvo sodeystviya Armii, Aviatsii, i flotu* [Volunteer Society to Support the Army, Aviation, and the Fleet]
FA	*Frontovaya aviatsiya* [Frontal Aviation]
GAZ	*Gosudarstvennyy aviatsionnyy zavod* [State Aircraft Factory]
GKO	*Gosudarstvennyy komitet oborony* [State Defense Committee]
Gv	*Gvardeyskiy* [Guards]
GVF	*Grazhdanskiy voydushnyy flot* [Civil Air Fleet]
I	*Istrebitel'* [Fighter]
IA	*Istrebitel'naya aviatsiya* [Fighter Aviation]
IA-PVO	*Istrebitel'naya aviatsiya protivovozdushnoi oborony* [Air Defense Fighter Aviation]
IAD	*Istrebitel'naya aviatsionnaya divisiya* [Fighter Air Division]
IAP	*Istrebitel'nyy aviatsionnyy polk* [Fighter Air Regiment]
KB	*Konstruktorskoye byuro* [Design Bureau]
Komsomol	*Kommunisticheskiy soyuz molodezhi* [Young Communist League]
La	Lavochkin, S. A.
LaGG	Lavochkin, S. A., Gorbunov, V., Gudkov, M.
Li	Lisunov, B.P.
MBR	*Morskoy blizhniy razvedchik* [Short-Range Reconnaissance Flying Boat]
MDR	*Morskoy dal'niy razvedchik* [Long-Range Reconnaissance Flying Boat]
MiG	Mikoyan, A.E., and Gurevich, M.I.
MTB	*Morskoy tyazhelyy bombardirovshchik* [Heavy Bomber Flying Boat]
NBAP	*Nochnoy bombardirovochnyy aviapolk* [Night Bomber Air Regiment]

ODVF	*Obshchestvo druzey vozdushnogo flota* [Society of the Friends of the Air Fleet]
Osoaviakhim	*Obshchestvo sodeystviya oborone, aviatsionnomu i khimicheskomu stroitel'stvu* [Society for the Support of Defense and Aviation and Chemical Construction]
Pe	Petlyakov, V.M.
Po	Polikarpov, N.N.
PTAB	*Protivotankovaya aviatsionnaya bomba* [Anti-tank bomb]
PVO	*Protivovoydushaya oborona* [Air Defense]
R	*Razvedchik* [Reconnaissance]
Revvoyensovet	*Revolyutsionno-voyennyy sovet* [Revolutionary Military Council]
SAD	*Svodnaya (smeshannaya) aviatsionnaya diviziya* [Mixed Air Division]
SB	*Skorostnoi bombardirovshchik* [Fast Bomber]
ShAD	*Shturmovaya aviatsionaya diviziya* [Ground-Attack Air Division]
ShAK	*Shturmovoy aviatsionnyy korpus* [Ground-Attack Air Corps]
ShAP	*Shturmovoy aviatsionnyy polk* [Ground-Attack Air Regiment]
Stavka	Shtab glavnogo/verkhovnogo komandovaniya [Headquarters/ Supreme High Command]
Su	Sukhoi, P.O.
TB	*Tyazhelyy bombardirovshchik* [Heavy Bomber]
TsAGI	*Tsentral'nyy aero-gidrodinamicheskiy institut* [Central Aero-Hydrodynamics Institute]
Tu	Tupolev, A.N.
U	*Uchebnyy* [Training]
UTI	*Uchebno-trenirovochnyy istrebitel'* [Fighter Trainer]
VA	*Vozdushnaya armiya* [Air Army]
VDV	*Vozdushno-desantnyye voiska* [Airborne Troops]
VIAM	*Vsesoyuznyy institut aviatsionnykh materialov* [All-Union Institute for Aviation Materials]
VK	Vladimir Klimov
VMF	*Voyenno-morskoy flot* [Navy]
VVS	*Voyenno-vozdushnyye sily* [Air Forces]
VVS-VMF	*Voyenno-vozdushnyye sily-Voyenno-morskoy flot* [Naval Air Force]
Yak	Yakovlev, A.S.
Yer	Yermolayev, V.G.
ZA	*Zenitnaya artilleriya* [Anti-Aircraft Artillery]
ZOS	*(Sluzhba) zemnogo obespecheniya samoletovozhdeniya* [Ground Assistance to Air Navigation Service]

Bibliography

This bibliography is a compilation of titles on pre-1945 Soviet air power. At its core—and representing the largest number of entries—is the expanding list of memoirs and histories of the Soviet Air Force (VVS) in World War II, or the Great Patriotic War, 1941–45. These Russian-language materials, most of which have appeared since 1960, constitute an important resource for the study of Soviet air power during the war. Grouped around this central theme are aviation titles dealing with tsarist antecedents, the birth of the "Red Air Fleet" under the Bolsheviks, the Soviet aeronautical scene in the interwar years, theories of air power, air defense, the airborne forces, civil aviation, and other relevant aspects of Soviet aviation. Excluded from the list are general histories of the war, histories of various wartime operations from a combined-arms perspective, and memoirs and histories which do not have Soviet air power as their major theme. A selection of English-language titles appears at the beginning of the bibliography.

For a general orientation to the Great Patriotic War from a Soviet perspective, there are several major works. One of the most ambitious contributions, published in six volumes, is P.N. Pospelov, editor, *Istoriya Velikoy Otechestvennoy voyny Sovetskogo Soyuza, 1941–1945* [History of the Great Patriotic War of the Soviet Union, 1941–1945] (Moscow: Voyenizdat, 1960–65). An abbreviated version, also under the editorship of Pospelov, is *Velikaya Otechestvennaya voyna Sovetskogo Soyuza 1941–1945 gg. Kratkaya istoriya* [The Great Patriotic War of the Soviet Union, 1941–1945: a short history] (Moscow: Voyenizdat, 1970). For an overview of the Soviet armed forces, see M.V. Zakharov, editor, *50 let Voorzhennykh Sil SSSR* [Fifty years of the armed forces of the USSR] (Moscow: Voyenizdat, 1968). Shorter pieces on the VVS, as well as other branches of the Soviet armed forces, have appeared in *Sovetskaya voyennaya entsiklopediya* [The Soviet Military Encyclopedia], 8 vols. (Moscow: Voyenizdat, 1976–1980).

Any bibliographic research on Soviet aviation should begin with A.A. Zhabrov's *Annotirovannyy ukazatel' literatury na russkom yazyke po aviatsii i vozdukhoplavaniya za 50 let, 1881–1931* [Annotated guide to Russian language literature on aviation and aeronautics for 50 years, 1881–1931] (Moscow: 1931). Zhabrov cites a wide variety of books and articles on aviation history, aeronautics, technical and engineering topics, air theory, and the political activities associated with Soviet aviation. A selection of more recent Soviet bibliographies (each with sections devoted to aviation) would include: *Istoriya SSSR, Ukazatel' sovetskoy literatury za 1917–1967. gg., Tom III* [History of the USSR: guide to Soviet literature, 1917–1967, vol. III] (Moscow: Nauka, 1977); V.I. Ezhako et al., editors, *O voyne, o tovarishchakh, o sebe. Velikaya Otechestvennaya voyna v vospominaniyakh uchastnikov boyevykh deystviy. Annotirovannyy ukazatel' voyennomemuarnoy literatury 1941–1945 gg* [About war, about comrades, about oneself: the Great Patriotic War in the recollections of combat participants: annotated guide to military memoir literature, 1941–1945] (Moscow: Voyenizdat, 1977); and *Velikaya pobeda, Rekomendatel'nyy ukazatel' literatury o VOV 1941–1945 gg* [Great victory: guide to recommended literature on the Great Patriotic War, 1941–1945] (Moscow: Izdatel'stvo Kniga, 1975).

Michael Parrish's two-volume *The USSR in World War II: An Annotated Bibliography of Books Published in the Soviet Union, 1945–1975* (New York: Garland Reference Library of Social Science, Garland Publishing, 1981) represents a major contribution in English to the growing body of reference materials on the Soviet Union in World War II. For bibliographic research the Parrish volumes are quite helpful. Part II, pp. 141–84, contains numerous headings, such as airborne, Soviet Air Force, naval aviation, and air defense; Part IV, pp. 311–16, lists a number of bibliographies dealing with the Great Patriotic War; and the Addenda, pp. 787–862, include a list of Soviet titles which appeared between 1975 and 1980, many related to Soviet aviation.

Soviet periodical literature provides another important avenue for research on the Soviet Air Force. *Voyenno-istoricheskiy zhurnal*, published since 1959, has become over the past two decades a vehicle for many significant articles on wartime Soviet air power. Other Soviet periodicals which deal with aviation themes include the following: *Aviatsiya i kosmonavtika, Istoriya SSSR, Krasnaya zvezda, Kryl'ya rodiny, Morskoy sbornik, Vestnik PVO,* and *Voprosy istorii.* Such periodicals have provided an opportunity for former air force commanders, aviation leaders, and historians to analyze the wartime role of the Soviet Air Force.

I. Selected English-language References

Alexander, J.P. *Russian Aircraft Since 1940*. London: Putnam, 1975.

Bialer, Serwyn, *Stalin and His Generals*. New York: Pegasus, 1969.

Baumbach, W. *Broken Swastika: The Defeat of the Luftwaffe*. London: Robert Hale, 1960.

Bekker, C. *The Luftwaffe War Diaries*. London: Macdonald, 1967.

Boyd, Alexander. *The Soviet Air Force Since 1918*. London: Macdonald and Jane's, 1977.

Cain, C.W., and Voaden, D.J. *Military Aircraft of the USSR*. London: Herbert Jenkins, 1952.

Carell, P. *Hitler's War on Russia*. London: Harrap, 1964, 1970.

Clark, Alan. *Barbarossa, The Russian-German Conflict, 1941–1945*. New York: Morrow, 1965.

Constable, Trevor J., and Toliver, Raymond F. *Horrido! Fighter Aces of the Luftwaffe*. New York: Macmillan, 1968.

———. *The Blond Knight of Germany*. Garden City, N.Y.: Doubleday and Co., 1970.

Craig, William. *Enemy at the Gates: The Battle for Stalingrad*. New York: E.P. Dutton and Co., 1973.

Deane, John R. *The Strange Alliance: The Story of American Efforts at Wartime Cooperation with Russia*. London: John Murray, 1947.

Deichman, Paul. *German Air Force Operations in Support of the Army*. USAF Historical Study, no. 163, USAF Historical Division, Research Studies Institute, Air University, 1962.

Erickson, John. *The Soviet High Command: A Military-Political History, 1918–1941*. New York: St. Martins Press, 1962.

———. *The Road to Stalingrad*. New York: Harper and Row, 1975.

Garthoff, R.L. *Soviet Military Doctrine*. Glencoe, Ill.: The Free Press, 1953.

———. *How Russia Makes War*. London: George Allen and Unwin, 1954.

———. *Soviet Military Policy: A Historical Analysis*. New York: Praeger, 1966.

Geust, Carl-Fredrik, et al. *Red Stars in the Sky*. Vols. I and II. Tietoteos, Finland, 1979.

Green, William, and Swanborough, Gordon. *Soviet Fighter of World War II*. Parts I, II. London: Macdonald and Jane's, 1977.

Grossman, V. *The Years of the War (1941–1945)*. Moscow: Foreign Languages Publishing House, 1946.

Higham, Robin, and Kipp, J.W. *Soviet Aviation and Air Power, A Historical View*. Boulder, Colo.: Westview Press, 1977.

Infield, G.B. *The Poltava Affair*. New York: Macmillan, 1973.

Jackson, Robert. *Red Falcons: The Soviet Air Force in Action, 1919–1969*. New York: International Publications Service, 1970.

Kilmarx, Robert A. *A History of Soviet Air Power*. New York: Frederick A. Praeger, 1962.

Leach, Barry A. *German Strategy Against Russia, 1939–1941*. Oxford: Clarendon Press, 1973.

Lee, Asher. *The German Air Force*. New York: Harper and Brothers, 1946.

Lee, Asher, ed. *The Soviet Air and Rocket Forces*. New York: Frederick A. Praeger, 1959.

Lee, Asher. *The Soviet Air Force*. New York: John Day Company, 1962.

Liddell Hart, B.H., ed. *The Red Army*. New York: Harcourt, Brace and Co., 1956.

Lukas, Richard C. *Eagles East: The Army Air Forces and the Soviet Union, 1941–1945*. Tallahassee: Florida State University Press, 1970.

Morzik, Fritz. *German Air Force Airlift Operations*. USAF Historical Study, no. 167. USAF Historical Division, Research Studies Institute, Air University, 1961.

Munro, Colin. *Soviet Air Force*. New York, 1972.

Nowarra, H.J., and Duval, G.R., eds. *Russian Civil and Military Aircraft, 1884–1969*. London: Fountain Press, 1971.

Overy, R.J. *The Air War 1939–1945*. New York: Stein and Day, 1980.

Plocher, Hermann. *The German Air Force Versus Russia 1941*. USAF Historical Studies, no. 153. New York: Arno Press, 1965.

———. *The German Air Force Versus Russia, 1942*. USAF Historical Studies, no. 154. New York: Arno Press, 1966.

———. *The German Air Force Versus Russia, 1943*. USAF Historical Studies, no. 155. New York: Arno Press, 1967.

Pokryshkin, A.I. *Red Air Ace*. London: Soviet War News, 1945.

Roustem-Bek, B. *Aerial Russia*. London: John Lane, 1916.

Rudel, Hans Ulrich. *Stuka Pilot*. New York: 1958.

Schwabedissen, Walter. *The Russian Air Force in the Eyes of German Commanders*. USAF Historical Study, no. 175. USAF Historical Division, Research Studies Institute, Air University, 1960.

Scott, H.F., and Scott, W.F. *The Armed Forces of the USSR*. Boulder, Colo.: Westview Press, 1979.

Seaton, Albert. *The Russo-German War, 1941–1945*. New York: Praeger, 1971.

Shores, Christopher. *Ground Attack Aircraft of World War II*. London: Macdonald and Jane's, 1978.

Shtemenko, S.M. *The Soviet General Staff at War: 1940–1945*. Moscow: Progress Publishers, 1970.

Sokolovskiy, V.D., ed. *Military Strategy*. 3d ed. Translated by Harriet Fast Scott. New York: Crane Russak and Co., 1975.

Stockwell, Richard. *Soviet Air Power*. New York: Pageant Press, Inc., 1956.

Strand, John. *The Red Air Force*. London: Pilot Press, 1943.

Suchenwirth, Richard. *Historical Turning Points in the German Air Force War Effort*. USAF Historical Study, no. 189. New York: Arno Press, 1968.

Uebe, Klaus. *Russian Reactions to German Air Power in World War II*. USAF Historical Study, no. 176. New York: Arno Press, 1964.

Unishevsky, Vladimir. *Red Pilot. Memoirs of a Soviet Airman*. London: Hurst and Blackett, 1939.

Vazhin, F.A. *Soviet Air Force*. Moscow: Novosti Press Publishing House, 1975.

Vodopianov, M. *Outstanding Flights by Soviet Airmen*. Moscow: Foreign Language Publishing House, 1939.

Voznesensky, N.A. *The Economy of the USSR during World War II*. Washington: Public Affairs Press, 1948.

Wagner, Ray, ed. *The Soviet Air Forces in World War II*. (The official history originally published by the Ministry of Defense of the USSR.) Translated by Leland Fetzer. Garden City, N.Y.: Doubleday and Co., 1973.

Werth, Alexander. *Russia at War, 1941–1945*. New York: Dutton, 1964.

Whiting, Kenneth R. *Soviet Air Power, 1917–1976*. Maxwell AFB, Alabama, 1976.

Yakovlev, A.S. *Aim of a Lifetime*. Moscow: Progress Publishers, 1972.

Ziemke, E.F. *Stalingrad to Berlin: The German Defeat in the East*. Office of the Chief of Military History, United States Army, Washington, 1968.

II. Russian-Language References

General

Alksnis, Ya. I. *Krepite shefstvo nad vozdushnym flotom* [Strengthen the air fleet]. Moscow, 1931, 1932.

Grazhdanskaya aviatsiya SSSR, 1917–1967 [Civil aviation in the Soviet Union, 1917–1967]. Moscow: Transport, 1967.

Izakson, A. M. *Sovetskoye vertoleto-stroyeniye* [Soviet helicopter construction] Moscow: Mashinostroyeniye, 1964, 1981.

Iz istorii aviatsii i kosmonavtiki [From the history of aviation and cosmonautics]. Vol. I. Moscow: Akademiya Nauk, 1964.

Kutakhov, P. S. *Voyenno-Vozdushnyye Sily* [The air force]. Moscow: Znaniye, 1977.

Moroz, I. M., ed. *V. I. Lenin i sovetskaya aviatsiya* [V. I. Lenin and Soviet aviation]. Moscow, 1979.

Obrazdsov, I. F., ed. *Razvitiye aviatsionnoy nauki i tekhniki v SSSR. Istoriko-naunicheskiy ocherki* [Development of aviation science and technology in the Soviet Union, historical-scientific notes]. Moscow, 1980.

Ordin, A. G. *Vozdushnyy flot strany Sovetov* [Air fleet of the Land of the Soviets]. Moscow, 1948 and 1949.

———. *Moguchaya stalinskaya aviatsiya* [Stalin's mighty aviation]. Moscow, 1950.

Popov, V. A. *Rossiya - Rodina vozdukhoplavaniya i aviatsii* [Russia—Motherland of aeronautics and aviation]. Moscow: Pravda, 1951.

Serebryakov, I. *Aviatsiya nashey rodiny* [Our Motherland's aviation]. Moscow, 1953.

Shavrov, V. B. *Istoriya konstruktsii samoletov v SSSR do 1938* [History of USSR aircraft design to 1938]. Moscow: Mashinostroyeniye, 1969, 1978.

———. *Samolety strany sovetov* [Aircraft of the Land of Soviets]. Moscow: DOSAAF, 1974.

———. *Istoriya konstruktsii samoletov v SSSR 1938–1950 gg.* [History of Soviet aircraft construction, 1938–1950]. Moscow: Mashinostroyeniye, 1978.

Shesterikov, L. *Daty istorii otechestvennoy aviatsii i vozdukhoplavaniya* [Historical dates of the Fatherland's aviation and aeronautics]. Moscow: DOSAAF, 1953.

Shipilov, I. F., ed. *Aviatsiya nashey Rodiny* [Our Motherland's aviation]. Moscow: Voyenizdat, 1955.

Shipilov, I. F., et al. *Zvezdy na kryl'yakh. Vospominaniya veteranov sovetskoy aviatsii* [Stars on the wings: reminiscences of Soviet aviation veterans]. Moscow: Voyenizdat, 1959.

Simakov, B. L., and Shipilov, I. F., eds. *Za chest' otechestvennoy nauki i tekhniki. Sbornik statey zhurnala "Vestnik vozdushnogo flota"* [In honor of Soviet science and technology: collection from the journal *Vestnik vozdushnogo flota*]. Moscow: Voyenizdat, 1949.

———. *Vozdushnyy flot strany sovetov. Kratkiy ocherk istorii aviatsii nashey Rodiny* [The Air Fleet of the Land of Soviets: a short sketch of our Motherland's aviation history]. Moscow: Voyenizdat, 1958.

Smirnov, M. D., et al. *Vozdushnyye sily i PVO* [The air force and air defense]. Moscow: Voyenizdat, 1936.

Sokoly [Falcons]. Leningrad: Lenizdat, 1971.

Spirin, I. T. *Zapiski aviatora* [An aviator's notes]. Moscow: Voyenizdat, 1955.

Tsykin, A. D. *Ot "Il'i Muromtsa" do raketonostsa* [From the Il'ya Muromets to missile-equipped aircraft]. Moscow: Voyenizdat, 1975.

Tumanskiy, A. K. *Polet skvoz' gody* [Flight through the years]. Moscow: Voyenizdat, 1962.

Valentey, I. A. *Aviatsiya ot legend do nashikh dney* [Aviation from legend to our time]. Moscow: ODVF, 1925.

Velizhev, A. A. *Dostizheniya sovetskoy aviapromyshlennosti za pyatnadtsat' let* [The achievements of the Soviet aviation industry over 15 years]. Moscow: ONTI, 1932.

————. *40 let sovetskoy aviatsii* [Forty years of Soviet aviation]. Moscow: Znaniye, 1958.

Vinogradov, R. I., and Minayev, A. V. *Kratkiy ocherk razvitiya samoletov v SSSR* [A short sketch of aircraft development in the USSR]. Moscow: Voyenizdat, 1956.

————. *Samolety SSSR* [USSR aircraft]. Moscow: Voyenizdat, 1961.

Vinokur, B. I. *Kryl'ya—Sbornik dokumental'nykh rasskazov i ocherkov ob aviatorakh* [Wings: a collection of documentary tales and stories about aviators]. Moscow: DOSAAF, 1972.

Voyenno-vozdushnyye sily [Air force]. Moscow: Voyenizdat, 1959.

Voyska protivovozdushnoy oborony strany. Istoricheskiy ocherk [The national air defense forces: a historical sketch]. Moscow: Voyenizdat, 1968.

Yur'yev, B. N. *Sovetskaya shkola aerodinamiki v akademii nauk* [The Soviet school of aerodynamics in the Academy of Sciences]. Moscow: Academy of Sciences Publishing House, 1945.

Air Theory, Tactics, and Operations

Algazin, A. S. *Obespecheniye vozdushnykh operatsiy* [Support of aerial operations]. Moscow: Gosizdat, 1928.

————. *Operativnaya rabota letchika-nablyudatelya* [Operational work of a pilot-observer]. Moscow, 1933.

————. *Taktika bombardirovochnoy aviatsii* [Bomber aviation tactics]. Moscow, 1934.

————. *Aviatsiya v sovremennoy voyne* [Aviation in modern warfare]. Moscow: Gos. voyenizdat, 1935.

————. *Osnovy operativnogo ispol'zovaniya Voyenno-vozhushnykh sil* [Fundamentals of air force operational employment]. Moscow, 1937.

Babilov, N. V., and Pistol'kors, S. F. *Kratkiy kurs bombardirovanniya dlya letchikov-razvedchikov i istrebiteley* [Short course in bombing for reconnaissance and fighter pilots]. Moscow-Leningrad, 1929.

Belousov, A. A., ed. *Vozdushnyye desanty i bor'ba s nimi. Ukazatel' Literatury* [Airborn assaults and how to counter them: a guide to literature]. Moscow, 1942.

Burche, Ye. f. *Maskirovka ob'yektov VVS* [Camouflage of air force installations]. 2d ed. Moscow, 1934.

————. *Vozdushnaya voyna i voyennaya maskirovka* [Air war and camouflage]. Moscow, 1938.

Ionov, P. P. *Obshchaya taktika Voyenno-vozdushnykh sil* [General air force tactics]. Moscow, 1934.

————. *Istrebitel'naya aviatsiya* [Fighter aviation]. Moscow, 1940.

Khripin, V. V. *Taktika bombardirovochnoy aviatsii* [Tactics of bomber aviation]. Moscow, 1934.

————. *O gospodstve v vozdukhe* [On air supremacy]. Moscow, 1935.

Kozhevnikov, A. *Taktika istrebitel'noy aviatsii* [Fighter aviation tactics]. Moscow-Leningrad, 1933.

Kulikovskiy, G. G. *Vestibulyarnaya trenirovka letchika dlya letnogo sostava* [Beginning flight crew training]. Moscow-Leningrad, 1939.

Kuz'menko, D., and Vislenev, B. *Teoriya aviatsii* [Theory of aviation]. Moscow, 1936; 3d ed., 1937.

————. *Zadachik po teorii aviatsii* [Problems of aviation theory]. Moscow, 1938.

Lapchinskiy, A. N. *Taktika aviatsii* [Aviation tactics]. Moscow, 1926; rev. eds. 1928–31.

————. *Krasnyy vozdushnyy flot, 1918–1928* [The Red Air Fleet, 1918–1928]. Moscow, 1928.

————. *Tekhnika i taktika vozdushnogo flota* [Air fleet equipment and tactics]. Moscow: Gosvoyenizdat, 1930.

————. *Vozdushnyye sily v boyu i operatsii* [The air force in combat and operations]. Moscow: Gosvoyenizdat, 1932.

————. *Vozdushnyy boy* [Air combat]. Moscow, 1934.

————. *Bombardirovochnaya aviatsiya* [Bomber aviation]. Moscow, 1937.

————. *Vozdushnaya razvedka* [Air reconnaissance]. Moscow: Voyenizdat, 1938.

————. *Vozdushnaya armiya* [The air army]. Moscow: Voyenizdat, 1939.

Martsinkovskiy, V. *Osnovnyye elementy deshifrirovaniya po aerosnimkam voyennykh ob'yektov i maskirovka* [Elements of deciphering aerial photographs of military installations and camouflage]. Moscow, 1925.

Maskirovka aerodromov [Camouflage of air bases]. Moscow, 1926.

Mednis, A. *Taktika shturmovoy aviatsii* [Tactics of ground-attack aviation]. Moscow, 1936 and 1937.

Mezheninov, S. *Osnovy voprosy primeneniya voyennykh vozdushnykh sil* [Fundamental questions about the application of air power]. Moscow, 1926.

————. *Vozdushnyye sily v voyne i operatsii* [The air force in war and in an operation]. Moscow, 1927.

Nikolskiy, M. N. *Rukhvodstvo po bombometaniyu s samoletov* [Training in air bombardment]. Moscow, 1924.

————. *Voprosy taktiki bombardirovochnoy aviatsii* [Questions of bomber aviation tactics]. Moscow: Aviaizdatel'stvo, 1925.

————. *Deystviya aviatsii protiv morskogo flota* [Air operations against naval forces]. Moscow, 1939.

Okovalkov, N. *Shturmavaya aviatsiya i eye boyevaya rabota* [Ground attack aviation and its combat work]. Moscow, 1931.

Pokrovskiy, S. N. *Boyevaya deyatel'nost' aviatsii* [Combat role of aviation]. Moscow, 1926.

Pokrovskiy, S. N., et al. *Boyevyye deystviya aviatsii protiv zemnogo protivnika* [Combat role of aviation against enemy troops]. Moscow-Leningrad, 1927.

Pronin, V. *Vozdushnyye desanty i bor'ba s nimi* [Airborne assaults and how to counter them]. Leningrad and Moscow: Ogiz, Gospolitizdat, 1941.

Rukavishnikov, S. *Vozdushnaya strel'ba. Uchebnik dlya letnykh shkol i stroyevykh chastey VVS RKKA* [Air gunnery: textbook for flying schools and Red Army air force line units]. Moscow: Voyenizdat, 1926; 2d ed., 1940.

Semenov, P. *Rabota shtabov VVS po upravleniyu boyem* [The work of air force staffs in battle management]. Moscow, 1933.

Sergeyev, A. K. *Strategiya i taktika krasnogo vozdushnogo flota* [Red air fleet strategy and tactics]. Moscow, 1925.

Shekhovtsov, N. I. *Sovetskoye voyennoye iskusstvo v Velikoy Otechestvennoy voyne* [Soviet military art in the Great Patriotic War]. Moscow: Znaniye, 1970.

Shomov, L. K. *Podgotovka shtaba aviatsionnogo polka* [The training of a regimental air staff]. Moscow: Voyenizdat, 1941.

Smirnov, M. *Aviatsiya i pekhota* [Aviation and infantry]. Moscow, 1931.

Smirnov, V. *Bombometaniye* [Bombing]. 2d ed. Moscow, 1938.

Sokolov, A., Zhuravlev, N., and Ban'kovskiy, G. *Taktika razvedyvatel'noy aviatsii* [Tactics of reconnaissance aviation]. Moscow-Leningrad, 1933.

Solov'yev, M. P., and Arbuzov, A. K. *Osnovy bombometaniya* [Fundamentals of bombing]. Moscow, 1940.

Spirin, M. *Kak borot'sya s vozdushnymi desantami vraga* [How to fight enemy airborne troops]. Moscow, 1941.

Svetlishin, N. A. *Voyska PVO strany v Velikoy Otechestvennoy voyny. Voprosy Operativno-strategicheskogo primeneniya* [Air defense troops in the Great Patriotic War: questions concerning their operational-strategic uses]. Moscow, 1979.

Taktika aviatsii [Aviation tactics]. Moscow, 1940.

Teplinskiy, B. L. *Vozdushnoye nablyudeniye* [Air observation]. Moscow, 1931.

————. *Aviatsiya v boyu nazemnykh voysk* [Aviation in ground combat]. Moscow: Voyenizdat, 1940.

————. *Osnovy obshchey taktiki Voyenno-vozdushnykh sil* [Fundamentals of general air force tactics]. Moscow: Voyenizdat, 1940.

Timokhovich, I. V. *Operativnoye iskusstvo Sovetskikh VVS v Velikoy Otechestvennoy voyne* [Operational art of the Soviet Air Force in the Great Patriotic War]. Moscow: Voyenizdat, 1976.

Vinogradov, N. *Taktika zenitnoy artillerii* [Anti-aircraft tactics]. Moscow, 1928.

Vislenev, B. V., and Kuz'menko, G. V. *Teoriya aviatsii* [Theory of aviation]. 4th ed. Moscow, 1939.

Yatsuk, N. *Taktika vozdushnogo flota* [Tactics of the air fleet]. Moscow, 1924.

Zhabrov, A. A. *Obucheniye polety* [Flight training]. Moscow, 1926.

Zhuravlev, N., and Sokolov, A. *Taktika aviatsii* [Tactics of aviation]. Moscow, 1934.

The Tsarist Period, Pre–1917

Baldwin, S. Vozdukhoplavatel'nyye dvigateli [Aeronautical engines]. St. Petersburg, 1909.

Barsh, G.V. *Vozdukhoplavaniye v yego proshlom v nastoyashem* [Aeronautics, past and present]. St. Petersburg, 1903.

Cheremnykh, N., and Shipilov, I. *A.F. Mozhaiskiy—sozdatel' pervogo v mire samoleta* [A.F. Mozhaiskiy—creator of the first airplane]. Moscow: Voyenizdat, 1955.

Duz, P. D. *Istoriya vozdukhoplavaniya i aviatsii v SSSR. Period do 1914 g* [History of aeronautics and aviation in the Soviet Union: pre–1914 period]. Moscow: Oborongiz, 1944; 2d ed. (abbreviated), 1979.

————. *Istoriya vozdukhoplavaniya i aviatsii v SSSR, 1914–1918gg* [History of aeronautics and aviation in the Soviet Union, 1914–1918]. Moscow: Oborongiz, 1960.

Ferber, F. *Aviatsiya, yeye nachaloi razvitiye* [Aviation, its beginnings and development]. Kiev, 1910.

Finne, K. N., *Russkiye vozdushnyye bogatyri I. I. Sikorskogo* [Russian aerial heroes of I. I. Sikorskiy]. Belgrad, 1930.

Glagolev, N. *K zvezdam. Istoriya vozdukhoplavaniya, Kn.1* [To the stars: history of aeronautics, book I]. St. Petersburg, 1912.

Golubev, V. V. *Sergei Alekseyevich Chaplygin* [Sergei Alekseyevich Chaplygin]. Moscow: TsAGI, 1947.

Iz neopublikovannoi perepiski N. E. Zhukovskogo [From unpublished notes of N. E. Zhukovskiy]. Moscow: TsAGI, 1957.

Lelase, L, and Mark, R. *Problema Vozdukhoplavaniya* [Problems of aeronautics]. St. Petersburg, 1910. .

N. E. Zhukovskiy—Bibliografiya pechatnykh trudov [N. E. Zhukovskiy: a bibliography of printed works]. Moscow: TsAGI, 1968.

Naydenov, V.F. *Aviatsiya v 1909 godu* [Aviation in the year 1909]. St. Petersburg: Tipografiya Usmanova, 1910.

Pamyati Professora Nikolaya Yegorovicha Zhukovskogo [Recollections of Professor Nikolay Yegorovich Zhukovskiy]. Moscow, 1922.

Popov, V. A., ed. *Vozdukhoplavaniye i aviatsii v Rossii do 1907 g. Sbornik dokumentov i materialov* [Aeronautics and aviation in Russia up to 1907: a collection of documents and materials]. Moscow: Oborongiz, 1956.

Prepodavaniye vozdukhoplavaniya v institute Putey soobshcheniya imperatora Aleksandra I [Teaching of aeronautics in the Alexander I Institute of Transportation]. St. Petersburg, 1911.

Rodnykh, A.A. *Istoriya vozdukhoplavaniya i letaniya v Rossii* [History of aeronautics and flying in Russia]. 2 vols. St. Petersburg: Gramotnost', 1911.

————. *Voyna v vozdukhe v byloye vremya i teper'* [The war in the air, past and present]. Petrograd: Delo, 1915.

Russkoye vozdukhoplavaniye Istoriya i uspekhi [Russian aeronautics: history and successes]. St. Petersburg, 1911.

S. A. *Chaplygin—Bibliografiya pechatnykh trudov* [S. A. Chaplygin: a bibliography of printed works]. Moscow: TsAGI, 1968.

Sher, A.S. *Kul'turno-istoricheskoye znacheniye vozdukhoplavaniya* [Cultural and historical significance of aeronautics]. St. Petersburg, 1912.

Shipilov, I.F. *Vydayushchiysya russkiy voyennyy letchik P.N. Nesterov* [Peter Nesterov—outstanding Russian military pilot]. Moscow, 1951.

Tiraspol'skiy, G.L. *Vozdukhoplavaniye i vozdukholetaniye* [Aeronautics and flight]. St. Petersburg, 1910.

Trunov, K.I. *Petr Nesterov* [Peter Nesterov] Moscow: Sovetskaya Rossiya, 1971.

Uteshev, N.I. *Zapiski po istorii voyennogo vozdukhoplavaniya* [Notes on the history of military aeronautics]. St. Petersburg, 1912.

Veygelin, K. Ye. *Azbuka vozdukhoplavaniya* [ABC's of aeronautics]. St. Petersburg, 1912.

———. *10–15 iyulya 1911 g. perelet S. Peterburg-Moskva* [Flight from St. Petersburg to Moscow]. St. Petersburg, 1911.

———. *Vozdushnyy spravochnik 1912 g. Sbornik spravochnykh svedeniy po vsem voprosam peredvizheniya v vozdukhe* [Air directory for 1912: collection of information on aeronautics]. St. Petersburg, 1912.

———. *Vozdushnyy spravochnik 1914 g. Yezhegodnik Imp. vseross. aerokluba* [Air directory for 1914: annual publication of the Imperial All-Russian Aero Club]. St. Petersburg, 1914.

———. *Put' letchika Nesterova* [Path of the flier Nesterov]. Moscow-Leningrad, 1939.

Vladimirov, L. *Sovremennoye vozdukhoplavaniye i yego istoriya* [Contemporary aeronautics and its history]. Kiev, 1909.

Vozdukhoplavaniye i letaniye. Russkiye letuny [Aeronautics and flying: Russian fliers]. St. Petersburg, 1911.

The Interwar Years, 1918–1940

Agokas, Ye. V. *Boyevyye sredstva aviatsii* [Aviation combat resources]. Moscow: Izdatel'stvo MAI, 1934.

Akimov, A. *Siluety Yaponcskikh samoletov* [Silouettes of Japanese aircraft]. Moscow, 1938.

Akopyan, G. *Velikiy letchiki: Valeriy Chkalov* [Great fliers: Valeriy Chkalov]. Moscow. 1940.

Aleksandrov, V. L. *Aeroplany* [Airplanes]. Moscow-Leningrad, 1930, 1931, and 1933.

Alekseyev, M., Batashev, M., and Malinovskiy, P. *Spravochnik po VVS* [Guide to the VVS]. Moscow, 1933.

———. *Spravochnyye svedeniya po vozdushnym silam* [Information guide for air force]. 2d ed. Moscow, 1935.

Alekseyev, M. V. *Spravochnyye svedeniya po aviatsii* [Guide to information on aviation]. Moscow, 1940.

Al'bom siluetov samoletov [Album of aircraft silhouettes]. Moscow, 1931

Antipov, L. *Groznyye ataki* [Cruel attacks]. Moscow, 1939.

Baranov, N., and Bobrov, N. *Nashi letchiki i nashi samolety* [Our fliers and our airplanes]. Moscow: Gosvoyenizdat, 1931.

Baydukov, G. *Nash polet v Ameriku. Zapiski letchika—shturman* [Our flight to America: memoirs of a pilot-navigator]. Moscow, 1937.

———. *Cherez polyus v Ameriki* [Over the pole to America]. Moscow-Leningrad, 1938.

———. *O Chkalove* [About Chkalov]. Moscow, 1939.

———. *Chkalov* [Chkalov]. Moscow: Molodaya gvardiya, 1975.

Bel'ts, V. *Vozdushnyy flot* [Air fleet]. Moscow, 1926.

Belopol'skiy, N. P. *Cherez polyus v Ameriki* [Over the pole to America]. Leningrad, 1939.

Belyakov, A. V. *Dva pereleta* [Two flights]. Moscow, 1939.

Bobrov, N. *Budni letayushchikh lyudey. Ocherki i rasskazy* [Everyday life of airmen, essays and stories]. Moscow-Leningrad: Mosk. Raboch., 1928.

———. *Kryl'ya sovetov* [Soviet wings]. Moscow: Mospoligraf, 1930.

———. *Zhizn' letchika* [Life of a pilot]. Moscow: Molodaya gvardiya 1931.

———. *Zemlya vnizu* [Land below]. Moscow-Leningrad, 1935.

———. *Lyudi ptitsy* [People of the bird]. Moscow, 1930.

———. *Khochu byt' letchikom* [I want to be a flier]. 3d ed. Moscow-Leningrad, 1936.

————. *Letchik Mikheyev* [Pilot Mikheyev]. Moscow, 1936.

————. *Oblachnyye dorogi.* [Pathways through the clouds]. Moscow, 1940.

Bogdanov, N., and Korobov, L. *Eskadril'ya geroyev* [Squadron of heroes]. Leningrad: Lenizdat, 1940.

Bor' pekhoty s vozdushnym vragom [Struggle of infantry with air opposition]. Leningrad, 1927.

Borodachev, N. *Taktika vozdushnoy oborony* [Tactics of air defense]. Moscow-Leningrad, 1927.

Borovikov, A. F. and Sedlenik, G. I. *Vooruzheniye samoleta* [Aircraft armament]. Moscow, 1941.

Brontman, L., and Khvat, L. *Geroicheskiy perelet "Rodiny"* [Heroic flight of the "Rodina"]. Moscow, 1938.

————. *Cherez okean—v Ameriku* [Over the ocean to America]. Moscow, 1939.

————. *Vladimir Kokkinaki* [Vladimir Kokkinaki]. Moscow, 1939.

Buzanov, G. *Voyskovaya aviatsiya* [Army aviation]. 2d ed. Moscow, 1932.

Chkalov, V., Baydukov, G., and Belyakov, A. *Tri dnya v vozduke* [Three days in the air]. Moscow-Leningrad, 1937.

————. *Nash transpolyarnyy reys Moskva-Severnyy polyus-Severnaya-Amerika* [Our trans-polar trip—Moscow-North Pole-North-America]. Moscow, 1938.

————. *Vysoko nad zemley. Rasskazy letchika* [High over the earth: stories of a pilot]. Moscow-Leningrad, 1939.

Chkalova, O. E. *Nash Chkalov. Sbornik Vospominaniy* [Our Chkalov recollections]. Moscow: Molodaya gvardiya, 1963.

Chudodeyev, Yu. V., ed. *V nebe Kitaya, 1937–1940* [In the skies of China]. Moscow: Nauka, 1980.

Dalin, S., and Zhabrov, A. *Proletariy, na somelet! Sbornik, posvyashchennyy voprosam shkol'noy podgotovki rabotnikov krash. Vosd. flota* [Proletarians, take to the air! collection of materials for training of workers of the Red Air Fleet]. Moscow, 1925.

Demchenko. A. *Sovety starogo pilota* [Advice of an old pilot]. Moscow, 1937.

Desyat' let voyennoy vozdushnoy akademii RKKA im. prof. N. Ye. Zhukovskogo 1922–1932 [Ten years of Zhukovskiy military air academy of the Red Army, 1922–1932]. Moscow, 1932.

Dubravin, A. K. *Samolety v arkticheskikh usloviyakh* [Aircraft into the Arctic]. Moscow-Leningrad, 1936.

Dzhardanov, A. *Vashi kryl'ya* [Your wings]. Moscow, 1937; 2d ed., 1939.

————. *Polety v oblakakh* [Flight into the clouds]. Moscow, 1940.

Eksler, K. *Geroicheskiy perelet* [Heroic flight]. Moscow, 1939.

Fyn Yu-Ko. *Zapiski kitayskikh letchikov* [Notes of Chinese fliers]. Moscow, 1939.

Gol'tsman, A. *Grazhdanskaya aviatsiya* [Civil aviation]. Moscow-Leningrad, 1932.

Grigor'yev, A. L., and Sergeyev, A. V. *Spravochnik po vozushnomu flotu dlya komsostava RKKA* [Reference book on Air Fleet for party staff of Red Army].Moscow, 1924.

Gusev, A. I. *Gnevoye nebo Ispanii* [The cruel skies of Spain]. Moscow: Voyenizdat, 1973.

Kamenev, K. *Vozdushnyy flot v sovremennoy voyne* [The Air Fleet in modern war]. Leningrad, 1933.

Kantorovich, M.M., and Ulanchev, V.F. *Zarubezhnaya aviapromyshlennost' i aviatsiya v 1940 g.* [Foreign aviation industry and aviation in 1940]. Moscow, 1940.

Karpov, I. *Pobedy Sovetskoy aviatsii* [Achievements of Soviet aviation]. Leningrad, 1938.

————. *Aviatsiya strany sotsializma* [Aviation of the Land of Socialism]. Leningrad, 1939.

Kartsev, A. *Istrebiteli mayora Denisova. Iz episodov voyny s belofinnami 1939–1940. gg.* [Fighter of Major Denisov: episodes from the Finnish War, 1939–1940]. Moscow, 1941.

Kaydarov, K. *Rasskazy letchika-parachutista* [Stories of a flier-parachutist]. Moscow, 1940.

Khripin, V. *Nash vozdushyy flot* [Our Air Fleet]. Moscow: Voyenizdat, 1931.

————. *Vozdushnyy flot. Voyenno-politicheskiy obzor organizatsii, vooruzheniya i primeneniya* [The Air Fleet: a military-political survey of its organization, armament, and application]. Moscow: Molodaya gvardiya, 1931.

Klyucharev, V. *Grazhdanskaya aviatsiya SSSR na poroge vtoroy pyatiletki* [Soviet civil aviation on the threshold of the second Five-Year Plan]. Moscow-Leningrad, 1933.

Klyucharev, V., and Tsekhanovich, A. *Grazhdanskiy vozdushnyy flot SSSR.* [The Civil Air Fleet of the Soviet Union]. Leningrad, 1933.

Kolkhozniky o protivovozdushnoy i protivokhimicheskoy oborone [Air defense and anti-chemical defense for collective farmers]. Moscow, 1940.

Khvat, L. *Amerikanskiye vstrechi* [American encounters]. Moscow, 1938.

Kokkinaki, V. *Kurs na vostok* [Course to the East]. Moscow, 1939.

Kol'tsov, M. *Khochu letat'* [I want to fly]. Moscow: Gosvoyenizdat, 1931.

Kossov, B. *Letat' vsekh vyshe, bystro, dal'she* [To fly higher, faster, further]. Moscow-Leningrad, 1939.

Kozhevin, N.V. *Aerovokzaly* [Airports]. Moscow-Leningrad, 1937.

Kreyson, P.M. *Samolety za 20 let* [Twenty years of aircraft]. Leningrad, 1934.

Kuzovkin, A., and Makarov, A. *Pod nami polyus!* [The North Pole beneath us!]. Moscow: Politizdat, 1977.

Langfang, A.I., ed. *Letchiki—sbornik rasskazov* [Fliers—collections of stories]. Moscow, 1938.

Lebed', D. *Ugroza voyny i protivovozdushnaya oborona* [Threat of war and air defense]. Moscow, 1936.

Leont'ev, B. *Budem krelit' krasnyy vozdushnyy flot i vsesoyuznomu dnyu aviatsii* [We will support the Red Air Fleet and All-Union Aviation Day]. Moscow, 1933.

Linnik, A. *Protivovozdushnaya oborona* [Air defense]. Moscow-Leningrad, 1932.

Linnik, A., and Popov, G. *Protivovozdushnaya oborona tyla* [Air defense of the rear]. Moscow-Leningrad, 1933.

Luchinin, V. *Protivovozdushnaya oborona voysk i tyla- Annot. ukazatel' literatury 1921–1930 gg* [Air defense troops and the rear: annotated index of literature, 1921–1930]. Moscow, 1931.

Lyakhovetsiy, D. *Protivovozdushnaya oborona. Al'bom risunkov* [Air defense album of illustratons]. Kharkov, 1934.

Malinovskiy, P., Alekseyev, M., and Batashev, M. *Spravochnyye svedeniya po voyennym vozdushnym silam* [Reference book on air forces]. 3d ed. Moscow, 1936.

Mazuruk, I. P. *Nasha aviatsiya* [Our Aviation]. Moscow-Leningrad, 1940.

Mednis, K. *Yakov Alksnis. Zhizn' v aviatsii* [Yakov Alksnis: a life in aviation]. Riga: Latviyskoye gosizdat, 1961.

Mednis, K., ed. *Komandarm krylatykh. Zhizn' Ya. I. Alksnisa. Sbornik vospominaniy* [Winged army commander: life of Ya. I. Alksnis: a collection of reminiscences]. Riga: Liyesma, 1967.

Mikhel's, V. *Ot Kremlevskoy do Kitayskoy steny. Perelet Moskva - Pekin* [From the Kremlin to the Wall of China: flight from Moscow to Peking]. Moscow-Leningrad, 1927.

———. *Ot kremlevskoy do kitayskoy steni* [From the Kremlin to the Wall of China]. Moscow-Leningrad, 1929.

Mikheyev, S. *Vozdushnyy flot* [Air fleet]. Moscow, 1925.

Molchanov, P. A. *Polety v stratosferu* [Flights into the stratosphere]. Moscow-Leningrad, 1935.

Morozov, S. *Oni prinesli kryl'ya v Arktiku* [They brought wings to the Arctic]. Moscow: Mysl', 1979.

Narusherich, A. *Vozdushnyye sily nashikh sosedey* [Our neighbors' air forces]. Moscow: Voyenizdat, 1931.

Nikol'skiy, M. N. *Deystviya aviatsii protiv morskogo flota* [Air action against naval forces]. Moscow, 1939.

Ordin, A. *Velikiy letchik nashego vremeni Valeriy Pavlovich Chkalov* [Valeriy P. Chkalov—great fliers of our age]. Moscow, 1949.

Ozerov, G.A. *Tsentral'nyy aero-gidrodinamicheskiy institut im. prof. N. Ye.*

    Zhukovskogo (TsAGI) Kratsiy obzor Zhukovskiy [Central Aero-Hydrodynamics Institute: short survey]. Moscow, 1927.

————. *Desyatiletiye TsAGI* [Ten years of TsAGI]. Moscow: Osoaviakhim, 1928.

Osokin, P. *Samolety* [Aircraft]. Moscow-Leningrad, 1933.

Rodimstsev, A.I. *Pod nebom Ispanii* [Beneath Spain's skies]. Moscow: Sovetskaya Rossiya, 1974.

Rodzevich, N. N. *Sovetskiy aviamotor 1917–1932* [The Soviet aero engine, 1917–1932]. Moscow-Leningrad, 1932.

Ruben, S. *Stalinskiyye sokoly v boyakh s belofinnami* [Stalin's Falcons in the Finnish War]. Moscow, 1941.

Ryabnikov, Ye., and Magid, A. *Stanovleniye* [Formation]. Moscow: Znaniye, 1973.

Rynin, N. A. *Zavoyevaniye stratosfery* [Conquest of the stratosphere]. Moscow-Leningrad, 1933.

Ryakhovskiy, V. *Komandir eskadril'i. Iz zapisok voyny s belofinnami 1939–1940 gg* [Squadron commander: notes from the Finnish War, 1939–1940]. Moscow, 1941.

Sergeyev, A. V. *5 let stroitel'stva i borby vozdushnogo flota, 1917–1922* [Five years building the air fleet, 1917–1922]. 2 books. Moscow: Aviaizdat, 1926.

Shaurov, N. I. *Razvitiye voyennykh tipov sukhoputnykh samoletov* [Development of ground support aircraft types]. Moscow: Voyenizdat, 1939.

Shingarev, S. *Pod nami Khalkhin—Gol* [Khalkhin-Gol beneath us]. Moscow: Moskovskiy rabochiy, 1979.

————. *Chatos idut v ataku* [I-15 Chatos on the attack]. Moscow: Moskovskiy rabochiy, 1971.

Shishkin, S. N. *Khalkhin-Gol* [Khalkhin-Gol]. Moscow: Voyenizdat, 1954.

Shpanov, N. N. *Osnovy vozdushnykh soobshcheniy* [Fundamentals of air communication]. Moscow-Leningrad: Gosudarstvennoye Izdatel'stvo, 1930.

Siluety germanskikh samoletov [Silhouettes of German aircraft]. Moscow, 1939, 1941.

Siluety samoletov Pol'shi i Rumynii [Silhouettes of Polish and Rumanian aircraft]. Moscow, 1939.

Siluety samoletov Rumynii, Bolgarii, Yugoslavii, Gretsii i Ventrii [Aircraft silhouettes of Rumania, Bulgaria, Yugoslavia, Greece, and Hungary]. Moscow, 1940.

Siluety samoletov SSSR [Silhouettes of Soviet aircraft]. Moscow, 1939.

Siluety samoletov (SSSR, Finlyandiya) [Aircraft silhouettes: Soviet Union and Finland]. Moscow, 1939.

Siluety samoletov Shvetsii, Norvetii i Danii [Aircraft silhouettes of Sweden, Norway, and Denmark]. Moscow, 1940.

Siluety samolety Turtsii, Irana, Iraka i Afganistana [Aircraft silhouettes of Turkey, Iran, Iraq and Afghanistan]. Moscow, 1940.

Simonov, N., and Sheleyet, K. *Bezmotornyy polet* [Motorless flight]. Moscow, 1938.

Smirnov, M. *Voyskovaya aviatsiya* [Army aviation]. Moscow, 1936; 3d ed., 1940.

Smirnov, M., and Vinogradov, N. *Aviatsiya i PVO* [Aviation and air defense]. 4th ed. Moscow, 1939.

Solytsev, I. I. *Ugroza voyny i zadachi PVO tyla* [The threat of war and the tasks of rear air defense]. Arkhangel'sk, 1932.

Spirin, I. T. *Polet' v oblakakh* [Flight into the clouds]. Moscow, 1935.

————. *Zapiski voyennogo letchika* [Notes of a combat pilot]. Moscow, 1939.

————. *Polety v Arktiku* [Flights to the Arctic]. Moscow-Leningrad, 1940.

————. *Sovetskaya aviatsiya* [Soviet aviation]. Moscow, 1940.

————. *Stalinskiye sokoly* [Stalin's Falcons]. Stalingrad: Oblastnoye knigoizdatel'stvo, 1941.

Stalinskiy marshrut prodolzhen Moskva-Severnyy polyus-severnaya Amerika [Stalin Route—Moscow-North Pole-North America]. Moscow, 1937.

Stolyarskiy, S.E. *Istoricheskiy ocherk po razvitiyu aviatsii russkogo flota* [Historical sketch of Russian Naval Aviation]. Moscow: UVMS, 1937.

Timofeyev, V. *Svyaz' samoleta s nazemymi voyskami* [Aircraft communication with ground troops]. Moscow, 1932.

Ust'yantsev, L.G. *Za 20 let aviatsii* [Twenty years of aviation]. Moscow and Leningrad, 1925.

Van si, *Kryl'ya Kitaya. Zapiski voyennogo letchika* [Wings of China: notes of combat pilot]. Moscow, 1940.

Vasyanin, V. S., and Borodin, V. G. *Paryashchiy polet* [Parachute flight]. Moscow, 1934.

Vereyskiy, G. S. *Krasnyy voyennyy vozdushnyy flot* [The Red military air fleet]. Moscow: Izdatel'stvo Tsk VLKSM, 1934.

Vladimirov, M. *Vozdushnyy flot yaponii* [Japanese Air Force]. Moscow-Leningrad, 1934.

———. *Voyennyye samolety inostrannykh gosudarstv.* Vol. I. *Angliya* [Foreign military aircraft. Vol. I—Britain]. Moscow-Leningrad, 1934.

Vernyye syny nashey Rodiny [Loyal sons of our Motherland]. Moscow, 1937.

Veygelin, K. E. *Vozdushnyy flot v mirovoy voyne. Ocherki i epizody vozdushnoy voyny* [The air fleet in the World War: sketches and episodes from the air war]. Leningrad: Voyennaya tipografiya, 1924.

———. *Aviatsionno—vozdukhoplavatel'nyy slovar'* [Aviation—Aeronautical Dictionary]. Moscow, 1926.

———. *Put' letchika Nesterova* [Path of the flier Nesterov]. Moscow-Leningrad, 1939.

———. *Ocherki po istorii letnogo dela* [Historical notes on flight]. Kiev, 1940.

Velizhev, A. A. *Dostizheniya sovetskoy aviapromyshlennosti za pyatnadtsat' let* [Achievements of Soviet aviation industry in the Five-Year Plan]. Moscow, 1932.

Vinogradov, N. *PVO voysk* [Air defense troops]. Moscow, 1932.

———. *PVO krupnogo punkta* [Air defense strong points]. Moscow, 1941.

Vishnekovskiy, B. *Letchiki—planeristy* [Glider pilots]. Moscow, 1934.

Vishnyakov, N.P., and Arkhipov, Ye. I. *Ustroystvo vooruzhennykh sil SSSR'* [The structure of the armed forces of the USSR]. Moscow, 1926.

Volkov, N. *SSSR. Velikaya aviatsionnaya derzhava* [USSR: a great air power]. Moscow, 1938.

———. *Nepobedimaya aviatsiya strany sovetov* [The invincible aviation of the Land of the Soviets]. Moscow, 1939.

———. *Moguchnaya sovetskaya aviatsiya* [Mighty Soviet aviation]. Moscow, 1940.

Volkovoynov, M. *Na samolete iz Moskvy v Yaponiyu cherez Pekin* [Flight from Moscow to Japan through Peking]. Moscow: Aviaizdat, 1926.

Voronim, V. *Komsomolets—na samolet* [Komsomols—take to the air]. Moscow, 1930.

Voyennyye samolety SSSR [USSR combat aircraft]. Moscow: Voyenizdat, 1941.

Yegorov, P., et al. *Potolok letchika* [Flier's ceiling]. Moscow, 1931.

Zarzar, V. *Grazhdanskaya aviatsiya kapitalisma i sotsializma* [Civil aviation of capitalism and socialism]. Moscow, 1932.

———. *Vtoraya pyatiletka grazhanskogo vozdushnogo flota* [The civil air fleet and the second Five-Year Plan]. Moscow-Leningrad, 1932.

Zhabrov, A. A. *Aviatsiya i vozdukhoplavaniye (istoriya, tekhnika, i primeneniye vozdushnogo flota)* [Aviation and aeronautics: history, technology, and application of the air fleet]. Moscow, 1925.

———. *V oblakakh, Rasskazy* [In the clouds: stories]. Moscow: "Federatsiya," 1931.

Zinger, M. E. *Vozdushnyye korabli* [Airships]. Moscow: Molodaya gvardiya, 1932.

Zvorkin, A. A., ed. *Istoriya aviatsii. Sbornik statey i materialov* [History of aviation—collection of articles]. Vol. 1. Moscow, 1934.

The Great Patriotic War, 1941–1945

Abasov, M. G. *Na kryl'yakh muzhestva* [On wings of valor]. Baku: Elm, 1975.

Abramichev, A. *Yevgraf Mikhailovich Ryzhov* [Yevgraf Mikhailovich Ryzhov]. Smolensk: Kn. Izdatel'stvo, 1960.

Abramov, A. *Ne radi slavy* [Not for the sake of glory]. Sverdlovsk: Sredne-Ural'sk. Kn. Izdatel'stvo, 1969.

———. *Dvenadtsat' taranov* [Twelve ramming attacks]. Sverdlovsk: Sredne-Ural'sk. Kn. Izdatel'stvo, 1970.

Akishin, A. A. *Komandir goluboy dvoiki* [Commander of the Blue Pair]. Moscow: Znaniye, 1965.

Alabin, N. I., et al. *Sovetskiye Voyenno-vozdushnyye sily* [The Soviet Air Force]. Moscow: Voyenizdat, 1968.

Aleksandrov, S. S. *Krylatyye tanki* [Winged tanks]. Moscow: Voyenizdat, 1971.

Andreyev, S. P. *Krylom k krylu* [Wing to wing]. Moscow: Znaniye, 1962.

Andryanov, S. V. *Ukroshcheniye "Uragana"* [Taming of "Typhoon"]. Moscow: Voyenizdat, 1969.

———. *Marshrut neizvesten* [Unknown path]. Moscow: Sovetskiy voin, 1972.

Arkhipov, P. *Siyaniye zvezd* [Halo of stars]. Moscow: DOSAAF, 1971.

Arlazorov, M. S., *Chelovek na kryl'yakh* [Man on wings]. Moscow: DOSAAF, 1958.

———. *Front idet cherez KB* [The front passes through the design bureau]. Moscow: Znaniye, 1969; 2d ed., 1975.

———. *Sovetskaya aviatsionnaya tekhnika. Fotoocherk* [Soviet aviation technology: a photo review]. Moscow: Mashinostroyeniye, 1970.

———. *Konstruktory* [The designers]. Moscow: Sovetskaya Rossiya, 1975.

———. *Artem Mikoyan* [Artem Mikoyan]. Moscow: Molodaya gvardiya, 1978.

———. *Doroga na kosmodrom* [Path to the cosmodrome]. Moscow: Politizdat, 1980.

———. *Vint i krylo* [Propeller and wing]. Moscow: Znaniye, 1980.

Aronova, R. Ye. *Nochnyye ved'my* [Witches of the night]. Moscow: Sovetskaya Rossiya, 1969, 1980.

———. *Letnyy kharacter* [Flying temper]. Moscow: DOSAAF, 1981.

Arsenin, N. *Klyuch ot Berlina* [Clue from Berlin]. Moscow: DOSAAF, 1970.

Artamoshin, Yu. N. *Lyudi geroicheskoi professii* [People of a heroic profession]. Moscow: DOSAAF, 1977.

Arykbayeva, K. *Timur Mikhailovich Frunze* [Timur Mikhailovich Frunze]. Kyrgyzstan, 1973.

Astashenkov, P. T., *Konstruktor legendarnykh Ilov* [The designer of the legendary "Ils"]. Moscow: Politizdat, 1972.

———. *Orbity glavnogo konstruktora* [The chief designer's world]. Moscow: DOSAAF, 1973.

———. *Glavnyy konstruktor* [Chief designer]. Moscow: Voyenizdat, 1975.

———. *Derzkiye starty* [Daring takeoffs]. Moscow: Politizdat, 1976.

Avdeyev, M. V. *U samogo Chernogo morya. Dokumental'naya povest'* [Right on the Black Sea: a documentary]. 3 vols. Moscow: DOSAAF, 1968, 1970, 1975.

Aviatsiya nashey Rodiny. Sbornik statey [Aviation of Our Motherland: collection of articles]. Moscow: Voyenizdat, 1955.

Azarov, I. I. *Nepobezhdennyye* [Unvanquished]. Moscow: 1973.

Babikov, I. N., *Gvardeyskiye zalpy. 8-y gvardeyskiy Yasskiy vozdushnodesantnyy-artiller. polk* [Guards volleys: the 8th Guards Jassy Airborne-Artillery Regiment]. Moscow: Voyenizdat, 1970.

Babiichuk, A. N. *Chelovek, nebo, kosmos* [Man, sky space]. Moscow: Voyenizdat, 1979.

Barinov, B. I. *Litsom k nebu* [Face to face with the sky]. Moscow: Moskovskiy rabochiy, 1980.

Barsukov, V. *Krylom k krylu* [From wing to wing]. Moscow: DOSAAF, 1981.

Batitskiy, P. F., ed. *Voiska PVO strany* [Air defense troops]. Moscow: Voyenizdat, 1968.

Batitskiy, P. F. *Voiska protivo-vozdushnoi oborony* [Air defense troops]. Moscow: Znaniye, 1977.

Baulin, Ye. P. *Syn neba* [Son of the sky]. Leningrad: Lenizdat, 1968.

Begel'dinov, T. Ya. *305 reydov* [Three hundred and five raids]. Frunze: Kyrgyzstan, 1963.

———. *"Ily" atakuyut* [The "Ils" are attacking]. Alma-Ata: Kazakhstan, 1966.

Belokon', K. F. *Surovoye nebo. Zapiski letchika-shturmovika* [The cruel heavens: notes of a ground-attack pilot]. Kharkov: Prapor, 1973.

Belostotskiy, I. V. *Boyevyye kryl'ya* [Combat wings]. Kazan: Tatknigoizdat, 1971.

Belyakov, A. V. *V polet skvoz' gody* [Flight through the years]. Moscow: Voyenizdat, 1981.

Beregovoy, G. *Ugol ataki* [Angle of attack]. Moscow: Molodaya gvardiya, 1971.

Berezovoy, I. N. *Tak srazhalis' qvardeytsy* [Guardsmen battled]. Moscow: Voyenizdat, 1960.

Beschastnov, P. I. *V ognennom nebe. Zapiski voyennogo letchika* [In the fiery skies: a military pilot's notes]. Alma-Ata; Kazakhstan, 1975.

Bezymyannyy, V. M., et al. *Na strazhe neba stolitsy* [Guarding the capital's skies]. Moscow: Voyenizdat, 1968.

Bizyukov, N. S. *Neistovaya dusha* [Fierce temper]. Petrozavodsk: Gosizdat Karel ASSR, 1962.

Bobrov, N. *Dvazhdi Geroy Sovetskogo Soyuza Vladimir Lavrinenkov* [Two-time hero of the Soviet Union Vladimir Lavrinenkov]. Moscow: Voyenizdat, 1950.

Bogatyri russkogo neba. Sbornik [Warriors of Russia's skies: a collection]. Khabarovsk: Dal'giz, 1943.

Bogdanov, N. G. *V nebe—gvardeyskiy Gatchinskiy. Iz zapisok letchika ADD* [Gatchinskiy guards into the sky: from the notebook of a long-range bomber pilot]. Leningrad, 1980.

Bondarenko, N. A. *Letim na razvedku* [We fly reconnaissance]. Moscow: Voyenizdat, 1976.

Borisenko, S. P. *Na trassakh voyny. Frontovyye zapiski grazhdanskogo letchika* [On the paths of war: front-line notes of a civilian pilot]. Moscow: RIO Aeroflota, 1947.

Boyko, V., and Verevkin, I. *Ispytaniye voli* [Test of will]. Archangelsk, 1973.

Boyko, V. *Kryl'ya severnogo flota* [Wings of the Northern Fleet]. Murmansk: Murmanskoye Kn. Izdatel'stvo, 1976.

Bukhanov, M. *Geroy Sovetskogo Soyuza Timur Mikhailovich Frunze* [Hero of the Soviet Union Timur Mikhailovich Frunze]. Moscow: Voyenizdat, 1953.

———. *Bessmertiye* [Immortal ones]. Vologda: Sev-Zap. Kn. Isdatel'stvo, 1971.

Burinda, I., *Posledniy patron dlya vraga* [The last cartridge for the enemy]. Donetsk: Donbass, 1972.

Burov, A., and Perepelov, L. *Leningradskaya aviatsiya* [Leningrad aviation]. Leningrad: Lenizdat, 1947.

———. *Ognennoye nebo* [Fiery sky]. Leningrad: Lenizdat, 1974.

Buzunov, V. K. *Aerodrom—Boyevaya pozitsiya aviatsii. Aerodromnotekhnicheskoye obespecheniye aviatsii* [The airfield—aviation's combat position: airfield technical support of aviation]. Moscow: Voyenizdat, 1969.

Chalaya, Z. *Anatoli Serov* [Anatoli Serov]. Sverdlovsk: Sredno-Ural'sk kn. Isdatel'stvo, 1970.

Chasovyye Leningradskogo neba [Sentries of the Leningrad sky]. Leningrad: Lenizdat, 1968.

Chechelashvili, O.G. *Na stal'nykh kryl'yakh. Zapiski letchika* [On steel wings: a pilot's notes]. Tbilisi, 1965.

Chechel'nitskiy, G.A. *Moskovskiy gvardeyskiy shturmovoy* [Moscow Guards Ground-Attack Regiment]. Moscow: Voyenizdat, 1960.

———. *Srazhalis' letchiki-istrebiteli* [Fighter pilots battled]. Moscow: Voyenizdat, 1964.

———. *Letchiki na voyne. Voyenno-istoricheskiy ocherk o boyevom puti 15-y vozdushnoy armii 1942–1945* [Pilots in war: a military-historical sketch of the combat path of the 15th Air Army, 1942–1945]. Moscow: Voyenizdat, 1974.

Chechneva, M.P. *Somolety ukhodyat v noch'* [Aircraft depart into the night]. Moscow: Voyenizdat, 1962.

———. *Boyevyye podrugi moi* [My combat friends]. Moscow: DOSAAF, 1975.

———. *Kryl'ya* [Wings]. Sukhumi: Alashara, 1968.

———. *Letali devchata v gvardeyskom* [The girls who flew in the guards regiment]. Cheboksary: Chuvashskoye kn. izdatel'stvo, 1968.

———. *Nebo ostayetsya nashim* [The skies are still ours]. Moscow: Voyenizdat, 1970; 2d ed., 1976.

Chereshnev, A.I. *Lyudi muzhestva* [Courageous people]. Moscow: Voyenizdat, 1971.

Cherevatenko, A.T. *My vernemsya, Odessa!* [We will return, Odessa!]. Odessa: Kn.

izdatel'stvo, 1963.

————. *Nebo Odessy* [Odessa's skies]. Odessa: Mayak, 1971.

Chernousov, S.I. *V nebe donskom* [The Don skies]. Rostov-on-Don: Kn. izdatel'stvo, 1974.

Chir'yev, V.N. *Zapiski voyennogo letchika* [Notes of a combat pilot]. Moscow: Voyenizdat, 1956.

Chukovskiy, N.K. *Rasskazy letchikov* [Pilots' tales]. Moscow: Voyenmorizdat, 1942.

————. *Na zashchite Leningrada. Letchiki-baltiytsy v boyakh* [Defending Leningrad: Baltic Fleet pilots in combat]. Moscow: Voyenmorizdat NKVMF, 1943.

Chutko, I. *Krasnyye samolety* [Red aircraft]. Moscow: Politizdat, 1978; 2d ed., 1979.

Damskiy, Ya. *Devushka iz legendy* [Girl from legend]. Kazan': Tatknigoizdat, 1966.

Davydov, I. *Podvig Nachinalsya v aprele* [The feat began in April]. Sverdlovsk: Sredno-Ural'sk. Kn. Izdatel'stvo, 1970.

Dazhin, F.A. *Vozdushnyy Taran* [Aerial Ramming]. Moscow: Voyenizdat, 1964.

Denisov, I., and Karpovich, M. *Trizhdy Geroy Sovetskogo Soyuza I.N. Kozhedub* [Three-time hero of the Soviet Union I.N. Kozhedub]. Moscow: Voyenizdat, 1948.

Denisov, N.N. *Dnevnik ofitsera svyazi* [Liaison officer's diary]. Moscow: Pravda, 1942.

————. *Boyevaya slava sovetskoy aviatsii* [Soviet aviation's combat glory]. Moscow: Voyenizdat, 1953.

————. *Aviatsiya na sluzhbe sovetskogo naroda* [Aviation in the service of the Soviet people]. Moscow, 1954.

Desantirovaniye i boyevyye deystviya 4-go vozdushnodesantnogo korpusa v tylu protivnika [Assault landing and combat operations of the 4th Airborne Corps in the enemy rear area]. Moscow: Voyenizdat, 1955.

Devyatayev, M.P. *Polet k solntsu* [Flight toward the sun]. Moscow: DOSAAF, 1972.

————. *Pobeda iz ada* [Victory out of Hell]. Saransk: Mordovskoye kn. izatel'stvo, 1974.

Devyat'yarov, A.A. *Zemlya pod krylom* [The land beneath the wing]. Izhevsk: Udmurtiya, 1973.

Dmitrevskiy, N.N. *Voyzdushnyy strazh* [On guard in the air]. Moscow: Voyenizdat, 1958.

————. *Zashchitniki neba stolitsy* [Defenders of the capital's skies]. Moscow: Voyenizdat, 1962.

Dorokhov, A.P. *Geroi chernomorskogo neba* [Heroes of the Black Sea skies]. Moscow: Voyenizdat, 1972.

Dospanova, Khivaz. *Pod komandovaniyem Raskovoy. Vospominaniya voyennoy letchitsy* [Under Raskova's command: reminiscences of a military aviatrix]. Alma-Ata: Kazgoslitizdat, 1960.

Dvazhdy Geroy Sovetskogo Soyuza N. Stepanyan [Two-time Hero of the Soviet Union, N. Stepanyan]. Yerevan: Ayastan, 1968.

Dvoryanskiy, Ye. M., and Yaroshenko, A.A. *V ognennom kol'tse* [In the fiery ring]. Tallin: Eesti raamat, 1977.

Dyrin, Ye. *Na boyevom kurse* [On the combat course]. Moscow: Voyenizdat, 1951.

————. *Delo, Kotoromu sluzhish'* [The cause we serve]. Moscow: Voyenizdat, 1960.

Dzusov, I.M. *V sem'ye otvazhnykh* [In the family of the brave]. Ordzhonikidze: Severo-Osetinskoye izdatel'stvo, 1960.

D'yachenko, G. Kh. *Nasledniki Nesterova* [Heirs of Nesterov]. Moscow: Voyenizdat, 1963.

D'yachkov, I. *Bogatyr' Krylatoy gvardii* [Hero of the winged guard]. Alma-Ata: kazgosizdat, 1962.

Falaleyev, F. Ya. *V stroyu krylatykh. Iz vospominaniy* [In the winged formation: reminiscences]. Izhevsk: Udmurtiya, 1970, 1978.

Fedorov, A.G. *Plata za schast'ye. Zapiski letchika-komandira* [Payment for happiness: a pilot-commander's notes]. Moscow: Molodaya gvardiya, 1963.

————. *Do poslednego starta* [Till final takeoff]. Moscow: Voyenizdat, 1965.

————. *Dorogami Muzhestva* [Paths of courage]. Moscow: Voyenizdat, 1968.

————. *Pyat' sosen* [Five pine trees]. Moscow: Sov. Rossiya, 1968.

————. *Vetram navstrechu* [Into the winds]. Moscow: DOSAAF, 1968.

————. *Aviatsiya v bitve pod Moskvoy* [Aviation in the Battle of Moscow]. Moscow: Nauka, 1971, 1975.

————. *Iz plemeni otvazhnykh* [From the tribe of the brave]. Moscow: Voyenizdat, 1971.

————. *Sud'boyu stalo nebo. Zapiski voyennogo letchika* [The heavens became our fate: notes of a military pilot]. Moscow: Moskovskiy rabochiy, 1973.

————. *Idu v pike* [I fly into a dive]. Moscow: Molodaya gvardiya, 1976.

————. *Letchiki na zashchiki Moskvy* [Fliers for the defense of Moscow]. Moscow: Nauka, 1979.

————. *Lyubimets polka* [Favorite regiment]. Moscow: Voyenizdat, 1981.

Filimonov, N.S. *Pavel Petrovich Karavay* [Pavel Petrovich Karavay]. Smolensk: Smolenskoye knizhnoye izdatel'stvo, 1958.

Frolov, M.L. *Krylataya gvardiya. Kniga-reportazh o letchikakh-geroyakh* [Winged guard: a book about heroic pilots]. Leningrad: Lenizdat, 1963.

Gai, D. *Profil' krylya* [Profile of wings]. Moscow: Moskovskiy Rabochiy, 1981.

Gallai, M.L. *Cherez nevidimyye bar'yery. Ispytano v nebe. Iz zapisok letchika-isputatelya* [Through invisible barriers: tested in the sky: from a test pilot's notes]. Moscow: Molodaya gvardiya, 1963, 1965.

Gamov, N.S. *Kryl'ya podviga* [Wings of a feat]. Voronezh: Tsentr-Chernozem. kn. izdatel'stvo, 1967.

Gareyev, M.G. *Shturmoviki idut na tsel'* [Ground-attack aircraft head for the target]. Moscow: DOSAAF, 1972.

Gasenko, I. *Pavel Mikhailovich Mikhailov* [Pavel Mikhailovich Mikhailov]. Smolensk: Kn. izdatel'stvo, 1958.

Gil'berg, L.A. *Pokoreniye neba* [Conquest of the sky]. Moscow: DOSAAF, 1977.

Gil'yardi, N. *Boris Safonov* [Boris Safonov]. Moscow: Voyenmorizdat, 1950.

Glukhov, M.K. *Voyenno-vozdushnyye sily* [The air force]. Moscow: Voyenizdat, 1959.

Glukhovskiy, S. *Kogda vyrastali kryl'ya* [When they were sprouting wings]. Moscow: Voyenizdat, 1965.

Golubev, G.G. *V pare s "sotym"* [Flying cover for "No. 100"]. Moscow: DOSAAF, 1974, 1978.

Golubev, V.F. *Shkola voyny* [The school of war]. Moscow: Voyenizdat, 1947.

Golubev, V.F., and Kalinichenko, A.F. *Kryl'ya Baltiki* [Wings of the Baltic]. Kaliningrad. Kaliningradskoye kn. izdatel'stvo, 1078.

————. *Kryl'ya krepnut v boyu* [Wings grow strong in battle]. Moscow: Sovetskaya Rossiya, 1980.

Golubeva-Teres, O.T. *Zvezdy na kryl'yakh* [Stars on the wings]. Saratov: Privolzhskoye kn. izdatel'stvo, 1974.

Golyshev, M.I., et. al. *Serdtsa Krylatykh* [Winged hearts]. Moscow: Voyenizdat, 1961.

Gorbatenko, D.D. *Ten' Lyuftvaffe nad Yevropoy. Iz istorii germanskoy aviatsii* [The shadow of the Luftwaffe over Europe: from German aviation history]. Moscow: Nauka, 1967.

Grebenyuk, I.F. *Na dalekikh rubezhakh* [On the frontiers]. Moscow: Voyenizdat, 1964.

Grigor'yev, G. *Dve zvezdy* [Two stars]. Moscow: DOSAAF, 1970.

Grigor'yev, N.F. *Krylataya Baltika* [The winged Baltic]. Moscow: Voyenmorizdat, 1940.

Grigor'yev, Pavel. *Na strazhe Zapolyar'ya. Boyevyye podvigi letchikov-severomortsev* [Guarding the polar regions: combat feats of North Sea pilots]. Moscow: Voyenmorizdat NKVMF, 1942.

Gubanov, N. *Letchik general Ostryakov* [Pilot General Ostryakov]. Simferopol': Krymizdat, 1959.

————. *Krylatyy general* [Winged general]. Simferopol': Krymizdat, 1971.

Gulyayev, V. *Na polevykh aerodromakh* [At a field air base]. Moscow: DOSAAF, 1977.

Guzhkov, A.A., ed. *Baltiiskiye zenitchiki* [Baltic air defenders]. Tallinn: Eesti raamat, 1981.

Il'in, N.G., and Rudin, V.P. *Gvardeytsy v vozdukhe* [Guardsmen in the air]. Moscow: DOSAAF, 1973.

Il'ina, Z. *Komissar Vera* [Commissar Vera]. Moscow: DOSAAF, 1981.

Inozemtsev, I.G. *Vozdushnyye tarany v nebe Leningrada* [Aerial ramming over Leningrad]. Leningrad: Znaniye, 1971.

————. *Krylatyye Zashchitniki severa* [Winged defenders of the north]. Moscow: Voyenizdat, 1975.

————. *Pod krylom—Leningrad* [Leningrad below]. Moscow: Voyenizdat, 1978.

Isayenko, N.F. *"Vizhu protivnika!"* [I see the enemy!]. Kiev: Politizdat Ukr., 1981.

Istoriya Voyenno-vozdushnykh sil sovetskoy armii [History of the Soviet Army Air Force]. Moscow: Voyenizdat, 1954.

Ivanov, A.L. *Skorost', manevr, ogon'* [Speed, maneuver, fire]. Moscow: DOSAAF, 1974.

Ivanov, F.P., and Silakov, A. *Podvig bessmerten* [Immortal feat]. Moscow: DOSAAF, 1959.

Ivanov, P.N. *Kryl'ya nad morem* [Wings over the sea]. Moscow: Voyenizdat, 1973.

Ivanskiy, A. *Orlinyye kryl'ya* [Wings of an eagle]. Moscow: Voyenizdat, 1973.

Ivich, A. *Mikhail Avdeyev* [Mikhail Avdeyev]. Moscow: Voyenizdat, 1947.

Izbekov, D.D. *Yakutiane v nebe frontovom* [Yakuts in the frontline skies]. Yakutsk: Yakutknigoizdat, 1970.

Kaberov, I.A. *V pritsele svastika* [Swastika in the sight]. Leningrad: Lenizdat, 1975.

Kalinin, A.P. *Istrebiteli nad "goluboy liniyey"* [Fighters over the "Blue Line"]. Moscow: Voyenizdat, 1963.

Kalinichenko, A.F. *V nebe Baltiki* [In the Baltic skies]. Moscow: Voyenizdat, 1973.

Kamanin, N.P. *Letchiki i kosmonavty* [Pilots and cosmonauts]. Moscow: Politizdat, 1971.

Kambulov, N.I., ed. *Krylataya yunost'. Ocherki i vospominaniya* [Winged youth: sketches and reminiscences]. Moscow: Voyenizdat, 1958.

Karavatskiy, A.Z. *Marshrutami muzhestva* [Routes of courage]. Minsk: Belarus, 1978.

Karpov, A. *V nebe Ukrainy* [In Ukrainian skies]. Kiev, Politzdat Ukr., 1980.

Karpovich, M.D. *Sovetskiye letchiki v Velikoy Otechestvennoy voyne* [Soviet pilots in the Great Patriotic War]. Moscow: DOSAAF, 1951.

Kazarinova, M.A. *V nebe frontovom. Sbornik vospominaniy sovetskikh letchits-uchastnits Velikoy Otechestvennoy voyny* [In the skies over the front: a collection of reminiscences of Soviet women participants in the Great Patriotic War]. Moscow: Molodaya gvardiya, 1962; 2d ed., 1971.

Kekkelev, L.N. *Taran chetyrekh* [Four rams]. Sverdlovsk: Sredno-Ural'sk. Kn. Izdatel'stvo, 1966.

Kerber, L.L. *Tu—Chelovek i samolet* [Tupolev—the man and the aircraft]. Moscow: Sovetskaya Rossiya, 1973.

Khakhalin, L.A. *Khozyain nochnogo neba* [Master of the night skies]. Leningrad: Lenizdat, 1961.

————. *Rasskazy o muzhestve* [Stories of courage]. Leningrad: Lenizdat, 1978.

Khapayev, A., and Shukanov, B. *Dvazhdy Geroy Sovetskogo Soyuza I.F. Pavlov* [Two-time hero of the Soviet Union, I.F. Pavlov]. Moscow: Voyenizdat, 1953.

Khar'kovskoye vyssh. voyen. aviats. uchilishche letchikov im. Gritsevtsa [The Gritsevets Khar'kov higher military aviation academy]. Khar'kov, 1969.

Khorunzhiy, A. *Orlinyye Kryl'ya* [Wings of an eagle]. Moscow: DOSAAF, 1966.

Kiknadze, M.G. *V nebe stolitsy* [In the capital's skies]. Moscow: DOSAAF, 1967; 2d ed., 1971.

Kin'dyushev, I.I. *K pobednym rassvetam* [Toward victorious dawns]. Moscow: Voyenizdat, 1978.

Komarov, M. Ya., ed. *Voiska PVO strany v Velikoy Otechestvennoy voyne 1941–1945 gg* [Air defense troops in the Great Patriotic War, 1941–1945]. Moscow: Voyenizdat, 1981.

Kondrat'yev, P.V. *Polet skvoz' gody* [Flight through the years]. Moscow: Moskovskiy Rabochiy, 1970.

Korets, L.B., and Ampleyev, N.I. *Bitva pod Moskvoy—deystviya Voyenno-vozdushnykh Sil* [The Battle of Moscow: air force operations]. Monino, 1956.

————. *Sovetskiye VVS v bitve pod Stalingradom* [The Soviet Air Force in the Battle of Stalingrad]. Moscow, 1959.

Korolev, V.D. *Gvardeytsy pervoy shturmovoy* [Guards of the First Ground Attack]. Moscow: Voyenizdat, 1980.

Korsunov, N. *Na boyevom kurse* [On combat course]. Moscow: Voyenmorizdat, 1945.

Kostenko, F.A. *Korpus krylatoy gvardii* [Winged guard corps]. Moscow: Voyenizdat, 1974.

Kostenko, I. *Boyevyye vzlety* [Combat takeoffs]. Moscow: Molodaya Gvardiya, 1976.

Koyander, Ye. V. *Ya.—"Rubin," prikazyvayu* [I "Rubin," Command]. Moscow: Voyenizdat, 1978.

Kozhedub, I.N. *Tri srazheniya* [Three encounters]. Moscow: Voyenizdat, 1945.

———. *Sluzhu Rodine* [I serve the Motherland]. Moscow: Voyenizdat, 1950.

———. *Vernost' otchizne. Rasskazy letchika-istrebitelya* [Fidelity to the Fatherland: tales of a fighter pilot]. Moscow: Voyenizdat, 1975.

Kozhevnika, T., and Popovich, M. *Pesn' vysoty* [Song of the heights]. Moscow: DOSAAF, 1980.

———. *Zhizn' - vechnyy polet* [Life—eternal flight]. Moscow: Voyenizdat, 1980.

Kozhevnikov, A.L. *Zapiski istrebitelya* [A fighter pilot's notes]. Moscow: Voyenizdat, 1961.

———. *Eskadril'i ukhodyat na zapad. Zapiski letchika-istrebitelya* [Squadrons depart for the west: a fighter pilot's notes]. Rostov-on-Don: Kn. izdatel'stvo, 1966.

———. *Startuyet muzhestvo* [Courage takes off]. Moscow: Voyenizdat, 1966.

Kozhevnikov, M.N. *Komandovaniye i shtab VVS Sovetskoy Armii v Velikoy Otechestvennoy voyne 1941–1945 gg* [Soviet army air force command and staff in the Great Patriotic War, 1941–1945]. Moscow: Nauka, 1977.

Kozlov, N.A. *V ogne srazheniy. Vospominaniya* [In the fire of battle: reminiscences]. Groznyy: Checheno-Ingushskoye kn. izdatel'stvo, 1968.

Kozlov, P. Ya. *Ily letyat na front* [Il-2s fly to the front]. Moscow, 1976.

Krasovskiy, S.A., ed. *Aviatsiya i kosmonavtika SSSR* [Aviation and cosmonautics in the USSR]. Moscow: Voyenizdat, 1968.

Krasovskiy, S.A. *Zhizn' v aviatsii* [A life in aviation]. Moscow: Voyenizdat, 1968.

Kravtsova, N.F. *Na goryashchem samolete* [In a burning aircraft]. Moscow: Moskovskiy rabochiy, 1968.

———. *Ot zakata do rassveta* [From dusk to dawn]. Moscow: Voyenizdat, 1968.

Krylataya pekhota [Winged infantry]. Moscow: Voyenizdat, 1956.

Krylatoye plemiya [Winged tribe]. Moscow: Voyenizdat, 1963.

Krylatyye bogatyri [Winged heroes]. Leningrad: Lenizdat, 1965.

Krylatyye syny Rodiny [Winged sons of the Motherland]. Monino, 1967.

Krylov, A.I. *Dal'nimi marshrutami* [On distant routes]. Moscow: Voyenizdat, 1969.

———. *Po prikazu stavki* [Orders from headquarters]. Moscow: Voyenizdat, 1977.

Kryl'ya [Wings]. Moscow: DOSAAF, 1971.

Kubarev, V.N. *Atakuyut gvardeytsy* [Guardsmen attack]. Tallinn: Eesti raamat, 1975.

Kuliyev, A. *Ognennoye nebo* [Fiery skies]. Baku: Gyandzhlik, 1970.

Kumanova, N.D. *Geroy Sovetskogo Timur Mikhailovich Frunze* [Soviet Hero Timur Frunze]. Moscow: Voyenizdat, 1955.

Kurguzov, I.P. *Nebo pokoryayetsya otvazhnym* [The skies are conquered by the brave]. Moscow: Voyenizdat, 1971.

———. *Zvezdy nad Pribaltikoy* [Stars above the Baltic Coast]. Moscow: DOSAAF, 1973.

Kurin, O. *V nebe nad Rovno* [In the sky over Rovno]. L'vov: Kn-Zhurn. izdatel'stvo, 1959.

Kurzenkov, S.G. *Pod nami zemlya i more* [The land and sea are beneath us]. Moscow: Voyenizdat, 1960; 2d ed., 1967.

———. *Osoboye zadaniye. Rasskazy o letchikakh* [Special mission: tales about pilots]. Moscow: Sovetskaya Rossiya, 1963.

———. *Vozdushnyy as* [Air ace]. Moscow: DOSAAF, 1966.

Kuzhevnikov, A.L. *Eskadril'i ukhodyat na Zapad* [Squadrons go west]. Rostov: Kn. izdatel'stvo, 1966.

Kuznetsov, N.F. *Front nad zemley* [The front above the earth]. Moscow: Voyenizdat, 1970.

Kuznetsov, P.I., et al. *Krylatyye bogatyri* [Winged warriors]. Leningrad: Lenizdat, 1965.

————. *Sokoly: Ocherki* [Falcons: sketches]. Leningrad: Lenizdat, 1971.

Kuznetsov, S.G. *Pod nami zemlya i more* [Land and sea beneath us]. Moscow: Voyenizdat, 1967.

Kuznetsov, V.A. *Stanovleniye letchika* [The making of a flier]. Moscow: Voyenizdat, 1963.

————. *Serebryanyye kryl'ya* [Silver wings]. Moscow: Voyenizdat, 1972.

Kuz'min, N. *Sergey Luganskiy* [Sergey Luganskiy]. Alma-Ata: Zhazushy, 1968.

Langman, M. *Etazhy neba* [Levels of the sky]. Donetsk: Donbass, 1970.

Larin, G.D. *Sovetskaya aviatsiya v boyakh za sotsialisticheskuyu Rodinu.* [Soviet aviation in the battle for the Socialist Motherland]. Moscow: Pravda, 1950.

Lavrinenkov, V.D. *Moi vozdushnyye boi. Zapiski letchika-istrebitelya* [My air battles: a fighter pilot's notes]. Moscow: Voyenizdat, 1943.

————. *Vozvrashcheniye v nebo* [Return to the skies]. Moscow: Voyenizdat, 1974.

Lavrinenkov, V.D., and Belorol, N.N. *Shpaga chest': Povest' o polke "Normandiya-Neman"* [Sword of honor: stories about the "Normandy-Niemen" Regiment]. Kiev: Politizdat Ukrainy, 1980.

Lazarev, L.L. *Vzlet* [Takeoff]. Moscow: Politizdat, 1978.

Lazukin, A.N. *Shkola Krylatykh geroyev* [School of winged heroes]. Chelyabinsk: Yuzh-Ural'sk. Kn. izdatel'stvo, 1971.

Lelyushenko, D.D. *Moskva-Stalingrad-Berlin-Praga* [Moscow-Stalingrad-Berlin-Prague]. Rev. 3d ed. Moscow: Nauka, 1975.

Lemberik, I.M. *Kapitan Starchak* [Kapitan Starchak]. Moscow: Voyenizdat, 1960.

Letchiki v boyakh za Sovetskuyu Rodinu [Pilots in combat for the Soviet Motherland]. Moscow: DOSAAF, 1958.

Levashov, M.A. *Krylatyye truzheniki* [Winged Toilers]. Alma-Ata: Kazakhskoye gosizdat, 1963.

Levin, K. *Rasskazy o polkovnike Rakove* [Stories about Colonel Rakov]. Moscow: 1941.

Lichak, G.K. *Bombardirovshchiki. Zapiski vozdushnogo strelka-radista* [Bombers: notes of an aerial gunner-radio operator]. Moscow: DOSAAF, 1959.

Lisov, I.I., ed. *Krylataya pekhota. Rasskazy, ocherki, vospominaniya* [Winged infantry: tales, sketches, reminiscences]. Moscow: Voyenizdat, 1956.

Lisov, I.I., et al. *Vozdushnyye desanty* [Airborne assault landings]. Moscow: Voyenizdat, 1959.

Lisov, I.I. *S vozdukha-v boi* [From the sky into battle]. Moscow, Voyenizdat, 1960.

————. *Sovetskiye vozdushno-desantnye voyska* [Soviet airborne troops]. Moscow: DOSAAF, 1967.

Lisov, I.I., and Korol'chenko, A.F. *Desantniki atakuyut s neba* [Airborne troops attack from the sky]. Moscow: Voyenizdat, 1980.

Litvinova, L. *Letyat skvoz' gody* [They fly through the years]. Moscow: Voyenizdat, 1965, 1975.

————. *Ulitsa Tat'yany Makarovoy* [Tat'yana Makarova Street]. Moscow: Moskovskiy rabochiy, 1976.

Lokshin, V.S., et al. *Shest' zolotykh zvezd* [Six Gold Stars]. Moscow: DOSAAF, 1976.

Luganskiy, S.D. *Na glubokikh virazhakh. Zapiski voyennogo letchika* [In steep banked turns: a military pilot's notes]. Alma-Ata: Zhazushy, 1966.

————. *Nebo ostayetsya chistym. Zapiski voyennogo letchika* [The sky remains clear: a military pilot's notes]. Alma-Ata: Zhazushy, 1970.

Lukashenko, A. *Dorogami vozdushnogo desanta* [On airborne landings]. Moscow: Moskovskiy rabochiy, 1971.

Lukashin, V.I. *Protiv obshchego vraga* [Against the common enemy]. Moscow: Voyenizdat, 1965.

Lushikov, F.A., and Vukolov, V.S. *Vernost'* [Fidelity]. Moscow: Voyenizdat, 1962.

L'vov, M.D. *Rasskazy o chetvertom gvardeyskom aviapolke, 1941–1942* [Tales of the 4th Guards Air Regiment, 1941–42]. Moscow: Voyenmorizdat NKVMF. 1943.

————. *"Boyevoy! Tak derzhat'" O A. Ya. Yefremove* [On the attack run! maintain course! about A. Ya. Yefremov]. Moscow: Moskovskiy rabochiy, 1973.

Magid, A.S. *"Il'yushiny" v boyakh za Rodinu* [Il'yushin aircraft in battles for the Motherland]. Moscow: Voyenizdat, 1952.

————. *Gvardeyskiy Tamanskiy aviatsionnyy polk* [The guards Taman' Air Regiment]. Moscow: DOSAAF, 1953; rev. 1956, 1960, and 1966.

————. *Kryl'ya pobedy* [Wings of victory]. Moscow: DOSAAF, 1958.

————. *Bol'shaya zhizn'* [Great life]. Moscow: DOSAAF, 1968.

Makeyev, V.F. *More v ogne* [Sea on fire]. Moscow: DOSAAF, 1980.

Makskimenko, Ye. *Dvazhdy Geroy Sovetskogo Soyuza Ye. M. Kungurtsev* [Two-Time Hero of the Soviet Union Ye. M. Kungurtsev]. Moscow: Voyenizdat, 1949.

Mal'kov D.K. *Podvig za podvigom* [Feat upon feat]. Moscow: DOSAAF, 1969.

Mares'yev, A.P. *Na Kurskoy duge* [On the Kursk salient]. Moscow: Voyenizdat, 1960.

Margelov, V.F. *Sovetskiye vozdushno-desantnyye* [Soviet airborne]. Moscow: Voyenizdat, 1980.

Mariynskiy, Ye. P. *Do zemli 15 sanitmetrov* [15 centimeters off the ground]. Moscow: Znaniye, 1963.

————. *Vnizu—peredniy* [Below—the forward edge of the battle area]. Moscow: Politizdat, 1966.

Markova, G.I. *Yunost' v ogne* [Youth under fire]. Moscow: Moskovskiy rabochiy, 1968.

Matveyev, N.S. *Burevestnik. Geroich. biografiya N.G. Stepanyana* [The stormy petrel: the heroic biography of N.G. Stepanyan]. Moscow: Molodaya gvardiya, 1971.

Mel'nik, V.K. *Istrebiteli* [Fighters]. Kiev: Derzhitvidav Ukraini, 1960.

Men', G. *Podvig* [Exploit]. Belgorod: Kn. izdatel'stvo, 1960.

————. *Istoriya odnogo podviga* [The story of one feat]. Minsk: Belarus', 1964.

Mikhalenko, K.F. *Sluzhu nebu* [I serve the skies]. Minsk: Belarus', 1973.

Mikhaylik, Ya. D. *Sokolinaya Sem'ya* [A family of falcons]. Moscow: Voyenizdat, 1971.

Minervin, B.I. *Na kryl'yakh Rodiny. Ocherki* [On the Motherland's wings: sketches]. Orenburg: Orenburgskoye knizhnoye izdatel'stvo, 1959.

Mineyev, N.F. *Chasovoy Leningradskogo neba* [Sentries of the Leningrad sky]. Leningrad, 1961.

————. *Pervaya pobeda* [First victory]. Leningrad: Znaniye, 1962.

————. *Stepan Zdorovtsev* [Stepan Zdorovtsev]. Leningrad: Lenizdat, 1963.

Mineyev, N.F., and Yalygin, M.I. *Za chistoye nebo* [Clear the sky]. Leningrad: Lenizdat, 1978.

Mironov, V.B. *Krylatyy divizion* [Winged division]. Saransk: Mordov. Kn. izdatel'stvo, 1973.

Mitroshenkov, V. ed. *Letchiki* [Pilots]. Moscow: Molodaya gvardiya, 1978.

Mitroshenkov, V., and Chugunov, N. *Kryl'ya Rodiny* [Wings of the Motherland]. Moscow: Politizdat, 1979.

Miroshnichenko, G.I. *Veter Baltiki* [Baltic wind]. Moscow: DOSAAF, 1972.

Moisyuk, M., and Khapayev, A. *Po ognennym marshrutam* [Along fiery paths]. Moscow: Voyenizdat, 1964.

Mokrousov, S.I. *Geroy Sovetskogo Soyuza Boris Pirozhkov* [Hero of the Soviet Union Boris Pirozhkov]. Perm: Kn. izdatel'stvo, 1959.

Molodchiy, A.I. *V pylayushchem nebe. Zapiski voyennogo letchika* [In the blazing sky: a military pilot's notes]. Kiev: Politizdat Ukrainy, 1973.

Molokov, V.S. *Rodnoye nebo* [Native skies]. Moscow: Voyenizdat, 1977.

Molotsev, V. *Filipp Trofimovich Demchenkov* [Filipp Trofimovich Demchenkov]. Smolensk: Kn. izdatel'stvo, 1962.

Moroz, I.M. *Dorogami ottsov* [On the paths of the fathers]. Moscow: DOSAAF, 1980.

Morozov, S. *Dvazhdy geroy Sovetskogo Soyuza T. Ya. Begel'dinov* [Two-time Hero of the Soviet Union T. Ya. Begel'dinov]. Moscow: Voyenizdat, 1948.

Moskovskiy, V.P. *Stalinskaya aviatsiya v boyakh za Rodinu* [Stalin's aviation in battles for the Motherland]. Moscow: Gosizdat, 1944.

————. *Stalinskaya aviatsiya v otechestvennoy voyne* [Stalin's aviation in the Patriotic War]. Moscow: Voyenizdat, 1945.

————. *Sovetskiye Voyenno-vozdushnyye sily v Velikoy Otechestvennoy voyne* [The Soviet Air Force in the Great Patriotic War]. Moscow: Voyenizdat, 1946.

Moskovskiy, V.P., ed. *Vosem' bogatyrey. Sbornik* [Eight warriors: a collection]. Moscow: Molodaya gvardiya, 1944.

————. *Voyenno-vozdushnyye sily SSSR, 1918–1948 gg. Kratkiy ocherk* [The Soviet Air Force, 1918–1948: a brief sketch]. Moscow: Voyenizadat, 1948.

Mozharovskiy, G.M. *Poka b'yetsya serdtse* [The heart beats]. Moscow: Voyenizdat, 1973.

Nalibaiko, B. *Na groznykh "Ilakh"* [In the formidable "ILS"]. Minsk: Belarus, 1981.

Nedbaylo, A.K. *V gvardeyskoy sem'ye* [In a guard's family]. Kiev: Politizdat Ukrainy, 1975.

Nekrasov, V.P. *Na kryl'yakh pobedy. Zapiski letchika istrebitelya* [On the wings of victory: a fighter pilot's notes]. Khabarovsk: Kn. izdatel'stvo, 1960; rev. ed., 1963.

Nikol'skiy, A. *Na boyevom kurse* [On combat course]. Moscow: Voyenizdat, 1961.

————. *Ogon' v litso* [Fire by sight]. Moscow: Voyenizdat, 1966.

Novikov, A.A. *V nebe Leningrada. Zapiski Kommanduyushchego aviatsiyey* [In Leningrad skies: an aviation commander's notes]. Moscow: Nauka, 1970.

Novikov, M.V. *Molnii pod krylom* [Lightning beneath the wing]. Moscow: Voyenizdat, 1973.

Novospasskiy, K.M. *Letchik Khol'zynov* [Pilot Khol'zynov]. Stalingrad: Kn. izdatel'stvo, 1951.

Oparin, V. *Odni protiv shesti* [Alone against six]. Petrozavodsk: Gosizdat. Karel ASSR, 1961.

Orlov, F.N. *Lyublyu ya svoyu Rodinu* [I love my Motherland]. Cheboksary: Chuvashgosizdat, 1943.

————. *Mest' "Goluboy dvoiki"* [Revenge of the "Blue Pair"]. Cheboksary: Chuvash. Kn. Isdatel'stvo, 1965.

————. *Ognennyye reyse "Goluboy dvoyki." Zapiski voyennogo letchika* [Fiery shorties of the "Blue Pair": a military pilot's notes]. Cheboksary: Chuvashizdat, 1975.

Osipenko. L.F. *Smelyy sokol* [Bold falcon]. Bryansk: Priok. Kn. Izdatel'stvo, 1969.

Ovcharenko, Ye. V. *Na frontovykh aerodromakh* [At the frontline airfields]. Moscow: Voyenizdat, 1975.

Ozerov, G.A. *Tupolevskaya sharaga* [The Tupolev internee design bureau]. Frankfurt/M.: Possev-Verlag, 1971.

Pakilev, G.N. *Sovetskaya voyenno-transportnaya aviatsiya* [Soviet military transport aviation]. Moscow: DOSAAF, 1974.

————. *Truzheniki neba* [Toilers of the heavens]. Moscow: Voyenizdat, 1978.

Perepelov, L. *Dvazhdy geroy Sovetskogo Soyuza Petr Pilyutov* [Two-time Hero of the Soviet Union Petr Pilyutov]. Leningrad: Voyenizdat, 1946.

Petrosyants, Kh. S. *V ryadakh sovetskikh aviatorov* [In the ranks of Soviet aviation]. Yerevan: Aistan, 1969.

Pevzner, G. Yu. *Zashchitniki Leningradskogo neba. Sbornik statey i ocherkov* [Defenders of Leningrad's skies: a collection of articles and sketches]. Leningrad: Leningradskoye gazetno-zhurnal'noye i knizhnoye izdatel'stvo, 1943.

Pinchuk, N.G. *V vozdukhe-Yaki* [Yaks in the air]. Minsk, 1977.

Pirogov, P. *Mushestvo pobezhdaet* [Courage triumphs]. Leningrad: Lenizdat, 1963.

Platonov, N.E. *Eskadril'ya. geroyev.* [Squadron of heroes]. Moscow: Voyenizdat, 1962.

Podvigi letchikov grazhdanskoy aviatsii v gody Velikoy Otechestvennoy voyny [Exploits of civil aviation pilots during the Great Patriotic War]. Leningrad, 1969.

Pogrebnoy, V.I. *Chelovek iz legendy* [A legendary man]. Moscow: Voyenizdat, 1963.

Pokryshkin, A.I. *Kryl'ya istrebitelya* [Fighter wings]. Moscow: Voyenizdat, 1944.

―――. *Kryl'ya istrebitelya* [Fighter wings]. Rev. ed. Moscow: Voyenizdat, 1948.

―――. *Nebo voyny* [The skies of war]. 6th ed. Moscow: Voyenizdat, 1980.

―――. *Na istrebitele* [Fighter pilot]. Novosibirsk: Novosibgiz, n.d.

Polevoy, B.N. *Povest' o nastoyashchem cheloveke* [Story about a real man]. Moscow: Khudozh. Lit., 1969.

Polukarov, N.T. *Atakuyet "chernaya smert'"* ["Black Death" attacks]. Tula: Priokskoye kn. izdatel'stvo, 1973.

Polynin, F.P. *Boyevyye marshruty* [Combat routes]. Moscow: Voyenizdat, 1972.

Ponomarev, A.N. *Sovetskiye aviatsionnyye konstruktory* [Soviet aviation designers]. Moscow; Voyenizdat, 1977; 2d ed., 1980.

―――. *Pokoriteli neba* [Conquerors of the sky]. Moscow: Voyenizdat, 1980.

Popova, L. *Dvazhdy geroy Sovetskogo Soyuza G.M. Parshin* [Two-time Hero of the Soviet Union G.M. Parshin]. Moscow: Voyenizdat, 1948.

―――. *Dvazhdy geroy Sovetskogo Soyuza Petr Afanas'yevich Pokryshev* [Two-time Hero of the Soviet Union Petr Afanas'yevich Pokryshev]. Moscow: Voyenizdat, 1953.

Potekhin, Ya. F. *Chelovek vysshei doblesti i geroystva* [A man of the highest valor and heroism]. Leningrad: Lenizdat, 1963.

Pozdnyakova, N. *V nochnom nebe* [In night skies]. Kishinev: Lumina, 1966.

Presnyakov, A.V. *Nad volnami Baltiki* [Above the waves of the Baltic]. Moscow: Voyenizdat, 1979.

Prussakov, G.K. *16-ya vozdushnaya. Voyenno-istoricheskiy ocherk o boyevom puti 16-y vozdushnoy armii, 1942–1945* [The 16th Air Army: a military-historical sketch of the 16th Air Army in combat, 1942–1945]. Moscow: Voyenizdat, 1973.

Pshenyanik, G.A. *Sovetskiye Voyenno-vozdushnyye sily v bor'be c Nemetsko-fashistskoy aviatsiyey v letneosenney kampanii 1941 g.* [The Soviet Air Force in the struggle against German-Fascist aviation in the summer-fall campaign, 1941]. Moscow: Voyenizdat, 1961.

Ptitsyn, B.G. *Voyenno-vozdushnyye sily v razgrome Nemetskikh voysk pod Moskvoy, 15 noyabrya—25 dekabrya 1941 g* [The air force in the rout of the German troops at Moscow, 15 November–25 December 1941]. Monino, 1948.

Puntus, V.G. *Krylatoye plemya* [Winged tribe]. Stalingrad: Stalingradksoye knizhnoye izdatel'stvo, 1961.

Puusepp, Endel. *Na dal'nikh vozdushnykh dorogakh. Vospominaniya* [Over long air routes: reminiscences]. Moscow: Voyenizdat, 1975.

Pyatkov, A. *Idu v ataku* [I attack]. Moscow: Voyenizdat, 1962.

Rakov, V.I. *Kril'ya nad morem. Zapiski voyennogo letchika* [Wings over the sea: a military pilot's notes]. Leningrad: Lenizdat, 1974.

Rechkalov, G.A. *V nebe Moldavii. Vospominaniya voyennogo letchika* [In the skies of Moldavia: a military pilot's recollections]. Kishinev: Kartya moldovenyaske, 1967.

―――. *Dymnoye nebo voyny* [The smoky skies of war]. Sverdlovsk: Sredne-Ural'skoye kn. izdatel'stvo, 1968.

Rudenko. S.I., et al. *Sovetskiye Voyenno-vozdushnyye sily v Velikoy Otechestvennoy voyne, 1941–1945* [The Soviet Air Force in the Great Patriotic War, 1941–1945]. Moscow: Voyenizdat, 1968.

―――. *Kryl'ya pobedy* [Wings of victory]. Moscow: Voyenizdat, 1976.

Rudneva, Ye. M. *Poka stuchit serdtse* [As long as the heart beats]. Moscow: Molodaya gvardiya, 1958.

Ryl'nikov, V.A. *Na kryl'yakh muzhestva* [On wings of valor]. Moscow: Voyenizdat, 1973.

Rytov, A.G. *Rytsari pyatogo okeana* [Knights of the fifth ocean]. Moscow: Voyenizdat, 1968.

Sadai, V.L. *Povest' o krylatykh druz'yakh* [A tale about flying friends]. Moscow: Voyenizdat, 1969.

Sadorskiy, A. *Starshiy pilot S.N. Fokanov* [Senior pilot S.N. Fokanov]. Moscow, 1941.

Sagaidak, P. *Krylataya pekhota* [Flying infantry]. Moscow: DOSAAF, 1963.

Sakharov, G.N. *2-ya vozdushnaya armiya v boyakh za Rodinu* [The 2d Air Army in battles for the Motherland]. Moscow: Voyenizdat, 1965.

————. *Povest' ob istrebitelyakh* [A tale about fighters]. Moscow: DOSAAF, 1977.

Sarkisov, A.F. *Dvazhdy geroy Sovetskogo Soyuza Nel'son Stepanyan* [Two-time Hero of the Soviet Union Nel'son Stepanyan]. Baku: Azerneshr, 1947.

Savitskiy, Ye. Ya. *V nebe nad maloi zemlei* [In the sky over the little land]. Krasnodarsk, 1980.

Schvartsman, Ya. S., ed., et al. *Sovetskiye letchiki v boyakh za rodinu. Sbornik materialov zhurnala "Kryl'ya Rodiny"* [Soviet pilots in battles for the Motherland: collection from the journal *Kryl'ya Rodiny*]. Moscow: DOSAAF, 1963.

Seidmamedova, Z. *Zapiski letchitsy* [Notes of an aviatrix]. Baku: Gyadzhlik, 1969.

Selenya, Ye. V. *V surovom nebe frontovom* [In the harsh frontline skies]. Minsk: Belarus', 1980.

Semenikhin, G. *Khmuryy leytenant* [Sullen lieutenant]. Moscow: Sovetskaya Rossiya, 1971.

————. *Vzlet protiv vetra. Povesti i rasskazy* [Takeoff into the wind: stories and tales]. Moscow: Voyenizdat, 1974.

Semenov, A.F. *Na vzlete* [Takeoff]. Moscow: Voyenizdat, 1969.

Semenov, A.F., et al. *Eskadril'ya "Mongol'skiy arat"* [The "Mongolian Shepherd" Squadron]. Moscow: Voyenizdat, 1971.

Semenov, G.K. *Parol' 'Ispaniya!* [Password—"Spain"]. Kharkov: Prapor, 1974.

Sereda, I. *Gruppa "Mech"* [Group "Sword"]. Kishinev: Kartya moldovenyaske, 1960.

Shadskiy, P. *Sovetskaya aviatsiya v boyakh za Rodinu* [Soviet aviation in the battle for the Motherland]. Moscow, 1958.

Shagalov, Ye. *Aleksandr Ivanovich Koldunov* [Aleksandr Ivanovich Koldunov]. Smolensk: Kn. izdatel'stvo, 1959.

Sharonshikov, I. Ya. *Golubyye dali* [Sky blue expanse]. Moscow: Voyenizdat, 1964.

Shatayev, K.N. *Rytsar' leningradskogo neba* [Knight of Leningrad's skies]. Leningrad: Obshchestvo Znaniye RSFSR, 1968.

Shcheglov, V. *A potom prishla pobeda* [And then victory]. Moscow: DOSAAF, 1980.

Shchutskiy, S. *Geroy Sovetskogo Soyuza Nikolay Gastello* [Hero of the Soviet Union Nikolay Gastello]. Minsk: Gosizdat BSSR, 1952.

Shelest, I.I. *S kryla na krylo* [Wing signals]. Moscow: Molodaya gvardiya, 1977.

————. *Krylatyye Lyudi* [Winged people]. Moscow: Moskovskiy rabochiy, 1980.

Shemenov, A. *Geroy Sovetskogo Soyuza G.A. Shadrin* [Hero of the Soviet Union G.A. Shadrin]. Moscow: Voyenizdat, 1948.

Shepelev, A.L. *V nebe i na zemle* [In the air and on the ground]. Moscow: Voyenizdat, 1974.

Shinkarenko, F.I. *Nebo rodnoye* [Native skies]. Kaliningrad: Kn. izdatel'stvo, 1965.

Shipilov, I.F. *Zhizn', otdannaya budushchemu* [A life dedicated to the future]. Moscow: Voyenizdat, 1962.

Shmelev, N.A. *Slovno rodnyye brat'ya. Rasskazy o boyevykh druz'yakh* [Like real brothers: tales of combat compatriots]. Moscow: Voyenizdat, 1960.

————. *Ravneniye na znamya!* [Line up on the banner!]. Ufa: Bashkir-izdat, 1962.

————. *V luchakh prozhektorov* [In searchlight beams]. Moscow: Voyenizdat, 1962.

————. *S malykh vysot* [At low altitudes]. Moscow: Voyenizdat, 1966.

————. *Ogon s neba. Vospominaniya* [Fire from the sky: reminiscences]. Yaroslavl': Verkhne-Volzhskoye kn. izdatel'stvo, 1972.

Shtepenko, A.P. *Osoboye zadaniye. Zapiski shturmana* [Special mission: a navigator's notes]. Moscow: Voyenizdat, 1944.

————. *Na dal'nem bombardirovshchike. Zapiski shturmana Kn. 1* [Aboard a long-range bomber: a navigator's notes, book one]. Moscow: Voyenizdat, 1945.

———. *Nochnyye okhotniki. Zapiski shturmana. Kn. 2* [Night hunters: a navigator's notes, book two]. Moscow: Voyenizdat, 1946.

———. *Tak derzhat'! Zapiski shturmana* [Maintain course!: a navigator's notes]. Moscow: Voyenizdat, 1951.

Shtuchkin, N.N. *Groznoye nebo Moskvy. Zapiski letchika-frontovika* [Moscow's stormy skies: a front-line pilot's notes]. Moscow: DOSAAF, 1972.

———. *Nad goryashchey zemley* [Over the burning land]. Moscow: DOSAAF, 1980.

Shur, N. *Geroy Sovetskogo Soyuza Grigoriy Taran* [Hero of the Soviet Union Grigoriy Taran]. Moscow: Redizdat, 1947.

Shutskiy, S. *Geroy Sovetskogo Soyuza Nikolay Gastello* [Hero of the Soviet Union Nikolay Gastello]. Minsk: Gosizdat BSSR, 1952.

Simeonov, S. *Zakalennyye kryl'ya* [Experienced wings]. Moscow, 1976.

Sivkov, G.F. *Gotovnost' nomer odin* [Readiness no. 1]. Moscow: Sovetskaya Rossiya, 1973.

Skomorokhov, N.M., et al. *17-ya vozdushnaya armiya v boyakh ot Stalingrada do Veny* [The 17th Air Army in battles from Stalingrad to Vienna]. Moscow: Voyenizdat, 1977.

Sled v nebe [Traces in the sky]. Moscow: Politizdat, 1971.

Smelyanov, N.V., et al. *Chasovyye leningradskogo neba* [Sentries of the Leningrad skies]. Leningrad: Lenizdat, 1968.

Smirnov, Ye. *Romantiki neba* [Romantics of the sky]. Moscow: DOSAAF, 1966.

———. *Plyvut oblaka* [The clouds float]. Moscow: DOSAAF, 1970.

Sofronov, G.P. *Vozdushnyye desanty vo vtoroy mirovoy voyne. Kratkiy voyenno-istoricheskiy ocherk* [Airborne assault landings in World War II: a brief military-historical sketch]. Moscow: Voyenizdat, 1962.

———. *Desantniki. Vozdushnyye desanty* [Airborne troops: airborne assault landings]. Moscow: Voyenizdat, 1968.

———. *Zemlya-nebo-zemlya* [Land-sky-land]. Moscow: DOSAAF, 1973.

Sofronov, G.P., et al. *Vozdushno-desantnaya podgotovka* [Airborne assault training]. Moscow: Voyenizdat, 1977.

Sokolov, V. *Moi druz'ya-letchiki* [My pilot friends]. Moscow: DOSAAF, 1969.

Solov'yev, A.G., ed. *V nebe—letchiki Baltiki* [Baltic pilots in the sky]. Tallin: Eesti raamat, 1974.

Soroka, A. *Severnaya legenda* [Arctic legend]. Arkhangel'sk: Kn. izdatel'stvo, 1963.

Sorokin, G. *Rasskazy kapitana Suslina* [Captain Suslin's tales]. Leningrad-Moscow: Voyenno-morskoye izdatel'stvo NKVMF, 1942.

———. *Dva, geroya* [Two heroes]. Moscow: Voyenizdat, 1956.

Sorokin, Z.A. *Net, ne otletalsya* [No, his flying days aren't over]. Murmansk: Kn. izdatel'stvo, 1960.

———. *Druz'ya-odnopolchane. Ocherki* [Friends from the same unit: sketches]. Moscow: Voyenizdat, 1962.

———. *Estafeta muzhestva* [Race of valor]. Moscow: GPU Sovetskoy Armii i Voyen-Mor. Flota, 1963.

———. *V nebe Zapolyar'ya* [In polar skies]. Moscow: DOSAAF, 1963.

———. *Khozyan sinikh vysot* [Master of the blue heights]. Moscow: Voyenizdat, 1964.

———. *Istrebiteli idut na perekhvat* [Fighters en route to an intercept]. Moscow: DOSAAF, 1965.

———. *Krylatyye gvardeytsy. Rasskazy i ocherki* [Winged guards: tales and sketches]. Moscow: Voyenizdat, 1966.

———. *Idem v ataku* [We go on the attack]. Moscow: DOSAAF, 1970.

Sovetskiye letchiki v boyakh za Rodinu [Soviet fliers in battles for the Motherland]. Moscow: DOSAAF, 1963.

Starchak, I.G. *S neba—v boy* [From the skies into battle]. Moscow: Voyenizdat, 1965.

Stefanovskiy, P.M. *Trista neizvestnykh* [Three hundred flights into the unknown]. Moscow: Voyenizdat, 1968.

Stepanenko, V. *Devyat' dney bez trevog* [Nine days without alerts]. Moscow: Sovetskaya Rossiya, 1977.

Strekhin, Yu., ed. *Den' pervyy, den' posledniy* [The first day, the final day]. Moscow: Sovetskaya Rossiya, 1966.

Stupin, Ye. *Moi brat* [My Brother]. Tula: Priok. kn. izdatel'stvo, 1968.

Sturikov, N.A. *Na kryl'yakh zhizni* [On the wings of life]. Moscow: Sovetskaya Rossiya, 1963.

Sukhachev, M.P. *Nebo dlya smelykh* [The sky for the brave]. Moscow: Molodaya gvardiya, 1979.

———. *Shturman vozdushnykh trass* [Navigator of the air routes]. Moscow: Moskovskiy rabochiy, 1981.

Sukhorukov, Ya. A. *Zhivaya pamyat'* [Living memory]. Moscow: Voyenizdat, 1967.

Sumarokova, T.N. *Proleti nado mnoy posle boya* [Overfly me after the battle]. Moscow: Politizdat, 1976.

Svetlishin, N.A. *Voiska PVO strany v Velikoy Otechestvennoy voyne* [Air defense troops in the Great Patriotic War]. Moscow: Nauka, 1979.

Talanov, A., ed. *Nad Berlinom. Iz zhizni letchikov aviatsii dal'nego deystviya* [Over Berlin: from the life of long-range aviation pilots]. Tashkent: Uzgosizdat, 1942.

Tarasenko, E.I. *Pod krylom samoleta* [Beneath the aircraft wing]. Stavropol': Kn. izdatel'stvo, 1968.

Telegin, K.F. *Ne otdali Moskvy!* [They did not surrender Moscow!]. Moscow: ovetskaya Rossiya, 1968; 2d ed., 1975.

Teplyakov, G.V. *Pobeg* [Escape]. Donetsk: Donbass, 1965.

Tikhomolov, B.E. *Na kryl'yakh ADD. Vospominaniya* [On the wings of long-range aviation: recollections]. Moscow: Voyenizdat, 1970.

Timofeyev, V.A. *Shturmoviki. Zapiski aviatsionnogo komandira* [Ground-attack aircraft: an aviation commander's notes]. Riga: Latgosizdat, 1953.

———. *Tovarishchi letchiki. Zapiski aviatsionnogo komandira* [Comrade pilots: an aviation commander's notes]. Moscow: Voyenizdat, 1963.

Timokhovich, I.V. *Sovetskaya aviatsiya v bitve pod Kurskom* [Soviet aviation in the battle of Kursk]. Moscow: Voyenizdat, 1959.

Tishchenko, A.T. *Vedomyye "drakona."* [The "Dragon's" wing-men]. Moscow: Voyenizdat, 1966.

———. *"Drakon" idet na tsel'* ["Dragon" hits the target]. Krasnodar: Kn. izdatel'stvo, 1969.

Tkachenko, A.K. *Zapiski vozdushnogo razvedchika* [An aerial scout's notes]. Leningrad: Lenizdat, 1970.

Tsupko, P. *Nad prostorami severnykh morei* [Over the expanse of the Arctic seas]. Moscow: Molodaya gvardiya, 1981.

Tsyrulev, A. *Morskiye vozdushnyye sily* [Naval air forces]. Moscow: 1935.

Ul'yanenko. N.Z. *Nezabyvayemoye. Zapiski letchitsy* [The unforgettable: an aviatrix's notes]. Izhevsk: Udmurtiya, 1964.

Ushakov, S.F. *Boyevyye budni* [Days of combat]. Moscow: Voyenizdat, 1946.

Utekhin, S.G. *Vo imya Rodiny* [In the name of the Motherland]. Moscow: Moskovskiy rabochiy, 1958.

———. *Viktor Talalikhin* [Victor Talalikhin]. Moscow: Moskovskiy rabochiy, 1961; 2d ed., 1965.

V Krylatoy pekhote [In the airborne forces]. Perm': Kn. izdatel'stvo, 1973.

V nebe frontom [In frontline skies]. Moscow: Voyenizdat, 1962; 2d ed., Molodaya Gvardiya, 1971.

V nebe letchiki Baltiki [Pilots in the Baltic skies]. Tallinn: Eesti raamat, 1974.

Vazhin, F. A. *Aviatsiya v boyu* [Aviation in combat]. Moscow: Voyenizdat, 1959.

———. *Vozdushnyy taran* [Aerial ramming]. Moscow: Voyenizdat, 1962.

Velichko, V. *Dvazhdy geroy Sovetskogo Soyuza V. I. Popkov* [Two-time Hero of the Soviet Union V. I. Popkov]. Moscow: Voyenizdat, 1948.

Verkhozin, A. M. *Samolety letyat k partizanam. Zapiski nachal'nika shtaba* [Aircraft en route to the partisans: a chief of staff's notes]. Moscow: Politizdat, 1964; 2d ed., 1966.

Vershinin, K. A. *Chetvertaya vozdushnaya* [The 4th Air Army]. Moscow: Voyenizdat, 1975.

Vinogradov, Yu. A. *Idu na Berlin* [I fly to Berlin]. Moscow: DOSAAF, 1980.

Vishenkov, S. A. *Dyazhdy geroy Sovetskogo Soyuza Stepan Pavlovich Suprun* [Two-time Hero of the Soviet Union Stepan Pavlovich Suprun]. Moscow: Voyenizdat, 1956.

Vishnyakov, I. A. *Na krytykh virazhakh* [In closed, banked turns]. Moscow: Voyenizdat, 1973.

Vodop'yanov, M. V. *Na kryl'yakh v Arktiku* [On wings to the Arctic]. Moscow: Izdatel'stvo geograficheskoy literatury, 1943.

———. *Krylatyye bogatyri* [Winged warriors]. Leningrad: Lenizdat, 1957.

———. *Sibirskiy kharakter* [Siberian temper]. Moscow: DOSAAF, 1958.

———. *Ural'skiy sokol* [Ural falcon]. Moscow: DOSAAF, 1964.

———. *Druz'ya v nebe* [Friends in the sky]. Moscow: Sovetskaya Rossiya, 1967.

Vodop'yanov, M. V., and Grigor'yev, G. *Letat' rozhdennyy. Dokumental'naya povest'* [Born to fly: documented stories]. Moscow: DOSAAF, 1969.

Vodop'yanov, M. V. *Povest' o pervykh geroyakh* [A story about the first heroes]. Moscow: DOSAAF, 1980.

Voinov, A. I., ed. *Krylatoye plemya. Vospominaniya o letchikakh trekh pokoleniy* [The winged tribe: reminiscences about three generations of pilots]. Moscow: Voyenizdat, 1962.

Volkov, A. *Samolety na voyne* [Aircraft in war]. Moscow, 1946.

Volynkin, I. T. *Nad pyat'yu moryami* [Over five seas]. Moscow: Voyenizdat, 1964.

Vorozheykin, A. V. *Istrebiteli* [Fighters]. Moscow: Voyenizdat, 1961.

———. *Nad Kurskoy dugoy* [Over the Kursk salient]. Moscow: Voyenizdat, 1962.

———. *Tverzhe stali* [Harder than steel]. Moscow: Voyenizdat, 1963.

———. *Rassvet nad Kiyevom* [Dawn over Kiev]. Moscow: Voyenizdat, 1966.

———. *Pod nami—Berlin. Vospominaniya letchika-istrebitelya* [Berlin beneath us: a fighter pilot's reminiscences]. Gor'kiy: Volgo-Vyatskoye kn. izdatel'stvo, 1970.

Vukolov, V. S. *Polk imeni Dzerzhinskogo* [The Dzerzhinskiy Regiment]. Moscow: Voyenizdat, 1961.

———. *Vysota [Altitude]. Moscow: DOSAAF, 1971.*

———. *Krylo boyevogo druga* [Wing of a combat friend]. Moscow: DOSAAF, 1974.

Vukolov, V. S., and Kon'kov, N. G. *Sovetskiye istrebiteli* [Soviet fighters]. Moscow: DOSAAF, 1973.

Vykhristenko, V. *Nebo v zvezdakh* [Stars in the heavens]. Murmansk: Kn. izdatel'stvo, 1969.

Yakimenko, A. D. *V atake—"Mech"* ["Sword" on the attack]. Moscow: DOSAAF, 1973.

Yakovlev, A. S. *Rasskazy iz zhizni* [Stories from life]. Moscow-Leningrad, 1944.

———. *50 let sovetskogo samoletostroyeniya* [Fifty years of Soviet aircraft construction]. Moscow: Nauka, 1968.

———. *Tsel' zhizni. Zapiski aviakonstruktora* [Life's goal: an aviation designer's notes]. Moscow: Politizdat, 1972.

———. *Rasskazy aviakonstruktora* [Stories of an aircraft designer]. Moscow: Detskaya literatura, 1964, 1974.

————. *Sovetskiyye samolety* [Soviet aircraft]. 3d ed. Moscow, 1979.

————. *Zapiski konstruktora* [Notes of a designer]. Moscow: Politizdat, 1979.

Yakushin, M. N., et al., eds. *Vozdushnyy boy pary i zvena istrebiteley. Sbornik* [Air combat by a fighter pair and flight: a collection]. Moscow: Voyenizdat, 1958.

Yar-Kravchenko, A. N. *Bor'ba za Leningrad. Letchiki* [The Battle of Leningrad: pilots]. Leningrad: Iskusstvo, 1944.

Yarynkin, V. *Dvazhdy geroy Sovetskogo Soyuza L. I. Beda* [Two-time Hero of the Soviet Union L. I. Beda]. Moscow: Voyenizdat, 1952.

Yefimov, A. I. *Nad polem boya* [Over the battlefield]. Moscow: Voyenizdat, 1976; 2d ed., 1980.

Yegart, M. *Dvazhy geroy Sovetskogo Soyuza A. N. Yefimov* [Two-time Hero of the Soviet Union]. Moscow: Voyenizdat, 1948.

Yekonomov, L. *Poiski kryl'yev* [The winged quest]. Moscow: Znaniye, 1969.

Yekonomov, Z. *Kapitan Bakhchivandshi* [Captain Bakhchivandshi]. Moscow: DOSAAF, 1972.

Yemel'yanenko, V. B. *Zapiski letchika-shturmovika* [A ground-attack pilot's notes]. Moscow: Voyenizdat, 1944.

————. *V voyennom vozdukhe surovom* [In the harsh combat airspace]. Moscow: Mol. gvardiya, 1972.

Yeremenko, A. I. *Na zapadnom napravlenii* [In the western sector]. Moscow: Voyenizdat, 1959.

————. *V nachale voyny* [At the onset of war]. Moscow: Nauka, 1965.

Zakharov, F. A., et al. *Letchiki Zapolyar'ya* [Pilots of the polar regions]. Arkhangel'sk: Oblizdat, 1943.

————. *V severnom nebe* [In the northern skies]. Arkhangel'sk: Sev.-Zap. kn. izdatel'stvo, 1968.

Zakharov, G. N. *Povest' ob istrebitelyakh* [A story about fighters]. Moscow: DOSAAF, 1977.

Zakharov, S. *Anatoliy Burdenyuk* [Anatoliy Burdenyuk]. Sverdlovsk: Sredno-Ural'sk. kn. izd., 1964.

Zankiskiyev, kh. *Syn gor-sokol Baltiki* [Son of the mountains—falcon of the Baltic]. Nal'chik: El'brus, 1971.

Zarakhovich, Ya, et al. *V nebe Sovetskoy Latvii. Sbornik ocherkov i rasskazov o letahikakh-geroyakh boyev za Sovetskuyu Latviyu* [In Soviet Latvia's skies: a collection of sketches and tales about heroic pilots in the battles for Soviet Latvia]. Riga, 1945.

Zarzar, V. A. *Vozdushnyye puti v SSSR i zagranitsey* [Air routes in the USSR and overseas]. Moscow: Osoaviakhim, 1929.

Zdravstvuy, Nebo! [Hail the sky!]. Moscow: Voyenizdat, 1966.

Zharov, F. I. *Podvigi krasnykh letchikov* [The feats of Red pilots]. Moscow: Voyenizdat, 1963.

Zholudev, L. V. *Stal'naya eskadril'ya* [The steel squadron]. Moscow: Voyenizdat, 1972.

Zhukov, yu. *Odni "MiG" iz tysyachi* [One "MiG" from thousands]. Moscow: Molodaya gvardiya, 1963.

Zil'manovich, D. Ya. *Na orbite bol'shoy zhizni* [In the orbit of a great life]. Vil'nyus, 1971.

Zvezdy na kryl'yakh [Stars on wings]. Moscow: Voyenizdat, 1959.

Zyuzin, D. V. *Ispytaniye skorost'yu* [The test of speed]. Moscow: Molodaya gvardiya, 1958.

Index